"Christian." She touched his lips with hers.

His arm circled her body, drawing her close, and she felt the heavy pounding of his heart against her breasts. She drew away, looking up at him, trying to read a message in his face. He pulled her back, his kiss suddenly searing, demanding, a hot pressure that startled yet excited her. Crushed against his hard chest she soon found herself kissing him back, her arms going up around his neck, heedless of the bedcover that had fallen away.

"Hannah," he whispered, his mouth resting on her cheek.

She couldn't speak. Held in thrall, heart beating wildly, she was unable to utter a sound. *Desire*, she thought. *I can't let him. I mustn't.*

But she did not struggle, could not bear to end this sweet, torturing ecstasy. . . .

Also by Fiona Harrowe:

PRIDE'S FOLLY*
BITTERSWEET AFTERNOONS
HONOR'S FURY*

*Published by Fawcett Books

DARK OBSESSION

Fiona Harrowe

FAWCETT GOLD MEDAL • NEW YORK

A Fawcett Gold Medal Book
Published by Ballantine Books
Copyright © 1987 by Fiona Harrowe

Library of Congress Catalog Card Number: 87-91023

ISBN 0-449-12899-7

Manufactured in the United States of America

First Edition: January 1988

Chapter I

A desolate cold rain fell on the little group of mourners huddled under black umbrellas. The needlelike downpour glistened on the trunks and branches of winter-bare elm and ash, streaking moss-covered tombstones and puddling the yellowed grass underfoot. The steady patter mingled with the droning voice of Preacher Wright, who spoke through the nasal intonation of a head cold.

"Ahm the Resurrection and the Life and whoso eber believedth in be shall . . ."

Hannah, her slender sixteen-year-old figure clothed in shabby black bombazine—the high-bustled skirt long out of fashion in this winter of 1892—listened with passive inattention to the preacher's garbled recitation. It held little meaning for her. Words like "resurrection" and "everlasting life," so often repeated, had become empty. There was no comfort, no significance, no relevance in this graveside sermon. The learned-by-rote scripture, as insubstantial as the mist rolling in from the creek, had nothing to do with her or the corpse that lay in the coffin.

". . . never die . . ."

Hannah did not want to think about death. She did not want to believe that in a few minutes her beloved grand-

1

mother would be lowered into that raw gaping hole, to
lie there for all eternity with the rain she would never
see or hear above her.

"Fo ahs in Ahdam all die so Chris' shall ahll be bade
ahlive . . ."

Hannah tore her attention from the coffin. Her eyes
roamed over the clutch of people: her older brother,
Travis; her father, Chad Blaine; her two younger brothers; and her little sister. To the left of the preacher stood
Aunt Bess, the youngest of Julia's five grown children
and the only one of them present at her mother's funeral. There were Mr. and Mrs. McCracken, next-door
neighbors to Julia; the Youngs, the Ashtons, the Burkes,
fellow church members; and lastly two strangers Hannah had never seen before. Her gaze lingered on them as
they stood bare-headed, partially sheltered from the rain
by the overhanging branches of a live oak. They were
both tall, one in his midthirties, perhaps, the other in
his twenties, both dressed in well-tailored riding clothes,
the sort of elegant attire one rarely saw in this semirural
part of Georgia. The older man was blond with vaguely
familiar features. A distant relative perhaps? The younger man was dark-haired, disturbingly handsome with an
aristocratic shape to his head, a straight nose, and a
thin, almost cruel mouth under a dark mustache. And he
was restless, perhaps bored. While the older man listened with rapt attention, his companion kept tapping
his muddied boots with his whip. Why had he—they—
come? What was Julia Page, an obscure country woman,
to them?

". . . prepared to meet her Lord and Maker . . ."

Hannah's eyes returned to the coffin, gazing at it, her
eyes slowly filling with tears. Pain constricted her heart
just as it had done when she first learned Granny Julie
had died of an apoplectic seizure. She couldn't go on
ignoring the preacher's oration, pretending the coffin
and open grave were for someone else. Granny was
gone. Her beloved grandmother was dead; her voice
silenced, her smile banished. *Granny . . . !* Hannah wept
silently.

Travis, holding her arm with one hand and the umbrella with the other, whispered, "All right, Sis?"

"Yes."

He couldn't tell. Was she weeping? Sick, feeling faint? Black folds of layered marquisette draped over her hat and falling past her black-clad shoulders hid her lovely face. What a to-do Pa had made over that veil!

"The womenfolks hereabouts in Bayetville, good country people, don't need none of them fancy doodads to show respect," Chad Blaine had argued volubly. "Wear a plain bonnet same as the others. No call to put on airs."

Hannah had said, "Granny Page would have wanted me to be dressed in proper mourning."

"Proper, my foot! *She's daid.* An' I don't give a hoot . . ."

But a defiant Hannah had worn the veil.

Travis smiled when he thought of it. Ever since she was thirteen and had voiced a desire to continue her education, Hannah and her father had been at odds. Travis vividly recalled the argument that had marked Hannah's first bid for independence. It had gone on for days, a tight-lipped, dry-eyed Hannah sticking stubbornly to her resolve, a ranting, threatening Chad lashing out at her.

"Yore gettin' too big for your bloomers. What you need is a taste of my belt buckle!" he had stormed.

"It won't change my mind, Pa."

"Damn you! Travis ain't been allowed more'n readin' and writin'. Why should a twit of a female have more larnin'? Eh?"

It wasn't the cost Chad had objected to, since Granny had offered to pay for Hannah's schooling at the Sisters of Mercy Convent in Atlanta. Hannah, Chad had protested, was needed at home. He couldn't spare her. Was he expected to run Stonebridge Inn with just himself, Travis, and a sick wife who was worse than useless? But Granny, hearing of his objection, had summoned him to her house on Asbury Street and in blunt terms reminded Chad that he was in debt to her to the tune of eight hundred dollars. And he hadn't paid his retail license fee yet, had he? She'd heard that this year it would be raised to one hundred and fifty dollars.

Chad, living on the edge of bankruptcy, "hog-tied by that old bitch," as he had put it, sullenly agreed to let Hannah go.

Hannah had been at the convent for two years, the happiest time of her life. Her letters to Travis—twenty months older than she and next to Granny her closest confidant—had bubbled with excitement. The friends she had made, the books, the music, the paintings she had been introduced to! "Oh, Travis, it's all so wonderful. The other girls complain about the food, the strict convent rules, the mean nuns. But I love everything! And I'm learning to talk like a proper lady. So different from Bayetville. If only you could be here with me . . ."

If only he could. Not for the schooling, because like his father, Travis didn't set much store by book learning (though he would never disabuse Hannah of the notion that he did), but simply to be able to get away. Thinking of those two years when Hannah had been absent from home, he remembered how miserable he had been. His one ally gone, he had been left to deal with his bullying, drunken father alone. Since childhood he and Hannah had formed a team, two against Chad's tyranny, closing ranks the instant they saw signs of a rampage.

What had made Chad that way? Travis, looking over at his father standing to the right of the preacher, saw a large man with a shock of gray-streaked auburn hair, bushy red sideburns, and the veined nose of the habitual toper. He might have been handsome once—as his mother had claimed—but it was lost now in slack flesh and puffy-lidded eyes. He was a man, Granny had once explained, who was bitterly disappointed in life. But why should he be? Travis had often wondered. When Chad had inherited from Grandpa Blaine the Stonebridge Inn, a property that had been in the Blaine family since the late eighteenth century, it had been a fairly prosperous establishment. Now it was little more than a low saloon, poorly run and sloppily kept. Chad had blamed Stonebridge's failure on the new turnpike, which diverted travelers elsewhere, and on the churchwomen's drive to make Bayetville "dry"—busybodies, prohibition bitches whose sole aim, according to him, was to put his tavern out of business. He was unable to see his own ineptness. Nor could he understand that he himself did not help matters by drinking up a fair share of the stock-in-trade or by the drunken irascibility that kept customers away. Men who came to imbibe expected a congenial host and a convivial atmosphere, a combination Chad seldom provided.

Travis watched him as he roughly yanked Sue Joy, who had begun to drift from his side, back under the umbrella. She, Bobby, and Colin, holding tightly to one another's hands, were still referred to as the "little ones," although they had now reached the ages of eleven, ten, and nine respectively. The younger Blaines had been born to Mary Louise after a series of miscarriages she had suffered following Hannah's birth. Pale passive children, they had learned early on to keep out of Chad's way, disappearing like wraiths the moment the first explosive curse issued from their father's lips.

Hapless tykes, Travis reflected. Their mother dead a short year ago and now Granny. The children, especially Colin, the youngest, had been bereft when Mary Louise, released at last from overwork, childbearing, and abuse, had passed on after a lingering illness. But Granny Julie from her house on Asbury Street had taken up the slack. Although Hannah had always been Granny's favorite, she had lavished love on all the Blaine children and her death was a blow.

Travis saw Colin's pale freckled face contort, his small mouth open. The howl that escaped momentarily overrode the preacher's voice, who, undisturbed, went on with his oration. Another howl brought Chad's hamlike hand chopping across the child's quivering shoulders. Colin clamped his mouth tightly shut as the tears streamed down his cheeks. Travis could almost feel the pain of those held-in tearing sobs. How many times had he himself been forced to stifle his weeping? Why had he endured it? Why had he not taken off years ago? Though he had told Hannah that he did not want to leave her and the younger children to the untender mercies of Chad,

the truth was that he was a coward. He was afraid to go
out into a world that might prove more hostile than
Chad. The thought of being stranded without money,
unable to buy his next meal or to pay for a roof over his
head, held him back. If he only had the wherewithal,
enough to tide him over until he found employment, he
would tell himself, he would go. The little he earned and
secretly kept in tips, he had tried unsuccessfully to par-
lay into larger sums, a method Hannah would have
certainly disapproved.

All three children were crying now, sniffling loudly,
despite Chad's threatening grumble.

Hannah, leaning close to Travis, said between gritted
teeth, "If he lays a hand on any of them again, I'll kill
him."

She was angry enough to mean it. She hated her
father. He had made life hell for everyone close to him
and the sight of him growling at the three grieving children had taken her mind from her own sorrow and
fueled her irritation. The drunk! The twitching eyelids
and the unsteady hand that held the umbrella, the tongue
flicking out and running over dry, cracked lips, were
unmistakable signs of alcoholic impatience. She knew he
could hardly wait to get back to the taproom and wet his
parched throat. It was a wonder he hadn't brought a hip
flask. Or had come at all. His dislike of Granny was no
secret. He had often enough called her a "goddamned
long-nosed bitch." Yet when financial disaster faced
him, as it did from time to time, he would go to her, hat
in hand, seeking a loan. She had given him money for
"the children's sake." It didn't make him any fonder of
Julie to realize he was beholden to her and she knew it.
More than that, she had taught Hannah to stand up to
him (something she had never been able to get Mary
Louise, her own daughter, to do) and for that alone she
had earned his ire.

Poor Mother, Hannah thought. She just didn't have it
in her to call Pa's bluff, to let him know she wasn't his
slave. Toward the last, Hannah suspected, her mother,
too, had taken to drinking, but on the sly. What a
wasted life, giving it all to a man who gave nothing in

return. If that was marriage, she wanted no part of it. Hannah remembered saying as much to Granny.

" 'Course you'll marry," Julie had said. "You'll meet a fine young man someday and fall in love and that will be the end of such talk."

"Did you love Grandpa?"

Harry Page had died in far-off Haiti before she was born. Harry had gone to investigate a coffee plantation deeded to him by a Yankee officer whose life he had saved during the Civil War and was killed there by a disgruntled squatter.

"Did I love your grandpa? 'Course I did."

She must have, Hannah thought now. Not only had she encouraged her husband to go on this chancy expedition, but she had accepted with cheerful composure the sudden appearance of Harry's grown, illegitimate son (the result of an alliance before the war). Together Harry and Page Morse had departed for Haiti, leaving Julie to cope with five children and the running of a general store. Yet never once through the years had Hannah heard Julie refer to the disastrous circumstances of her husband's death with a single word of recrimination.

Why did people like Julie have to die? Noble, fine, generous, courageous, loving people, while others who were mean-minded and cruel lived on. Oh Granny, I miss you, Hannah mourned silently, clenching her fist to keep fresh tears from flowing. She mustn't wail like Colin, though she desperately wanted to. She must be as much like Granny as possible. Tomorrow she would take up her life and go on as best she could. She would return to teaching in the one-room school where the children would be waiting for her, from little Nancy in pink-bowed braids stumbling over the first reader to bright cowlicked William Pratt who had already gone through every text twice.

Thank God for Pine Tree School. Ever since her mother's death, when she had been called back from Atlanta, the school had served as a haven, a place where for a few hours each day she could put whatever troubled her aside. There had been no question of resuming her education. Chad had refused to be outargued again, saying that her brothers and sister needed her. But instead of lending a hand in the taproom as her father wished, she had taken the position as schoolmistress at Pine Tree. Her decision had thrown him into a tantrum, calmed only when she had promised to turn over her pittance of a salary to him.

"Ahhhchoo!" Preacher Wright's explosive sneeze drew Hannah's attention away from Chad. The clergyman blew his nose loudly on an oversized, wrinkled handkerchief. He had finished his oration and was looking around the assembly with watery eyes.

"Is there anybody here who wishes to say a few words?"

Aunt Bess stepped forward, her face stern under the depths of a black umbrella. What she was thinking or feeling Hannah could not guess. Aunt Bess was never one to share her emotions. A tall, thin woman with pale hair and pale lashes, she had never married. She had lived with Granny, doing fine embroidery and sewing for the local ladies for pocket money. Aside from going regularly to Preacher Wright's church, she did not mingle socially. In a rare moment of confession, she had told Hannah that she wasn't good enough for "quality folks" and she could not stoop to associate with "crackers." To her, all those—including Chad Blaine and Preacher Wright—who did not live in one of the fine houses on Pecan Hill or Cedar Street were crackers.

Aunt Bess read from the Bible: "So that as Christ was raised from the dead by the glory of the Father . . ."

Hannah's eyes, skimming past Bess and Preacher Wright, fell on the two strangers again. The dark one was frowning, his black brows drawn together with a look of restrained ferocity.

She nudged Travis. "Who are those two men?"

"I don't know," he whispered. "The dark one maybe looks like the devil come to see if there's another soul he can collect."

Hannah shivered. "Don't say that, not even in jest."

After each of the mourners had spoken briefly on the virtues of the departed (including Chad, whose laudatory

remarks were the height of hypocrisy) Hannah laid a
wreath of winter berries on the coffin and it was lowered
into the trench. Unable to look, she closed her eyes and
waited until the awful clumping sound of the gravedigger
filling the hole with dirt had ceased.

"Travis! Hannah!" Chad called. The two strangers
had crossed over from the tree and were shaking hands
with him. "Come and meet some kin."

Hannah, picking up her skirts, followed Travis to where
the group stood. "Here's my two oldest," Chad said.
"Hannah 'n Travis, meet your ma's half-brother, Mr.
Page Morse. And this here is Mr. Christian Falconer, his
brother-in-law."

Travis shook hands, Hannah nodded.

So this was Page Morse, her mother's half-brother—on
the other side of the blanket, as Granny would have
said—the same Page Morse who had gone off with her
grandfather to Haiti. Hannah could see now why she
thought Page, with Mary Louise's blue eyes and fair
hair, looked vaguely familiar.

The other, the dark one, Christian Falconer, was close
enough to Hannah for her to smell whiskey on his breath.
A drinker, she thought with scorn. Handsome devil, but
a drinker and arrogant. Well, handsome is as handsome
does. Like Chad, he'll soon lose his looks.

"Y'all—Mr. Morse and Mr. Falconer, too—come to
Stonebridge," Chad loudly invited. "Grandma's wake at
my place." To Travis he said, "Ain't forgot my manners. You and Sis run along and open up."

While Travis lit the coal stove and raked up the fire
on the large stone hearth, Hannah hurried upstairs to the
tiny boxlike room she shared with Sue Joy. She removed her hat and veil, peering into the mirror to see if
her weeping had swollen her face. Except for a pinkness
at the lower lids, her gray eyes framed in dark curling
lashes were crystal clear. The smooth, damasklike cheeks
with their tinge of healthy flush showed no signs of her
grief either. She wasn't vain, she told herself as she
patted a strand of hair into the dark chestnut coiled
mass at the nape of her neck, she simply didn't want her

father chiding her about the veil again, saying she only wore it to hide her sniffling.

When she returned to the taproom, the guests were starting to arrive. Hannah did not linger but went quickly through the passage to the kitchen, where she and the hired girl, Lacey, had prepared the cold meats and cakes brought in by Julie's friends and neighbors the night before. Lacey was not there now, having been unexpectedly called home to tend her sick mother, and it was left to Hannah to serve the guests. Not that clumsy Lacey would have been much use, Hannah reminded herself as she arranged plates on lacquered trays, though she might have helped with the washing up.

Hannah brought the food out to the tables, which had been pushed together, covered with Mary Louise's best cloths and set out with glasses. The guests had already seated themselves on hard, backless benches along either side of the table. Chad, still fairly sober, and for once the genial host, dispensed beer and spirits. The ladies, except for Bess, a teetotaler, were served sherry. The smell of wet wool and mothballs rose with the warmth generated by the stove and the fire leaping and crackling from its bed of pine and maple logs on the hearth. Everyone was chattering now. The solemn business of putting Julie Page underground over, the mourners helped themselves to food and drink as if it were a reward well earned. Mrs. McCracken congratulated Preacher Wright on his fine oration. Bess concurred with a nod of her head, the bedraggled feather plume on her hat dipping in time to Mrs. McCracken's words.

Hannah, seated between Travis and Page Morse, spoke to Morse. "We are pleased to have you at Granny's funeral, but—forgive me for asking—how did you know of her death?" Hannah remembered Julie saying that her half-uncle lived at Wildoak, a plantation in Virginia.

"By pure chance," he answered. "Christian—Mr. Falconer—and I were in Crawford looking at some brood mares when a drummer passing through happened to mention it."

"That must have been old Ben North," Travis said. Ben was a sometime customer at Stonebridge.

"As soon as I heard," Page went on, "I wanted to pay my respects. Miss Julie was responsible for my getting started at Wildoak. I breed thoroughbreds."

"Yes, Granny mentioned that. But how did she help?"

His suntanned face lit up with a smile. "Bless her. She returned some money she said was a loan. I had thought of it as a gift. But she insisted. You see, when her husband, my father, and I went off to Haiti . . ." He paused, looking down at her with warm friendliness in his blue eyes. "You do know about Haiti? Good. Well, Harry, your grandfather, couldn't afford to make the trip, so I staked him. It was money I had been given to buy my first stud, but it didn't seem as important to me at the time as going to Haiti and seeing what Harry had been left. Well, the coffee plantation had long since been settled by squatters and Harry gave up on it. In fact we were riding back down to Port-au-Prince when he was killed." He paused again, a distant melancholy look in his eyes, as if reliving an unhappy scene that had left its mark on his memory.

"And . . . ?" Hannah prompted.

His gaze returned to Hannah and for a few moments she thought he was going to tell her how his father died. But when he spoke, he said, "And . . . ? Yes. Well, then—Harry had also been deeded an interest in a Haitian rum distillery. Before I came back to the States I saw to it that his shares were signed over to Julie. Several months later she sent me a bank draft, repayment of the loan I had given her husband, she said. I didn't want to accept it, but she insisted. Someone else wouldn't have bothered. I'll always be grateful to her for that kind of integrity."

"She wasn't one to—"

"Hannah!" Chad bellowed. "Hannah! Ain't we got no more for these folks to eat?"

Chad's crudeness, always an irritant, was never more grating to Hannah than tonight. She knew that the larder had been emptied of all but hard Stilton and a few loaves of the bread she had baked. She had been able to purchase only a limited supply to add to the largess of neighbors with the few dollars Chad had given her. Even this

small amount, Chad's willingness to foot the bill for a
wake, had been a surprise until she realized that Chad
was expecting a bequest from Julie.

"Hannah!"

"Yes—at once. Pardon," she said to Page Morse. As
she rose from the bench, her eyes met Christian Falconer's. Sitting diagonally across the table between Bess
and Mrs. McCracken, he was staring at her in a way that
could only be described as lewd. His eyes were shamelessly, deliberately undressing her, flicking up from her
narrow waist to her high, pointed breasts. Anger stained
her cheeks. How dare he! Then, as if guessing her
thoughts, he smiled, amused, his eyes caressing her
breasts again. She lifted her chin, darting him a look full
of scorn. Yet beneath her scorn and outrage something
stirred, a tiny flame of excitement that burned for a
heated moment before it died.

That flicker of excitement disturbed her. When other
men had stared at her in a provocative way, she had
ignored them or with a chilling word had put them in
their place. She had learned to do that on the few occasions she had helped out in the taproom. I should have
ignored him, she thought as she hurried through the
passage to the kitchen, instead of blushing like a ninny.
She gathered loaves from the warming shelf above the
oven and cut the Stilton into wedges. She wondered
how long he and the other guests would stay. She was
getting tired of the meaningless chatter, of Preacher
Wright's sanctimonious pronouncements and Bess's acid
remarks and disapproving glances. In addition Chad was
getting drunk, very drunk.

Would her father invite Page Morse and Mr. Falconer
to remain overnight? It was still raining and too late for
them to take to the road. Stonebridge had an extra room
reserved for travelers, a holdover from the days when it
had truly been an inn, a crossroads halt on the way to
Atlanta. Now the room was rarely used. Most people,
chiefly drummers passing through, put up at the Colley
Hotel on Allison Street. Perhaps the two men would
prefer the amenities of such a hotel. She hoped so. The
thought of Christian Falconer under the same roof as

herself disturbed her. And it upset her even more to
realize that this man with his superior airs, the insulting
stare, and whiskey breath could evoke the slightest feeling except revulsion.

She picked up the heavy tray and started back to the
taproom. Halfway through the passage, a man's figure
loomed, coming toward her.

"May I help you, Miss Blaine?"

It took her a moment to overcome shock, to steady
her voice. "Thank you, Mr. Falconer, but I can manage."

"Please."

He was blocking her way.

"If you would let me pass," she said stiffly.

"Allow me." His hands covered hers, warm, strong,
possessive hands. The tiny flame again, shooting up now
like a lighted torch. She felt her mouth go dry. He
smelled of brandy and beer. That should have put her
off, but somehow didn't. Close up, his handsomeness
was almost diabolical—dark, dark hair, tanned skin, black,
black brows. His eyes were hazel, tiger eyes flecked
with green and gold, and the look in them was avid.
They were gazing at her hungrily, with a greedy desire
that made her heart pound.

"You're very pretty," he said, leaning closer. His
breath was hot on her skin. His mouth, thin and sensual
under the mustache, curved in a smile revealing white
teeth. Hannah felt a thrill of fear mingled with fascination. Was he going to kiss her? "Pretty," he repeated
softly, "lovely skin, charming, sweet, sweet mouth."

She had backed herself up against the damp, sweating
wall and the chill penetrating to her spine suddenly
broke the spell.

"Mr. Falconer!" She drew herself up as much as her
awkward position would allow, for he still held on to her
hands. "I am not the barmaid here. And I resent your
actions, your lewd behavior and speech. Here!" She
shoved the tray into his midriff as hard as she could, so
that he had no alternative but to grasp it. "Since you
wanted to help, you might carry that into the taproom
while I go back to the kitchen for the pot of mustard I've

forgotten. Please—don't follow me. I warn you. If you
do I'll take a knife to you."

He laughed, stepping aside, his amused eyes stripping
her once more.

She returned to the kitchen, leaning on the deal table
to steady her trembling legs. She felt so foolish she
could weep. Never had she had such an encounter or
met such a man, one who both repelled and attracted
her. The thought suddenly struck her that he might be
married. That would compound her mortification, for
Hannah, though she scoffed at Preacher Wright and his
speechifying, was thoroughly imbued with his philoso-
phy, the Ten Commandments having given her a strong
sense of right and wrong. And here she had gone all silly
and weak, wanting the man to kiss her. Yes, it was true.
For one awful moment she had actually yearned for
those mobile lips to press hers.

When a composed Hannah got back to the taproom,
Travis, now standing at the bar, beckoned to her.

"Has that bounder been annoyin' you?" he asked.

"What bounder?"

"Mr. Falconer. I saw him foller you into the kitchen."

"He offered to help."

"Right helpful, ain't he?"

"I can deal with him."

"No, you cain't. What does a convent-bred girl know
about fancy men like Falconer?"

"I'm not convent-bred, Travis. You forget I've spent
most of my life living over a tavern."

"This fellah's different than the sots you've seen here.
He's an aristycrat, one of those spoiled rich sons with
nothin' better to do than play cards, drink, and run after
women. Them kind has appeal for innocent girls."

She laughed. "Travis, you sure seem to know a lot
about innocent girls for someone who's two months shy
of nineteen."

"More'n you think. It don't take a whole lot of sense
to size Falconer up. 'Sides, Ben North, who's got folks
in Richmond, says he's heard Falconer's got a black
reputation. Footloose and fancy free. Not even a wife to
hold him down."

So he wasn't married. Hannah glanced over to the table, and as if by prearranged signal, Falconer looked up and their eyes met again. She put all the contempt she could summon into a long, cold gaze and had the satisfaction of seeing him turn away.

"Pa is taken with them two," Travis said. "Uncle Page—I guess he's our uncle—is fine, but Falconer—well, you know Pa: when he sniffs money he starts to neigh. They're both rich. He's asked them to spend the night."

"And they accepted?"

"Yeah. He wants you to make up the room. But keep out of Falconer's way, you hear?"

"Oh, Travis, you're such a worrywart. Trust me. Besides, they'll be gone in the morning."

And I'll never see Christian Falconer again, she thought. Thank God for that.

But she did see him again. Perhaps if she had known that this man would become the storm center of her life, a demon lover whom she would love and hate with equal passion, she might have made a more determined attempt to avoid him. Perhaps.

Chapter II

Christian Falconer lay on the bare, uncomfortable cot listening to the rain gusting at the windows. On the ceiling above him a zigzag crack ran past a damp spot where water now oozed drop by drop, falling with a slow, hollow plunk on the wooden floor below. The room, its furnishings almost nonexistent, smelled of damp and mold and stale sweat. On the adjoining bed Christian's brother-in-law was snoring, a sound that irritated Christian as much as the plunking of water and the cold draft chilling the back of his neck.

Lucky fellow, that Page Morse, Christian thought. Asleep the minute his head hit the pillow. Not a care in the world. But why should he have cares? Owner of Wildoak at thirty-seven, married to my sister, Sabrina, the apple of Papa's eye, father of a healthy eighteen-month-old son. What did Page have to feel unhappy about?

Christian shifted and, rising on an elbow, punched up the lumpy pillow. He tried once more to compose himself for sleep but his busy mind kept swinging from one thought to another.

Why had he come to this backwater village in the first place? Restless. He had left his home in San Francisco for an extended stay at Wildoak. Growing bored with it, he had intended to move on when Page suggested he accompany him to Georgia to look at a brood mare. Then the news of the old woman who had been the mother of Page's half-sister had brought them to Bayetville.

And now he was here, wide-eyed at two in the morning and desperately wanting a drink. Could he slip downstairs to the taproom? More likely than not, the old cracker, Blaine, was still stretched out on the table where he had last seen him when he and Page had gone up to bed. How could such a crude lump be the father of something so exquisite as Hannah Blaine? He smiled to himself as he thought of her clear gray eyes, the petal-like skin, the pink cheeks, the pert, almost delicate nose, and the lush red lips that spoke of a sensuality of which, he was sure, Hannah was unaware.

And her figure! Despite that ugly, unfashionable boned bodice, caged bustle, and aproned skirt, he could discern the narrow waist and ripe breasts pushing against the ebony-buttoned fichu. How he would have loved to undo those buttons, part the camisole, release the white mounded flesh to seeking hands and tongue. If she weren't a relative of Page's (what was it—half-niece?) he would have pursued her. And what a pursuit! Little wench, giving him that scornful look.

He turned over on his side, closed his eyes, and was finally drifting down into blessed sleep when a loud crash and the tinkling of broken glass from down below brought him sharply up. A few moments later he heard footsteps hurrying past his door and someone's voice—Hannah's—call from the top of the stairs.

"Pa? Pa, is that you?" And then an exclamation, "Oh, my God!"

Christian got into his riding breeches and shirt, shot a glance at the still-sleeping Page, and let himself out.

"Pa?" he heard Hannah question as he came down the stairs.

Chad Blaine was stretched out on the stone floor, blood trickling down his forehead. Hannah, kneeling beside him, was trying to stop the blood with a cloth.

"What happened?" Christian asked. "Is he out?"

"Yes. He must have rolled off the table and taken a glass with him. It broke and—"

"Here. Let me look. Do you have another clean cloth? Some alcohol?" When she hesitated he said, "It's all right. I'm a doctor."

She got what he wanted and he cleaned the wound.

"Is it deep?"

"Afraid so. I should sew it up. Get me a stout needle and thread."

She went off and was back in a few minutes. "I'm surprised the noise didn't wake the children or Travis," she said.

"Page slept through it, too." Christian wondered if she had been as sleepless as he had been.

"Does he feel it?" she asked.

"I doubt it. He's too full of whiskey to feel anything. He'll have a big headache in the morning."

"Do you think we could get him upstairs?"

"That hulk of a man? A pillow under his head and a blanket will do him until morning."

She sped away to fetch pillow and blanket. He had finished his task when she got back. He slipped the pillow under Chad's head. Hannah knelt beside him and gently dabbed the blood from Chad's brow. As she worked her arm brushed his and he was surprised how that accidental touch sent a thrill of excitement through his veins. Her body, so close to his, emanated a sweet warmth, the faint fragrance of lilac—or was it violets? She was wearing a quilted wrapper that hid her figure. But his imagination unclothed her as it had done earlier, and as she leaned forward he pictured her breasts, their smooth, silky firmness cupped in his hands, his thumbs caressing the nipples, making them taut with desire.

She rose abruptly, almost as if she had divined his thoughts. Her eyes briefly held a startled look like a doe's, aware that it is being stalked.

"Thank you, Mr. Falconer."

"You're welcome. Oh"—he held out his bloodied hands—"I wonder if I could wash these."

"There's a pump in the kitchen." She pointed with her chin.

Not that dark passage again for her, he thought. "May I have some brandy? To drink, that is."

"Certainly. Help yourself."

He gave her a wry smile. "You're not being very hospitable to someone who's just saved your papa from bleeding to death."

"I did thank you, Mr. Falconer. And when Pa comes to, I'm sure he'll do the same." She looked down at her father's face. "Perhaps his gashed head might even be a lesson to curb his thirst in the future."

"You don't think much of your papa, do you?"

"I don't think much of men who drink to excess."

"And can't hold their liquor?"

"Yes."

"I see." She didn't much like her father—or him. She wasn't pretty, he decided, she was beautiful. Her brown hair, highlighted with glints of chestnut, was let down for the night. It fell over her shoulders in dark waves, framing her lovely face, the pert nose, the pouting lips. What was such a rose doing in this cabbage patch? Probably longing to get out, but no money. Poor. Everything about Stonebridge, from its broken shutters to the scarred countertopped bar, the cracked glassware, and the meager supper they had been served, screamed poverty. "May I ask an impertinent question?"

"No."

"I'll ask it anyway. How is it that you speak without the local accent? Your grammar—"

"I'm not a country bumpkin," she interrupted haughtily, "as you might think. I've had the advantage of a little education. And I would remind you, sir, not to patronize me."

He smiled. He couldn't help it. What was she, all of sixteen, seventeen? And putting him in his place.

"I apologize if my manner seemed disrespectful."

"It has been from the first."

"A double apology." He smiled again. Honest, too. Forthright; said what she thought. "I'm afraid I've acted like less than a gentleman." How could he help but look at her with desire, he wanted to add, when she was so desirable? "And now I'll go along and wash up. There's soap and a towel, I presume?"

She tucked in her mouth. "I'll show you." Hannah lifted the old lamp from the counter and led the way. In the kitchen she found a bar of yellow soap and a faded flour sack.

The pump over the soapstone sink groaned and squealed as Christian worked it. When he was through, Hannah handed him the towel. Their hands touched. He resisted the impulse to grasp hers and saw the slight flush rising from her throat to her cheeks. She was feeling, then. She might dislike him, but she found him physically attractive. The thought buoyed him, made him bolder.

He said nothing as he slowly dried his hands. She had stepped away, the doe again, alert, wary.

"If you'll excuse me." She turned to go.

"Wait! Miss Blaine . . ." He paused. "Why are you afraid of me?"

It was not what he meant to say. He had thought to hold her with some inconsequential remark, another petty request, not his truth matching hers.

"Afraid of you, Mr. Falconer? You flatter yourself."

What dignity she had! How beautiful, how irresistible she looked in that graceless wrapper.

"Do I?" He stepped closer. "Perhaps I'm mistaken then. Perhaps you merely detest me."

"I don't detest you, Mr. Falconer," she said in a low voice. "I have no feelings about you one way or the other."

He expected her to leave then, but she didn't. Perhaps she did detest him, but there was something else there, something between them that pulled like a compelling magnet, an animal instinct, the mating call, male and female, that had nothing to do with like or dislike, love or hate.

"So I'm of no consequence. I'm truly sorry you feel that way."

She was tense, but the hostility had gone. Her eyes were fixed on his. He held her gaze, not moving, hardly daring to breathe, just looking, losing himself, drowning

in those wide gray eyes. Behind him he was faintly
conscious of rain spattering the window.

"Hannah . . ."

"Don't come any closer," she warned, her voice
trembling. "I—I don't trust you. I must go."

But she could not pull herself away. Nor could he.
Neither of them spoke. The silence grew in intensity, a
taut expectancy, a wordless suspense. Her hand went to
her throat but her eyes remained fixed on his face.

"Stay," he pleaded softly. He took a step, two, three.
Again he was reminded of the doe, the tremulous, tiptoe
fear held in thrall by a fascination it did not understand.
Her very timidity, her seeming defenselessness filled
him with a compelling sexual desire that paled his earlier
fantasies. He wanted her, he must have her. Damn the
scruples.

"Hannah . . ." He reached out, the tips of his fingers touching her wrapper.

"Don't. Please."

"Come to me, Hannah."

"No, I cannot."

He saw the pulse beating in her throat, could almost
hear the thump of her heart.

Slowly, as though he were moving under water, he
pulled her into his embrace. Softly, softly so as not to
frighten her, his lips tenderly brushed hers. He felt her
shiver. His mouth closed over hers and for a split second he felt her stiffen, but then as his kiss deepened she
went lax. He wanted to ravage those honey-sweet lips,
to pry them open, to taste her, to have his tongue
explore, to press, to bruise, to leave that scarlet mouth
swollen with his kisses. But he held back, the air catching
in his lungs, waiting for the soft pressure of Hannah's
mouth to tell him he could go on.

She sighed in his arms and then made the first tenta-
tive move, a feather touch on his mouth. He kissed her
again, quick little kisses on the lips, on the cheek, his
hands sliding inside the wrapper. Her slim body trembled, but she did not push him away. Blindly he sought
her breasts, the firm mounds through her cotton gown,
the clothed nipples. She was shivering, leaning against

him, exciting him more and more, his arousal pulsing. He wanted her, he wanted her as he had never wanted a woman before.

He lifted his head and looked wildly about. Where? On the stone-flagged floor? Where could he take her, rip off that ugly wrapper, the gown, crush her nakedness to his chest, splay the thighs apart? Oh, he must have her! "Don't," she whispered as his hands moved down her rounded hips, pushing at the gown, seeking, seeking. He would take her here, now. She would make no objection. Her "don't" was for form's sake. She was his. In another moment he would have what every fiber of his being craved, cried out for.

"Hannah!" a voice suddenly shrieked. "Hannah, where are you?"

They sprang apart. Hannah, her face a fiery red, quickly rebelted her wrapper.

"Hannah!" A pigtailed Sue Joy in nightdress stood in the kitchen doorway. "Why is Pa lying on the floor?"

"He—he hurt himself," Hannah stammered, fighting to regain her composure. She did not look at Christian. She couldn't. "Pa—Pa cut his forehead and Mr. Falconer was kind enough to fix it." She swallowed, making another attempt to control the tremor in her voice. "What are you doing out of bed?"

"There's a mouse in our room. It woke me."

"Come along, then, we'll take care of the mouse. Good night, Mr. Falconer," she added, glancing quickly in his direction, wishing he would disappear, sink into the floor, prove to be a bad dream, anything but have him stand there in the flesh, his eyes upon her.

"Good night, Hannah."

She was still trembling, her knees like water, shaking so badly she clung to Sue Joy's small hand. She felt weak, giddy, sick. How could she have behaved in such a disreputable, vulgar fashion? No decent woman would have allowed a man, especially a stranger, to take such liberties.

"How long is Mr. Falconer and Uncle Page going to stay?" Sue Joy asked.

"They're leaving tomorrow."

In the morning she must get up and wait on them. Lacey, the hired girl, usually helped to cook and serve the household's breakfast, but since she was gone Hannah would be obliged to do it on her own. How could she face that devil, that Christian Falconer who had roused such desire in her, such animal passion as to blot out her good sense? How could she meet his eyes, speak to him? She could hide in the kitchen. But having to skulk there among the pots and pans would be a further humiliation.

She slept poorly the rest of the night, slipping in and out of dreams where Christian Falconer tormented her with his kisses, his rough hands, his husky voice. In one awful nightmare he and Granny fought over her, Christian pulling on one arm, Julie on the other. When dawn came she rose, dressed in the same faded black gown, and went downstairs. Chad was already sitting at the table, holding his head.

"I see you're up," Hannah said dryly. He looked terrible, the bags under his eyes dark gray pouches, his hair in greasy spikes.

"Where else would I be?" he replied irritably. "Get me a tot of whiskey, will you, Sis?"

"Haven't you had enough? You passed out last night."

" 'S that why I couldn't remember? Must have hit my head."

"You split it open."

"I need a drink, Sis." She went behind the counter and poured him a shot glass of corn whiskey. He drank it in one greedy gulp. "Our company still sleepin'?"

"It's not yet six."

"Give 'em a good breakfast. See that Lacey doesn't boil the coffee till it tastes like piss. And get the side of bacon out of the smokehouse."

"The bacon's gone."

"Oh, Christ. You young uns are eatin' me out of house and home."

Harsh words crowded her tongue. But to give vent to them would be an exercise in futility. "Why don't you go upstairs and sleep it off?" she suggested acidly.

"Naw. A good dousin' under the pump and I'll be

right as rain. I'm not about missin' sayin' good-bye to
Page and Mr. Falconer."

Hannah started for the kitchen.

"Sis, now lissin, afore you leave. If they offer pay I
want you 'n Travis to keep your mouths shut."

"Pa! They're guests!"

"Beggars can't be choosers."

"We're not beggars!"

"Speak for yoreself, gel. Get me another tot of that
white lightnin'. Whyn't you bring the bottle over and
save yourself some trouble."

Hannah ignored him and, turning on her heel, went
through the passage to the kitchen to find Lacey had
unexpectedly returned from her mother's bedside. "She
ain't that near dying as Brother put on," Lacey said as
she fumbled over the stove.

"Here, let me!" Hannah said impatiently. God, she
thought, if I could only get away, if only Granny left
me some money. She hated to think of herself as looking
forward to money when Julie's body was hardly cold in
the grave. But Granny would understand. Julie herself
had once hinted that as soon as Sue Joy was old enough
to care for her brothers she'd send Hannah to the convent for another year.

"You can find you a good husband in Atlanta," she
had said, "not some local lout who'll work you to the
bone and get you in pup as regular as a bitch dog.
Nothin' but a gentleman for you, Hannah, my dear."

Yes, a gentleman, Hannah thought, her heart searing
with shame. A gentleman's toy.

She started a fire going in the iron stove, feeding the
growing flame from the woodbox. "The kettle,
Lacey." Then, "Have you brought the eggs in from the
henhouse?"

Every morning it was the same. The woodstove to
light, the kettle; Lacey, have you brought in the eggs?
Lacey was willing but not very bright. She must be told
what to do each time, though she had gone through the
same routine for a year now. A lumpish girl of eighteen
with a pudding face, she was the daughter of a domestic
worker with a stepping-stair brood, their various fathers

unknown. Hannah would have fired her months ago, but she pitied the girl.

Breakfast was ready at six-thirty. Page Morse wanted an early start. Chad, red-eyed and already tipsy, sat at the head of the table, the children at the foot. Hannah, bringing in dishes from the kitchen, platters of cornbread and honey, hominy and fried eggs, avoided looking directly at Christian. But the sight of the back of his black head, the broad shoulders, filled her again with mortification. She still felt his kisses burning her mouth, the hot lips resting in the hollow of her throat, kisses that made her bones melt like candle wax thrust into fire. He could have done anything with her and she would have been willing. Anything. Were it not for Sue Joy she probably would no longer be a virgin, but a used woman, a whore.

Page said, "Won't you sit down and join us, Hannah?"

"I must help Lacey."

"Lacey will do all right," her father growled. "You ain't the kitchen maid. Not with all that fancy schoolin'. Yore uncle ast you to sit. It's bad manners to say no."

Hannah sat between Page and Travis. Christian was directly across from her. She kept her eyes lowered.

Page said, "You must come and visit us at Wildoak, Hannah."

"Thank you, Uncle, but I have obligations here. There is the school and I'm also needed at home."

She would never go to Wildoak as long as there was any chance of Christian being there. She was afraid of him, afraid of herself.

"Now, Hannah," her father said, "you make too much of yoreself. We ain't needin' you. Sue Joy is gettin' to be a big gel and there's Lacey, not much help, but some. And Travis give us all the hand we need."

Hannah looked at her father with surprise. He wants me to go, she thought. Why?

"It'll be right nice to meet yore Virginny kin," he went on. "Ain't no call to pass up a chanc't at meetin' quality folk 'cause of a little ole teachin' job, now, is there?"

His manner was unctuous, disgusting. His reasons

for wanting her to go to Wildoak were all too plain. He wished to ingratiate himself with his late wife's rich relatives, with that other gentleman, Christian Falconer, who had once or twice looked at his daughter with the kind of craving he understood. Hannah could almost read his mind. He was thinking that short of finding herself a rich husband, she might become mistress, perhaps to this man here, who, being an honorable man in Chad's eyes, could be persuaded to marry her if she became pregnant.

Hannah had never hated her father more.

She turned to Page Morse. "I thank you for your kind invitation. I shall think it over."

No cause to get into a nasty argument where her father might end up bellowing curses and smashing the crockery. But she would be a long time "thinking it over." In the meanwhile she was sure her father's befuddled mind would forget the two men from Wildoak, and, she hoped, in time she would, too.

Chapter III

The family had gathered at Julie Page's house on Asbury Street for the reading of her will. Chad, trying not to appear anxious, sat with the others on dusty fiddleback chairs, while Tom Baxter, Julie's friend, chief clerk at the Bayetville Bank, spelled out the terms of Granny's last testament. It was short and succinct. She had left everything, except her pearl brooch, to her daughter, Bess, who had lived with her mother for thirty-eight years in an unarmed truce.

Chad was fit to be tied.

"It's all legal, folks," Tom Baxter said. A thin, elderly man with a squint, he had handled Julie's financial affairs since the death of her husband. It was he who had negotiated the sale of the small general store when she had chosen to retire, getting a decent (some said outrageous) sum for it. "You can holler all you want. But ain't a danged thing I can do about it."

Chad loosened the top button of his shirt. He had dressed up for the occasion, the country-inn landlord about to inherit money. "I don't believe it. She was rich, I tell you, *rich*! Enough for everybody. Now you claim she left all her shares in that rum company in

27

Haytee and every penny of her cash to Bess. And you won't even say how much."

"That was Julie's wish. She didn't think it was anybody's business 'cept hers and Bess's."

"That so? You shore you ain't had yore hand in the cookie jar, Tom, afore she passed on? Or mebbe after?"

Tom Baxter drew himself up. His grammar and education may not have been up to the standard of the young men coming into the bank these days, but he knew his job. He took pride in his accumulated knowledge and ability, and above all, his honesty.

"I ain't goin' to honor that with a reply. My records are at the bank, Chad Blaine, if you want to look 'em over, go 'head. You'll find they balance to the penny. Mrs. Page was obliged to sell some of her stock four years ago for personal use, but otherwise nothing's been touched."

Four years ago, Hannah thought. That's when I went off to school. The Sisters of Mercy, though vowed to poverty, had charged high fees. And Granny had paid them without once hinting that she had sacrificed a portion of her income to do so.

Though Hannah herself had been somewhat disappointed in Granny's will, she understood. Aunt Bess, unmarried, without a man to look after her, needed to be provided for. Hannah had received *her* bequest when Granny was still alive.

And there was the brooch to treasure—and a letter.

Dear Hannah:
   I never had much scooling, so I hope you excuse my speling and so forth. . . . I really wished to leave you shares of Rum stock but I was affeard Chad would get his hands on it. None to you . . . You were so like me at thirteen, big eyes wide with hope and a hole life ahead to look forward to. Well, for me, the futcher turned out to be no bed of roses. Tell the truth I lied bout a few things. I loved your grandpa when I married him. That was honest-to-goodness. A big blond hansum man. Then one day Page Morse showd up, Harry's son. First

I knowd Harry had gotten some lady named Deedee Morse at a place called Wildoak with child. (First he heard bout the baby too, or so he said. I think between you and me the lady's folks run him off.) I didn't mind. Everybody knows how men be when they is away from home. Howsoever when Harry took off with his son and left me to fend with the store, I tell you now I ain't ever forgive him. He put that bastard ahed of his own true family and that was something no man, whatsoever his faults, ought to do.

One thing I want you to remember, Hannah, is I love you. I want you to marry a good man, one that will stand up for you and be there when you need him. Protect your virtue. Its the only thing a poor girl with no money has to offer.

God bless you, my dear. Granny.

Hannah reread the letter a half-dozen times before she folded it and put it in the japanned box where she kept her valuables.

Chad, on the other hand, continued to rant and rave. He felt cheated. *Cheated.* As Mary Louise's husband, the father of Granny Julie's grandchildren, he deserved something. So certain had he been of receiving a substantial sum from Julie that he had borrowed money on the strength of it, laying in a stock of malt lager, buying himself a fancy watch with a solid gold fob. In his disappointment he soon began to consume the lager and was quickly forced to sell the watch and fob (at a loss) to keep his creditors from closing him down.

The following September Chad received a letter from Page Morse at Wildoak. Chad, who could barely decipher large print, asked Hannah to read it for him.

"Dear Chad, forgive me for being neglectful in thanking you for your hospitality—"

"For which he paid," Hannah interposed.

"Never you mind. Go on."

"I think I may have an offer which will be of interest

to your daughter. Our local school is in need of a mistress come this October. The children are from neighboring families, well behaved and eager to learn. The schoolhouse is newly built and is amply supplied with readers, composition books, slates, desks, and such. The pay is fifteen dollars a month—"

"Fifteen dollars a month!" Chad expostulated. "Holy Mother!"

Hannah read on. "I hope that Hannah looks upon this situation with favor. She could also be of use by privately tutoring some of the backward students, for additional recompense, of course. With your permission, Chad—"

"I'm not going," Hannah said, putting the letter down.

They were sitting at the kitchen table. Travis was in the taproom serving the local blacksmith, who had stopped by for a pint. The children were outside, below the window, shouting and squabbling over a game of stone jacks.

"Are you daft? Clean out of your head? Fifteen dollars . . ."

"I don't want to go to Wildoak."

"Goddammit! You'll go, if I have to . . ."

"I can't. I haven't any decent clothes to wear." Chad might understand that. It was the only explanation she could think of.

"All righty," he said, calming. "Git yoreself some goods from Hawkinson's on credit. Make up a gown or two."

"We already owe him, Pa. He won't put a cent more on the books. And both Sue Joy and Bobby need shoes. That comes first."

"Let 'em go barefoot. Tell you what, I think I can scrounge up five dollars, a feller owes me. You take it and fix yoreself some duds."

"No, Pa."

"Don't argue. Is the letter done?"

"Just a few lines." She read on, "Sabrina will be delighted to have Hannah. For once we are without guests since Christian returned to his home in San Francisco two months ago." Hannah paused. Was it true?

She reread the sentence. ". . . returned to his home in San Francisco and the house seems empty. Please tell Hannah to give this serious thought. With best regards, Page Morse."

"There 'tis," Chad said. "And I want no sass. Tonight you sit yoreself down and answer that letter and say you'll be happy to come. If you don't—so help me, I'll . . ."

But Hannah wasn't listening. The last two lines of the letter had opened a door for her. For the first time she dared to think that this was her way out of Stonebridge. Christian had been the obstacle at Wildoak and he wasn't there. She didn't care about the fifteen dollars. Let Chad have it. Her only regret would be in leaving Travis. Perhaps she might be able to procure some work for him at Wildoak, too, something far more elevating than drawing beer. Not right away. In another year, perhaps, when Sue Joy got a little older and could care for the younger children. If both she and Travis sent money home, Chad could hardly object.

All sorts of possibilities began to present themselves to Hannah. She would live with gentlefolk, hear soft words spoken, eat at a linen-covered table with kin who did not gobble their food or let it dribble down their chins, cultured people who did not get roaring drunk. She would wake in the morning, not at cockcrow but at a respectable hour, and would come downstairs to a warm dining room, not to a cold kitchen with a half-wit waiting to be told what to do.

"Are you goin' to fetch pen and ink, or shall I do it?" her father asked.

"Let me talk to Travis first."

"What's he got to do with it?"

"I don't want him to feel I'm running off without asking what he thinks."

Travis, as she had guessed, was delighted. "Why should I mind? God Almighty! Gettin' away from here is what you've always wanted. And a job to boot. You'll be beholden to nobody."

"Oh, Travis, I do feel guilty."

"No reason to. I'll be gone myself 'nother year or

two. Let Bobby or Colin have Stonebridge, what's left
of it time Pa gets done. It ain't for me."

"Travis, I want you to make something of yourself."

He hugged her, holding her for a long moment.
" 'Course I will."

Hannah came to Wildoak in mid-September on a warm,
golden afternoon. A buggy had been sent to fetch her at
the train station in Richmond. Driven by the Wildoak
servant, Isaiah, a large black man with a thatch of crin-
kly white hair, the buggy rumbled over a rutted road
following the Pamunkey River, which shimmered in the
dazzling sunlight as it ran its course between banks
overgrown with Black-eyed Susans. Isaiah pointed out
the various properties that had been plantations before
the War Between the States: The Willows, Glen Ivy,
Fairchild, names which seemed to resound with a romantic antebellum past. She craned her neck to catch a
glimpse of what she imagined would be magnolia-shaded
mansions, but all she saw was a few chimneys rising
above the treetops and the burnt-out shell of a house on
the river's edge.

As the buggy turned into the long, carefully raked
gravel drive that led to Wildoak Hannah's heart beat
with renewed excitement. When the last tree fell away
and she caught sight of the house set back from a green
velvety lawn, she exclaimed, "Oh! It's so grand!"

It was everything she expected and more. Built of
brick, mellowed by the wind and weather of two hundred and fifty years to a dusty pink, it rose from a
white-pillared veranda in two stories. Fragrant jasmine
buzzing with bees bloomed at the foot of the shallow
brick steps.

Page Morse and his wife came out to greet her. "My
dear," Page said, handing her down from the buggy, "so
glad you could come. Darling, this is Hannah Blaine."

"Welcome to Wildoak," Sabrina said, kissing Hannah. "We've heard so much about you."

Sabrina, except for the dark, glossy hair, bore only a
slight resemblance to her brother, Christian. She was a
beautiful woman with a heart-shaped face and delicately

molded features. Dressed in what Hannah assumed was the height of fashion—a russet skirt pinched at the slender waist with a buckled silk belt and above it a white shirtwaist ruffled down the front—Sabrina's easy poise and sweet smile exuded self-confidence and happiness that pierced Hannah with envy.

By contrast Hannah felt shoddy, dated, though the gown she had copied from a picture in the *Atlantic Times* at home had seemed stylish at the time. She had added little bows and fancywork braid down the front because she had thought it gave the dress a needed fillip. Now she could see that Sabrina's attire without adornment was much more pleasing to the eye. Like its owner, it had an air of simple elegance.

"Come, let us go in."

Hannah tried to behave as though visiting homes like Wildoak was an everyday occurrence. She did not want to seem like the country cousin. But the interior of the house, like the exterior, awed her. The staircase itself was a thing of grace, winding up from the entryway, sweeping upward in a spiral before it disappeared beyond the ceiling.

"Isaiah will take your hat."

Sabrina led Hannah into the parlor. "Please . . ." She motioned to a green rococo sofa. The room smelled of beeswax and roses. A wide blue jar filled with yellow and red blooms stood on a polished table behind the sofa and another had been placed on the closed lid of the piano. There were chairs covered with green damask and a flowered damask loveseat on which Sabrina sat. There were painted china lamps, oil portraits and landscapes on the walls, and underfoot a thick umber carpet, strewn with smaller Oriental rugs. Again Hannah tried not to stare, pretending that she sat on rococo sofas in charming, richly furnished rooms every day of her life.

"Would you like some refreshment?" Sabrina asked. She had a low, musical voice. "You must have had a tiring journey. Tea, perhaps?"

"Tea would be fine."

Sabrina pressed a china handle set in a wall covered

with green, flocked paper. She inquired politely after Hannah's family.

"We'd only been married two years, you know," Sabrina explained as they waited, "when Page barely got Wildoak started. He did well this past year and we are hoping he will continue to do so. Then perhaps we can enlarge the parlor, get new furniture. But in the meanwhile, we'll make do. Ah, here's the tea."

Hannah watched as Sabrina poured. To the manor born, such grace, so in command. And this beautiful woman in this beautiful house with a husband who adored her and a young son was hinting (she was too much the lady to complain) that because of strained finances they would have to make do. Hannah tried not to feel bitter. There was no cause to, she told herself; making do was different for different people.

"I mustn't chatter so much," Sabrina said. "One lump or two?"

"Three, please." Sugar had been a luxury at Stonebridge.

Tarts were served with the tea, fresh peach tarts baked with a crispy crust and spiced generously with ginger and cinnamon. Hannah could have easily eaten the whole platter but restrained herself to a decorous two.

Sabrina said, "Would you like to meet little Miles? I believe he must be up from his nap by now."

Little Miles, held by a servant, a young black girl of fourteen or fifteen, was sobbing and wailing when they entered the nursery, his face screwed up, tears falling from his blue eyes.

"He wan' his sugar tit," the servant said.

"Well, he can't have it." Sabrina took him into her arms. "Do you want to grow up a milksop?" She kissed the wet face and gradually the crying went into long gasps and ceased. "Is that the way you behave for our guest?" The child gazed at her out of tear-misted eyes. "Say hello to Cousin Hannah."

Miles looked at Hannah and said, " 'Upper. I wan' 'upper."

"Presently," Sabrina said.

When they left the room the child began to wail again. Even paradise, Hannah thought, has its imperfections.

Sabrina led Hannah down a short corridor and, opening a door, said, "This will be yours, Hannah."

The room was good-sized, twice as large as the one Hannah had shared with Sue Joy. The wide-planked floor was strewn with patchwork rugs, the bed curtained in white eyelet to match the window hangings. A large vase of fragrant pink roses graced the dressing table. Hannah's cardboard case had been brought up and stood on a low bench. It looked cheap, shabby, out of place in this pretty room.

"I'm sorry," Sabrina apologized, "but Daisy, our servant girl, is occupied at the moment and there is no one to help you unpack."

"I can manage, thank you," Hannah said, glad that no one, not even a servant, would be able to view her pitiable belongings, the harsh, homespun cotton underclothes and her one other gown.

Sabrina stood for a moment looking at Hannah with something close to pity in her eyes. "I hope you won't be homesick."

"No, no, not at all," she said, a shaft of nostalgic pain suddenly piercing her heart. Everything was so strange and she felt so alone. This was far different from her first foray into the world. At the convent school the rooms were austerely furnished, the girls dressed alike, all reduced to the same level. Here she felt out of her element, the poor relation who must watch her speech, her manners, who would daily be reminded of the contrast between Wildoak and Stonebridge.

"I'll go and let you have a rest," Sabrina said at the door. "You must try and feel at home, Hannah dear."

"I already do," Hannah said, standing very straight, too proud to admit how she felt. "You've been so kind."

When Hannah took her place in the schoolroom the following Monday morning, she did so with an outward calm that belied her inner uncertainty. All those eyes staring at her, sizing her up, children in starched pinafores and pressed, patchless trousers, not a pair of bare feet or a torn overall among them.

Riverview, like Pine Tree, was a one-room school. But there the similarity ended. Newly built for its specific purpose, Riverview exuded the fragrance of planed wood and fresh paint. The windows were whole—not cracked or grimy with handprints—the desks, as yet, unscarred, gleaming with varnish. It was well supplied, as Page Morse had written. The shelves along one whole wall held neat stacks of McGuffy Readers, Noah Webster's Elementary Spelling Books, Palmer's Writing Method, copybooks, boxes of pens and pencils, and slates. Her pupils were the sons and daughters of planters and prosperous farmers; most were destined to go on to academies of higher learning.

It did not take Hannah long to discover, however, that except for their speech, clean faces, and well-shod feet these children differed little from her pupils at home. There were the dummies, the plodders, the bright ones, and the troublemakers. Billy Carstairs, big for his age and a bully, was the worst. In the schoolyard he pinched and cuffed the younger boys, threatening them if they did not buy him off with sweets or money. Inside, he threw paper darts behind Hannah's back, distracting her other pupils, often making them break into nervous laughter with his antics.

One afternoon Billy got too much for Hannah. He had dumped one of the younger boys in the rainbarrel and nearly drowned him. Hannah closed the school early and took Billy home in the trap.

In the drawing room at Grenfield—a huge mansion said to have been purchased by Carstairs from the proceeds of ill-gotten blockade money—Hannah confronted Tom and Bertha Carstairs. Either Billy mended his manners or they must keep him at home.

Mrs. Carstairs, a large-bosomed young woman, swept Hannah head to foot with scathing eyes.

"Now, just who are you to give instructions?"

"I'm sorry, but I can't have him disturbing the other children."

"He stays and that's final."

Mr. Carstairs, a tall man with lank brown hair and a large nose, fondled his heavy mustache but said nothing.

"I was put in charge of that classroom to teach," Hannah said firmly. "I can't do it with Billy there. I don't want him to come back unless he shows me he can behave. Promises won't do."

"Are you dictating terms to me?" Bertha Carstairs demanded.

Billy snickered. Tom Carstairs gazed at Hannah with interest.

"Yes," Hannah said. "And *that* is *my* final word."

She went out of the house. She was getting into the trap when Tom Carstairs came running down the steps.

"A moment, Miss Blaine."

She sat and waited, the reins in her hands.

"You mustn't mind Mrs. Carstairs. She's gone on the boy and believes he can do no wrong."

"I'm sorry, but I can't agree with her."

"Could you," he said, leaning close, "see your way to giving him private lessons, perhaps?"

"I don't think so. Besides, I believe it would be best if he started to learn how to get along with other people. He won't go far in this world if he doesn't." She realized after she spoke how ridiculous her words must seem to Tom Carstairs. Billy, because of his father's wealth, would never have to get along, and as for going far in the world, he had already arrived.

"That's true, my dear." His voice had taken on an intimate tone. "Perhaps you'd care to tutor me instead?" He laughed, an offensive hee-haw that jangled Hannah's ears.

"I don't know what you mean."

"I mean you and I can have a romp together when Bertha goes off to her women's club on Thursday afternoons. We'd have the house all to ourselves, including the big bed upstairs." Leaning closer, he put his hot, moist hand over hers. "I'd make it worth your while."

She gave the horse a smart smack with the reins and the buggy jolted forward, nearly upsetting Tom Carstairs. Hannah did not look back.

* * *

With Christmas approaching, school was in recess for a month. Page Morse had offered Hannah the fare to go home but she had refused. By this time she had made it plain that she would accept nothing she hadn't earned. No charity. Sabrina had tried to give Hannah gowns she claimed she had outgrown, having gained weight since little Miles's birth. But Hannah, too proud to appear in hand-me-downs, suggested that perhaps Sabrina could donate the clothing to the missionary society sponsored by local churchwomen. She did, however, accept a length of blue shot silk in payment for helping Page with his business correspondence in the evening. Using this fabric, she decided to make up a dress copied from an illustration in a fashion magazine of Sabrina's, a gown that had little puffed sleeves, a scooped neck, and from its narrow waist a skirt that fell in peplums, stiffened with chamois, to the floor. It was extravagant attire for someone of Hannah's status and means, not practical in the least. But Hannah, for once in her life, wanted something extravagant. She wanted to own just one thing that had no earthly use except to make her pretty. When the girls at convent school had talked of parties and velvet dresses and satin-striped jaconets and pert little hats, she had thought them frivolous. Now she understood. Frivolity was that part of her girlhood she had missed. I'll make up for it, she thought, standing in front of the mirror, holding the blue shot silk up to her chin. I'll wear it on Christmas Eve.

Outwardly Hannah's social position at Wildoak held no ambiguity. She was one of the family, not a governess or impoverished relation but a niece who just happened to be teaching school. Hannah explained this in her numerous letters to Travis, which were as exuberant as the ones she had sent to him from Atlanta, and, had she but known, as alarming. Travis, who had hinted at it more than once, was afraid such fine living, such aristocratic company, would create a chasm between them that eventually could not be breached. He needn't have worried. No matter how kind Sabrina and Page were, how politely their friends behaved toward Hannah, she still felt she didn't belong, the girl from a farm town in

central Georgia whose father belched at the table and
considered it normal for his guests to hawk and spit on
the floor.

Sabrina and Hannah were sitting in Page's little office
writing Christmas cards.

"I always forget how many relatives Page and I have
until the holidays come around," Sabrina said with a
sigh.

Hannah's list had been much shorter. She was now
helping Sabrina by addressing cards to Page's business
acquaintances.

Sabrina ran her pen down the list at her elbow, ticking
off names. "Well, that takes care of Mother and Father,
Brother Arthur and family, Aunt Deirdre and that crew.
I suppose I ought to send a few cheerful words to
Christian, although *he* never writes. The scalawag." She
shook her head. "I really don't know what's to become
of him. Papa says he's given up on Christian, but then
Papa is short on patience. Especially with Christian."

Hannah listened to this with more interest than she
cared to admit.

"You've met my brother, Hannah. Would you ever
guess that he's a qualified doctor?"

"Not if he hadn't told me." In fact the news had
come as a surprise. She had thought of Christian as a
rich ne'er-do-well, more handsome than any man had a
right to be, with little thought but to enjoy himself. "My
father," Hannah went on to explain, "well, my father
had a little accident while Mr. Falconer and Uncle Page
were visiting and Christian—Mr. Falconer—tended a cut
on Pa's head."

"Christian's good at tending people, much better than
he thinks. But I'm afraid he went into medicine not
because he had a bent for it but to spite Papa, who
wanted him to study law. Christian is always doing the
opposite of what Papa wants." She smiled ruefully.
"And his escapades while a student—but I won't go into
that. However, he did obtain his degree and actually
went into practice with a Dr. Baumgard. But not for
long."

"Didn't he care for it?"

"It wasn't that." Sabrina frowned. "He became—how shall I put it?—disillusioned. I can't say that I really blame him. Dr. Baumgard was an ignorant man, a butcher, according to Christian. He'd operated on a child and accidentally hit an artery. They couldn't stanch the blood and she died. Christian said it was sheer ineptness, but what really made him furious was the doctor walking away from the corpse saying, 'It was only a charity case.' Of course Christian raised quite a fuss, at one point promising to strangle the surgeon and commit general mayhem among the hospital staff. Naturally this did not go down well with Christian's colleagues and they threatened to drum him out of the profession."

"Perhaps if he had used tact, he might have accomplished more," Hannah suggested.

"I'm sure of it. Christian can be very tactful, very charming when he sets out to get what he wants. As long as his temper isn't ruffled, that is. Page says he should have been a stevedore, a boxer, a mercenary soldier, a pirate on the high seas, pillaging, kidnapping, and ravishing women at the point of a sword. And perhaps Page is right. Christian's my brother and I do love him, but I wish he had a more serious purpose in life."

Sabrina sat gazing thoughtfully into space while Hannah waited for her to go on, curious about Christian, wanting to know more. But when Sabrina picked up her pen and, dipping it into the cut glass inkwell, said, "I suppose I will send him a card, after all," Hannah knew the subject was closed.

Houseguests had been invited to Wildoak for the Christmas holidays. The Fairchilds, Mortimer and Hetty, were the first to arrive. They were a middle-aged couple, he with bushy iron-gray hair and old-fashioned sidewhiskers, Hetty, large, stout, her generous figure corseted tightly in rustling brown taffeta. The Coxes came a day later. Amanda Hastings Cox was Page's second cousin, a golden-haired beauty in her twenties. Her husband, Burnwell, was much older than she, a heavy-jowled man with close-set, red-rimmed eyes and a bullet-shaped bald head.

It didn't take long for Hannah to realize that Sabrina did not particularly care for the Coxes. For one thing, Amanda flirted outrageously with Page, fluttering her golden eyelashes, smiling seductively, leaning toward him as he spoke and in the process showing much white bosom. Burnwell was an arrogant man. Obviously accustomed to being waited on, he told Page: "More servants altogether is what you need."

Page smiled. "Can't afford them. When I get as rich as you, perhaps I'll be able to employ a larger staff."

"It's a damned shame," Burnwell said, "the blacks have to be paid. They're not worth it, of course. Lazy lot."

Hannah wondered why the Coxes had been invited at all until Sabrina told her that Burnwell, the descendant of a long line of bluebloods, had one of the best horsebreeding farms in Virginia. It seemed that Burnwell had offered Page free stud service—one of Page's mares bred to a Cox prize stallion. He had waived the stud fee, saying he couldn't accept money from a relative. Sabrina felt that the least they could do in return was to provide Christmas hospitality.

If Amanda flirted, Burnwell had a roving eye. It explained why Sabrina treated him with icy courtesy. But somehow the cold, "If you please, Mr. Cox," Sabrina used so effectively did not work for Hannah. The man cornered her on the stairs, in the parlor, once even following her as she took a morning stroll.

One night he boldly walked into her bedroom while the others were downstairs at cards. Hannah, who had excused herself to work on her dress, was so shocked to see him, she could not speak.

"Good evening, Miss Blaine," Burnwell said in a low, ingratiating voice. "I thought you might want company."

"If you please, Mr. Cox . . ." she began.

"I know you do. Lonesome, isn't it? And so far from home."

"Mr. Cox . . ."

"You're too lush a peach to go unpicked."

Hannah put her sewing aside. "I think you'd best leave." She got up and started for the door. But Burnwell caught her arm, bringing her around, crushing her to his chest. His breath was hot and sour-smelling.

"Don't cause trouble, wench. Do as I say, you'll be happier for it."

"Turn me loose!" She tried to struggle but his grasp was iron-tight. His lips sought hers and she twisted her face away. His mouth came down hard on her cheek, then found her lips. It was terrible, horrible, like drowning in a cesspool, a wet, slobbering kiss that went on and on and on. He tried to pry her mouth open with his corrosive tongue while one hand tore at the buttons down her back. If only she could scream, but her attempts to do so were no more than strangled growls in her throat. Oh, God! she begged in silent desperation.

Then suddenly she remembered the scissors she wore around her neck on a long ribbon. She forced herself to go limp. Burnwell's hold relaxed. Hannah brought the scissors up, pointing the tipped blades under his chin. He released her.

"I know how to use these," Hannah said, her voice trembling with anger. "Now get out! Get out! I will not mention what happened here if you keep your mouth shut. Good night, Mr. Cox."

He left, muttering an obscene curse.

After that Hannah was never again to envy the rich, to feel deprived because she had not been born an aristocrat. She would never again think of a blueblood as above her or feel ashamed because she had come from humble origins. Burnwell Cox and Tom Carstairs (and Christian Falconer for that matter) were no different from the men who drank at Stonebridge, no different from her crude father with his hand up Lacey's skirts. Carstairs and Cox (and Christian, who had somewhat refined the art of seduction) had mercifully cured her of any inferiority she might have felt. There were decent people and there were scoundrels, whether rich or poor. Hannah, without being smug, knew she was among the decent, just as Travis was and Page and Sabrina. There was really no gulf between them. This episode had taught her that. It was a lesson she would never forget.

Chapter IV

One blustering, sleet-lashed night a week before Christmas as the household was sitting down to supper they heard a heavy pounding on the outer door. Before Isaiah could reach it, the door was flung open and a hearty voice shouted, "Merry Christmas!"

A stunned pause—and then Amanda sprang to her feet. "Why, it's Christian!"

He strode into the dining room, hat in hand, his sweeping black cape glistening with droplets, white teeth flashing in a dark, handsome face.

"Christian!" Sabrina clapped her hands in delight. "What a wonderful surprise! I never expected . . . Oh, Christian, how good to see you! Come, take your cape off. We'll make a place for you."

Hannah could only stare in dumb amazement while her heart sank like lead in her breast. The worst had happened. She never dreamed Christian would reappear at Wildoak. San Francisco was a continent away, a distance that seemed safe. What had brought him here? God, oh God!

She felt trapped. There was no possibility of flight, ignoble as it would seem. Why had he come? She had not forgotten him, but as more and more time passed he

had receded from her thoughts. The Morses rarely spoke
of him. If they received letters from Christian, they
never mentioned it. Sabrina had remarked that she loved
her brother but wished he had more ambition. Hannah
remembered how Page referred to Christian as the "devil's own" and how Wildoak bored him.

Why then this sudden appearance? She forced herself
to look at him. Isaiah was helping him off with his wet
cape. Christian moved quickly to where Sabrina sat and
kissed her.

"Sabrina, dear. Page." He shook his hand. "And who
have we here?"

"Hannah Blaine, dear," Sabrina explained. "I believe
you've already met."

"Hannah . . . ? Yes, yes, of course. Let me think.
Bayetville, was it? How could I forget. Cousin Hannah."

He came around to her chair and kissed her on the
cheek just as he had done with Sabrina. His lips were
cool, his breath smelled of whiskey. Hannah, to her
dismay, blushed to the roots of her hair. He was kissing
Amanda now, and then Hetty, his ebullience infecting
everyone so that when he finally sat down to a place
hastily set for him next to Amanda, the dining room rang
with talk and laughter.

Presently Hannah's panic subsided. He'd forgotten
her, in fact had only remembered when Sabrina mentioned her name. Not for him the long nights of haunting
dreams, the remorse, the battle to banish a face from his
thoughts. Obviously he had put hers from his mind the
moment he had left Stonebridge.

"You naughty boy," Amanda cooed. "Not letting us
know. Not even your sister."

"I'm a poor correspondent, am I not, Sabrina? There,
you see. I don't write letters. It's another one of my
vices."

Sabrina said, "You must admit it's a bit of a shock.
San Francisco is not just beyond the next bend in the
road. Have you come directly? Mama and Papa said
something about business in Richmond that you might
be sent to attend to for them, the sale of some property,
but they intimated it wouldn't be until next spring."

"The date was moved up unexpectedly. Yes," he said, turning to Isaiah, "please, more wine. Once in Richmond it didn't seem right not to visit Wildoak. I hired a horse and here I am."

"We'd have felt very put out if you hadn't come," Sabrina said. "How are Father and Mother?"

"Tolerably well. I don't see much of them since I've moved into my own quarters. They send love, Christmas greetings, and several packages to be opened on Christmas morning. How is little Miles?"

"Splendid," Page said.

Christian looked at Hannah. "And you, cousin, are you visiting for the holidays?"

Why had he taken to calling her cousin? As near as Hannah could determine they weren't actually related. "I'm afraid I'm a permanent guest," she said, surprised at the evenness of her voice.

Page explained. "Hannah is teaching at our new school."

"Ah." Christian smiled benevolently. "How fortunate for her pupils."

There was no hint either in look or words that he felt anything but polite interest, none of the earlier brash lewdness, the desire that had burned in his eyes. He seemed only casually interested. She was merely someone he had once met in a Georgia country town, and the scene in the kitchen when he had held and kissed her so passionately, arousing her to yearning need, had apparently faded entirely from his mind.

Hannah told herself she was grateful. It would make Christian's visit so much easier for her.

Stealing a glance at Christian, she saw his eyes resting on golden-haired Amanda with that deep sensual look he had once directed at herself. Someone like Amanda is more to his taste, Hannah thought—sophisticated, clever, not averse to an affair perhaps, certainly not one to guard her chastity with bulldog tenacity. Yes, she decided, there's no call for me to be alarmed. All my fears are groundless. I am no more to him than a shadow.

And yet beneath her thoughts there lurked a tiny thread of disappointment. Feminine vanity. Every woman likes to be noticed. Even by a philanderer such as Christian Falconer.

In the days that followed, Christian spent a good deal of time with Amanda, riding out with her early in the morning along the river, playing bezique, gossiping. They seemed like long-separated lovers who had finally been reunited—Amanda on Christian's arm, her face looking up at his, smiling into his eyes. Was her husband blind? Had he no control over this woman? Perhaps he didn't care. Perhaps the two of them had an arrangement in which each was left free to pursue their own immoral adventures.

After supper on the third night of Christian's stay Sabrina was persuaded to play the piano for her guests. She had done so for the family on many previous evenings and her mastery at the keyboard had come to Hannah like a revelation. She found these impromptu concerts thrilling and tonight was no exception. Sabrina had chosen a selection from Liszt. Hannah closed her eyes, giving herself over to the exquisite sound that Sabrina coaxed from the ivory keys, her blood singing to the soaring, crashing crescendos and the thrum of counterpoint. Just as the thunderous finale came pouring out, Hannah opened her eyes to find Christian staring at her, with a hot hungry look that startled her. It was gone in a moment, passing so quickly she wondered afterward if she had imagined it or if Christian, too, had simply been affected by the music.

The next night the people at Wildoak went to a party given by the Plummers, who now owned the Fairchild plantation. Hannah had begged off. She hadn't finished her gown. There were a few more touches, some handwork, and the interfacing still to be put on. Actually she looked forward to a few hours alone, to peace and tranquillity, a respite from the holiday hubbub that had been going on without pause for over ten days.

Since the air was too chilly and the light poor in her room she had come downstairs to the parlor with her sewing. She was threading her needle when she heard the knob of the outer door rattle. A few moments later Christian stood in the doorway of the parlor.

"Oh!" he exclaimed, surprised. "I hope I'm not disturbing you."

"Not at all."

He came in and removed his cape and threw it down on a chair. "I couldn't face another moment of the Plummers and their Richmond crew." He went to the table at the back of the sofa and poured himself a whiskey. "Boring hypocrites, the lot of them. All seeking political favors, trying to find a way to get the state legislature to dance to their tune, calling it 'influence' when they know it's pure bribery."

"Perhaps it's just talk." Hannah stuck her needle in the pincushion, put it back in her sewing basket, and gathered the unfinished dress in her arms.

"I'm not chasing you off, am I?" Christian asked.

"No, I was leaving anyway."

"My company that distasteful?" he asked with a lopsided grin.

"Of course not."

"Then sit and chat awhile."

She leaned back. "What would you like to talk about, Mr. Falconer?"

"Cousin Christian," he corrected. "Talk about? You. Me. Anything." Drink in hand, he went to the fireplace and stood with his back to Hannah, staring down at the smoldering logs. He kicked them and a flame shot up, dancing in orange-red brightness, silhouetting his strong booted legs. He turned to face Hannah. "Did you ever ask yourself, what do I want out of life?"

Hannah, though surprised at his direct question, answered without pause. "I know what I want, Mr. Falconer." She hadn't meant to sound prim or schoolmarmish, but it was exactly how she felt.

"And what is that?"

"I would like to continue my education," she replied. "Become a proper teacher in a large school, a women's college if I'm good enough."

"And?" When she didn't answer, he went on. "You must have thoughts of a husband and children. Isn't that what most women want?"

"Oh, yes. But that will come later."

"I see."

"And what about you, Mr. Falconer?"

He sighed. "I don't know. That's the hell of it, I don't know. I've been a pleasure-seeker all my life, I like high living, easy, comfortable, without strain. But now I find something's missing." He shrugged. "A good woman, I suppose."

"I'm sure you'll meet her, Mr. Falconer."

"Christian. Do you find it so hard to use my name?" She did not answer.

"Well, then," he continued, "the question is whether a good woman will have me."

"I don't see why not." Was he fishing for compliments? Why was he asking such questions? The conversation was getting too personal for comfort.

"Oh, come now, you can see I drink too much. Isn't that true?"

She flushed. "It's something you could control, Mr. Falconer." She could not call him Christian. She felt she must keep their talk on a formal basis. For subtly, or suddenly—she was not sure which—the atmosphere in the room had changed. She was aware of him now as a man, an awareness that perhaps had been there all along. His rampant masculinity had never seemed more apparent. Or was it her? Was she the lascivious one? Was she imagining it, creating an erotic fantasy where there was no basis for one? Was there something in her that craved . . . No, she dismissed the thought at once. She didn't like Christian Falconer, she decided again. He brought out these thoughts, brought out the worst in her.

"Control," he repeated, a quizzical, amused expression on his face. "But I'm known for my lack of control. At least that is what my father claims. And I'm almost certain Page and Sabrina concur."

"Control can be cultivated," she said stiffly.

He laughed. "Like a garden? Like love, pity, honor, passion? I doubt it."

He stood, legs apart, hands behind his back, observing her. The fire on the hearth crackled noisily, dancing and leaping, casting a red, moving glow across the carpet.

"Did you know I once killed a man?"

"Why, no," she answered, taken aback.

"It happened two years ago. He accused me of cheating at cards. I do a lot of things of which I am not proud, but cheating isn't one of them. So I hit him. I'm good with my fists. He pulled a knife and slashed at me. I managed to get the knife from him, only to have him draw a small pistol from his pocket. Before he could shoot, I killed him with his own knife. Not a pretty tale, is it?"

"Why are you telling me all this?"

"Because I want you to know what sort of person I am."

"What difference should it make?"

He looked at her without answering, a look that seemed to challenge, to cut through Hannah to the girl behind the stuffy facade. She felt the blood surge to her cheeks. Now she was really confused. What kind of cat-and-mouse game was he playing?

"I don't really know why it should make a difference," he finally said. "Except that I want you to like me. I know you disapprove of me, and I feel you have a right to. The fact is," he went on, his voice suddenly becoming low and tense, "since I met you I haven't been able to get you out of my mind."

Was it true or merely a ploy? "Really, Mr. Falconer . . ."

"No, wait. I behaved badly at Stonebridge. I want to apologize. You will accept my apology?"

So he did remember. Which only made things worse. "Yes. And now if you'll excuse me."

He made no move to detain her.

"Good night, Mr. Falconer."

She was at the door when he said, "Hannah . . . please . . ."

She turned. He was looking at her now with eyes that blazed with a frightening intensity in the reflected firelight. "Won't you stay?"

The burning magnetism of those amber eyes reached out across the room, igniting a spark, a tiny flame that common sense told her was dangerous. Though she tried to quench the threatening fire, she felt its heat rising in her blood, scorching her cheeks. Her heart raced, thudding with fear and excitement. Christian said nothing but kept staring, his eyes caressing her now, going over her, coming back to meet her own, drawing her, compelling her to come to him. No words were uttered, yet volumes were spoken, meanings and messages sent, an electrifying current charging her senses, her will. She remembered his kisses, his hot breath on her cheek, his warm hand on her breast, and for a moment, a brief moment, was tempted.

Taking advantage of her hesitation, Christian started to move toward her.

Alarmed, she turned and went out of the parlor without another word, hurrying up the staircase as if Satan himself were on her heels.

Hannah's gown was finished in time for the Christmas Eve party. Looking at herself in the mirror, patting the peplum in place, arranging the little sleeves, Hannah had to admit she had done an excellent job. And the deep blue suited her; it gave her gray eyes a soft, misty glow and set off her skin. Now she need not feel inferior to any of the female guests. Her only uneasiness was in having to face Christian again. She had not seen him since their meeting in the parlor and she did not look forward to having him remind her—whether by a knowing glance or words—that she had stood poised, for one single, terrible moment ready, willing, to meet his desire with her own.

When she came down the stairs to the already filled and overflowing parlor, she saw him speaking to Amanda near the punch bowl. He looked up as she entered, nodded, and went back to his conversation. Again Hannah felt that curious drop in her mood. She didn't want to call it disappointment, but she had expected some sort of acknowledgment, that knowing glance, a flash of admiration in his eyes, perhaps, but apparently he had reverted to his former self. He was going to ignore her, treat her as if that strangely intimate scene between them had never happened.

"Hannah, dear." Sabrina came forward and took her arm. "How lovely you look. I want you to meet some of our friends."

The room had been made smaller by an enormous tree hung with ornaments and draped with tinsel. On the side table next to the punch bowl was a tray set with a whiskey decanter and glasses and a siphon of soda. Platters of chicken salad, cold pork and beef, baskets of bread and cheese, and an assortment of cakes tempted the appetite.

Hannah was taken around. Burnwell Cox eyed her with naked hunger. One man, whose name she promptly forgot, held her hand overlong, blinking at her. She pretended she didn't notice.

"And this is Mr. Allan Bainbridge," Sabrina said, introducing Hannah to a young man of about twenty-five with sandy hair and pale eyes.

"I didn't know Page had such a pretty niece. May I bring you a glass of punch?"

He was attentive and pleasant. She sat with him and Hetty Fairchild and old Mr. Ramsey, a safe trio, on the sofa, while Mortimer Fairchild sat on a chair facing them. Allan Bainbridge regaled them with gossip from Richmond.

"Yes, the Parkinsons are having trouble. I don't know exactly what, but they quarreled rather openly in the foyer of the Grand Theater last Saturday night. Money, I think. That's the root of all evil, isn't it? And speaking of evil, have you been following the trial of Lizzie Borden? It's been in all the Richmond papers."

"Borden?" Hetty repeated. "Isn't she the spinster from New York who hacked her mother and father to death with an ax?"

"She claims she didn't do it," Allan Bainbridge said.

Hetty wiped a crumb from her lips with a lace-edged handkerchief. "Very few culprits confess to their guilt. The jails are full of them."

"Now that you mention jails," Allan said, again leading the talk from topic to topic. "Two of our desperadoes escaped from Richmond prison a few days ago. They were convicted of killing a man in a bank robbery. Apparently they stole a wagon that had been delivering bread to the jail and got out in it."

"Goodness!" Hetty remarked. "Goodness! We'd best lock our doors and windows, hadn't we?"

"Now, Mother," her husband soothed, "there's no reason to believe they're in this neighborhood."

"Quite right," Allan Bainbridge said. "They've been sighted in Crozier. It's believed they're heading for the Blue Ridge and should be captured before they reach the foothills."

"Well, that's a consolation," Mr. Ramsey said in his creaky voice.

The talk went on to the Foresters, newlyweds who had just returned from a trip around the world, reporting that their honeymoon had been spoiled by thieves in Venice who had stolen their luggage and pickpockets who had fleeced them in Delhi.

Christmas day dawned with a flurry of soft snowflakes, a feathery downfall that melted into wetness as it reached the ground. By one o'clock when dinner was announced, the sun had come out, peeping through a ragged hole in the clouds. Christian did not appear for the meal. He had gone out riding alone, Sabrina said, and had probably forgotten the time. Amanda pouted. "Isn't that like him?" Hetty Fairchild clicked her tongue. Page said, "Would you care to give the blessing, Mortimer?"

It was a heavy meal—roast goose, suckling pig, assorted breads, puddings, yams, and greens swimming in grease. Hannah, looking at the groaning board, watching the plates passed around, thought of Stonebridge and the lean dinner her own family would be sitting down to—pork, if they were lucky, pone, and beans. If she could only scoop up what was left on the plates, she thought, and whisk it home. Looking at the wine-flushed faces, listening to the loud, jarring voices and tipsy laughter, she had the sudden desire to escape as Christian had done, to take a ride in the buggy or simply to walk in the fresh brisk air.

So when Sabrina said, "Oh, dear, I did say I would help Isaiah deliver Christmas baskets this afternoon, didn't I?" Hannah offered to go in her stead.

Sabrina, anxious to establish customs that were her own at Wildoak, had for the past two seasons taken baskets to the stableboys and horse trainers who lived in the renovated slave cabins on the rear of the property. She had also included on her rounds several poor farming families in the neighborhood, independent, courageous souls who were trying to eke out an existence on five- or ten-acre plots. Among these were the Trotters, the last on her list. They were renting Alder House, which had once belonged to Beasley Morse, Page's stepfather. Hannah had never been there, but she understood from Isaiah that even in Page's time the house had been rundown, the fields running fallow and overgrown with dock and thistle. The Trotters, though they diversified their crops and worked like moles, did not prosper. The soil was poor, they could not afford fertilizer, and the weather always seemed against them—either too much or too little rain. They had three children, none of whom went to school because they were needed at home.

As the buggy in which Isaiah and Hannah rode clattered over the rutted dirt road that led down through a small valley to Alder House, Isaiah, who had been humming an old spiritual, suddenly pointed to the sky.

"Turkey vulture." He crossed himself.

"Must be after a dead rabbit or possum."

"No. He flyin' too high for dat. Someone daid."

The buggy rumbled on, entering the woods, the dark alders and pines closing around them. The wind dropped and it suddenly grew bitterly cold. Hannah, shivering, drew her coat collar up around her neck. Isaiah sat grim-faced, staring ahead.

"The Trotters will be glad to see us," Hannah said, by way of cheering him up. "And we can warm ourselves at their fire before we start for home."

"Ain't no fire, Miz Hannah." The chimney was now just visible above the trees. "I doan see smoke. Only dat buzzard."

"Maybe they haven't lighted one." Poor families conserved their fuel for early morning, the bitterest part of the day.

But Alder House as they drove up was strangely quiet. Not a sound came from behind the closed door or peeling walls. No face appeared at the window, no barking dog rushed out to meet them.

"Dar big yaller houn' dog must have run off," Isaiah said.

Hannah raised her eyes and thought she saw a curtain twitch in an upper window.

"They might be ill," she said. "I'm going in to see."

"Miz Hannah, doan go. I doan lak the look of dat place."

"Nonsense. If something's wrong they might need help."

Isaiah handed her down from the buggy. He stood by it while she went up the three sagging steps of the wooden porch. A pair of muddy boots stood by the door. She knocked on it, waited, then knocked loudly again. When there was no answer, she turned the knob, surprised to find it gave easily.

It was dim inside, and chilly, the stale cold air smelling of cooked cabbage and onions. Somewhere a clock ticked in the silence, the sound like the tap of a light hammer. Hannah made out a coatrack, a worn, patched jacket and a floppy hat hanging from it. Beyond the rack an uncarpeted staircase disappeared upward into shadow. Overhead a floorboard suddenly creaked. Hannah's nerves jumped. She glanced back at Isaiah, who stood where she had left him, an anxious look on his face. Hannah pushed the door open a little wider.

"Mrs. Trotter!" she called. "Mrs. Trotter!" Her voice echoed strangely in the silence.

Could they have gone somewhere? she wondered. Perhaps they were visiting friends or relatives. But why would they leave the door unlocked? Perhaps because they felt they had nothing to steal. And the dog must have followed them wherever they'd gone.

"Mrs. Trotter!"

The clock ticked on. Did she imagine it or did she hear someone breathing? The shadows at the foot of the staircase seemed to shift and move. Hannah could make out part of a wall, the paper faded and stained. A picture hung there, but what it portrayed she could not tell. It was obvious there was no one home. She had imagined the curtain twitching in the window. Should she go in, leave the basket with a note in it? Or perhaps it would

be more proper to simply set it on the porch. She was
somehow reluctant to go into the house. Standing on the
threshold in the silence with the clock ticking gave her a
queer, uneasy feeling.

She tried one last time. "Mrs. Trotter!"

A hand shot out from the other side of the door and
grabbed her wrist, pulling her across the threshold. A
bearded face leered at her and she screamed. She was
roughly thrown to the floor.

"The niggher," a voice said. "He's coming, better get
him."

Hannah, lying facedown on the musty carpet, her
heart hammering wildly, heard a shot. Isaiah! She rose
on an elbow. My God! My God! Isaiah! Between booted
legs she saw the porch steps where Isaiah lay sprawled,
blood oozing from his white poll.

"Isaiah!" she screamed.

Chapter V

"Close the door, Jasper." The voice was refined, speaking with a slow, cultivated drawl.

Hannah looked up. The speaker, though unshaven and dressed in an ill-fitting jacket and mud-splattered boots, carried himself with a poise and assurance that spoke of breeding. Hannah knew instinctively that this was not Mr. Trotter. Nor did the long pale face, the blondish hair, and aristocratic bearing seem to belong to a man who could order someone shot in cold blood. Jasper's face and bearing, however, did. He was unshaven also, his beard scraggly and patchy, his skin greasy, his squashed-up features pugnacious and mean.

"Kill her, too?" he asked, waving his gun at Hannah.

"I think it might be a good idea. But wait."

The man held out his hand to lift Hannah. She ignored it and shakily got to her feet, her legs so weak they threatened to collapse under her. Yet when she spoke her voice was firm.

"How dare you shoot my servant?" She was frightened, but angry, too.

"He's a nigger," the elegant blond replied smoothly. "Besides being a danger to me. As you are."

"How a danger? What have you done to the Trotters? Who are you?"

"Questions, questions. Isn't that like a female?" Jasper snickered.

"You won't get away with this."

They both laughed.

"Who are you?" she demanded again.

"Since you're going to die in any case, I see no harm in telling you."

"Now, lookee here, Arthur," Jasper remonstrated.

"Mr. Palmer, if you please."

"Mr. Palmer. Best not say anything."

"I don't see where it would hurt. Miss . . ." He turned to Hannah. "It *is* Miss? What's your name?"

Hannah, a sick feeling in the pit of her stomach, remained silent. Now that the initial shock was over she no longer trusted her voice. She was afraid to speak, afraid an unwanted quaver might betray her abysmal fear. They were going to kill her; they were discussing it. In a matter of moments Jasper would shoot her. She wondered if the bullet would hurt. Had Isaiah died instantly? What if he were still alive, but slowly bleeding to death?

"Cat got your tongue?" Palmer peered at her. "Pretty thing. Pretty, isn't she, Jasper?"

Jasper licked his lips, gazing at Hannah, a sudden greed lighting his eyes. "Ast her to take off that coat."

"Surely. Miss, would you kindly remove your coat?"

"I will not."

Jasper waved his gun at her. It was a long-barreled, blue-steel piece, as deadly-looking a weapon as she had ever seen. Her experience had been with hunting rifles filled with shot, guns that could kill rabbits or possums, nothing like this revolver that had stopped Isaiah with one bullet.

"Well, you gonna do as I say?"

She undid the top button of her coat. Take your time, she told herself. Stay calm. The longer I can keep them talking, the better. Perhaps I can persuade them to let me go. Perhaps they will spare me, just tie me up until they get away. The second button went, the third. I won't think now, I won't think about the Trotters, what happened to them or who these two culprits are or that this might be my last conscious act.

"Good," Palmer said as she eased herself out of the coat. "I'm glad you have chosen to obey." He took the coat from her and threw it to Jasper.

Jasper, staring at Hannah, caught it mechanically. "Jeez." He licked his lips. "Mighty purty."

"You see," Palmer went on, "we're desperate men. Three days ago we escaped from a Richmond prison. The authorities are looking for us, but in the wrong direction. We deliberately left a trail to Crozier then passed around their rear flank. They think we're heading for the mountains, a logical place for men on the run to hide. All those gullies and caves. But we're not playing their game. We're doing the illogical, going right for the seacoast. Don't you think that's clever of us?"

Hannah, feeling faint with fear and with the terrible effort to hide it, said, "May I sit down?" She had to get off her feet before she lost what little control she had.

"Certainly. Get her a chair, Jasper."

"Why? She ain't goin' to need—"

"Get her a chair."

Jasper and the gun disappeared into the room beyond the entryway. For one wild moment Hannah thought of fleeing, but the moment passed and Jasper was already returning with a hard-back chair. She sat. Jasper flicked his gunpoint at a breast. "Purty," he repeated. "Purty."

"Would you like to have her, Jasper? A plaything for you?"

"Yeah. Great jeezabubb! Look at them tits!"

Hannah tried to sink within herself, away from the dirty leer in his squeezed-up eyes.

"All right, I reckon we can spare a few minutes, Jasper. But in return I want you to do for me."

"Now, Arth . . . I mean, Mr. Palmer . . ."

"Without complaint. Look at her. Can you imagine her in the nude? And if you're good," he added, "we might even take her with us."

"Well, now, that ain't such a bad idee."

Jasper reached over and with a dirty, clawlike hand ripped the neckline of her dress downward, exposing breasts mounding over her corselet.

"Whoooeee! Apples!" A thread of spittle had caught

in his beard. "Ripe apples for lickin' and suckin'." He pursed up his mouth and made a horrible slurping noise. " 'Less go upstairs where there's a real bed. Ain't had a woman on a real bed for a coon's age."

Hannah clutched her torn bodice together with clammy hands. She was going to be raped. She couldn't believe it, she couldn't believe any of this: Isaiah dead on the steps, the man with the elegant manners offering a chair as if she had come for a social call, Jasper's hideous, gargoyle face, the reddened eyes peering at her. It all seemed so unreal. A dream, a nightmare. But it was no dream. Jasper's hand was on her bare shoulder, lifting her from the chair. He turned her about, poking the gun into her spine.

"Up them stairs!" he ordered.

The Trotters. But she mustn't let her mind dwell on the Trotters. Think of other things—the stairs, the wallpaper, the picture she had seen earlier. It was a faded watercolor of a vase of roses. Roses.

"Cain't you go a little faster?" The gun prodded her. She stumbled, then went on. The stairs were worn bare of varnish in the middle; the sides still held nailed shreds of what was once carpet. Many feet had passed over these steps. The Trotters and at one time the Morses . . .

"Git along, now."

They came into a bedroom. Against one wall stood a four-poster hung with dirty chintz so faded and thin it was almost transparent.

"Git your clothes off," Jasper commanded, unbuckling his belt and shoving his trousers down. "Go on, git!"

But Hannah's fingers refused to obey.

Palmer, who had followed them up, came to her side. "May I?"

She wanted to fight, to raise fisted hands and beat him off. But she couldn't. She was frozen with fear. Palmer undressed her, chucking petticoats, corselet, hose, shoes to the floor while she stood shivering at his cold touch. "Nice," he said, but there was no masculine interest in his voice or eyes.

Jasper, his breeches down about his ankles, his man-

hood protruding stiffly, was unable to control himself
any longer. Pushing the revolver into Palmer's hands, he
threw Hannah on the bed. As Jasper tried to lower
himself, Hannah suddenly came to life. She screamed
and struggled, jabbing at his face, beating his arms, his
shoulders, her knees coming up, thumping at his legs.

"Stop that!" The dirty hand cracked her across the
face in a tooth-jolting blow.

Palmer, leaning over the foot of the bed, laughed. "I
like that. Let her fight. I like to see the little bitch
fight."

Hannah lay still. She wasn't going to give either of
them pleasure, although her whole being screamed out
to resist. Oh, if she only had a knife, a gun, a club, a
weapon, something to hit out with. Never in her whole
life had she imagined that she could so passionately
want to kill a man.

She felt the coarse hair of Jasper's chest, smelled the
rank odor of corn whiskey and unwashed flesh, and
thought, I'm going to vomit. When he brought his face
close, attempting to kiss her, a blackness came over
Hannah. If only she were dead, if only she were in her
grave at the Bayetville cemetery, asleep under the elms,
unable to feel, to suffer. Why hadn't she fled during that
moment when Jasper had gone to fetch the chair? A
bullet in her back would have been better than this. She
couldn't breathe, she was dying. . . .

Suddenly she felt the mattress shake violently. A shout
from Jasper as his weight was flung from her. She rolled
over on her side. Still in shock, she tried to sit up. She
saw Palmer reeling under the blows of a man who was
going after him in a fury. Where had he come from? His
back was to her, but the dark hair, that coat, those
shoulders . . .

Christian! Christian Falconer!

He pummeled Palmer, bouncing him against a huge,
scrolled wardrobe. Hannah heard the cracking sound as
Palmer's head hit wood. His knees sagged and he sank
to the floor.

Meanwhile Jasper had pulled up his breeches and was
fumbling in the bedclothes for his gun. Christian kicked

Palmer aside. Shucking his jacket, he went for Jasper, catching him with a bone-crunching jab to the side of the head. Jasper flicked it off as a dog would shake water from its hide and sprang to his feet. He sent his hairy fist smashing into Christian's jaw. Christian's head went back and for one terrible moment Hannah thought he would fall. He staggered but righted himself, coming back, his arms lifted, dancing around Jasper, moving, weaving, flicking one fist under Jasper's nose, then the other. His leonine eyes held a maniacal gleam.

This was a Christian Hannah had never seen. The indolent, sneering gentleman with a taste for whiskey and women had disappeared. In his place was a savage with a ruthless look on his face, the lips drawn back in a snarl. The rage on his dark handsome face, the ruthlessness with which he went after Jasper, should have repelled if not frightened her. Instead it sent a thrill of inexplicable excitement shivering down her spine. She felt a resurgence of the animal passion, the yearning to kill Jasper, she had felt earlier. She wanted the convict torn to bits, mashed to a pulp for what he had done to her.

Christian continued to dance around Jasper, fists poised, making little jabs, taunting the outlaw. He feinted, then with a quick dive hit Jasper's face with a rapid tattoo of blows. The convict's right eye was bleeding but he showed no sign of fatigue, no sign that Christian was making headway. The two men circled one another cautiously, Christian, lithe, graceful, wary, and calculating. Jasper, his eyes mean little slits, was still taking Christian's blows without any visible effect, every now and then lashing out wildly, thrusts that Christian managed to duck. But one heavy, lightninglike punch to the cheek connected, knocking Christian against the wall. Jasper was on him in an instant, his large hands clamping around Christian's throat. Christian tried to throw him off, his hands scrabbling at the deathlike grip. Jasper grunted and squeezed harder.

Hannah could see Christian's struggles were weakening. Desperate, close to panic, she got up on her knees, the bedcover which she had drawn up around her fall-

ing as she searched blindly for the discarded revolver. A
moment later her hand closed around it. It was heavy.
She hadn't realized that a handgun could be that heavy.
She brought it up and aimed it at Jasper's back. The
question of whether she could kill a man never occurred
to her. Her finger pressed the trigger. The empty click
seemed to go off in her head like a small explosion.
Blank; no bullets. After killing Isaiah, Jasper hadn't
reloaded it. She had been terrorized by a useless gun.
Black rage gave her arm strength and she hurled the
revolver at Jasper's back. The shock of the flying heavy
object loosened his grip for a fraction of a moment and
Christian, taking advantage of it, lifted his knees, striking Jasper in his groin. With a howl of pain Jasper let go.

Christian went after him, raining blow after blow on
the outlaw. Jasper's bleeding eyes were half closed now,
swollen to an ugly purple. Christian, recovered from
near asphyxiation, fought on with bulldog tenacity. The
fiery glitter in his eyes had intensified. How strange,
Hannah thought, that fear for her own personal safety
had vanished. Now she was only afraid for Christian.

Then out of the corner of her eye she saw Palmer
getting to his feet. He flattened himself against the wall,
a knife poised in his raised right hand.

"He's got a knife!" she shouted.

With a movement so quick it seemed to happen before
she was aware of it, Christian came in close to Jasper,
hugging him, whirling him about just as Palmer plunged
with his knife. It caught Jasper in the back. He went
down with an odd gurgle, the blood pouring from his
wound.

"C'mon!" Christian shouted to Palmer. "Would you
like to be next?"

Palmer licked his lips, edging around Christian, then
suddenly bolted through the open door. Christian was at
his heels. There was the sound of battering blows, followed by that of a falling body hitting the stairs, a
thump, a crash, then sudden silence.

Hannah waited, her breath at the top of her lungs.
Presently she heard slow, heavy footsteps on the stairs.
Panicky fear returned, damp, cold sweat breaking out on

her forehead as she stared at the open door. If Palmer
had emerged the victor, he would surely kill her now.
The footsteps got louder, nearer. She clutched the bedcover in her hands, kneeling on the bed, her eyes starting
from their sockets.

Christian came through the door. She sank back. He
did not look at Hannah. Grasping Jasper's limp arms, he
dragged him from the room. Hannah could hear the
body rolling down the staircase.

She was safe.

And suddenly the enormity of what she had just lived
through hit her. The entire ugly, frightening episode
from first to last came back to her in an overwhelming
tide of horror. Trembling, every limb shaking uncontrollably, she covered her face and burst into sobs. When
Christian sat down beside her, she was only dimly aware
of his presence.

"Hannah, Hannah, it's all right now," he said softly,
taking her in his arms, holding her aganist his chest
where she continued to weep.

"It was horrible, so horrible. Christian, I wanted to
die," she sobbed.

"It's all right, darling. Did they . . . ?"

She shook her head.

"The sons of bitches didn't deserve to live."

His arms held her tightly. She rested her head on his
chest until her quaking subsided. She felt his lips in her
hair and she lifted her tearstained face to look into his
eyes. They were soft and tender, gazing down at her
with a gentle smile. It seemed the most natural thing in
the world for him to brush her lips lightly, to kiss her
tear-streaked cheeks, the swollen eyelids.

"Christian, you have no idea how grateful I am, how—"

"Hush." He put his finger to her lips. "I don't want
thanks of any kind for what I've done." Again he kissed
her, and the feel of his lips on her sent a rush of warmth
through her body. Good Lord, she suddenly realized,
I'm naked. I must get dressed. It's indecent to sit here
like this. But his arms were a sanctuary and she needed
to feel sheltered.

"Oh, Christian . . ." It was a sigh like a whisper of

wind at the casement. His mouth lingered on hers, the pressure increasing. A languid helplessness stole through her, a willingness to forget time and place.

Her hand resting on his arm suddenly felt sticky and she drew away.

"Why, you're hurt, Christian, you're bleeding."

"Scratch. I don't feel it."

"Let me see. Please, take off your shirt. Please."

He unbuttoned his shirt and she was surprised at the sight of his muscled arms. The hair on his chest, too, a dark mat, that struck her as erotic. She blushed. He didn't notice. He was looking at his arm.

"You see," he said, "it's nothing to get excited about."

With a delicate finger she touched the spot where the blood had clotted. He grasped her hand, turned it palm-up, and kissed it.

"When I think what might have happened . . ." he began.

"Yes, yes. Thank God you came." Tears welled up in her eyes again. She understood now why women referred to rape as a fate worse than death. And Christian, risking his life, had delivered her.

"Christian." She touched his lips with hers.

His good arm circled her body, drawing her close, and she felt the heavy pounding of his heart against her breasts. She drew away, looking up at him, trying to read a message in his face. He pulled her back, his kiss suddenly searing, demanding, a hot pressure that startled yet excited her. Under his insistent prodding she opened her mouth to the invasion of his tongue, a possessive exploration that made her dizzy and weak. Crushed against his hard chest, she soon found herself kissing him back, her tongue imitating his, her arms going up around his neck, heedless of the bedcover that had fallen away.

"Hannah," he whispered, his mouth resting on her cheek.

She couldn't speak. Held in thrall, her heart beating wildly, she was unable to utter a sound. But when his hand went up, cupping the soft, firm mound, she gasped aloud in astonishment. The touch of his strong fingers caressing her bare, sensitive skin brought goose pimples to her arms. She could feel the pink crest growing rigid. He lowered his head and captured the stiffened bud in his mouth, sucking then licking, his tongue describing a tantalizing circle around it before he took it in his mouth again. Drawing on the nipple, his lips created a sweet, sharp, poignant stab at her loins. Desire, she thought. I can't let him. I mustn't. But she did not struggle, made no attempt to push him away or stop him, had no will to end this sweet, torturing ecstasy.

For a few fleeting moments she wondered what had happened to the Hannah she knew. Where had the girl who had guarded her virtue so fiercely gone? Earlier she had experienced a savage surge of passion, wanting to kill a man, and now a desire such as she had never known, never imagined, tore through her with the force of a raging storm. She trembled as Christian took the other breast in his hand, kissing and sucking the ruched crest so that it soon matched the other. His hot breath excited her. While his mouth and tongue drifted from breast to hollow to breast, he pushed her gently down on the bed. Hovering over her, he fanned her loose hair out on the pillow. "Lovely, my lovely."

"Christian, it isn't . . . I mustn't . . ."

But the words were meaningless, empty. He had stopped them again with his mouth, grinding fiercely into hers, bruising her already swollen lips. His kisses, frantic now, traveled downward again, stopping briefly at her breasts, burning a path of fire across her stomach, going lower to the thatch that shielded her womanhood. His hand cupped the moist warmth, his finger going inside, to pet and tease the little button.

"No! No, Christian!" God, what was he doing? She was aflame, every nerve and muscle crying out for what she could only dimly guess. She was powerless in his grasp, powerless to curb her own mounting frenzy. Her wildly beating heart rang in her ears, her breath came as a ragged gasp, half whimper, half moan. "Christian, don't. I can't." But he went on with his sensual torment while her hips arched against him, the coiled spring inside her growing tighter and tighter until one last flick and the world seemed to explode in a thousand brilliant lights, jerking her into spasm after spasm. Oh, she loved him, she loved him!

Lifting himself, resting on his elbows, he gazed down at her with a look so dark, so full of intense passion she had to turn her own eyes away.

"Forgive me," he murmured hoarsely. He threw himself on her, his hands grasping her bare shoulders, splaying her legs apart with a knee. The next moment his rock-hard manhood plunged deep within her, the sharp, jarring thrust piercing her with a pain that brought a cry to her lips. He buried his face in the hollow of her neck, moving back and forth, plumbing deeper into her very soul, it seemed, until he, too, gave a sudden startled cry and with an involuntary shudder lay still, his sweat-soaked body lying over hers.

She was no longer a virgin. In giving herself to this demon lover she had lost what Granny had warned her was her greatest prize. But at that moment, lying in Christian's arms, his hand tenderly brushing the damp hair from her forehead, she didn't care. She was his. He had possessed her as no man had before or would again. If she had sinned, God would forgive her, for wasn't it written that love forgave all?

She wrapped her arms around him, happy, content, her heart singing.

Chapter VI

They descended the stairs together, Christian's arm held protectively around Hannah's waist.

"Don't look, darling," he said.

But she couldn't help seeing them. Jasper lay sprawled at the foot of the clothesrack, the knife still in his bloodied back. Palmer had fallen over his legs, his head and neck at a queer angle.

Hannah, a sour lump in her throat, averted her head. "The Trotters?"

"Most likely dead. They're not upstairs. I had a quick look while you were dressing. There were bloodstains on the kitchen floor."

"Bloodstains! Oh—how horrible!"

"I'll put you in the buggy, then see if I can find them."

"No. Don't leave me. I'll go with you."

Hannah and Christian followed a bloody trail out the back door and down the path leading to the barn. On the way they had to step over the corpse of the yellow dog, the hound that Isaiah had wondered about.

"It doesn't look good," Christian said.

Inside the barn, stacked like cordwood, were the five bodies of the Trotter family. To Hannah that seemed the final horror, those stone-cold bodies, the little girl with her bonnet still on. Hannah's stomach heaved, and darting outside, she was sick against the barn wall.

Christian came after her and gently wiped her face with his handkerchief, holding her until her shuddering ceased.

"Why?" she asked. "Innocent children, why? I can't conceive of anything so inhuman. And Isaiah, who never harmed a fly."

"Sometimes there are no answers." Christian took her arm. "Are you going to be all right?"

"Yes, yes. I think so."

They made their way to the buggy. Isaiah still lay where he had dropped, the black-coated figure with arms reaching out as if to embrace the worn, wooden steps. Hannah had a dark moment, the nausea returning. She clung to Christian's arm.

"Poor sod," Christian said. "Never had any kind of life of his own. Dutiful slave, faithful servant, and in the end shot for his trouble."

"Can we take him with us?" Hannah asked. She did not want to leave Isaiah lying there with the buzzards—three of them now—lazily circling over Alder House.

"I'll tie him across the saddle of my horse."

They rode under the trees in silence. Hannah felt strangely dislocated, as if her head were detached from her body. So many things had happened, unreal things, horror, murder, violence—and love. Her mind tried to sort events out, tried to put the worst behind her. Christian had already explained how he had come to Alder House. Riding in from the river's edge, he had cut across country when he noticed the turkey buzzard. Curious, he had put the horse into a canter to see what sort of game the scavenger was after. At the end of the Trotters' drive he found the Morse buggy, Isaiah dead.

"I suppose they'll put me in the dock again, this time for killing two men," Christian said with a rueful quirk to his lips as he turned to Hannah on the buggy seat beside him. "Even though it was Palmer who actually stuck the knife in that dark-haired ruffian, I would have gladly done it myself."

"It was in self-defense, Christian. You called Palmer by his name. Did you know him?"

"Only slightly. He came of a good family. Well-to-do plantation owners on the James River. The Civil War wiped them out and Palmer grew up in genteel poverty. His father couldn't adjust to the loss. Nothing like my own father, who learned early on in his life how to make his way—with great success, I might add."

Hannah caught the note of bitterness. "Do you resent your father for that?"

"Not as much as I once did, I suppose. At least he had gumption, which is more than I can say for poor Palmer."

She stole a sidelong glance at Christian. How handsome he looked! The dark skin, the dark hair, the sculpted profile. Christian, whom she had resented so vehemently, whom she had sworn to hate, had come to her in her hour of need, had fought to save her, and in so doing had shown her a Christian she had not remotely imagined. Strong, courageous, tender, and passionate, a man so close to her romantic ideal she wondered how she could have misjudged him so thoroughly. That night when he had spoken to her as he stood in front of the fire, he had virtually confessed that he was dissatisfied with the kind of life he had been leading. A good woman was what he needed, he had said. The rakehell image Christian presented to the world was a camouflage, not a true picture.

Did she really love him?

How could she not? It was like a revelation to her that love should come when and where she least expected it. And with Christian Falconer.

But he himself had said nothing about love. Or had he? He had called her darling, had whispered "my dearest." Perhaps somewhere among those murmured endearments as his hands went over her body, he had said he loved her. She wanted to know, longed to know, to be reassured that he did not look upon her as a common whore. She wanted him to understand that though she may have given herself in the heat of the

moment, what she felt now was love. I love you, she
yearned to say; to ask, do you love me?

As if divining the turmoil in her mind Christian turned
and gave her a gentle smile.

"Christian," she said hesitantly, encouraged by the
smile, but still not daring to come to the point,
"back there, at Alder House, I may have acted shamelessly. . . ."

"My dear, I would never in a thousand years accuse
you of shamelessness. Never. It is I who should feel
ashamed."

"Oh, Christian, no."

"I should have restrained myself. I'm older, the man,
more experienced. I've not behaved well, my darling."

It was not exactly what Hannah wanted to hear. She
wanted him to confess that he could not have helped
himself because he loved her, that he had been swept
along by a physical passion as well as a spiritual one.

Yet he had held her so tenderly, had stroked her hair,
had asked her forgiveness. Could she doubt those signs?
There hadn't been time to declare his love, to say, "Now
you are my wife in the eyes of God, we will make it so
before the world."

Still there were niggling questions that plagued her.
Why had he been so chilly, so indifferent to her at
Wildoak? Except for that one time in the parlor when he
had looked at her with desire, he had practically ignored
her existence.

And there was Amanda.

But she wasn't going to think about Amanda. Perhaps
Christian had not realized he loved her until he saw her
at the mercy of that awful Jasper. Perhaps his love was
as sudden as hers. She would ask him. Later, when things
calmed down, they would talk to one another and all the
little doubts and mysteries would be made clear.

"We're getting close to Wildoak," Christian said. "Let
me tell the others what happened."

"Oh, yes. Please. But I'd rather . . ." She blushed
deeply.

"I will only give them the facts," he said. "You don't

think I'm cad enough to tell them I lost my head and took advantage of you, do you?''

"Oh, no. I was thinking of the convicts, of what was happening when you arrived.''

"Of course, Hannah, my dear. I have no intention of embarrassing you. I shall say that I came upon you as you were being held at gunpoint.''

"Thank you, Christian.'' Oh, how she had wronged him!

He leaned over and kissed her forehead. "Dear Hannah,'' he said.

Now, she thought, heart thumping, now he will say something, tell me he never realized how much he loved me.

But he said nothing and they rode the rest of the way in silence.

Despite Christian's account of the incident, Amanda and Hetty kept looking at Hannah with speculative eyes. Amanda went as far as to knock on Hannah's door one late afternoon and invite herself in. She inquired after Hannah's health, something she had never remotely been interested in before.

"I'm glad to hear you are well,'' Amanda said. "I don't know if I should have survived such a nasty ordeal.''

"It was frightening,'' Hannah admitted. Outwardly composed, sitting very still, hands folded in her lap, she resented the greedy curiosity in Amanda's eyes.

"Sometimes,'' Amanda said, smiling, showing widely spaced teeth, "it helps to talk to another woman. Instead of keeping the ugliness bottled inside.''

"Everything has been said, Amanda. It *was* ugly. No one who comes upon a scene of murder can claim otherwise.''

"But didn't those brutes try—try to force themselves on you?''

Why was Amanda so interested? Was she expecting some kind of lurid confession? An obscene tale of assault? In her own way she was just as perverse as Palmer. "No one touched me,'' Hannah said stiffly.

"You're fortunate. I've heard of women who were

brutally raped by outlaws, forced to submit to unspeakable indecencies, their clothes torn off, their private parts invaded, their—''

"I was spared that," Hannah interrupted. "Mr. Falconer saved me from such humiliation, if that was what the rogues intended. However"—how easily the lies flowed, Hannah thought, one fabrication leading smoothly into another—"I think they were more interested in shooting me as they had done with Isaiah and the Trotters than anything else."

"Really." She gave Hannah a quick up-and-down look. "How fortunate. I don't suppose if it were me I'd be that lucky. Of course I would simply die to have savage hands tearing, ripping my clothes off, fondling my breasts." She shuddered, as if the thought excited rather than frightened her.

"And so Christian rescued you. And I suppose you are grateful."

"Very grateful." What is she leading up to? Hannah wondered. What does she want?

Amanda leaned forward. "He didn't exact any payment, did he?"

"I don't know what you mean."

"Well, I know Christian of old. He's a scoundrel. God knows he's been after me to break my marriage vows, cornering me on the stairs, begging for kisses—and more."

"Mr. Falconer was a perfect gentleman."

"Oh? Nevertheless, I feel it is a kindness to forewarn you. You seem to be inexperienced in the ways of life and Christian is an attractive as well as a very persuasive man. He is quite skilled in the art of seduction. He's had affairs not only with notorious courtesans but with women highly placed in society. It would mean nothing to him—''

"He had no designs upon me," Hannah interrupted, angry now, so angry she wanted to slap the false smile from Amanda's pretty face. "Nor I upon him. Furthermore I think this conversation is an impertinence."

"Well!" Amanda exclaimed huffily. She got to her feet. "I must say this is poor thanks for letting you know—''

"I'd rather do without the knowledge. And now, if you'll excuse me, I'm busy."

Amanda paused at the door. "Whatever you say, whatever you might think, I want you to remember one thing. Christian Falconer is mine."

Hannah thought it a stupid thing to say. A married woman, who earlier had deplored Christian's uncalled-for advances, painting him as a lecher who went from bed to bed, she was now claiming a proprietary interest in him. Hannah was more inclined to think that it was simply a question of sour grapes. Amanda had flirted outrageously with Christian, had been rebuffed, and was taking out her anger by needling a girl whom she thought was either a rival or a possible one.

Let her fume, Hannah thought, hugging the memory of Christian's embraces, his kisses, the tender words whispered in her ear. He was not Amanda's.

Early on Saturday morning, shortly after breakfast, Hannah had gone out for a stroll along the river's edge when Christian caught up with her. This was the first time since the events at Alder House that they were alone. Hannah, afraid of tongue-wagging, had prevailed upon Christian to keep his distance until things "had been settled." She, of course, had meant until he made a formal declaration, never dreaming that his understanding was quite different.

"I would prefer keeping the episode from Father," Christian said. "Page has promised not to mention it in his next letter, but I'm sure some busybody here will see it as their duty to inform him."

"But surely he would understand."

"No. He will think: 'Like the other one.' He will lump the man I killed over cards with the convicts, saying I've a black temper and am prone to violence. I can almost see the way his brows will come together, that angry frown that was the bane of my childhood. No. He won't like this."

"Will he disown you?"

Christian laughed. "How quaint you are, my darling. In a manner of speaking he already has. But if you mean will he cut me off without a penny, no. Years ago he set up a trust for each of his children. I came into it when I reached twenty-one. There's nothing he can do about that, thank God."

Christian certainly had never appeared to be a man who lacked funds. Since arriving at Wildoak, he had bought himself a horse, a sleek chestnut gelding that must have cost a great deal. He was always turned out in the finest broadcloth and shoe leather, smoked expensive cigars, and seemed to find no reason to seek gainful employment. Just how rich he was Hannah could not guess, but she would have loved him if he had been as poor as a traveling tinker.

"My dear," he said, taking her hand, "enough of irrelevancies. It's you I've been concerned about. I've had no opportunity to talk to you without half a dozen people in the room. And this"—his hand swept toward the river, dull gray under a cold, lowering sky—"is not conducive to intimate conversation." He stroked her gloved hand. "I want to talk to you, kiss you, and I don't want to do it on the run, or furtively, in some corner of the house."

"Christian, I would like that, too." He wanted to talk to her, kiss her. Privately. That could only mean one thing. He was going to declare himself. Perhaps even present her with a ring.

"There's the overseer's cottage," Christian said, "on the other side of the front paddock under a large elm. It has a red tile roof. It's vacant now. Do you know which one I mean?"

"Yes."

"Can you meet me there? After supper, around nine?"

"I don't know . . ."

"Please, Hannah. It means so much to me. Nine o'clock?"

"All right." She smiled. "I'll be there."

Shortly before nine Hannah left the house, letting herself out of a side door. *When I come back*, she thought happily, her mind projecting the future, *I'll be an engaged woman, Christian's fiancée*. The prospective

Mrs. Christian Falconer. She pictured the stir her news would make. Sabrina would kiss her and want to know when. Page would smile and say, "What a wonderful surprise! It's the best thing that could have happened to Christian." They'd be married at Wildoak, and she would come down that graceful staircase trailing white satin on Chad's arm—Chad, who would be sober for once. Travis wouldn't be too pleased, he didn't like Christian, but he'd come around. And Amanda—Hannah smiled to herself as she hurried past the white-fenced paddock— would be green with envy.

He was waiting for her, standing in the small parlor window, the red ember of his cigar glowing in the dark. The moment she entered he put the cigar down and took her into his arms. His kiss was hot, feverish, his mouth lingering long on her eager lips. Breathless, she leaned against him as he caressed her hair.

"I can't see you," he said. "I want to see you."

She heard him draw the curtains, strike a match. A pink light bloomed under a glass lampshade, throwing shadows on the low whitewashed ceiling. The air was chilly. It smelled of camphor and liniment, as if it had been used as a sickroom.

"Are you cold?" Christian asked. "I could light a fire but I'm afraid the smoke might attract attention."

"I'm not cold." How could she be cold with Christian looking at her that way, his eyes devouring her face.

"Here, let me feel your hands." He rubbed her hands, turning them palms-up, kissing them.

"Christian—I . . ." She stood on tiptoe, softly brushing his lips with her own.

He drew her into his embrace, claiming her mouth in a long, long kiss. She threw her arms about his neck, closing her eyes, holding him tightly. He kissed her cheeks, her lips, her forehead, his mustache tickling her skin as he returned to her mouth again. His hands began to undo the buttons at the back of her dress.

"Christian, wait . . ." Her voice trembled. This was not how she had imagined their meeting.

"I can't wait," he said, pulling the pins from her hair. His hands caressed the tumbled cascade. "You've been in my mind every waking hour, in my dreams at night, wherever I look I see your face, your eyes. You haunt me, darling.''

His eyes, shadowed with desire, looked down at her. He traced a trembling finger along her cheek, her upturned chin. "You've enchanted, enslaved me." He kissed the tip of her nose. Then, winding his arms about her waist, he pulled her close and began kissing her with passionate urgency. She surged against him, his possessive mouth, the pressure of his hard thighs against her driving everything from her mind. She did not protest when he finished undoing the buttons, sliding her out of her clothes, taking her breasts in his hands, his thumbs flicking the coral nipples, bringing them to aching rigidity.

"Oh, God," he moaned, resting his lips between the white, satiny mounds. She caressed his dark, springy hair, stooping to press her mouth to the black crown.

He raised his head and kissed her throat. "Hannah," he whispered, his mouth nuzzling her ear, blowing into it, sending a warm rush of blood to her face.

Swinging her off her feet, he carried her across the room through a door. She was dimly aware of a curtained window, a bureau, and the bed on which he lowered her. The parlor lamp cast a faint path of pink light through the open doorway. She wanted to tell him, to ask him, now in these moments while he was hurriedly undressing, if he loved her, but again a strange timidity hampered her tongue.

"Christian," she began tentatively as he lowered himself over her supported by his hands.

"What, my love?"

Wasn't that enough—*my love*?

"There's nothing to be afraid of, Hannah. Put your arms around my neck, darling."

Her arms circled his neck as his body pressed upon hers. His nakedness against her, the furred chest, the feel of rippling muscles under her hands as she stroked his back banished all scruples. He was hers, as she was his. They belonged to one another. She wanted to know every part of him, to explore him as he was exploring her, tonguing her breasts, her belly, lips tantalizing, teasing, softly touching the hollows of her hips, boldly questing for her nipples again. What were words? Why speak? This was the ecstasy, this intoxicating river of fire she was destined for. With this man and no other. She was lost in him, softly moaning under his touch, growing hot and cold as his mouth scorched the soft skin of her inner thighs.

When he parted her pubic hair she whimpered, "No. No, Christian," remembering the loss of control, the utter mindless rapture she had experienced before, wanting it, yet afraid.

He brought his mouth to the mound, his tongue darting inside. He began to lick and suck, flicking the swollen love button rapidly.

Hannah, feeling herself on the edge of an abyss, grasped Christian's black hair, throwing her pelvis against him, begging for release. When it came with a bursting rush, she shook convulsively, a tide of rapture that spread to her very fingertips. Christian, raising himself slightly, entered her, moving, plunging, spiraling down, down, grinding into her. Again the world seemed to drop away, everything blotted out except Christian and herself. Her lover and she joined, one joy, one bliss, one body, one soul, together climbing into dazzling light.

When it was over Hannah wept with happiness.

Christian kissed away the tears. "Hannah, my darling, my sweet."

She smiled up at him with misted eyes.

He moved and brought her head to his shoulder. She felt safe, protected in the cradle of his arms.

"Christian," she said, after a long while, "I should feel ashamed, but I don't. Perhaps it's because I love you so much."

"My darling," he said. "My sweet."

"What's to become of us?" she asked, more to herself than to him.

"I don't know. It's all been so sudden, hasn't it, my darling?"

"Yes, oh, yes."

"I never thought to give up my bachelorhood. And now . . . I don't know."

That was it, Hannah thought. It had been too sudden; too much has happened all at once. The outlaws, the terrible fight, the horror of the murders and their love all mixed, it seemed, inextricably. She must allow him time to think.

He leaned over and kissed her tenderly on the lips. "I only know I can't give you up. You're like wine, an intoxicant. You're in my blood, Hannah, my lovely Hannah."

When they both had dressed and were embracing one last time, he said, "You will come tomorrow night, won't you, sweetheart?"

She came to him the next night and the next and the next, giving herself to joy, to passion and a happiness she had never known. She did not ask again: What's to become of us. She felt certain Christian would know. She trusted him.

Nor was Hannah dismayed when Sabrina, seeing her brother ride off one morning, said, "I wish he'd decide what to do with himself. Mama, of course, is hoping he'll make a sensible marriage. She feels a well-bred wife of good family can settle him down."

Hannah knew she was only a poor village girl and lacked what the Falconers would consider good family and breeding. But her experience since leaving Stonebridge had shown her that family and breeding could be empty attributes. Amanda and Burnwell Cox and the Carstairs—and Palmer—were cases in point. Furthermore, in her present state of euphoria Hannah felt that love would conquer all. Even the thought of Christian's parents living in far-off San Francisco no longer dismayed her. She felt sure that once they met, her humble origins would not matter, that all barriers would be breached.

By the last two weeks in January the Fairchilds had left Wildoak. The Coxes, however, stayed on, Burnwell giving way to Amanda who did not wish to return to Charles where there was "nothing to do." She had resumed her friendship with Caroline Dinwiddie, the wife of a neighboring planter, a silly girl with a long nose and a foolish laugh. Together they would sit for hours in the parlor, sipping sherry, playing bezique, chattering about the latest French fashions and the private lives of their friends.

Hannah, impervious to their prattle, moved in a world of her own. She had not forgotten her ordeal with the convicts, but it had faded, the stark memory growing dim. Sometimes it seemed as if the whole episode had happened to someone else. She had become a new and different person.

She was a woman now, a woman in love. Everything she saw—the gray winter sky, the wet, unplowed fields, the muddy paddocks, the denuded trees along the drive— was bathed in a golden light. Wildoak became a palace peopled by nobility, the dining room with its polished table and heavy gleaming silver a hall fit for kings. A fire on the hearth, the musical chime of a clock, little Miles laughing, everyday things gave her joy. She was in love. Love transformed, made the ugly beautiful, and the beautiful radiant. When she looked in the mirror she saw shining eyes, cheeks glowing with health. Even her hair had taken on a new sheen, the deep chestnut tresses demurely tamed into their proper bun ready at the slip of a pin or two to be set free, falling, tumbling waves about her shoulders. In love. The food she ate took on a delicacy of flavor, the water she drank became ambrosia. Sabrina at the piano was angelic, transporting her to empyrean heights. The words and music of a popular song hummed in her head. *Drink to me only with thine eyes and I will drink with mine.*

She had been careful not to meet Christian's eyes, not to seem too interested, not to touch, to be polite, yet distant, as she had been before. It would be unseemly to act loverlike in public before Christian announced their engagement. He had said nothing about it, nothing definite, but she knew it was simply a matter of time. No man could tell a woman he couldn't do without her and not want her to be his wife.

In the meanwhile she had returned to her duties at Riverview with a buoyant heart. It seemed to her that all her pupils had become brighter, more eager to learn. Even Phillip Dinwiddie, whom she had despaired of teaching to read, began to pick out letters, a word here and there. She decorated the walls with children's works of art, taught them songs she had learned as a young girl in Georgia. One child brought a sack of apples and she distributed them to the others, saving a few for a copper bowl she found in a cupboard. The sweet pungent scent of apples would follow her home at night.

In the midst of her lighthearted happiness she heard surprising news from Travis. Lacey had married!

> *Who'd ever think* [Travis wrote] *such a thing could happen? But old Crawley took her as wife. You know Crawley, he farms just this other side of Bayetville. His wife died and he was left with six brats. He needed someone and she, the dimwit, was the only one who'd have him. She'll probably get in the family way right quick, if she isn't that way already.*

The term "family way" gave her a twinge. She had missed her monthly. She had never been late before but the excitement, the horror, then the lovemaking had somehow delayed this natural function. It was not until February when she missed it the second time that she realized her breasts were abnormally swollen and that she had been feeling queasy in the mornings.

She wasn't unduly alarmed but she did castigate herself for not remembering that male and female coupling, even those in love (especially with those in love) resulted in the making of babies. She may have been virginal and inexperienced but she wasn't ignorant. Her condition would mean that a definite wedding date had to be set—and soon. The engagement would be a short one, perhaps dispensed with altogether. They could be married quietly, returning to Christian's home in San Francisco, leaving Wildoak, where there might be the counting of fingers when the baby arrived.

She had no difficulty in arranging a meeting that evening in the cottage. For once she was early and Christian late. He arrived somewhat wine-flown, having imbibed freely at the supper table, and greeted her with the usual long, delicious kiss that still—would always, forever—send little shivers of delight down her spine. When he began to undo her waist, she moved away. Better let him know now, she thought, while she had the courage and could speak rationally.

"Wait—Christian. I have something to tell you." His hazel eyes looked at her questioningly. "Well, you see— well—I'm going to have a baby." She had not meant to blurt it out. The words just seemed to come of their own, awkward and precipitate.

He looked shocked. "Are you sure?"

The age-old question. She nodded dumbly.

He sat down. "Of course. I thought . . ." He shook his head. "I don't know what I thought."

It was not the answer she had anticipated. For the first time since she had realized her condition, a cold finger of apprehension touched her heart. She had been certain that he would say without hesitation, "This puts a different light on the matter. We'll be married at once." Of course it was a surprise, a shock, and he had to collect himself. Even a husband, she had been told, the last person to be surprised, often was.

"It's a situation I should have expected." He gave a wry smile. "But somehow didn't."

"Neither did I. But now, I thought you and I—we could . . ."

"Marry? I'm not quite ready for it, Hannah. Or at least I haven't been. Dear, sweet Hannah, don't look so dismayed." He held out his arms and she came to him. He drew her onto his lap and caressed her hair. "Let me think about it. You mustn't worry, darling. Everything will turn out all right." He kissed her. "You will trust me, won't you, sweetheart?"

"Yes, Christian." For now she had to be content with that.

That night, unable to sleep, she sat up mending a torn petticoat. It was cold in the room despite the fire. She had thrown a coat over her nightgown to keep warm. She was half through with her task when she ran out of white thread. There was none in her basket but she remembered a spool she had left on the treadle machine in the sewing room.

Buttoning her coat, she let herself out as the clock on the lower landing chimed one. The house was very quiet, steeped in a somnolent silence that seemed to breathe in the dark. Treading lightly in her slippers, she descended, pausing momentarily at the foot.

The sewing room was at the far end of the hall. When there was an overflow of guests, it was used as a spare bedroom, although the bed in it was hardly more than a narrow cot. As Hannah started toward the room she was surprised to see a shaft of light coming from the partially opened door. Curious as to who would be in the sewing room at one o'clock in the morning, she moved on, her heart beating loudly, for it occurred to her it might be thieves. Ever since the episode of the escaped convicts, people had been warned by the local magistrate to safeguard their homes against marauders.

As she approached on tiptoe a baritone rumble and a woman's voice became more distinct. She was a few inches from the door when, peering through the crack, she saw Amanda in a man's arms. He had his back to her, but that back, those shoulders, that thick dark hair at the nape was as familiar as her own. Christian Falconer. Christian—her man, her lover, her would-be husband, the father of her unborn child—and Amanda.

"I thought you'd never come," Amanda said. "Oh, Christian, my darling . . ."

Hannah, shrinking back in the shadows, did not wait to hear more, but turned and on noiseless feet crept back along the hall to the foot of the staircase. She stood for a moment looking up at its disappearing height, the polished banisters reflecting a glimmer of upper-story lamplight, and wondered how she could make the climb. Amanda's voice still rang in her ears. She felt as though some great earthquake had occurred, that walls and buildings and chimneys had fallen crashing all around, miraculously leaving her standing alone, an empty shell.

She began to ascend the staircase, the same ones she had descended only minutes ago, a young girl full of foolish illusions. Now she felt old. She had aged. "I thought you'd never come." A few words, a man and a woman in an embrace, and Hannah Blaine, the girl she had known all her life, had changed, had become a stranger to herself.

In her room again Hannah sat dry-eyed, rocking back and forth. Gradually her numbness wore off and the pain filtering through her body became so acute she screamed. But the scream was a silent one, a howl in the echoing tumult of her thoughts. I should have known! she raged inwardly. I should have known! Everything was there for me to see but I was too besotted, too blind. He never once spoke of marriage, of love. Love! Oh, my God, when I think of it! How could I have been such a fool? "He's a scoundrel," Amanda had said. I wouldn't believe her. I thought it was sour grapes. My God!

From the first when I met him at Stonebridge I knew what he was, selfish, a drinker, a womanizer. But then because he saved me from the horror of rape, I put a golden halo around his head. But the devil was there, the devil with horns and tail. How could I have been so dense when everything about Christian Falconer, even his own words, was so obvious? At Alder House I should have understood that he had stumbled unaware into a situation where he had no choice but to fight to save his own life. How easily he seduced me, how willingly I came naked to his lust. And I reveled in his carnality, the unspeakable things he did to me, because I thought he loved me. Love. Was there ever such a sentimental child, such a goose? I, who had seen how men could act, had watched and listened to their talk of conquests at Stonebridge, should have known better. But sense went out the window when he kissed me and said "my darling." He was full of "darlings," "sweethearts," and "my loves" and I took those false utterances and blew them up into undying declarations. He never loved me. He never wanted to marry me. Even if I had been a half-wit, I should have realized that. "You must not worry, sweet, everything will be all right. Trust me," he had said, and all the time he was sleeping with Amanda, going from my bed to hers, loving her, kissing, caressing her, tasting her voluptuous breasts, her . . .

Hannah rose abruptly. She couldn't continue in this manner. She would go mad. She had to do something. In the whirlpool of her mind one thing was clear. She could not stay at Wildoak. The thought of having to face Christian, no matter what the circumstances, filled her with revulsion. She never wanted to see his face again. Never. She must leave, now, at once. Where she would go was irrelevant.

She drew out her worn suitcase from under the bed and began to pack. She could not get all her belongings into the case. She had prospered at Wildoak. She would have to leave some of her things: a hand mirror, a few books, a pair of shoes, and the gown she had made for the Christmas Eve party. She would not have an occasion to wear it again. She was going to have a baby. In her pain, the shock of disenchantment, it had momentarily slipped her mind. She would grow large, ungainly, with melonlike breasts and protruding belly. *Pregnant.* Her transgression would show for all the world to mock and scorn.

Oh, God, God! What am I to do?

A dizzy nausea overcame her and she clung to the bedpost for a moment before the room righted itself. Slowly she began to dress. When she had finished, she braided her hair, twisting the thick plaits into a bun at the back. She stood for a moment rubbing her hands on the sides of her skirt, contemplating the case, closed now and locked. Her purse lay on the bed beside it. She opened it and counted her money, fifteen dollars, her school salary, which as yet she had not sent home, and five more dollars she had earned tutoring the Dinwiddie child. There were ten additional dollars under the bureau scarf, thirty dollars in all. She folded the greenbacks in a handkerchief and pinned it to the inside of her corselet.

Next she sat down and wrote a note to Sabrina and Page. It was not an easy message to compose. What could she say? How could she phrase an explanation of a hasty departure, no good-byes, a vanishing act in the wee hours of the morning? The Morses had been so kind. They had taken her in, made her one of the family.

To run off in this way seemed an insult. And the children at school . . .

Yet to remain was unthinkable.

At last she made up a story, farfetched, but the best she could do. She said that she had received a letter (unopened until she returned to her room that night) from Travis, saying that her father was desperately ill and needed her. She had decided she must go at once without delay. She begged them to forgive her haste. She did not know when she would return. She would write. "Many thanks for everything you've done for me, for kindnesses and affection. Fondly, Hannah."

A mile from Wildoak a bonneted farm woman and her son taking a load of milk, eggs, and butter to the Richmond market picked her up. The woman was wild with curiosity to see a lady, satchel in hand, at such an ungodly hour. But Hannah repeated her story about a sick father and soon the woman went on to talk about her own problems, her arthritic bones, her worthless husband, and the hens that were laying poorly.

She was kind enough, however, to deposit Hannah at the train depot. It was busy, even at five in the morning. People were sitting about on hard-backed benches, whole families, the wife asleep on the husband's shoulder, the children curled up in their laps. Somewhere a baby was crying. A group of men were playing cards, squatting over a blanket. Hannah, threading her way past sleepers, string bags and portmanteaus, discarded banana peels and paper bags, went up to the ticket window.

"Where to, miss?"

Where? As far away as she could go. She glanced over the ticket seller's shoulder and saw the names of cities posted: Petersburg, Norfolk, Savannah, Cleveland, Chicago.

"How much is it to Chicago?" she asked, picking the city at random.

"You'd have to change trains," he said.

"Yes. But all together, how much?"

"Ten dollars and fifty cents in coach."

"One ticket, please."

It did not matter that she knew no one there, that she would arrive with very little money, without a place to stay or any notion of what she would do. She would be far from Wildoak, miles and miles, a world away from the man who had betrayed her.

Chapter VII

Christian awoke abruptly to a heavy knocking on his bedroom door. "I say, Christian," Page called, "are you going to sleep all morning?"

The gilded, glass-windowed clock on the mantel said five past ten.

"You slugabed," Page accused, coming into the room. "I've already given Shaizar his morning workout, gone over some paperwork, answered a letter, and had my breakfast. Half the day is gone."

"So it is." Christian's eyes ached. He didn't like to be reminded how energetic his brother-in-law was in contrast to his own indolence. And although he realized Page was not boasting when he enumerated his early morning activities, the recital irritated him.

"We were to ride over to the Ferris place to look at a mare," Page reminded. He looked disgustingly healthy, cheeks ruddy, eyes clear and eager.

"I'd forgotten," Christian said, sitting up. "Sorry. Best go along without me. I had too much port last night and my head is in a miserable state."

Page made a commiserating sound in the back of his throat. "Shall I have Daisy fetch you coffee?"

"No, thank you. I'll be all right."

After Page left, Christian sank back on the pillows and closed his eyes. Hannah's news had jolted him, though if he'd had his wits about him through this affair, it shouldn't have surprised him at all. But he had reacted like an ignorant schoolboy, as if her announcement of impending motherhood was some kind of bolt from the blue.

And if that hadn't been enough for one night, Amanda had threatened him with blackmail.

Two years earlier, on one of his visits to Wildoak, attracted by Amanda, who had sent him unmistakable signs of her willingness to share his bed, he had been indiscreet (or stupid) enough to write her a note urging her to meet him at an old abandoned mill about a mile from the house. Unfortunately she had kept the note. And now she was holding it over his head.

"You've been neglecting me," Amanda had said, cornering him in the parlor after supper. "There's another woman. Don't try to deny it. You're too virile to remain celibate. I'll be in the sewing room. At midnight. Be there, Chris."

He had gone with no specific plan in mind, no idea what he was going to say to placate her. The simple truth was that she had palled. Her chatter, the thin, babylike voice that tinkled on and on, saying nothing that was worth listening to, had finally gotten on his nerves. She had also grown demanding, dictatorial, and her white flesh, the little pear-shaped breasts and inviting loins that once had titillated and excited him had lost their charm.

She had been waiting for him, and before he could pull the door to she had flung herself at him, linking her arms in a stranglehold about his neck, covering his face with kisses. When he tried to pry her loose, she clung all the tighter.

"Let go, Amanda."

But she hadn't. "Chris, I thought you'd never come, my darling Chris." And another torrent of kisses.

"At least let me close the door."

He thought he saw the tail end of a shadow moving

along the corridor and was going to step out to make
sure no one had overheard or seen them when Amanda
pulled him roughly back into the room and shut the door
herself. She immediately began to undo the pearl buttons down the front of her blouse.

"No," he said. "Amanda, you must listen to me."

"We'll talk later." She pressed her half-exposed breasts
to his chest. "I'm on fire, Chris. I want you inside me.
Now."

"You must listen. I can't."

"What?" Her green eyes narrowed. It was then she
had told him of the note, threatening to present it to
Burnwell.

The odd thing was that they were both aware that
Burnwell suspected their liaison. But as long as the
cuckolded husband was not presented with irrefutable
evidence, he could pretend to ignore it. What he would
do if Amanda showed him the note was open to conjec-
ture. Christian did not think Burnwell would challenge
him to a duel (that romantic and rather foolhardy age
had long since passed) or come after him with a pistol.
But there would be an uproar of some kind, a scandal
that would incidentally involve Page and Sabrina, two
people who were closer to him than his own father and
mother.

"Well, Chris?"

An inspiration came to him. "I—I've a confession,
one I hoped I wouldn't have to make." He managed to
look sheepish. "I've contracted a disease."

She sat down abruptly on a cane-bottomed chair. "You
what?"

"An indiscretion. A bordello in Richmond. Sorry to
say its reputation for cleanliness among its girls proved
false. It's an embarrassment. A physician is treating me.
Fortunately he says it is not a bad case, but you can
see . . ."

"Yes, yes." Her round green eyes were accusing.
"How could you? How could you patronize one of
those awful places?"

"My dear, you've known all along I'm no saint. It

happened on impulse, one that I deeply regret.'' He
picked up her hand and gallantly kissed it.

Somewhat mollified, she gave him a weak smile.

"Admitting I'm in the wrong," Christian went on, "I
nevertheless feel disappointed in you, Amanda."

"Why me? I assure you, there's been no one else. A
flirtation or two, but nothing more."

"A woman who professes to love a man as you do
does not threaten to expose him—to put a polite term on
blackmail."

"Oh, Chris, sweetheart, I was desperate, desperate!
Do you think for a minute I'd show that note to—"

"You said you would."

"I didn't mean it, believe me."

"But you didn't burn or destroy it? No. Instead you
kept it like a weapon. Does that indicate love?"

"But, Chris, darling . . ."

"There's no other way to interpret your action. However, if you are bent on showing the note to your husband, I suppose I can't prevent it. There will be a to-do,
of course. Knowing Burnwell, he will probably divorce
you, set you adrift without a penny or— "

"Oh, stop it! Stop it!" She reached into her bosom
and drew out the offending note. Leaning over the oil
lamp on the table, she touched it to the flame. The smell
of burning paper filled the room. "There, you see!"

"My darling," he said.

She grasped his hands. "You must promise the moment you are cured we'll be together again."

"I look forward to it with great longing."

But five minutes after he had left her and climbed the
stairs to his room he had forgotten his promise and her.
He had spent most of a miserable night imbibing port
and thinking of Hannah.

Lying on his bed, fully awake now, he tried to sort out
what was happening to him. Why had Hannah become
such a disturbing (and, admit it, Christian, a little frightening) part of his life? How had she crept into it? What
was there about Hannah's face, her voice, the direct

wide look under straight dark brows that he could not dismiss, that no amount of wine could dim or vanquish? He wasn't ready for love, for one woman, for marriage. He had promised himself he never would be. Hannah—damn her!—had caught him by surprise.

He refilled his glass from the port bottle on the side table and drank slowly, recalling the women he had known in the past. At twenty-four he could look back on dozens, few of them memorable. There had been Kate Kinsley, his first. One did not forget the first. She had been a luminary at Mrs. McAllister's sporting house, a skilled and knowledgeable whore. He was fifteen at the time, she at least twice his age, a woman with a square jaw, bushy dyed hair, and a husky, whiskey voice. But to his callow eyes she had appeared beautiful, a goddess. When she disrobed to reveal the marble perfection of her large ripe breasts, the nipples rouged provocatively, the curve of her ivory-fleshed hips, and the thatch of pubic hair, black in contrast to the bright red of her head, he had been overcome with awe. He remembered how she had praised his manliness (limp and dangling between his legs out of shyness), his good looks, his broad shoulders (he was large for his age). She had fondled and kissed him and, when that failed to evoke a response, had gone down on her knees and taken his flaccid member in her mouth. He had never in his whole life imagined—or come close to imagining—such an electrifying sensation as when those sucking lips, the teasing tongue swirled and coaxed him into a hard, throbbing erection. She had brought him to bed, then, and guided his pulsing organ between her legs, not a moment too soon. His ejaculation had been like the eruption of Vesuvius, a spine-jarring ecstatic burst.

In the next few weeks he had come to her as often as he could. She was a good teacher. Her lessons had included the various ways to approach a woman, how to win her through the art of subtle flattery, how to make love to her, bringing her to moaning excitement. She taught him the trick of using his tongue and lips to touch, to kiss the parts of a woman's body that would

give her pleasure. She showed him how the clitoris
when properly manipulated could reduce a woman to
quivering eagerness. She coached him in restraint, how
to hold his climax back, a discipline indispensable to an
accomplished lover.

He never forgot her. She was well paid for her lessons and demanded nothing more from him. When they
parted, it was with friendly affection. There were many
women after Kate—high-priced courtesans as well as
high-class matrons; a few ladies of the theater; now and
then girls he'd met in expensive shops. With his swarthy
good looks and his charming manners, seduction had
come easily. Sometimes—more frequently than he had
anticipated—women had seduced him. Marguerite Chesney came to mind. Mrs. Sinclair Chesney, a San Francisco socialite who together with her husband had
been occasional guests at his parents' home. How old
was he when she took him into her mauve bedroom with
the Irish lace curtains and lace-tatted pillows? Seventeen? No, eighteen.

On the plump side, but firm of flesh, she had taught
him a few turns that Kate had somehow missed. She
enjoyed having him lie flat on his back, his erection an
inviting, fleshy spike as she straddled him. Slowly lowering herself, she would enclose his turgid penis in her
moist velvety sheath. Holding it there, she would rock
slowly from side to side, back and forth, then up and
down, her head flung back in ecstasy until, bringing him
to ejaculation, she shuddered to her own climax with a
wild cry.

And there was Amanda. A vixen, a heathen who had
met him halfway in mutual attraction. She had been
willing to try anything; the more violent, the more excited she became. She had once asked Christian to beat
her. This he refused to do. He may have been a hedon-
ist, debauched beyond redemption, but an innate sense
of balance, the influence of his own upbringing, which
proscribed striking the "weaker sex," turned him away
from such a perversion. Amanda had never suggested it
again. He did not love her and knew she did not love

him despite her protestations. He also knew that she, too, would fade from memory like the many faceless women he had known, the sophisticated matrons, the shop girls, the actresses, the respectable but unhappy hausfraus. Yes, he could easily forget them all.

But not Hannah.

There was something about her he could not explain, although, God knew, she seemed simplicity itself. The daughter of a drunken tavern keeper, utterly lacking in the smooth, polished finish of the girls of his class, minimally educated, virtuous with the kind of prim morality that ordinarily set his teeth on edge, she nonetheless had captured his fancy.

It was more than her beauty that bedeviled him, although he could not disparage the luminous skin with its rosy flush, the supple, expressive mouth, the pure curve of cheek, the smooth forehead and the torrent of reddish-brown silky hair, the feel of it remaining in his fingers long after he had caressed it. Yet he had known beauties in the past, one or two even surpassing Hannah in looks. Why Hannah? What was there about her that caught at his thoughts? The tenderness, the sweet temperament, her pride as absolute as the line from throat to jaw?

After the Stonebridge funeral he had gone back to San Francisco thinking ruefully of his unsuccessful conquest. It hadn't been for want of trying or for want of reciprocation but because of an unfortunate interruption at the precise moment when Hannah would have fallen, a ripe plum, into his arms. He had thought that she would quickly disappear from memory. And was surprised that she had not.

Then, when he had seen her again at Wildoak, he could hardly believe his good fortune. This time, he had promised himself, he would be more subtle, play the game with more patient cunning, track her in a way that would leave her unaware of pursuit until he had her naked beneath him. Hannah had been an intriguing challenge. How cleverly he had feigned indifference, how cleverly he had pretended to be involved with Amanda, how cleverly he had aroused Hannah's sympathy with his talk of needing a good woman. And all the while he felt through some kind of odd telepathic communication that she was willing or would be willing if only he could find the right moment.

It had come at Alder House under horrific circumstances. Seeing Hannah spread-eagled on the bed with those two bastards at her had ripped loose a fury he hadn't felt in years. And after he had disposed of her attackers (he could have killed them each a dozen times over) it seemed the most natural thing in the world to take her into his arms and comfort her and that that comfort should ease into lovemaking.

He had been surprised at her sensuality, at the passion he had released from this prim little schoolteacher. He had suspected some of it, but nothing like the outpouring of wild kisses, the quivering response of her untried virginal body to his. She had seeped into his mind and blood. He had become obsessed with her, a madness, he reassured himself as he waited each night for her in the overseer's little cottage, that would pass as other obsessions had.

And now she was pregnant. He blamed himself for being such a fool, for not anticipating such a calamity. A man who had bedded so many women should have known better. It was true that most of his mistresses had been experienced, had been familiar with devices to prevent conception. He himself on several occasions (at the insistence of his partners) had used a sheath, but he hated the things. They took all pleasure from the act. Yet he could have procured one of those contraceptive sponges used by women and instructed Hannah how to insert it even if such a contrivance did take a little of the spontaneity from their lovemaking. Better a diminution of spontaneity than the unpleasant reality of a baby—his—growing in her belly.

He sighed as he reached for the bottle, tipping it into his glass. A poor antidote, he thought. The more he drank, the soberer he seemed to become.

What was he to do?

He could leave, of course, sneak off, and take the next train to San Francisco and forget Hannah and his dilemma. But he knew he couldn't. He had tried to forget her before and failed. Marry her? Out of the question. For one thing, he had no means to support a wife. He had lied to Hannah about his trust. He would not come into it until his twenty-fifth birthday. In the meanwhile he was living on the interest, a substantial income in itself, but unfortunately not enough to keep up with his debts. He owed money to his tailor, to the man from whom he had bought his chestnut mare, and considerable sums to several of his card-playing cronies. He was too proud to borrow from his family. Though he were at death's door, he would not ask for a penny from his father, who had lectured him more than once on prudence, forgetting that he himself had been less than prudent in his salad days.

Even if he had the wherewithal to take on a wife, Christian was not too sure he wanted one. To be tied to a particular woman for the rest of his life when there were so many yet untried did not appeal to him. Domesticity was not his forte. Yet he could not abandon Hannah. He had not sunk that low. Nor could he recommend one of the midwives who plied another side of their trade in the dark shadows of Canal Street, women who by means of a strong potion or a crochet hook could rid an unfortunate girl of her embarrassing burden. Too many had died of such ministrations. As a doctor, perhaps he could perform the abortion himself. But somehow he found the idea repellent.

He turned again to the port, draining the last of it from his glass. What should he do about Hannah? He had promised her he would think of something, that "things would work out." How? Perhaps he could send her away, establish her in a small hamlet in the mountains, West Virginia or Kentucky, where she could pose as a widow and have her child. He would get the money somewhere, sell his gold watch, several sets of valuable cuff links, a diamond stickpin he had recently bought on impulse and never worn. Afterward, if Hannah chose not to keep the child, he could arrange for its adoption.

The more Christian thought about this plan, the more it

seemed like a good one. Now he had only to convince Hannah. She would be rebellious, stubborn, refusing to be persuaded, but in the end he felt sure she would agree.

The household did not miss Hannah until the next evening. It had been her habit to rise early, before the others, to breakfast lightly alone (sometimes with Page, who was also an early riser) and to leave with her papers and box lunch for school. No one thought it unusual that the trap she sometimes rode in inclement weather had not been taken out that day. Hannah often walked the two miles to school. The note she had written and left propped on the mantel in her room was not found until suppertime when Daisy had been sent up to inquire why she had not appeared at the table.

Both Page and Sabrina were shocked, then mystified. Even for a serious illness, it seemed an abrupt way to leave. But in talking it over, they concluded that Hannah must have been too distraught to think clearly. If her father were dying, she would have wanted to leave at once without fuss or further explanation. It was a conclusion that was hardly satisfying and left several unanswered questions. How had she reached Richmond, where she must have taken the train? Why hadn't she wakened Daisy or Cook if she hadn't wanted to trouble her hosts? However, Sabrina felt sure these blanks would be filled in once Hannah reached Bayetville and wrote to them as she had promised to do.

Christian did not for one moment believe the reason Hannah had given for her precipitate departure under cover of darkness. He had met her father, had seen the disdain in Hannah's eyes, heard her voice when she addressed him. Chad's ailment, a deathbed illness, could have conceivably impelled her to return to Stonebridge. But never on the spur of the moment.

She had left Wildoak in haste because of her condition, because of shame. When she had stood before him, her face flushed with confusion, telling him that she knew for certain she was carrying his child, he had consoled her and dried her tears. He had even professed his love in a weak, almost mechanical way. Wasn't the shame his also?

Her flight—it was nothing less—had been totally unexpected. She had run home to her besotted father and her inept brother rather than have Christian go on with his equivocating half-truths.

Still, he couldn't help thinking that Hannah's action might be for the best. Perhaps she could resolve the matter by letting her family take care of her. There would be repercussions, no doubt. Her father or brother might come after him, shotgun in hand, in true backwoods Georgia style, and force the issue. But this possibility held no fear for him. He had faced irate papas and brothers before. News of Sabrina and Page's horror and anger at such cavalier repayment of their hospitality would surely reach his father. By now Christian thought he should be immune to his father's opinion. Miles Falconer had made no bones about his feelings, calling his son wastrel, drunkard, card sharper, and libertine. What would one more calumnious name mean? Yet deep in his heart there remained a remnant of the boyhood wish to please, to be praised by his father, to be loved. Try as he might to cut away completely from his father, he could not.

In the end, after much self-debate, Christian decided to go after Hannah. He would find her and suggest his plan. If she rejected it, perhaps he would even do the gentlemanly thing and offer to marry her. But marriage would be the last resort.

A stinging, sleetlike rain was falling as Christian drove up to Stonebridge in the trap he had hired at the Atlanta train station. As he got out and tied his horse to a hitching post he wondered if Georgia, and Bayetville in particular, ever had anything but foul weather.

The taproom was deserted except for a seedy character slumped over a table in the corner. Christian shook the bell on the bar counter. In a few seconds Chad Blaine appeared, bleary-eyed, his step somewhat un-

steady, but he was far from ill or dying. His eyes opened
wide when he saw Christian.

"I do declare if it ain't the gentleman who come to
Granny's funeral. Christian Falconer, ain't it?"

He extended a dirty hand in a frayed sleeve. Christian
shook it, repulsed by the fawning look in Chad's eyes.
Again he wondered how a flower like Hannah could
have been sired by such a noxious creeper as Chad
Blaine.

"A drink, Mr. Falconer?" Chad asked, going behind
the bar.

"Thank you. Whiskey would be fine."

Christian would not have thought it possible but the
inn seemed to have deteriorated even more since he had
last seen it. The flagged floor was strewn with refuse—
peelings, crusts, chicken bones, stubbed cigars, clotted
tobacco juice, spittle, and, under one trestle, dog droppings. On the bar an array of unwashed mugs stood in
puddles that stank of stale beer.

"How's your health?" Christian asked, just to make
sure.

"Never better." Chad belched and patted his paunchy
stomach. "What brings you to these parts, Mr. Falconer? Passin' through?"

Christian set his glass down and contemplated the
dead spider floating in his drink. "No, as a matter of
fact I came to see Miss Blaine. Is she about?"

Chad's look of astonishment was not feigned.

"Hannah? Here? Ain't you heard she's at Wildoak?"

"She was at Wildoak until a few days ago but left.
Said you were ill and needed her."

"Said that, did she? But it ain't true. You can see I'm
hale and hearty. If she done left Wildoak, she ain't come
here."

"Perhaps her brother would know more. I believe she
corresponds regularly with him."

"Mebbe so. Travis!" he bellowed. "Come here,
Travis!" Chad disappeared through the archway that led
to the kitchen.

A few minutes later both Travis and Chad strode into

the taproom, the shoulders of his shabby coat wet with rain, his cracked boots streaked with mud. He had a sour look on his face.

"Pa here tells me you been lookin' for Hannah. What fer?"

"I'd like to talk to her."

"What about?"

"That's my business."

"She ain't here."

Undaunted by Travis's surly tone, Christian said, "Is she at her aunt's? Anywhere in Bayetville?"

"Why should she be? She been teachin' school near Wildoak. Ain't you heard?"

Evidently Hannah had not written to Travis about Christian's presence there. "She *was* at Wildoak," Christian said, "but she left saying your father had suddenly taken ill."

"How'd you know that?" The eyes were suspicious.

"I happened to be a houseguest at my sister's."

"Is that right?" Travis contemplated Christian, the fawn-colored breeches, the braided jacket. "Mebbe she decided she didn't like bein' in the same house as you."

Insufferable jackass, Christian thought.

"You ain't laid a hand on her, have you?"

"I'd like to talk to her."

Travis bristled, his face turning an angry blotched red, his fists clenched at his sides.

"You ain't told me yet what about."

Travis was halfway to violence now. If he should guess the real reason for Christian's visit, his violence would erupt with disastrous consequences—not for Christian but for Travis. The boy was no match for Christian, who could be a mean fighter when necessity arose. So he invented a lie.

"Since you press me, I have been commissioned to deliver some money owed to Miss Blaine by several parents whose children she has tutored."

Chad banged a mug on the counter and cried, "Money! Did ya say money? Then give it here, young man. Give it here. I'm her pa and in charge of her wages."

"I realize that, but I was specifically instructed to give it into her own hands."

Travis eyed him dubiously. "And you come all this way for that?"

"I had business in Atlanta. At any rate I don't see why I should have to account for my movements or motives."

"My sis's just a girl. It's my duty as her brother to see no wrong come to her."

"Yes—and very commendable. But this debate seems to be complicating a very simple matter. May I see Miss Blaine?"

"She ain't here. She ain't at Aunt Bess's. She ain't nowhere in Bayetville. Why did she leave Wildoak?"

"We thought it was because of your father. . . ."

"You can see for yoreself ain't nothin' wrong with Pa."

"Then I don't know."

Christian put up at the Dalton House in Bayetville to wait for Hannah. After three days passed and there was no sign of her, he rode back to Atlanta. He stayed a week, going down each morning to the train station to meet the northbound B&O on its once-a-day run. He would stand a little back from the crowd, anxiously scanning the women passengers who debarked, looking for the familiar face with its widely spaced eyes and classic nose. There were a few minutes on the third day when he was sure he had found her. A woman swathed in a plaid shawl speaking to an elderly man as the train huffed and steamed was so like Hannah his heart turned over. He hastily made his way through knots of people, rudely elbowing them away, intent on reaching the woman who, by now, had become fixed in his mind as Hannah. But before he got to her she turned her head. Not Hannah. Not Hannah by any stretch of the imagination. The mouth too large, bulging over protruding front teeth, the eyes close-set. His disappointment was so keen he felt sick.

That afternoon he took a solitary walk to the outskirts of the city. It was a chilly, windy day, the sun sailing in and out of white, cottonlike clouds. The fields on either side of the road had a damp, earthy smell, the moist promise of returning spring. He asked himself again, as he had so many times in the past few days: Why am I so determined to find her? Why should I care? He searched his soul for the answer, the most profound soul-searching he had ever done in his life.

Why does she haunt me so? Because she is more than a beautiful face, a lovely body? Yes. It must be. She represents so many virtues I have pretended to despise but secretly admired. Honesty, duty, loyalty. And pride. That cool, elegant pride. She is my better self. Could I marry her? There is a difference in our social status, but has social status ever mattered to me? No. Can I see myself waking each morning to the same face on my pillow? Hers, yes. Until death do us part. That face, those intelligent eyes, that sweet, encompassing smile.

Could it be, he thought, stopping suddenly, startling a flock of crows into whirling flight, that I love that girl? I, Christian Falconer, the eternal sophisticate, in *love*? He broke into impulsive, crazy laughter. A man leading a dog on a leash passed, looking at Christian curiously. He thinks I'm drunk. Or mad. Maybe I am. No, no. I've never been saner.

I'm in love with Hannah Blaine! How curious, how strange! Astounding, but true. I'm in *love*!

He hurried back to town and wired Richmond, instructing that his message be relayed to the Morses at Wildoak. Had Hannah returned? Could they let him know where she had gone?

The answer came back the next morning. HANNAH NOT HERE. MUCH CONCERNED.

Christian paid a visit to the Convent of the Sisters of Mercy where Hannah had received her education, hoping that perhaps she had sought sanctuary there. But the sisters had received no word from her in over a year. With persuasion (his charm brought into full play) he managed to worm two names of Hannah's former schoolmates from the nuns. They too could give him no clue as to where she might be.

He did not want to think that she had done away with herself. Hannah was too resolute, too strong, to seek suicide as a solution, he kept reassuring himself, though that fear remained in the dark recesses of his now-guilty heart.

At the end of the three weeks he was forced to admit failure. But only temporarily. He would not give up his search though it seemed that Hannah had vanished without a trace.

Chapter VIII

Hannah, coming through on the Baltimore and Ohio, reached journey's end at the Randolph Street station in Chicago. Weighted down with her suitcase, she joined the debarking throngs as they jostled and pushed their way up from the lower level past a high iron fence designed to keep would-be travelers without tickets from boarding trains. Funneled through the upper gates, Hannah entered a vast, noisy waiting room echoing with the babble of voices, stentorian announcements of departures and arrivals, whistles, hoots, shouts, cries, and the distant huff of released steam. Trying not to feel small and lost, she managed to find a place on a bench where she could sit and think what to do next.

The station was crowded with more people than she had ever seen in her life. Men and women, old and young, milling about, sitting or sleeping on the hard wooden benches, a few crouched on the floor clasping their rope-tied bundles; glassy-eyed, frightened, and bewildered immigrants headed west to homestead the wilderness, children with their names pinned to their clothes, mothers with screaming babies, fresh-faced country girls and boys arriving like herself to escape the past and seek the future. The rest of the nation might be on the

verge of a financial panic, but Chicago, preparing for its
Columbian Exposition, was booming.

She was hungry. From the counters and stalls that
lined the walls of the station came the tantalizing odors
of frying meat, roasting hams and chickens, and brewing
coffee. Should she have something to eat before she
found a lodging for the night? She had ten dollars left in
her purse. She thought she had been hoarding her money
and was surprised how quickly it had melted away.
Perhaps now was as good a time as any to start disci-
plining herself to do without. But her empty stomach
kept rumbling in protest.

Looking around, she saw a booth that advertised coffee at two cents a cup, doughnuts, a penny each. Surely
three pennies would not put too great a dent in her
funds. The old phrase "two to feed" surfaced as she
gave her order, but she quickly pushed the thought
back. She would not allow herself to dwell on the life
that had started inside her, that one day soon her dis-
torted figure would announce her disgrace to the world.
She wanted to forget for as long as she could that the
man she believed she loved had played her false.

First things first.

Standing at the counter, she ate and drank slowly,
savoring every bite and sip. Presently she became aware
of a woman a few feet from her who was also drinking
coffee. When Hannah looked up the woman smiled.

"Noisy place, isn't it?"

"Indeed," Hannah said.

The woman was richly if a bit flamboyantly dressed.
She wore a maroon cape trimmed generously in fur and
a wide-brimmed maroon hat on which a jade-green bird
had been anchored in midflight. Earrings that sparkled
like diamonds dangled from her ears. Her longish face
with its pouched eyes and deep nose-to-mouth lines was
no longer young but it was a pleasant one and the smile
warm.

"I've just seen my sister off for Washington, D.C.,"
the woman said. "I shall miss her. My husband's a dear,
but there's nothing like blood kin—someone you've grown
up with, you know."

"Yes," Hannah said, thinking with a pang of Travis.

"Are you departing or arriving?" the woman asked.

"I've just come in on the B&O from Virginia."

The woman was friendly without seeming to pry. She introduced herself as Mrs. Corinth.

"You've never been to Chicago before?"

"This is my first time. I—I'm a schoolteacher and have heard the pay is good here in the city, much better than in Virginia."

"A schoolteacher—fancy that! Why, I have a friend who just the other day was asking whether I knew of a qualified person who could teach first through third grade. Miss—is it Miss or Mrs.?"

"Mrs. Bush," Hannah said quickly, using the name she had already decided on. During one of her stopovers she had bought a cheap brass wedding band to confirm her status. "I'm a widow," she added, the lie part of her rehearsed story. "My husband died several months ago."

"How sad! And your family?"

"I have a brother. He's married and has five children. I did not wish to be a burden on him." A half-truth she hoped would explain her venture to Chicago.

"You are a plucky sort," Mrs. Corinth said. "I can see that. And what a fortunate coincidence that we should meet. I'm a good judge of character and just from our short acquaintance I feel you are well suited for the position. Of course my friend, who is superintendent, must have the final word, but I can foresee no difficulty." She smiled again at Hannah.

"Why, thank you, Mrs. Corinth."

"Lillian. Please call me Lillian and I shall call you . . . ?"

"Hannah."

"Now, Hannah, I won't think of you putting up at a hotel. No. You must come and stay with us until you get settled. I insist. And I know Mr. Corinth will feel the same."

Hannah could hardly believe her good luck. A roof over her head—at least for the time being—and the promise of a job. About her pregnancy she would keep mum. Wearing stays and voluminous skirts, she could hide her condition until perhaps the sixth month. By then she might have enough money to see her through her ordeal. Beyond that she could not think.

The Corinth residence was on South Dearborn Street, a large, three-story brownstone with a flat roof. Though it was nearly midnight when Mrs. Corinth's carriage pulled in under a side portico, the house was ablaze with lights.

Mrs. Corinth clucked disapprovingly. "I'm afraid the going-away party we had for my sister is still in progress. You must be worn out after your long train ride. Perhaps you'd prefer retiring to your room at once?"

"Oh, yes." Hannah hadn't had a decent night's sleep since before leaving Wildoak and she was exhausted.

As they ascended the back stairs, Hannah could hear a piano crashing out a rollicking rendition of "Home Sweet Home," joined a moment later by a chorus of male and female voices singing in loud and tipsy disharmony.

"I hope my guests won't disturb you," Lillian Corinth said. "I shall soon send them all packing."

The room to which Hannah was shown was furnished with a wide brass bed, an ornately carved bureau and commode, and a pier glass. The walls were covered in flocked crimson paper, the floor in a thick carpet of a darker red shade.

"I'll have Betsy bring you a cup of hot chocolate."

"Oh, please don't. The coffee was quite enough."

"My dear, it's no trouble to me."

Mrs. Corinth tugged at the crimson tassel pull over the bed. Meanwhile Hannah's suitcase was brought up by the black man who had driven Mrs. Corinth's carriage. As soon as he left a black maid wearing a neat gray uniform and a lacy cap on her head entered, carrying a tray with a cup of steaming chocolate.

Hannah thanked the maid. "Put it on the bureau, please. I'll have it later."

"My dear," Mrs. Corinth said, "why don't you have a sip now. See if it's to your taste. Not sweet enough perhaps."

Hannah obliged. The chocolate was gritty but she smiled and said, "Delicious."

"Ah, but you've hardly drunk enough to tell."

Again Hannah sipped. "Yes, it's fine."

"Good. Now I'll leave you. Betsy will wake you around nine with a cup of tea—if that's all right. Then good night, my dear." She kissed Hannah's cheek, the lily-of-the-valley perfume Hannah had noticed on their ride from the train station wrapping her momentarily in cloying sweetness.

After Mrs. Corinth and the maid left, Hannah opened her suitcase and removed her nightgown. But halfway through undressing a disabling, dog-weary fatigue overcame her. Her limbs felt like weights, every movement an effort, her eyes so heavy-lidded she had to struggle to keep them open. Stretching out on the bed, she immediately fell into a deep sleep.

When she awoke, the lamps were still burning. Her head ached and she had an excruciating thirst. Dulled with sleep, she looked around, puzzled by her strange surroundings until she remembered Mrs. Corinth and their encounter in the train station. On the bureau a small gilded clock supported by two naked nymphs said four.

Hannah got up and went to the window, drawing the curtains aside. It was still dark, and by pressing her nose to the glass, she could see that it had started to snow.

She shivered in the cold. I must have a drink of water, she thought. But the pitcher on the commode was empty and the remains of the chocolate, overlaid with scum, looked unappetizing. She tugged at the bellpull and waited. And waited. Betsy had probably long since gone to bed.

Her thirst continued to torment her. She got into her skirt and waist and, letting herself out, padded down the corridor in her stocking feet. The doors on either side were closed. Behind one she heard the rumble of low voices but could not distinguish whether they were female or male. Then there was silence.

She continued on until she came to a staircase carpeted in burgundy red. Bracketed gas lamps lit the way down. At the bottom she paused before mauve velvet draperies through which she again heard subdued voices. Had the Corinths' guests not left yet? She hated to intrude. It would be awkward trying to explain her presence, but she had come this far and by now she could only think of relieving her thirst. Slipping through a gap in the draperies, she hesitated, surveying the scene before her.

There were four women sitting on two facing settees at the far end of a very large room. They hadn't heard or seen her, so she stood there in puzzled silence. Three were in negligees. One wore lacy drawers but nothing above the waist except a tiny gold cross on a chain that dangled between overripe breasts.

The room, lit by crystal chandeliers, was opulently furnished in satin-covered sofas and chairs. There was a large grand piano—the one Hannah had heard earlier—covered by a fine Spanish shawl. On it stood a three-foot gilded Venus de Milo and a vase of white mums. Over all hung the odor of stale cigar smoke and the same lily-of-the-valley perfume that Mrs. Corinth wore.

"He was a beast, Clara, I tell you," the half-naked woman said. "A beast. He wanted me to get down on all fours while he rode me with a whip."

"You don't have to put up with that," the woman called Clara replied. Her yellow hair, falling untidily down from its pins, was dark at the roots. "Not here. That's one thing I like about Lillian Corinth. She keeps a decent house. That kind of vulgar play, the beating and whipping and burning with cigar ends, goes on in the cheap knocking shops, and anyone trying it here would be shown the door."

"That's what I told that elegant cocksman. I said I'd lick his balls but I'd be damned . . ."

Hannah, dumbfounded, her thirst forgotten, stepped noiselessly back through the heavy curtains. Carefully, without making a sound, she hurried up the staircase. Once back in her room she sat on the bed, her heart beating loudly. How could she have been so naive? She had succumbed to one of the oldest games in the world. A procurer's ruse: the nicely dressed, matronly woman meeting a train, picking out an innocent-looking small-town girl who was traveling alone without a relative or friend to meet her and approaching her in a natural, "accidental" fashion with an offer of shelter and work.

She had been lured into a bordello. No mistaking it. No one reared above a tavern, no matter how well shielded, could escape hearing about the seamier side of life. From talk by drummers who had passed through Stonebridge on their way to or from a large city she had understood early on what a whorehouse was and how lavishly some of the better ones were furnished.

Mrs. Corinth was a madam and Hannah had been recruited to serve in the "trade." Exactly how Mrs. Corinth would accomplish this, Hannah had no idea. It was apparent from the way the woman had reacted to Hannah's widowhood that she preferred girls who had some experience with men to virgins. The chocolate, Hannah was certain now, had been drugged. Why was not clear. Perhaps Mrs. Corinth wanted to make sure Hannah would sleep through the night and not go wandering about. Chances were her so-called benefactor would keep up the deception of a teaching job (which, of course, would never materialize), meanwhile suggesting that four times as much money could be made by entertaining men.

Hannah put on her shoes, closed and locked her suitcase. She did not know whether Mrs. Corinth would keep her against her will but she was taking no chances.

With suitcase in hand, she moved cautiously along the corridor until she found the back stairs. Down below she tinkered with the locks on the door, pulling back the bolt, which grated so loudly she was afraid the entire household would be awakened. At last, working hastily with stiff nervous fingers, she managed to undo the chains and twist the key.

It was bitterly cold outside, the snow falling thicker now. And pitch dark. Hannah waited for a minute or two and then, guided by the feeble glow of a street lamp, began to move quickly, her shoes crunching annoyingly on the graveled drive. Once on the street, she turned to the left. She did not know where she was going. Anywhere, she thought, as long as it was away from the house. What other dangers might lurk in the deserted streets behind shadowy hedges and dark tree trunks she would not let herself consider. Nor did she care to remind herself that this was the second time in a week she was fleeing, suitcase in hand.

She walked on, the wind slapping at her face, tearing at her jacket, threatening to blow the hat from her head. Her thin clothing was no defense against the snow, which swirled and danced in cold gusts, beading her lashes and freezing her nose. The case dragged at her arm. She switched it to the other hand, numb now like her feet in their flimsy-soled shoes. Presently she saw a dim light coming from a building next to a darkened church. It was set back from the street and surrounded by an iron fence. Hannah assumed it was the rectory. She had a tussle with the gate while the wind snatched at and worried her skirts. Finally the gate creaked open.

She went up to the door over which a gas light flickered and yanked at the bell. She waited for what seemed an interminable length of time and yanked again. Finally a small panel slid open and a woman's face framed by a nun's wimple looked out.

"P-please," Hannah stuttered, fighting the vibration of her lower jaw, "may I come in? I'm lost. Just to sit until daybreak?"

"Who are you?"

"Mrs. B-Bush, a widow. I'm a newcomer to Chicago."

The door was opened and she entered the warmth of a starkly furnished parlor.

"We have no accommodations for outsiders," the nun said. She was a large woman with a knobby forehead. "But you may sit until morning. I'm sorry I cannot do better."

Hannah fell asleep, her head sunk forward on her chest.

In the morning she was awakened by the same sister, who brought her a cup of weak tea.

"You girls will come to the city," she lectured. "Even if you are a widow, you're still a girl, you know. There's thousands of you tramping the streets, looking for work and getting into mischief."

"But I have a profession," Hannah said. "I'm a schoolteacher. I was hoping I could find something along that line."

"Ah—a schoolteacher," the nun said, her stern face relaxing. "That puts another light on the matter. Have you ever taught the little ones—kindergarten, for instance?"

"Oh, yes, I've had all ages in Bayetville, Georgia, and at the Riverview School in Virginia."

"Well, Miss Addams of Hull House might be interested. There would be little pay, if any, but you would get your room and board. It might tide you over until you could find something better. Have you heard of Hull House?"

"No, I'm afraid not."

"It's a settlement house started by Jane Addams and her friend Miss Starr. Both women are devoting their lives to the poor, mainly European immigrants who find it difficult to adjust to their new life. You would be teaching their children."

"But if they are foreigners, how will I communicate? English is my only language."

"Oh, you'd be surprised how quickly the little ones pick it up. And there's always sign language. Are you interested?"

"By all means."

"Good. As soon as one of the lay sisters arrives, I'll have her take you there. You can speak to Miss Addams yourself."

The lay sister came at nine o'clock, a stout woman wearing a black toque and a man's overcoat buttoned to the chin. A long woolen muffler was wrapped about her throat. She was somewhat aghast at Hannah's lack of warm clothing for a Chicago winter and insisted that Hannah at least wear her muffler.

They traveled by horse car, changing twice, jolting and rumbling along through mile after mile of streets, past factories belching dark clouds of coal smoke, the car's clanging bell warning pedestrians and horse-drawn wagons plodding through the dirty, melting snow to make way. The lay sister kept up a running commentary.

"We are doing much building now in the city," she

said as they went by a construction site where men clambered over wooden frames. "And see the tall buildings with plate-glass windows? That's the newest, those windows."

They passed shanties and shops and row after row of clapboard houses standing behind iron grillwork fences. The narrow pavements were busy with pedestrians—no leisurely strollers here, but men and women who seemed in a great hurry to reach their destinations.

They did the last two blocks on foot, Hannah lugging her suitcase, trying to keep up with her energetic guide as they plowed their way through an open-air market. Crowds were gathered about pushcarts and overturned crates and upended barrels heaped with merchandise. "Cheap! Cheap!" a hawker cried. "Over here, the best pair of pants in the city!" Secondhand clothing, pots and pans, dry goods, baskets of potatoes, harnesses, shoes, iron bedsteads, and crockery were haggled over while money changed hands with cheerful briskness.

Hull House was situated on Halstead Street, a brick building with a pitched roof and dormer windows. Hannah had expected an institutional sort of interior—bare floors, a waiting room with straight wooden chairs and a scuffed desk. Instead she found the wide entry hall, with its scattered rugs, open fireplace, and its few pieces of lovely mahogany furniture, as welcoming as any drawing room.

It was a setting that befit Jane Addams. Hannah had never met a sweeter, kinder, more gracious woman. Miss Adams's deep-set eyes, so full of interest and concern, put Hannah at ease, making the interview much less of an ordeal than she had anticipated.

"You say you have taught school in a rural area, but I must warn you this will be quite different. Your pupils will come from Italian families mostly. They are a good people but their standards and customs, especially in bringing up children, are not quite the same as ours. Don't be too shocked if you find several of your little ones intoxicated. The habit of feeding children wine-soaked bread for breakfast is hard to break. But the children are bright, for the most part, and willing to learn.''

Hannah was installed on the top floor, sharing a dormer room with another young woman, Carrie, a titian-haired, thin girl with a squint. Carrie was friendly, kind, and inordinately curious, wanting to know about Hannah's dead husband, why she had come to Chicago, her family, educational background. Hannah found herself going deeper and deeper into a morass of lies, inventing answers to all of Carrie's questions.

She had not been entirely candid with Miss Addams either, although Miss Addams hadn't pressed for details, only the basic facts of experience and education. Still Hannah's conscience bothered her. She had been at Hull House two weeks when she decided to tell Miss Addams the truth. Hannah, meeting with her mentor privately, had planned beforehand to give only a bare-bones account of what had happened, but soon she found herself making a full confession. Jane Addams listened attentively, her head to one side, and offered no comment until a flushed and shamefaced Hannah had finished.

"My dear child," she said, "you needn't think you are the first sinner in the world. Or certainly not the first to come to Hull House. Rest assured your secret will be kept. When your confinement draws near, we will be here to help."

But Miss Addams's offer of help came sooner than expected, for a few days after this interview Hannah had an accident.

Descending the wide wooden stairs to the lower hall, she tripped on the hem of her gown. She felt a moment of weightless disbelief as she clutched for nonexistent support. Then to her horror she was falling, tumbling over and over, scrabbling wildly at each smooth, worn step, at the banisters beyond her reach, at the empty air, pain jabbing her elbows, head, back, hips, knees, until she finally reached the bottom. Helping hands picked her up. Miraculously she had broken no bones. But her entire body seemed one throbbing bruise while her stomach contracted and dilated with violent cramps. Assisted into a room, she lay on a leather couch, biting her lip to keep from screaming. Moments before the doctor arrived, she felt the rush of sticky fluid between her legs and knew she had miscarried.

A great deal of sympathy was shown by the people of Hull House. Carrie, the other teachers, her pupils and their mothers (who were told that Mrs. Bush had lost her late husband's baby) brought or sent her little gifts while she lay abed. Miss Addams was concerned for Hannah's health but did not dwell on the aborted child. It was her opinion, voiced privately, obliquely, and in kindly terms, that the accident, though painful, had relieved Hannah of a burden. Hannah tried to share this feeling, but could not. She knew that life would be easier without an illegitimate child to raise, without having to go on with lies that would compound themselves when her son or daughter got old enough to ask questions. And she hated the father. Nevertheless her loss saddened and depressed her.

Hannah, knowing her brother would be worried, finally brought herself to write. She pondered a long time over what to say, her mind vacillating between truth and fiction, until she settled on something halfway between.

> *Dear Travis,*
> *I left Wildoak on the spur of the moment, although it had been in the back of my mind for some time to do so. Mr. and Mrs. Morse were kindness itself, Sabrina like a sister, Page like a brother. But as you may know from my letters, they have a considerable number of guests.*
> *I am sorry to say, though the Morses themselves are of the highest moral caliber, some of their male friends are not. They made sly advances toward me—one in particular was quite obnoxious. I could not tell my benefactors. It was the sort of accusation that would cause embarrassment all around. You can understand that, can't you? I thought it best to invent an excuse to explain my hasty departure. I said Pa was desperately ill and*

*needed me. Please, please, don't let the Morses
know the real reason. This letter must be in strict-
est confidence. Tell Pa I've gone to Atlanta and
am teaching there. I will write to the Morses but
send my letter to you and you can put it in another
envelope and have one of the drummers mail it
from Atlanta. I am well and happy and teaching at
Hull House in Chicago but I want no one to know
my present address. Travis, I trust you. Write. For
reasons above I have changed my name to Mrs.
Bush. I think of you constantly.*

*Much love,
Hannah*

What Travis would make of the farfetched jumble,
Hannah could only wonder. A week later when Travis
replied, he asked whether one of the Morses' male friends
had been Christian Falconer, since he had come to
Stonebridge looking for her. Hannah, surprised that Christian made the effort trace her, decided he had done so
only out of curiosity. In all probability he had business
in Atlanta and had made the side trip to Bayetville as an
afterthought. To Travis she wrote that yes, Christian
was one of the "obnoxious" males. But she would never
tell her brother about her pregnancy, never tell him that
she had willingly given herself to Christian with shameful eagerness. That was one secret, one confidence, she
and Travis would never share.

A month after Hannah had fully recovered from her
miscarriage she had supper with Jane Addams, Miss
Starr, the Reverend Plunkett, and a young guest, Guy
Hartwell. He, like Miss Addams, had been born in
Cedarville, Illinois, and the families there had known
each other. Guy had come to Chicago a year earlier to
help build the Columbian Exposition. A skilled cabinet-
maker and carpenter, he had also volunteered to assist
Miss Addams with repairs and any add-on construction
she might have at Hull House. Guy was a tall, attractive
young man of twenty-five with very expressive blue

eyes and a mustache and sidewhiskers a shade darker
than his light blond hair.

The meal was served in one of the small upstairs
dining room; a simple repast of poached whitefish, potatoes, and bottled greens. The conversation focused on
one-room schools, the subject of a projected study by
the Reverend Plunkett, and Hannah's opinions were attentively noted. However, before long Hannah could
feel that Guy, though he made several pungent comments, was drawn to her, not for her opinions but as a
woman. It put her on the defensive. Guy was pleasant as
a table companion, but Hannah wanted no entanglements. She had gone through too much to feel anything
like sexual attraction to any man, no matter how
appealing.

But she had reckoned without the impression she had
made on Guy. Later he was to tell her that he had fallen
in love with her the moment she had entered that small
dining room, her beautiful, sad face touching his heart.

Two days after this first encounter he sent her a note
asking to her to take supper with him. She refused. But
he turned up at the appointed hour, carrying a single red
rose wrapped in green tissue. Where he had obtained
(and how much he had paid for) that rose during a
Chicago winter, Hannah could not guess. She was em-
barrassed if not a little chagrined when she saw him
standing in the hall holding the wrapped rose in one
hand and his fedora in the other. She looked upon his
presence as an invasion of her privacy.

"I'm sorry to be so brash," he said apologetically.
"But if you don't want to go out for supper, perhaps we
could sit and talk for a few minutes."

Hannah, with words of dismissal on her tongue, hesitated. She could tell by his voice and the entreaty in his
eyes that he was lonely, perhaps as lonely as she. She
recalled that he, too, had come from a small town, and
though he had been in Chicago longer, he probably still
felt uncomfortable in a city whose teeming multitudes
seemed unfriendly and indifferent.

"Or do you think me too forward?"

"No," she said, relenting, smiling.

They sat on a hard sofa by the fireplace. As they spoke together on a variety of nonpersonal subjects, Hannah felt warmer toward him. Guy was an easy person to be with. In some ways he reminded her of Travis: the way he kept brushing the cowlick from his eyes, the earnest way he pronounced his words, the respect with which he listened to her. The few minutes of conversation ran quickly into an hour.

When Guy got up to leave he said, "Mrs. Bush, thank you so much for a pleasant evening." He twisted the hat in his hand. "I have a suggestion, if it meets with your approval, of course. Tomorrow is Sunday, a free day for me. Could I show you some of the city?"

Hannah found it hard to refuse.

He came the next morning at ten. He had hired a trap and they set off to what he called the "prettiest part of town," the Gold Coast on the North Side. Here the rich had built their homes: imitation castles and chateaux, villas and huge rambling Victorian residences with gingerbread verandas. Passing a surrey drawn by a pair of sleek, docked bays, Hannah glanced inside the nickel-boxed interior and saw a young woman dressed in a fur cape, her velvet hat turned up at the side to reveal a haughty profile. Beside her sat a man in a black derby, his gloved hands holding a gold-headed cane. The trap turned into a driveway where iron gates were swung open by a keeper. Beyond the gates Hannah glimpsed a lawn where even in this near-freezing weather a fountain played. Farther back sat a T-shaped brick mansion, its bay windows gleaming in the sunlight. Hannah wondered what it would be like to live in such a house, to be waited on by servants, to have nothing on her mind when she woke in the morning but what dress to choose, what shop to visit, or with whom to have tea or dinner. It was an idle thought that vanished when she suddenly recalled her days at Wildoak. While Wildoak did not resemble the thirty-room palace she had just passed, nor was it staffed by a host of servants, it was a substantial if not imposing residence. She had lived there and knew the facade never told the story within.

"Mrs. Bush," Guy Hartwell said. "You're so quiet. Of what are you thinking?"

"Of the rich and the poor."

"Ah, yes. There is an unfortunate gap, no doubt, but it's nowhere more apparent than here. On the farm, people at least can grow their own food and can breathe clean air. They don't have to put up with the bad odors of the city."

He was referring to the stench of the stockyards where cattle waited to be slaughtered and dissected to provide meat for America's tables. On any given day when the wind blew from the southwest, the smell of animal droppings, blood, and decaying carcasses pervaded neighborhoods miles from the yards. In addition the Chicago River, whose two forks joined at Lake Street, was a gigantic cesspool. Hannah and Guy had crossed it on their drive, Hannah holding a handkerchief to her nose. Its greasy waters clogged with sewage, garbage, dead cats and rats, broken bottles and rotting timber reeked intolerably, a stench that had the Gold Coast people moving farther and farther north. Were all large cities like this, Hannah wondered, with so much beauty, so much squalor existing side by side?

They ate their dinner at the old Windsor dining room on Monroe Street. Hannah, examining the menu, was shocked at the prices: half a broiled chicken, seventy-five cents; steak with mushrooms, one dollar and twenty-five cents; ham, eighty-five cents. The whitefish with hash-brown potatoes and asparagus seemed the cheapest. She was about to order it when Guy said, "I'd recommend the steak. It's very good."

Obviously he had been at the Windsor before. He must be rich, she thought, if he could dine in such a sumptuous place. And what must he be spending today, renting a trap and now this dinner?

"I don't often come here," he said as if reading her thoughts. "Only on special occasions with special people." His smile lit up his deep blue eyes, which looked at her with fond amusement. He was a handsome man, she decided again, a wonder he hadn't already been spoken for.

"And not out of charity?" she couldn't help asking. "Treating the girl from the country to a good time?"

"By God, no. I give charity in alms or by fixing a cabinet. You, Hannah—and may I call you Hannah?—have given me more pleasure today than anything I could possibly put a price on."

"Tell me," she said when their steaks arrived, "a little about yourself. I don't mean to be patronizing, Mr.—"

"Guy."

"Guy. Have you always been a carpenter?"

"No. My father wanted his boys to be professional men and I was destined for the ministry. But a year after I was at the seminary I knew theology wasn't for me. I enjoy working with my hands, making things. So I apprenticed myself to a master carpenter. But, Hannah, that's not what I really want." He leaned forward. "What I wish for most of all is to have my own piece of land. My uncle Hooper is a farmer and as a boy I spent my summers with him. Getting in the hay is one of my happiest memories. But farmland in the Midwest has become too dear. Out of the question. The only acreage someone like me can afford is out west."

"A ranch?"

"Yes. I have my eyes on a spread in Monterey County bordering the seacoast of California. It was advertised several years ago in the *Farmer's Gazette*. I wrote to the man and he sent pictures. Then he changed his mind. But just last week I heard from him again. He asked if I was still interested."

"And?"

"I haven't answered him yet. He wants only a small down payment. I've saved up some money since I've been working at the exposition and have more than enough."

"If that's what you want, Guy, I think you should buy it."

"Well—yes. I would have snapped his offer up if he'd written a month earlier, but something has happened in the meantime." He paused, a faint flush creeping into his wind-burned cheeks. "I met you."

Hannah looked away from his direct blue gaze. She had sensed what was coming, but not this soon. She tried to make light of it.

"Me? I can't be as important as a lifelong ambition."

"I never thought to meet a girl who was," he said. "But I was wrong. Oh, Hannah, I know a gentleman is supposed to court a lady for months, perhaps even a year, before he speaks his mind. But . . ." He put his hand over hers and she did not draw it away. "I'm as sure now of my feelings as I will be twenty years from now. I love you, Hannah."

His sincerity touched her. She didn't know what to say. His declaration had come too quickly. She wanted time to think, to go over it in her mind. He was not at all like Christian. (And would she have to tell him about that affair? She shuddered inwardly when she thought about it.) Guy's open, honest face, his lack of pretense, his avoidance of false flattery appealed to her. But love? Could she ever love in that feverish, all-consuming, heart-breaking, ecstatic, agonizing way again? The pain and the joy. No, thank God, that could happen only once in a lifetime.

"I don't want to go out west unless you come with me as my wife," Guy was saying.

"But you hardly know me," Hannah protested.

"Hannah, I suppose it would sound banal if I said I feel I've known you all my life. But the strange thing is I do. You remind me a little of a picture my mother had taken when she was a young girl. The same soft smile at the corners of her mouth, the same clear eyes. I'm convinced if she were alive now and met you, she would feel that she had known you too. And loved you."

"Marriage is for a long while."

"I hope forever."

Hannah looked down at her plate where the last bit of steak lay in congealing gravy. He wanted to marry her, wanted her to be his wife. To go away and make another life in a far distant place. It would mean leaving the city behind and the last remnants of a memory that bound her to the unhappy past.

He said, "I'm being very selfish, aren't I? I haven't

even asked about your feelings, if you could possibly care for me. You are so lovely—and a lady—and I'm—well—I'm just a plain carpenter."

"You mustn't say that. You mustn't even think it. It's simply—so sudden. I'm not sure . . ."

"Of course you aren't. It's not a life of luxury and ease that I'm promising."

"No, no, it isn't that."

"Still, a woman must consider it. The first year or two might take a little getting used to. But you see I'm positive I can make a go of it. I plan to raise cattle, prime beef for the table d'hôtes of the best restaurants in San Francisco and for the settlements and cities all up and down the state. California is growing, Hannah; people are flocking there. They'll want meat. And it's fine cattle country. They don't have our terrible freezing winters, and the central section where the Sycamore Ranch is located gets plenty of rainfall. I can raise my own feed. I can't lose, Hannah." He touched her hand again, then squeezed it. "There is a house and several outbuildings, and two or three deep, working wells, so we won't be starting from scratch." A small nervous smile curved his lips. "I say 'we.' I hope with all my heart it's going to be 'we.' "

"Guy, there's something you must know." She couldn't let him go on without telling him she wasn't the widow she pretended to be. He was too candid, too straightforward, too fine a person to be led into believing she was the lady he thought she was. He would be disillusioned, of course, but better now than later. "Guy—my name is not Mrs. Bush. I've never been married. My name is Hannah Blaine. Last year . . ."

She told him everything except Christian's name. When she had finished, he asked only one question.

"Do you still love this man?"

"I despise him!" she replied with honest vehemence.

"Then we'll not talk of this episode again."

"But surely you can't mean that you still—"

"Yes." He cut her off. "It would be a poor love that died so easily. Hannah, more than ever, I want to make it up to you, to erase the unhappiness I saw in your eyes when I first met you. I want you to put the past behind you. All that was ugly and painful. It's done and over with. Now is what I want you to think about. Will you promise me that?''

"Oh, Guy, I promise."

When he drew up to Hull House, he halted the trap. Shyly he put his arm about Hannah's waist, and when she made no resistance drew her closer and gently kissed her on the lips. She felt no tremor of excitement, no thrill. Her bones did not melt, the blood did not rush to her face. But what she did feel was a deep affection. She knew that she could trust Guy with her life, that he would be honest, faithful, hardworking, a true husband in every sense of the word. Perhaps someday she might even come to love him.

"I'm not going to press you," Guy said. "I want you to get to know me better. I do have hope. You haven't said no outright."

She laughed and on impulse reached up and planted a kiss on his cheek.

"Oh, Hannah." His lips claimed hers again in a kiss that was stronger than the first. "My darling," he whispered. "I want to see you tomorrow night and the night after that. We have so much to talk about. I still can't believe my good fortune—to think I might never have met you if I hadn't come to dinner at Hull House." He kissed her again. "You will consider my proposal, Hannah?"

"Yes, Guy, I will."

And in the days that followed, seeing Guy almost every evening, she thought more and more seriously about becoming Mrs. Guy Hartwell. She believed she was actually falling in love with him and felt that he held the key to her—as well as his—future happiness.

Chapter IX

Christian was still at Wildoak when the Morses received a letter from Hannah postmarked Atlanta. In it she apologized for her hasty departure.

> *My father is much better, but I feel I should accept a teaching post at the Grayson School in Atlanta . . . I do hope you will extend my sincerest apologies and regret to the Riverview School board. . . .*

The letter, Christian suspected, was a fabrication. Chad Blaine had not been ill and Christian doubted very much that Hannah was teaching in Atlanta. He said nothing to the Morses about his suspicions. They had no inkling of his relationship with Hannah, nor were they aware of his recent trip to Bayetville. Since he came and went at Wildoak with relative frequency, they accepted without question or curiosity the excuses he gave to explain his arrivals or departures. He had kept his involvement with Hannah a secret, first out of the knowledge that he was behaving in a rather swinish fashion by seducing her, then because of remorse at what he had done.

The next day he left for Atlanta.

Once there he set out to search for the Grayson School.

Inquiries soon revealed there was no such place. He had a detective agency scrutinize the teaching rosters of both private and public schools in the city. Thinking Hannah might have changed her name, he also supplied the agency with a description of her and asked that they investigate all likely leads. Nothing came of it. A return visit to Hannah's former convent school produced the same negative results as it had earlier.

Stonebridge now seemed his only hope. His plan was to corner Chad alone. Travis, he knew from past experience, would be antagonistic and refuse to talk about his sister, but Chad might be persuaded to part with Hannah's address.

In some respects Christian felt like a thief returning to the scene of the crime—if one could call Stonebridge the scene and his first lustful desire for Hannah a crime. He did not enjoy lurking about, wearing a peaked hat pulled low over his eyes to hide his face, waiting for Travis to leave the inn. It was not Christian's way. He would have much preferred accosting Travis, grabbing him by the coat lapels, shaking (or knocking) the information from him. But he knew how fond Hannah was of her brother and that punching Travis about would only be another black mark against him.

He caught Chad in the taproom after he had seen Travis come out and drive off in a donkey cart, presumably on some errand.

Chad was amazed but happy to see Christian again. A gentleman, he said, was always welcome at Stonebridge. It gave the inn a good name (as well, Christian surmised, as added cash—for Christian was a generous tipper).

"What'll it be, brandy or beer?" Chad asked, rubbing his hands together.

"Brandy would be fine. And have one for yourself as my guest." The drinks were poured and good health wished on both sides. Christian said, "I'm looking for your daughter. My sister and brother-in-law have received a communication from her, but the school she gave as her place of employment is fictitious."

"Is what?"

"Made up. There is no Grayson School."

Chad scratched his two-day-old-whiskered chin. " 'S that so? First I heard."

"I was wondering if you would know her present whereabouts."

"Ain't got a clue. It's Travis she writes to. You bent on getting together with my gel?" he asked in a tone that Christian supposed Chad thought was fatherly concern.

"Yes." He could not bring himself to say, I'd like to marry her. The prospect of Chad calling him son was one he would rather not think about. "Has she written to Travis lately?"

"Can't rightly say."

Christian brought out his pigskin wallet and extracted two crisp ten-dollar bills.

Chad's eyes fastened on the bills. "Well, now . . ."

"I'd make it worth your while if I could have her address."

"Fair 'nough."

He went out of the taproom and disappeared up the stairs. Christian drank his brandy and helped himself to another. It was of poor quality, tasting of burnt sugar and the cask. He was surprised at how nervous he was, how impatient.

Minutes later Chad returned with an envelope in his hand. "This is from my gel," he said. "Ain't it queer? She's not in Atlanta like Travis told me, but in Chicago. Now what the hell is she doin' there? And she calls herself Mrs. Bush."

"Let me look at it." Christian copied the number quickly: Hull House, 600 Halstead Street.

He handed Chad the bills. "It's most important that you say nothing to Travis about this. Do I have your word?"

"What d'you take me fer? I ain't no tattletale. See you do right by my Hannah."

Christian did not ask what Chad meant by doing "right."

Although no stranger to Chicago—he had graduated from Rush Medical College there—Christian had not known such a place as Hull House existed until he saw

Hannah's letter. But then he had traveled in circles far removed from the poor or from the people like Jane Addams who tried to alleviate their lot. His college years had been spent with cronies who were rich and dissolute, with little thought—aside from an occasional perusal of their textbooks—except to enjoy themselves.

Troy Woolridge, scion of a wealthy furniture manufacturer, had been his particular friend. Of medium height with sandy hair and lively blue eyes, he, like Christian, was a rebel against parental authority. Nothing had given the two students more pleasure than to compare the injustices of their respective fathers, their stodginess and the narrow path they expected their sons to follow.

It was Troy who had usually taken the initiative when they had made their rounds of debauchery. "What say we go down the line tonight?" he would suggest. Going "down the line" was a euphemism for a raunchy tour of the Levee. Located in the first ward, just a few blocks square, the Levee, so named from pre–Civil War days when high-rolling gamblers debarked from packets from downriver close by, ran wide-open whorehouses, poker palaces, dance halls, barrel-house joints, and peep shows in addition to legitimate hock shops, oyster bars, and livery stables.

Troy and Christian had visited only the best of the bagnios, leaving the dives to the less affluent or particular. They had favored flesh peddlers like Lizzie Allen's and the French Elm, with their much-admired gilded chamber pots and mirrored walls and ceilings. Occasionally they had given the House of All Nations their custom. Here "clean" girls of various colors and talents in the more exotic modes of love-for-sale could be bought for an hour or a night.

If intercourse had not been their immediate pleasure, the two young bucks would find a table at Freiberg's Dance Hall, where they could listen to first-rate jazz bands imported from New Orleans. Or they might purchase stall tickets at Saint Jack's, where they could watch chorus girls in tights capering and singing bawdy songs to loud music. When the gambling bug bit them, they would attend the meets at Washington Park Race-

track, rubbing elbows with the *nouveaux riches* who
claimed to be society and who made such a fuss when
Lillian Russell—an "actress!"—appeared in their midst.
If the pair wished to indulge in other forms of betting,
they would spend an evening at the faro houses on Clark
Street, losing (more often than winning) large sums to
the click of the roulette wheel and the rattle of dice.
They would sip Rhine wine at Schlogel's and champagne
at the exclusive Calumet Club or get roaring drunk at
Chapin and Gore.

But Hull House? Who had ever heard of it?

Christian, now walking the streets of Chicago, was
plunged into gloom. He had already called at Hull House
and been told by Miss Addams's secretary that no one
by the name of Mrs. Bush or Blaine was known to them.
The description he had given did not match any of the
teachers in residence, she had said.

Where was Hannah, then? Where had she gone?

Dreadful possibilities had immediately occurred to him.
He knew too well how a young girl without funds, friends,
or family could fall into the trap of prostitution. It did
not make him feel better to think that because of her
beauty she might be enticed or tricked into becoming a
fixture of one of the plusher bordellos where at least she
would not be brutalized. The idea of Hannah going from
man to man, that lovely innocent body (yes, innocent,
for Hannah was knowledgeable only in how to give
herself in love) subject to the pawing, to the uncaring
lust of some fornicator interested only in the pleasure of
his cock, sickened him.

That she was pregnant only worsened the bleak picture of Hannah's fate. Either she had gotten rid of the
child—*their* child—or she would ply the prostitute's trade
until her condition became obvious. God knew what
would happen to her if she fell into the hands of an
unscrupulous whoremaster or pimp. As he traced his
way through the noisome labyrinth of the Levee, past
tintype picture galleries, penny arcades, flophouses, and
the cheaper establishments where the girls displayed
themselves in the windows, he saw it all with new eyes,

with a mixture of disgust, pity, and anxiety, emotions he would have shrugged off six months earlier. It was not that he had transformed himself overnight into a reformer, a pious moralist, but suddenly he had become aware of the human waste, the exploitation of dull-witted plug-uglies, the dog-eat-dog atmosphere, the blatant greed. In the past, when he and Troy had gone merrily from one pleasure to the next, he had hardly noticed the grosser aspects of Van Buren and State streets: the men reeling drunk or spread-eagled face-down in their own vomit on the sidewalks; the tarts taking their customers into reeking alleys, where, backed up against a damp sweaty wall, they would open their legs wide to receive a male organ in exchange for cash; the rapacious con men with their sleazy "boaters" and celluloid collars. He realized that corruption was not confined to the Levee, that Chicago had one of the most venal city governments in the United States, that aldermen could be bought for as little as a box of cigars, a bottle of whiskey, or a "piece of ass."

When he imagined the possibility of Hannah becoming part of this tawdry, bestial scene, he wanted to tear the Levee, the whole city, apart with his bare hands. He had the insane desire to shake up the entire rotten system, to bring down the corrupted pillars of city hall who profited from this decadent underworld.

But he was no crusader, nor did he have any wish to be one. Troy, with whom he was staying, and to whom he had confided his love, had laughed at first but, seeing his friend's earnestness, had tried to help. They both had gone in search of Hannah on the Levee, each taking a section, visiting every cathouse, crib, and bordello—a prodigious undertaking as there were some two hundred such establishments within the Levee district alone.

After an exhausting week Troy gave up. There was no trace of Hannah. He was joining a friend on the Continent and offered Christian the use of his house while he was abroad.

Christian would not—even remotely—consider defeat. He knew Hannah was in Chicago; she had to be. He went back to Hull House. This time he insisted on seeing Jane Addams herself. Seated in her office, he told her his name, that he was related to her family (how, he didn't specify), and that he had urgent business with Mrs. Bush.

"She doesn't want to see me, does she?" Christian asked when he had finished and Miss Addams remained silent. From his brief encounter with Jane Addams he had divined that she knew who he was and that if asked a direct question she would answer truthfully. He was right.

"No," she said at last. "She doesn't. I would advise you to go back to wherever you came from and forget all about her, as she has forgotten about you."

"But she can't have," he insisted. "She's carrying my child."

"She lost the baby—an accident."

He took the news with a mixture of shock and anger, as if in some way his seed, his manhood, had been found wanting and been rejected.

"But she can't have . . ." he blustered and stopped. A stupid thing to say.

"She did. Furthermore she has made quite a satisfactory life for herself here. She has privacy and a much happier future ahead of her."

What future? he wanted to ask. Hull House in itself was acceptable. But the surroundings! The mean, dirty streets littered with refuse and horse manure, peopled by refugees from the poorer slums of Europe. This was not the life he wanted for Hannah. He wanted to dress her in rustling silks, to put pearls and diamonds at her throat and ears. He wanted to establish her in a fine house or a smart flat with deep-pile carpets and brocade draperies and works of art on the walls. And he could do it when he came into his trust, now only four months away.

But in the meanwhile Miss Addams was asking him to go back "to wherever you came from" because Hannah had a happier future without him.

"Am I to assume," Christian said, putting on his most authoritative air, "that Mrs. Bush—or Miss Blaine, as I know her—has found another attachment?"

"You may assume nothing, young man," she said
with asperity. "And now I really must get on with my
work."

He had been dismissed.

Damn her, he thought, the prudish do-gooder! Didn't
she know what it meant to be in love? Even if Hannah
had given instructions not to reveal her presence, that
earnest woman should have shown some compassion,
some understanding. Well, he would do as he pleased.
Miss Addams might be in charge of Hull House but not
the street outside.

He had tied up the trap he had borrowed from
Woolridge across the street. Shooing a cluster of gawk-
ing urchins away, he positioned himself behind the equi-
page and waited. At four o'clock, his nose reddened by
the sharp wind, his toes and fingers frozen to insensibil-
ity, he saw Hannah emerge from the house. Her shabby
appearance wrung his heart. She was wearing the same
plaid shawl, the same blue skirt she had worn at Wildoak.
Yet how proudly she bore herself! She turned without
seeing him and started down Halstead Street on foot. He
followed for half a block before he allowed himself to
call, "Hannah!"

She stopped short, her back going rigid. Then slowly
she turned. "Christian! My God! What . . . ? No, oh, no!
Please, go away."

She tried to walk on but Christian caught up with her
and took hold of her arm.

"Let go! Turn me loose or I shall summon the police."

"There are no police in this part of the city. Hannah—I
must talk to you."

"You've done more than enough talking already. Take
your hand away."

"Not until you give me a hearing. You must listen, if
only for a few minutes. Dammit, even the lowliest, most
dastardly criminal has a right to speak."

People were passing in the street, some peering at
them with curiosity. A paunchy man in a moth-eaten fur
cap paused and in a thick Italian accent wanted to know
if the lady was having trouble. They both ignored him,

staring at each another, one in anger, the other in challenge.

"I'm glad you have some inkling as to your true nature," Hannah said tartly.

"We can discuss that, too. Hannah . . ."

"All right, then, have your say."

"Here? On the street? I have a carriage. . . ."

"No."

"You're afraid to be alone with me?"

She drew herself up. "There is no reason to fear you, Mr. Falconer. The foolish attraction I once felt for you no longer exists. You see," she added maliciously, "I'm in love with a fine, decent man. Really in love. He wants to marry me—and I plan to do so in a few weeks."

"My congratulations." He gave her a slight, mocking bow. "Then if that is so, all the more reason why you should not mind me speaking my piece. Unless you wish to make a public scene. And I'm quite capable of that, I assure you."

By this time the man in the moth-eaten fur cap had been joined by two women with shopping bags who were staring at Hannah with interest. To escape their curiosity she said, "However you wish."

Once in the trap he drove slowly away from Hull House.

"I want you to be frank with me, Hannah, as I will be with you."

She remained silent.

"Very well. Why did you leave Wildoak so suddenly? I won't admonish you for not bidding a proper adieu to your hosts, to your schoolchildren, or to me—who, I may add, was left completely baffled."

"I'm surprised that you ask, Mr. Falconer." She turned to him, her voice trembling with anger. "You knew my situation, you knew . . ." She bit her lip, then, taking a deep breath, went on. "And yet you fobbed me off with an evasive answer. You cannot imagine—but then, how could you, not being a woman—what it means to be in the family way, unmarried, a sinner, with the man treating you as though you were less than nothing, a pleasurable toy to be discarded lightly."

"Hannah, that is not—"

"Let me finish. Because he has another toy handy." Her eyes flashed with burning hostility. "All the time this man was making love to this stupid girl he had a mistress, one that he had never given up, had no intention of giving up."

"If you were anyone else, I wouldn't bother to deny such a lie. It simply isn't true."

"Don't protest. No matter how vehemently you deny it, Christian, I _saw_ you. I saw her in your arms, I heard her, I heard you. . . ."

"Who? What? When?"

"Amanda Cox. On the night I left Wildoak. You and she were in the sewing room."

"Ah—I see." He gripped the reins, smacking them over the horse's rump. "So that's what it was all about. Amanda Cox." The hussy, he thought, the damned hussy. "Did you know," he said, "that events we sometimes witness with our own eyes are not always what they seem?"

"Nothing could have been plainer."

"I'm sorry, but you are grossly mistaken. Shall I tell you what really happened between myself and Amanda that night?" He saw the skepticism on her face and wanted to shake her. "I swear," he went on, "to God—or whoever you would have me swear to—that from the moment you and I were intimate I had nothing to do with Amanda. Nor have I since."

She said nothing. Turning her face to the side, she gazed out at the passing street. Her profile under the worn cloth hat was so faultless, so beautiful, he was tempted to carry her off and damn the explanations.

"I swear Amanda means nothing to me." He went on to tell her what had happened, how Amanda had lured him to the sewing room by her threat to tell her husband of their past alliance, how she had embraced him, how he had broken away.

When he had finished, Hannah, still with an averted face, remained silent. He did not know what she was thinking, whether she believed him or not. He halted the horse while a crowded trolley clanged past on the cross street. They drove another block before Christian pulled the horse to a stop at a curbside.

"Hannah," he said in a gentle voice, "Miss Addams told me you lost the baby."

"Yes," she said, her tone hard. "Through no fault of my own. It was God's will. Poor mite with no father and a mother who had made a fool of herself. Perhaps it was for the best."

"I do not think so," he said.

She turned and gave him a sharp look.

"The child was mine, too," he said. "Would you believe me if I said I grieve for it?"

"No."

"You believe nothing I've said? You think I'm merely going through this exercise to get you back in my bed?"

She did not answer.

"Did it occur to you that there must be a reason why I've spent the past two months searching for you, that I've gone back and forth from Wildoak to Stonebridge to Atlanta, that I've covered miles and miles, looking into every face, hoping that a figure glimpsed ahead of me in a crowd might be yours? That I've . . ." He caught himself, his voice dangerously on the edge of anger.

"How *did* you find me?" Hannah asked. "Ah—don't answer. I can guess. You bribed Pa to snoop. Travis would never tell you."

"What difference does it make who told me? You are evading me, Hannah. I wonder that you've heard anything I've said."

"It makes no difference to me now what you say. There was a time when I would have listened and believed—God help me. But that time is over."

Christian frowned, his anger rising again. Damn her for being so stubborn. Why did she persist with this cold, implacable attitude? Though he had anticipated hostility, he had thought that once they had ironed out whatever misunderstanding had sent her on her flight and he had explained how earnestly he had sought her, then she would smile at him in the old way, looking into his eyes with the warmth and love she had shown before.

"Is there nothing I can do to convince you?"

"I can't think of what. Oh—perhaps you'd like to tell me you've changed," she said with biting sarcasm. "My father was a great one for swearing he'd changed. All men do it when they wish to be forgiven."

"And I have much to be forgiven for. I won't debate that." It was humiliating to eat humble pie. And for a woman. Why was he doing it? Again he resisted the urge to whip up the horse and ride off with her. "If you would try to understand . . ."

She faced him with a bitter look. "I'd rather not discuss it. Why bring it all back? It's too painful. For me, perhaps not for you. And now if you are finished, please take me back to Hull House."

"No!" He hadn't meant to shout and he struggled to lower his voice. "I'm not through. I haven't come all this way merely for conversation. I came to tell you that when you left and I could not find you . . ." And now he was stumbling for the right words, irritated by Hannah's unyielding manner and annoyed with his own sudden, surprising, and confusing ineptness. "Dammit! You don't make it easy, Hannah. The truth is—I love you. Yes, dammit, I love you!"

Hannah, an acid retort on her tongue, was stopped by the look on his face. Was he telling the truth? He had murmured words like "love" many times in the heat of physical passion, but never like this, never with his throat working and his eyes blazing. If he had tried to draw her into his arms, made a movement to kiss or fondle her, she would have suspected his sincerity. But he did not touch her. He sat glaring at her in fierce defiance, their eyes locking until hers softened and she looked away.

"Well, speak up! Have you nothing to say, Hannah?"

"No," she answered uncertainly.

Oh, why had he come back into her life? Why had he suddenly appeared just when she thought she had put him and the past behind her? It wasn't fair. It wasn't right. Again she wished she had never met him, that chance had not brought him to Granny's funeral. Failing that, she wished that there had been some magic potion

she could have taken, could take now, to cure herself of
this man. But there was no such esoteric dose. From the
moment he had settled himself in the trap beside her,
she had felt the aura of his masculinity. She had thought
if she ever saw him again she would hate him, that his
good looks, his magnetism would have no effect whatsoever on her. But the pull, the irresistible draw was there
all the same. Arrogant devil, she had thought, repeating
it over and over in her mind while he spoke. Did he
think she was still the simpleton he had seduced at
Wildoak? Yet despite her determination not to listen,
she had heard. And now he was saying he loved her. He
was saying it with a sudden tender earnestness she once
would have gone down on her knees and thanked God to
hear.

"I love you, Hannah," he repeated simply, his anger
and defiance vanishing as quickly as they had come.
"There's never been a woman I've loved. Never—until
you." He took her unresisting gloved hand and, lifting it
to his lips, kissed it. Then added the stilted, the worn
but heartfelt words, "You would make me the happiest
man alive if you'd do me the honor of becoming my wife."

It was a formal proposal. Christian Falconer, the rep-
robate, who once claimed he wasn't ready for marriage,
intimating that he never would be, was proposing. He
was courting her in the time-honored mànner. He wanted
her to become his wife. He was serious; no humor lit his
eyes, no hint of mockery edged his voice. "I would be
the happiest man alive . . . I have never loved another
woman." If he had only said that months ago when she
was at Wildoak, alone, afraid, uncertain. But he hadn't
realized he loved her until after she had gone. And he
was saying it now.

"Hannah?" he asked softly.

Tears sprang to her eyes. All the feeling, the passion,
the yearning, the love for this man she had thought she
hated returned in a flash flood of overwhelming emotion. Had her dreams been empty of his face, her mind
refusing to remember? She knew it wasn't so. He had
never left her.

"Christian . . ." Her throat ached, the taste of tears

lay on her tongue. She tried again. "Christian . . ." And suddenly she began to cry.

He took her in his arms while she sobbed in the protective circle of his embrace. She did not know why she should weep. Relief? Joy? She heard the beat of his heart, felt him remove the hat from her head, felt the soft brush of his lips in her hair.

"Then I'm forgiven?"

She nodded mutely.

"I will never forgive *myself* for hurting you, do you believe that?"

Again she nodded.

He lifted her chin and tenderly kissed away her tears. "But we won't talk about that again. It's behind us. We've the future to think of. My darling, darling Hannah."

He captured her mouth in a long hungry kiss. Her lips parted to his exploration, her whole being surging against his taut chest. He loved her; Christian Falconer loved her. She clung to him in giddy exhilaration, a feeling she'd expected never to experience again. Poor Guy, she thought fleetingly, who could never make her tremble so, who could never bring such wild excitement to her heart.

"There are so many things we must talk about," Christian murmured against her cheek. "The wedding—how, when? And, darling, since you are going to be my wife, I must be honest. We'll have to stretch things at first. I won't come into my money until September. I have debts, foolish debts."

"I can guess at your vices." She laughed.

"Yes. All true. However, you've made a new man of me. But, Hannah," he said, drawing away, "you haven't said yes."

She kissed him again and again for an answer. "Doesn't that say it?"

He held her long, close, lovingly. "I want to give you a ring to seal our engagement. Now, this very day. I'm staying at a friend's house. He and his family are away and my things are there. I have a small ring that belonged to my mother. I'm sure it would fit you. It's temporary, a stopgap until I get one you deserve. But

you must wear it. It will mean that you are promised to
me.''

She could hardly believe it was the same Christian.
He *had* changed. Her fingers traced his cheek.

"Yes, I will wear it, Christian."

Guy Hartwell also wanted to give her a ring. What
could she tell him? That she had met her old lover? That
it was he she truly loved, not Guy? It would hurt him—
and how well she knew the pain of rejection. But wasn't
it better to tell him the truth? Wouldn't it be wrong to
marry a good man like Guy loving Christian? For she did
love Christian. That she had the power to change this
man who once claimed lifelong bachelorhood suited him
gave her love a new dimension.

"We'll fetch the ring now. Or must you hurry back?"

"No. I have the afternoon and evening off." Guy
would be working until midnight every night for the next
two weeks and she would not be seeing him. It would
give her time to compose a gentle way of letting him
down. "But I must be in by ten o'clock."

"We have time, then."

At the Woolridge house the butler let them in. He was
a tall, imperious man with a large nose. "Good evening,
Mr. Falconer."

"Evening, Jones. This is my fiancée, Miss Blaine."

Fiancée! How lovely that sounded.

The butler's haughty expression did not change, but
his close-set eyes took in Hannah's shawl, the faded
skirt, the worn shoes.

"Will you and Miss Blaine be staying for dinner?"

"Hannah? No, I think not. We'll dine out."

Christian ushered her into the drawing room. It was
twice the size of Wildoak's parlor, furnished with heavy
oak and mahogany pieces, the floor laid with priceless
Chinese rugs.

"Wait here, darling," Christian said. "I'll only be a
minute."

Perched on an uncomfortable Queen Anne sofa, Hannah gazed about her. The ceiling was bordered by intri-
cately carved friezes and hanging from it was a large,
many-tiered, ornate brass and wrought-iron chandelier.

Glass lights set in sockets shaped like dragons and sea serpents glowed with electricity, a new invention that had been adopted by the wealthy.

Hannah felt diminished by the magnificence of the room, the high ceiling, the paintings on the walls, the tables cluttered with crystal, ivory, and gold-leaf knick-knacks, the marble mantel shelf with an alabaster clock, its golden pendulum ticking in precise motion.

When Christian returned, his smile, the light in his eyes, somehow made the room shrink. In possession of love, her surroundings did not matter. He had only to look into her eyes and everything else dropped away.

He sat down beside her and took her hand.

"My darling, you're sure . . . ?"

"Yes," she whispered.

He placed the ring on her finger, then kissed her on the lips. She leaned her head on his shoulder.

"Where shall we live?" he asked. "I've been thinking of going back to medicine. And since I know San Francisco best, or at least I have connections there, that would be the logical place. Would you mind? It would mean a separation of many miles from your family."

"Travis is the only one I care about. Perhaps—perhaps after we've settled in, we can send for him. I'm sure he'll have no difficulty in finding employment."

"Anything you say, my darling."

He leaned over to kiss her, his lips touching hers tenderly at first, then deepening until with a shuddering half sigh, half moan he crushed her to his chest, his mouth moving on her lips, prying them open, his tongue plunging inside. She returned the tongue play, eager to give and receive, her hands grasping his thick black hair, as if she could press him into her very soul.

"Hannah!" Breathless, he rested his cheek on hers. "These past few weeks I'd have given the world for such a kiss."

"I never thought . . ." She looked into his eyes and saw a passion there that matched her own. He kissed her again. The shawl fell away as his hands found a breast. She could feel the nipple harden, the ache in her loins.

"We mustn't," he said, drawing away. "We must do everything right this time."

"Yes," she whispered, baffled, not understanding why she suddenly didn't want to do anything "right," why she felt swept away just as she had before in Christian's arms. But now it didn't matter, she told herself. They would be husband and wife.

She caressed his face, the beloved face. Yes, she belonged to him. Though she might have hated, cursed, condemned him in the past, Christian had remained part of her.

"Come, Hannah, I will take you back to Hull House." He stood up and gave her his hands.

She turned as he placed the shawl about her shoulders. When he bent to kiss the side of her neck, the warm touch of his lips made her tremble. His mouth shifted, pressing a sensitive vein, the lobe of her ear. Gasping, she whirled about, flinging her arms about him. They stood together a long time, locked in an embrace, heartbeat to heartbeat. He began to kiss her again, his urgent mouth moving from cheek to forehead to lips and cheek again. She tightened her grasp, kissing him wildly now.

"Hannah . . ."

"I know, I know. It's my fault this time. But I can't seem to let you go. Oh, the hours I swore to hate you, the revenge I dreamed of—and it's all vanished like smoke." A tear trembled on her eyelash and he kissed it away.

"We'll be married as soon as I get a license and a justice of the peace. Hang the wedding. Is that all right with you?"

"Yes, oh, yes!"

They began to kiss again passionately, desperately. The electric lights above them flickered and mysteriously dimmed but they hardly noticed. Hannah felt the rigidity of Christian's stiffened manhood through the stuff of her petticoats and skirt. Excitement rose in her; she wanted him with a burning heat, a desire that made her forget time and place.

"Come upstairs," he whispered. "We can be alone there."

And she went without a second thought. With his arm about her waist they climbed the shadowed staircase, their footfalls deadened by the thick, pile carpet. Her step matched his. There was no reluctance or maidenly hanging back. Later she was to wonder at Christian's sorcery, the way he could make her discard restraint and acquiesce to the needs of her body, the upsurge of desire, to the storm that raged within her at his touch.

Her clothing came away in his hands, peeled like skin after skin—the jet buttons, hooks and eyes undone, the whalebone stays tossed aside, the petticoat, the storm ruffle flung after it. He did it all slowly, savoring every moment, planting a kiss each time a strip of white naked flesh appeared, touching burning lips to the mounded breasts released to his cupped hands. Stripped to the skin, she lay on the bed, watching with half-closed eyes as he quickly divested himself of his clothing, admiring again the rippling muscles of his chest and arms, the hard columns of his legs. And he was aroused. She didn't look away but smiled at his manhood, the proof of her desirability.

It was as if she were two Hannahs, two personalities. Some remnant of guilt still lurked in the darker shadows of her mind. She had promised herself never to go to bed with a man unless she wore his wedding ring. But it seemed the promise had been made by someone else. (Besides, she told herself, she *did* have Christian's ring. She was engaged. She had been proposed to and would soon be Mrs. Falconer, tomorrow, perhaps.)

When Christian lowered himself on the bed, leaning on his hands over her, his deep-set eyes luminous with love, all thought of sin fled from her mind. He brought his head down to her breasts, his mouth covering one rosy nipple, then the other, going back and forth, tasting until both peaks were rigid under his tongue. Every movement of his hands and mouth had meaning. The languorous caress of his fingers, mouth, and tongue, the gentle fondling became more heated, more urgent. Her excitement rose with the increased tempo of his lovemaking and soon she was rocking and arching under him, longing for the feel of his manhood inside to ease the aching desire.

When he finally entered her, she moaned, wrapping her legs about his hips, lifting herself to meet him. She felt scorched, burned, wanting, yearning to be consumed in the flames of his passion. She heard him pant as his thrusts became deeper, wilder, their bodies united, merging into one as Hannah's whole being seemed to erupt in a golden shower of fiery sparks.

"Hannah, my sweet, my darling." He kissed her moist brow. "You'll not get away from me again."

He would come for her tomorrow in the late afternoon. He wanted to take her shopping. He wanted to buy her clothes, everything from the skin outward: lingerie, petticoats, gowns, hats, and shoes. "And a decent coat. Something of fur, marten or lambskin. Never mind, I shall borrow the money."

The next morning Hannah received a note from Christian delivered by hand.

Hannah, darling. I cannot come today. I'm to meet with a banker friend to arrange a loan. Forgive me, but I shall be at your doorstep bright and early on Thursday.

Hannah had said nothing to Miss Addams about this latest turn of events. In order to avoid embarrassing questions she wore his ring on a ribbon around her neck tucked inside her waist. She wanted her marriage to be a fait accompli before she announced it. A romantic elopement. It would be easier to explain that way.

In the early afternoon Miss Addams sent her on an errand.

"I'd like you to deliver a letter to Mr. Abraham Finley at the Palmer House. Mr. Finley is from Philadelphia, a philanthropist who has shown an interest in contributing a substantial sum of money for a project of mine. I'm thinking of adding a small apartment building onto Hull House, one that would be suitable for single working girls. The letter contains facts and figures regarding cost.

It isn't necessary to see him in person. Just leave the letter at the desk."

Hannah was glad to be commissioned to run this little errand. It would make the day go faster. Tomorrow, when she would see Christian again, seemed an eternity away, the hours until then interminable.

Palmer House, rebuilt after it had been destroyed in the Great Chicago Fire of '71, was famous for its elegance. Hannah had passed it several times but had never been inside. A favorite stopping place for the rich, it boasted among other things a plethora of mirrors, deep-cushioned sofas, and a twenty-five-foot-high rotunda. When Hannah ascended the marble steps to the crowded lobby, it was abuzz with voices, men collected in little groups holding earnest discussions, women who had met for tea after a busy day of shopping, travelers checking in or out, their luggage borne by a troop of uniformed porters. She was approaching the desk when she was startled to see Amanda Cox in conversation with several people, standing at the foot of the wide staircase that led to the rooms upstairs. A moment later Christian descended those same stairs. Unmistakably Christian. He took a proprietary hold of Amanda's arm and they walked away, disappearing into the crowd.

Hannah felt as though she had been run through, shot, murdered. She wondered how she managed to keep standing, her knees trembled so. She was terrified lest the scream lodged in her chest burst from her lungs. She wanted to faint, to lie down on the hard marble floor, to sleep, to die.

But she did none of these things. Propelled by some inner will, she moved like one of those dolls that are wound up by a key in the back.

At the desk she addressed a clerk. "Pardon, but would you kindly see that this letter is given into the hands of Mr. Abraham Finley? It is from Miss Jane Addams of Hull House and is important."

"Yes, madam. Is there a message that goes with it?"

She put her trembling hands on the counter to steady herself. "No message, but . . ." She bit her lip. "Can you tell me if a Mr. Christian Falconer is registered here?''

"A moment, please." She watched as if hypnotized as his finger went down the register. "Ah, yes. A Mr. and Mrs. Christian Falconer came in last Tuesday. From San Francisco. Would you care to—"

"No, thank you."

Somehow she had willed her numb legs to carry her from the hotel, for she found herself outside on the sidewalk, standing there, baffled, not knowing what to do, where to go as people jostled past her.

There could not be two Christian Falconers from San Francisco. Besides, she had seen him. He and Amanda Cox had been together. Arm in arm. Mr. and Mrs. Had Amanda divorced that sly, pompous husband of hers and married Christian? In so short a time? Oh, God, what difference did it make? They had been together. Since last Tuesday. Since before yesterday, since before Christian had waited for her outside Hull House, since before he had sworn he loved her, begged her to marry him, since before she had given herself to him. Once more.

She reached into her bodice and brought the ring out. It winked at her like some malevolent eye. She tore it from the ribbon and tossed it into the gutter. To Hannah, Christian was dead.

Ten days later she was married to Guy Hartwell. It was a simple ceremony attended only by Miss Addams and Miss Starr. Gazing up into her new husband's flushed, adoring face as he lifted the short marquisette veil to kiss her, her heart filled with gratitude. She vowed that she would make every effort to be a good wife, to see to it that Guy never felt a single moment's regret for having chosen her as his bride. She would make him happy, no memories would come between them, she would be his helpmeet, his love, and someday, God willing, she would grow to love him, too.

Chapter X

On a bright day in April—one of those beautiful early spring days when the wind, instead of blowing from the odorous stockyards, had veered to the east bringing fresh lake breezes—Hannah moved into Guy's room at his boardinghouse on Cottage Grove Avenue. Since the newlyweds would be leaving for California in May, they felt it would be an extravagance to rent a flat or to put up at a hotel for the five- or six-week interim.

So Hannah's wedding night was spent in a cramped room, on an iron bedstead designed for a single occupant, with the sounds of snoring sleepers, muttered curses, footsteps, and slamming doors coming through the paper-thin walls. Though Guy was no better a lover than she had anticipated, she nevertheless was disappointed at the speed with which he performed his conjugal duties. Except for a brief, almost shy kiss planted on her breasts, he made no attempt to caress her, to fondle or bring her to desire, but separated her legs almost at once, entering her, grunting to a hasty climax, and leaving her cold and unfulfilled. She would not let herself think of Christian's fiery kisses, the fever and the passion he had aroused in her. She did not want to compare the lovemaking ability of her husband, who had led a virtuous life, and a

144

rakehell who had made bedding women a vocation. Furthermore, present circumstances, she told herself—the lumpy mattress, the narrow bed, the walls that had ears—were not conducive to any real intimacy. With time and a more private environment their sexual responses to each other would improve.

Apart from Guy's poor performance as a lover, he was the most considerate, the most adoring and attentive of husbands. He was impatient for them to be on their own, to set up housekeeping and start raising a family. The transaction to obtain Sycamore Ranch had been completed through the mail. A down payment had been made, terms agreed upon, papers signed. Mr. McAllister, the owner of Sycamore, had assured Guy that he would leave the ranch in the hands of a competent caretaker until Guy arrived. Now Guy and Hannah had only to wait until May, when Guy's contract with the exposition terminated, to leave Chicago.

Hannah wrote to Travis, telling of her marriage and of their plans to settle on the West Coast.

As soon as I'm able I will send for you. Guy agrees. He says he would welcome an extra hand. You would earn your keep and then some, so there's no worry on that score. (Later you'll be able to go up to San Francisco and get more schooling, learn a profession.) The photographs we've seen of Sycamore show it to be a beautiful place, the house in good repair. I am looking forward to this new venture. You will like Guy. He is steadfast, honest, hardworking, the sort of man any woman would be proud to have as a husband. . . .

The World's Columbian Exposition of 1893 opened on the first of May. Hannah, by virtue of Guy's employment, was among the one hundred thousand guests who had been invited to attend the initial ceremonies. Clinging to Guy's arm, she stood on tiptoe, craning her neck over the heads of the tightly packed cheering throng to get a better view of the carriage procession. Guy had told her that President Grover Cleveland would be lead-

ing the parade, but all Hannah could see as the span of
glitteringly caparisoned horses drew abreast was a fleeting glimpse of a top hat. The occupants of the other
carriages (twenty-three, Guy counted) were supposed to
include dignitaries such as Carter Harrison, mayor of
Chicago; the Marquis de Harbales; Princess Eulalia; the
Infanta of Spain (representing the nation that had sponsored Columbus's voyages); and the Duke and Duchess
of Veragus. But the richly attired men and women who
rode past were unidentifiable to Hannah as well as to
Guy, and the people around them could not agree as to
which was the princess or the infanta.

Once they were admitted inside the gates, Hannah
and Guy stood for a few minutes trying to decide where
to start on their tour of the grounds. There was so much
to see, so many pavilions and exhibits. Dubbed the
White City, the fair had been planned around man-made
lagoons, grassy lawns, and gardens. The buildings were
an architect's dream (or nightmare, as a few carping
critics called them). Constructed in Romanesque style,
porticoed like Greek temples or tiered like white wedding
cakes, each represented a different nation, a state of the
union, or housed the latest in agriculture and industry.

Guy, who was fairly familiar with the layout, suggested they visit the German building, where among
other things a giant globe of the Earth was on view.
From there they went to the French pavilion to sniff at
exotic perfumes and taste the wines of Medoc and the
Chateau de Rothschild, then on to the Machinery Hall
where they marveled at the latest in typewriters, tele-
phones, and the horseless carriage.

After a late lunch in a Chinese restaurant (whose
exotic food Hannah now tasted for the first time) they
strolled the midway, the entertainment core of the fair.
There, barkers stood at the doors of their tented show-
places cajoling the crowds to enter the Congress of
Beauties, to watch James J. Corbett, the boxing cham-
pion, working out, or to see the exotic temptress, Little
Egypt, do her sensual dance. They rode a huge wheel
George Washington Ferris had erected. Strapped into
one of its gondolas, they went up and up, holding tightly

to the bar in front of them. As they rose slowly to a great height they could look out over thousands of acres of parkland dotted with silver lagoons reflecting golden domed buildings, the palazzos with their pseudo-marble statues, the columned grandeur of the Court of Honor. At dusk, as they limped tiredly back to the outer gates, electric lights suddenly blazed on, fountains sprouted and splashed, turning the entire exposition into a magic fairyland.

"It's so beautiful, like a dream," said Hannah in wonder. "And to think you had a part in making it come true."

"A very small part," he admitted with a modesty Hannah found endearing.

A week later Guy and Hannah boarded the Overland to San Francisco to begin their journey across half a continent, a long, tiresome, and dusty ride. Since they had to watch every penny, they could not afford the luxury of the new Pullman cars, but sat up in the day coaches, eating their meals from food Hannah had packed in a wicker hamper. As mile after mile of countryside and towns slipped by, Hannah tried to share Guy's eager anticipation. But the distances they traversed seemed limitless, like crossing an uncharted ocean, each hour, each day taking her farther away from Travis and the world she had known in Bayetville. It was a feeling she could not understand. No one had been more impatient to leave home than she. Her school years in Atlanta had been a happy hiatus, her invitation to Wildoak welcomed, and when disaster overtook her there, she had not thought of returning to Stonebridge but had gone to Chicago. Why then should she feel this tug, this vague malaise?

The reason for her strange mood became clear when they reached San Francisco. She was pregnant. Exhausted, gritty with soot, debarking from the train on unsteady legs, Hannah wondered if she ought to tell Guy. Though he wanted a family, she wasn't quite certain how he would accept a pregnancy before they had the chance to settle in. She knew he was counting on her to help with the numberless tasks of putting their new home in order. But with her history of a miscarriage he might insist on shouldering the entire load himself.

However, her secret was impossible to keep.

Guy guessed at her condition when he came upon her being very sick in the early morning as she bent over the commode in their hotel room. He fussed over her like a mother hen. She must get right into bed. Should he call a doctor? Did she think she could go on with the journey or ought they to stay in the city a few more days until she rested up? He was overjoyed, delighted. To him Hannah's pregnancy was the best of omens: his already sown seed had taken root, promising the best harvest of all, a son.

"He shall be a native-born Californian," he said gleefully.

Hannah, buoyed by his high spirits, gently reminded him it might be a girl.

"Doesn't matter," he said magnanimously. "She'll be the finest-looking filly in the state."

McAllister had written that there were three possible means by which they could reach Sycamore Ranch. One was by passenger ship to Monterey. From there they would have to travel on foot or horseback some fifty miles down the Coast Trail. Or they could wait for an infrequent supply ship that anchored off Partington Cove, a wait that might be as long as six months. The third route, and the one Guy favored, was by way of King City. There they could purchase a wagon and horses and come over the switchback Nacimiento Trail through the Santa Lucia Mountains.

So on a clear, fogless morning, they caught the stage-coach to King City, a small, hot, dry cattlemen's town on the Salinas River, to the east of the coastal mountains. Here Hannah and Guy bought a wagon and two horses, paying much more for them than Guy thought reasonable. But the hostler, a gruff, unfriendly man with a handlebar mustache, would not come down on his price—"not a penny, sir"—and Guy had no choice. The one thing McAllister said he could not provide was a wagon; any horses that Guy acquired, he had written, could be added to the herd (four stallions and two mares) already at Sycamore. In the general store on Main Street, Guy bought flour, sugar, coffee, rice, and some tinned vegetables to tide them over until the produce from their own kitchen garden was available. Meat he expected to procure with his rifle. He had been given to understand that there was an abundance of deer, rabbit, and squirrel in the forest surrounding Sycamore.

Though his wallet had been greatly depleted, Guy's optimism was not shaken. They would arrive at the ranch in time to put in their vegetables. The place came with chickens, ducks, geese, and a milch cow. They would have food and shelter and in the fall—when the fattened cattle were driven to market and sold—ready cash.

It was the best time of the year to be traveling. The land, still fresh from the winter and spring rains, was green and golden; the orange poppies and purple lupin, scattered on hillsides or growing in thick clumps, half hidden by the tall prairie grass, made the plain and the softly swelling hills beyond a tapestry of color. A fairly good road skirted the valley, passing several ranch houses tucked under live oak, madrones, and pepper trees. But soon the road became a trail, snaking and backtracking up the mountain. They rode under tall bays and maples and the ever-present live oak, which spread thick, gnarled limbs over their heads. Occasionally they heard the gurgle of a stream; at one point it crossed the road and they splashed through cool crystal water.

As the climb became steeper they had to make frequent stops to rest the horses. Rounding one bend, they came to a halt before a fallen giant sequoia that barred the way. Guy had to unhitch the horses and lead them to the other side of the trunk. Then the wagon had to be unloaded and pulled around in the same fashion. He would not allow Hannah to do any heavy lifting, so it took over an hour for them to resume their journey.

Nightfall found them still far from the ranch. The crude map McAllister had sent them showed they had another five or eight miles to go. "As the crow flies,"

Guy said. "How many by horse and wagon I wouldn't care to guess."

They camped on the edge of a stream that cut betwen vine- and fern-covered banks, careful to avoid the poison oak that grew in abundance among the trees. It was the first time Hannah had spent a night in the open and the sounds of the nocturnal forest were a little frightening. Guy laughed when she started at the hoot of an owl and the yip-yip of a coyote. Later she cried out, creeping to his side, when a pair of brilliant eyes appeared suddenly on the far side of their campfire.

But the stars! Oh, the stars, shimmering on high! Galaxies of stars, shining in clusters and milky streams and far-off nebulae. Brilliant and hard, they were like scintillating diamonds thrown carelessly across a jeweler's black cloth, the universe displayed to awe and wonder. Hannah felt that by stretching out her hand, she could catch one in her hand, and in her dreams that night she did, only to find that it was made of ice, cold and melting to the touch.

They had an early start the next morning. Now the trail became so potholed Hannah found it easier to walk behind the slow-moving, jolting wagon. She wondered how the early pioneers had managed to make their long wagon-train trips across country, day after day, week after week, traversing plains, fording rivers, and climbing the much steeper and tortuous range of the Sierra Nevada.

At last they reached a fork in the trail where a painted sign, faded by wind and weather, indicated that the Sycamore Ranch was to the left. Journey's end. Hannah peered anxiously through the trees as they rattled on. Here under the dark gloomy oaks and sycamores, the road was deeply rutted in mud and the horses strained against the harness to keep the wagon wheels from bogging down. Thin shafts of sunlight shooting down through needled and leafed branches lit patches of oxalis and climbing ivy. A bird shrilled from a bush and flew off with a clap of fluttering wings. The track twisted upward around a sharp bend, then upward again. Guy spoke to the lathered horses that were panting audibly. Just as he

was about to call them to a halt the road ended abruptly.
Before them a crooked, moss-covered fence sagged against
a gate.

"This must be it," said Guy.

He got down and unfastened the gate by pulling sharply
at a rusty lock that gave at the first yank. They rode
through, emerging shortly from the trees to look down
into a cupped, oval-shaped valley of rippling grass bright
with sunshine, yellow daisies, and wild mustard. In the
center on a slight elevation stood an adobe ranch house
with a shadowed porch and recessed windows. Three
chimneys rose from a tiled roof, just as pictured in the
photograph McAllister had sent, except that many of the
tiles were missing. Behind the house were two separate
wooden structures. The compound stood bare of trees.
There was no lawn, no hedge, no bushes, no flowers to
soften or shade the mud walls of the main house or the
adjoining weatherbeaten shacks.

Guy, whose uncle Hooper had made his tree-shaded
farmhouse a bower of green-growing and blooming plants,
said, "I suppose these old adobe houses were placed a
distance from the woods so there would be no surprise
attack from the Indians."

"Indians? But they've long since disappeared from
this area."

"That's true. But Mr. McAllister wrote that this house
was built by a hidalgo at the time of the Spanish land
grants. I imagine in those days such precautions were
necessary."

Except for a few cattle standing under an isolated
live oak gazing bovinelike at them, there was no sign of
life.

"Mr. McAllister said there'd be a caretaker." Guy
shaded his eyes against the sun. "Well, let's go see."

As they approached the house Hannah noted that in
addition to the missing roof tiles, one chimney was half
destroyed and a side window was broken.

"Needs some repair," Guy commented.

As he spoke a little runt of a man with a wispy
mustache and bowed legs emerged from the shadow of
the deep porch. He removed a battered, greasy som-

brero from his head. "Mr. and Mrs. Hartwell? I'm Billy
Ostler, the caretaker." He squinted up at Guy. "Didn't
think you'd get here so soon."

"Didn't seem soon enough for us." Jumping down,
Guy helped Hannah from the seat of the wagon.

"Did you bring some 'baccy with you? I run clean
out."

"Sorry. I don't smoke or chew."

As the two men spoke, Hannah, impatient to see her
new home, stepped up to the porch and pushed open the
heavy oak door. It took her a few seconds to get accustomed to the gloom, for the small, deep-set windows let
in little light.

What she saw filled her with dismay. The room she
looked on was a shambles, the splintered wooden floor
littered with refuse, the few pieces of hand-hewn furniture chipped and gouged, the walls stained where rain
had leaked in. There were no rugs, no pictures, no light
fixtures, only a few brass candlesticks, a blackened oil
lamp, and dusty beer bottles holding waxy stumps. The
fireplace was heaped with ashes, the fanned adobe bricks
above it blackened by smoke, indicating a poor draw.
Not even Stonebridge could rival the squalor that confronted her.

She moved through the main room and stepped in to
what she assumed was the dining room. An ancient
sideboard thick with dust stood against one wall, a scarred
table and heavy chairs in the center.

Beyond was a door. She hesitated a moment before
she opened it. Sun poured through grimy glass to reveal
a cot, a chair, an upturned keg, and an assortment of
dirty clothing hanging from hooks screwed into the plas-
tered walls. The filthy trousers and torn shirts and the
odor of stale, sour sweat told her that Billy had claimed
this room as his own.

He'll have to go out to the barn or the bunkhouse or
wherever, she thought grimly. I'm not having that smell
in my house.

The kitchen, reached through a short passage, seemed
to have been tacked onto the rest of the house as an
afterthought. Hannah assumed it was once a separate

building. The Spanish dons, she remembered reading, had built them that way from fear of a spreading kitchen fire, and also because they liked to enjoy their meals without having the smell and heat of the preparation too close. In the intervening years some woman apparently had decided that both the improbable threat of fire and the inconvenience of having to carry food in from the outside were reasons enough to make the kitchen part of the house.

A woodburning stove had replaced the hearth fire, its jointed pipe disappearing into the dark maw of the fireplace and up the chimney. The black, ugly stove, encrusted with the grease of countless fryings, the spillage and spatterings of numberless soups, stews, and roasts, emitted the rank odor of mutton fat. A soapstone sink without faucets or water pump was filled with unwashed crockery. The floor—earthen here—was best not looked at. A large larder revealed cobwebbed shelves holding a few jars of unidentifiable, moldy contents.

The door to the kitchen led to a courtyard flanked on three sides by a series of rooms that Hannah guessed were the bedrooms. Only one, the largest, contained a bed. So much for the furnishings McAllister had written were "not fancy, but ample for your needs."

The courtyard itself, where not a single blade of grass grew, was strewn with rusty, discarded implements and horse and cow droppings. How animals had managed to get into the enclosure, Hannah could not guess. In the center stood a pump. When Hannah took hold of the rusty handle and wrenched it free from its frozen position, it groaned and screeched, but did not bring up a single drop of water. Either something was wrong with the mechanism or the well had gone dry.

Hannah was surveying the scene wondering if there was another well close at hand when Guy joined her. The jaunty air with which he had first gazed on Sycamore Ranch had disappeared. He looked sober, subdued. "It's bad, isn't it? I can't understand how Mr. McAllister could have left the house in such terrible condition. It seems as though it hasn't been lived in for years."

There was no milch cow. The geese McAllister had promised had been eaten by coyotes, according to Billy Ostler. There were a dozen or so scrawny chickens and a red-combed rooster in the henhouse. When Billy brought the "herd" of horses in for inspection, Guy found there were four, only two fit to ride. Of the remaining pair one was a gelding with the gall and the other a mare with a limp.

The next day when Guy, with the help of Billy, finished counting the cattle, he found he was twenty-five short of the one hundred he had been assured went with the ranch.

"I've been had," he told Hannah. She had managed to clear the worst of the filth from the house and they were sitting at the table in the dining room. "The man bilked me. Pure and simple."

His sunburned face had a beaten look about it.

"Isn't there anything we can do?" Hannah asked. "We must have some recourse. A lawyer perhaps could help us."

"Lawyers cost money, Hannah. And I have barely enough to keep us in flour and coffee until we can fatten some of the heifers and drive them to market."

"Then we'll just take the money for the twenty-five steer, the furniture we were supposed to have, the ducks and the geese and the horses, not to speak of the milch cow, out of our monthly payments."

The payments, deferred until market time in October, were to be made to the First National Bank in San Francisco. McAllister himself had given them no address other than the bank's. Nevertheless, Guy wrote him, listing all the shortcomings of Sycamore and how he felt he had been cheated.

In the meanwhile Guy, buoyed up by Hannah's assurance that all was not lost, set to work, mending fences, repairing the barn, the house roof, seeing that the bulls were properly penned, that the little heifers did not sicken or stray. Fortunately there were two other wells in good working order, a cool spring at the bottom of the slope where the house stood, several streams that ran through deep-cut canyons, and a pond on the far forty from which the cattle could drink. Guy labored like ten men with a minimum of help from Billy. The small, bowlegged man made a great show of industry when watched but as soon as "the boss" was out of sight he would find a convenient spot to take his siesta. More than once Hannah found him curled up in the henhouse. Guy threatened to fire him, but both Billy and he knew such threats were empty. Billy was working for room and board (Hannah had banished him to the loft above the barn and succeeded in having him wash his hands before he came to the supper table) and the pledge of future wages. No one else, were there such a person in this out-of-the-way place, would work very long or hard under such an arrangement.

Billy did manage to plow a piece of ground where Hannah could put in her kitchen garden. She had never realized how much physical labor went into the planting, watering, and weeding of several rows of corn, beans, and tomatoes. At Hull House, when Guy had spoken of the wonders of eating their own produce, Hannah had looked forward to gardening as a pleasant, rather enjoyable occupation, one she would busy herself with between other tasks. She had anticipated neither the backbreaking toil nor the voracious creatures that seemed waiting to pounce on and devour her handiwork. From the crows picking at the newly set seeds to the gophers who burrowed underground and swallowed plants whole, to the rabbits, squirrels, and dainty-footed deer who nibbled, gnawed, and chewed on the tender green growth when her back was turned, it was a never-ending struggle to keep her garden from sinking out of sight. A fence went up, a scarecrow erected, and still the enemy persisted. At night, lying in bed, Hannah imagined she could hear the persistent chomping of teeth.

There was very little time or energy for lovemaking. The few efforts Guy made ended in his quick satisfaction, leaving Hannah frustrated and incomplete. She tried not to be resentful, telling herself that the physical side of marriage did not matter. It was far better to have a

loving husband who cared deeply than one who could
skillfully caress and kiss—and betray.

Guy did everything he could to make things easy for
her. He took care that she did no heavy lifting, and one
of the few times he became angry was when he found
Hannah instead of Billy hauling water from the spring.
For Hannah's sake he tried to appear more optimistic,
making light of the lack of a decent plowshare, of leaky
water troughs and broken windmills, but she knew Sycamore had been a disappointment, that Guy found ranching in a remote area far different from the farm life in the
settled Midwest. Sometimes when he sat opposite her at
the supper table after working until the last glimmer of
twilight had faded, she wished he would be frank, complain, or even curse, rather than pretend all was well
with a forced smile.

"You could use another pair of hands," she told him
one evening. "Perhaps we ought to send for Travis."

"I can't spare the money for his fare right now,
darling."

"How much do we have left?"

"Now, honey, you're not to worry yourself about
that. You have the baby to think of."

As if she could forget. It was not due until late January or early February, a long way off, it seemed, but
Hannah knew how quickly time flew, how each day her
waist seemed to expand, her body change. Where would
she have it? How? Like their other miscalculations they
had simply assumed they had only to make a short
journey down the mountain (on the map King City was
twenty miles away, Monterey forty-nine) a week before
the baby was due and receive medical attention. She had
been told in King City that a Dr. Roberts made a horseback circuit twice a month in the coast area, but how
and when to get word to him Hannah did not know.

She wondered about neighbors and if there was a
woman close by should she need her. Mr. McAllister
had mentioned that the adjoining ranch was owned by
people named Barlow, but Guy, as yet, hadn't found the
time to seek them out. Hannah, though unfamiliar with
the countryside and still an inexpert horsewoman, thought

of trying to make contact with the Barlows but kept putting it off.

The extent of her travels had been a ride over the ranch. Its scenic beauty would have impressed her all the more were she and Guy not trying to wrest a living from it. The solitary copses of live oak on rolling hills, the bluebonnets and Indian brush, the smell of sage, the streams that rushed over boulders at the bottom of folded canyons were far more beautiful than the pictures McAllister had sent.

Only in describing Sycamore's physical attributes had he spoken the truth. The greatest wonder—the ocean—he hadn't mentioned at all. Topping a rise, she could look out over the blue Pacific, the horizon lost in a gray haze where the fog sat, a cloud bank of gray, waiting to roll in. Far, far down below at the base of the cliff, the long green combers broke in white foam against a cluster of rocks sculpted by wind and sea into high tabletop and conical shapes. In the afternoons a group of seals could be seen sunning themselves on these rocks, their whiskered heads occasionally rising to emit a barking yelp. To the left of the rocks was a small, sandy cove where sandpipers and curlews stepped daintily into the lacy froth of the sea, peckin for tiny crabs and shrimp. A trail led down to the cove but it was so steep Hannah was afraid to venture on it.

Except for an infrequent excursion around the ranch, Hannah kept close to home, where the garden, the chickens, and the task of keeping house under primitive conditions took all her time and energy.

It was Flavia Barlow who found Hannah. Sweet-faced, flaxen-haired, of the same age as Hannah, she had come riding down from the trail through the still-broken gate hallooing at the front step of the house.

Hannah had never been so glad to see anyone in her whole life. She brought Flavia into the house, made her sit while she rushed out to the kitchen for the pot of coffee kept warm on the back of the stove.

"I'm sorry I can't offer you better than a mug," Hannah told the girl, "and no milk, but we do have sugar."

"Thank you. Black will be fine." Flavia had a freck-led nose that wrinkled then she smiled. "So you're the new owners of Sycamore. We wondered if it had been sold again. The people who bought it last—the Parkin-sons—couldn't keep up the payments and McAllister foreclosed."

"When was that?"

"About six, seven months ago."

"Mrs. Parkinson wasn't much of a housekeeper, was she?"

"Didn't have time, I expect. She had a dozen children and they still kept coming. Poor thing. But you've done right good." She looked around. "Don't think I've ever seen the place looking so nice."

"Thank you. There's so many things I've wanted to know. Billy Ostler, that's our hired man"—calling Billy a hired man was like calling an oaf quick-witted, but she had no other way to explain him—"says that you can send and receive mail at Limekiln."

"That's right. But Pa and my uncle, Mr. Anderson—he's got his spread near McIntyre Canyon—take turns once a month going into King City. They'd be glad to take your mail or get any supplies you need. Pa would like to visit, say howdy—Ma, too—but right now we're getting ready for the branding. Three of us families in this section do it together. And that's why I'm here. To invite you folks to come, too. It's pretty hard branding on your own."

"I'm sure of it. We appreciate the invitation. Guy just hasn't had the opportunity to do much else but feel his way along. Thank you."

"You come, too. The branding is one of our few get-togethers. Will you?"

"I'd be delighted."

Hannah, preparing for her first outing since coming to Sycamore, squinted into the clouded mirror, unhappy with what she saw. Her skin! How tan it had become. Her hands, too, roughened by work and hard water, were a sight. Should she wear gloves? Would she seem overdressed if she let out the seams in her wedding gown and went in that?

Looking over her scant wardrobe, she finally decided on her old calico, refurbishing it with a clean lace collar and silk rose at the waist. Later, when she arrived at the Barlow ranch and was introduced around, she was glad she hadn't dressed more elaborately. Both men and women wore their workaday clothes, for the branding was not a frolic but a serious business. While the men collected their calves and heifers and brought them down to the large corral set aside for marking their stock, the women occupied themselves with cooking over an outdoor campfire. There were four married women, their numerous children, a grandmother, and a girl who was engaged to be married to a shopowner in King City.

"No rancher for me," she said. "I swore if I'd ever marry, it'd be a town man. And I got him." She was Mel Anderson's oldest girl, Tess Barlow's niece, a pert redhead with a longish nose and high cheekbones.

"Hog-tied him, you mean," Flavia teased, and everyone laughed.

Hannah, observing the older women, could guess why Sue Anderson was so anxious to exchange ranch life for the city. Hardship was written in these women's weatherbeaten faces, the graying, carelessly pinned-up hair, their red clawed hands. Mrs. Anderson, Tess's sister, was in men's riding trousers and slouch hat. Tess Barlow, a tall, plump woman, wore a sack apron over a shapeless gray dress. No frippery, no silk roses or lace collars. But if their appearance and their voices were somewhat harsh, they made up for it in kindliness. Even if Hannah had come in her done-over wedding gown, her neighbors would have made her feel comfortable. Still, when Hannah caught Tess Barlow looking at her with pity, her heart sank. Did these women reflect a picture of her own future? Was she to become like them, old before her time?

It didn't have to be, she told herself. She would remember to wear a wide-brimmed hat in all weathers, to use the cucumber cream Carrie had given her as a going-away present. She would be less of a perfectionist, get more rest. But wasn't it vanity? She *was* a rancher's wife; she had freely chosen to be one. Why worry about

how she looked? None of her new friends took much
notice of their appearance. They were, on the whole, a
happy lot. They laughed and joshed one another, genuinely enjoying this rare occasion to visit.

Tess Barlow, guessing at Hannah's condition despite
the many petticoats and full skirt, assured the younger
woman she had no need to fear being alone when her
time came.

"I've helped with the birthing of a dozen or more
babies. Never lost one."

The men were just as kind as their wives. Mr. Anderson and Leonard Barlow had offered to help Guy with
the courtyard well, feeling sure that by digging a few
more feet they would strike water again. Leonard also
informed Guy that he had trees growing in his canyons
that could provide a valuable crop of tanbark used in the
manufacture of dyes. "When you're ready to harvest,
just give a holler and I'll come by and give you a hand."

Returning home from the branding, Guy and Hannah
felt as if they had been given a new lease on life. Hannah attacked her chores with new vigor, singing a tune
as she fed the chickens, hung out her wash, worked in
the garden, cooked and mended and scrubbed. She hadn't
forgotten her vow to wear a hat or to use her cucumber
cream, but the uneasy prospect of growing old had faded.
She had friends, she had neighbors; she and Guy were
no longer alone.

In August another event broke their daily routine. A
ship—the *Argo*—anchored off the small cove, rocking
on the water beyond the reach of the pounding surf. It
had brought supplies from San Francisco ordered through
the mail by the coast ranchers some six months before.
Hours earlier Abel Trout had sighted it inching its way
down from the north and had ridden from homestead to
homestead announcing the news. Now, men, women,
and children gathered on the edge of the cliff in a high
state of excitement, the men taking turns to peer through
Mr. Anderson's binoculars while standing by at the winch,
the women yelling at Johnny or Timmy not to get too
close to the dropoff, the children playing tag or casting
stones that fell far short of the sea.

Because landing by small boat through the rough seas was dangerous if not impossible, the cargo was removed by means of a cable thrown from the mesa to the ship's deck. Once secured, a sling of goods was hooked on to the cable and the men on the cliff working a windlass drew it up over the breaking waters to the top, where it was eagerly detached and returned for another load.

In addition to the ordered items, tagged with names (Tess received her long-awaited new stove), the *Argo* had brought a miscellaneous cargo of harnesses, plow blades, crockery, nails, knives, boots, palmetto hats, bolts of cloth, scissors, and pins and needles. These items were laid out on blankets over the grass. The ranch folk bartered for their selections with fresh milk, eggs, butter, produce, animal hides, and tanbark. Hannah, having managed to harvest an abundance of garden vegetables, traded her surplus for a length of calico for herself, and flannelette and several skeins of yarn for her baby's layette.

After the ship departed, the men and women stood around visiting for a brief spell, the men discussing new breeds of stock and the price of beef, the women comparing purchases and catching up on the local gossip. Before they dispersed, Tess Barlow reminded Hannah, "Now don't you forget to call on me when your time comes."

"Thank you, I won't. But it's still a long way off."

In September Guy, together with Billy, and his neighbors drove their cattle down the mountain to King City. Hannah was left alone for two weeks, but she was so busy preserving wild blackberries, tomatoes, and the last of the corn, she hardly had time to miss Guy. She never asked herself whether she regretted her decision to marry him, never asked herself whether she loved him or whether she was happy. Happiness was relative. If she compared her present life to life before Guy, she supposed she was happy. He was a good man, a companion, a friend, the father of her child. His forced cheerfulness sometimes bothered her, but she supposed it was better than having him go about with a long face.

She did not allow herself to think of Christian. If something—a falling leaf, a bird in flight, the sight of a horse galloping across the valley—suddenly, for some obscure reason, brought him to mind, she would quickly switch her thoughts. The dreams in which he appeared were confused, so that what she felt when she woke was a lingering sadness with no real memory of Christian.

The country-wide depression of '93 had not yet reached King City, and Guy did fairly well at the cattle sale. Uplifted by his success, he brought back a milch cow, ticking for a new feather bed, another bedstead, miscellaneous chairs, a brace of live ducks, and an old sewing machine he had picked up at an auction yard.

"I've enough money left over," he told Hannah, "for you to take a run up to Frisco when Tess Barlow goes next month." Tess and Flavia made this trip an annual holiday. "Do a little Christmas shopping. Buy yourself something nice."

"Oh, Guy, I'm not one for shopping. I know most women love to do the stores, but it's not my favorite pastime." This was true—to a certain point. Hannah had never had much money to spend on herself, and without money, looking at merchandise she could not possibly afford was far from pleasurable. The silk gown she had fashioned at Wildoak had been her one extravagance. But now, with a few dollars in her purse and the prospect of a change from her routine at Sycamore, she would have enjoyed the excursion—were it not to San Francisco.

She had nothing against the city itself, but it was Christian Falconer's home and that was enough to make it a place to avoid. During her overnight stay in San Francisco with Guy, en route to Sycamore, she had told herself it was ridiculous to fear a chance meeting with Christian in a city that boasted some three hundred thousand souls. He was in the city; she had seen his name on a list of practitioners Guy had procured from the desk clerk when he had discovered she was pregnant.

DR. CHRISTIAN FALCONER,
THE PRACTICE OF MEDICINE AND SURGERY.

She did not want a doctor, she had told Guy firmly, in a voice that refused debate. She had not wanted to risk even one chance in three hundred thousand of meeting him. She wanted to get out of the city as quickly as possible and never to return.

"Why don't we send that money to Travis?" Hannah suggested. "Is there enough?"

"Not quite. Maybe this spring when the mare foals we can manage it."

In the first week of January a squall blew in from the Pacific. Gathering speed and intensity, it soon took on the proportions of a gale. The furious wind and lashing rain racing across the valley, whipping through the sere summer grass, sent the small animals scurrying for their holes. It knocked the windmills down, uprooted trees, tore at the roof tiles, smashing the wagon against the side of the barn where Guy, Billy, and Hannah had just managed to bring the horses, the milch cow, and two heifers to shelter. The horses were all atremble, their eyes rolling, their tails swishing as the wind savaged the walls and the roof. Billy Ostler, though a slacker when it came to hard work, nevertheless had a gentle way with animals and he soon had the horses quieted and the cow chewing contentedly at a heap of hay.

Guy and Hannah beat their way to the house through the howling chaos, reaching the door breathless and drenched through. It was then that Hannah felt the first pangs of approaching motherhood. She thought to wait until the pains came closer together before sending Guy to fetch Tess Barlow. By then she hoped the storm would have abated or blown itself out. And it seemed she was right, for presently the rain and wind slackened. An hour went by without as much as a twinge. False labor, Hannah thought, reaching back into her memory of when her mother, overdue with her fourth (later to be stillborn), complained of such symptoms, impatient for the actual process to begin.

At five o'clock in the afternoon dark purple clouds suddenly moved in again, scudding before a beating wind. Once more the outside world became a storm-tossed frenzy, the wind shrieking around the corners of the house and the rain drumming a tattoo on the roof. Crashing, banging sounds echoed through the house. Guy, peering through a side window, saw the henhouse hurtle past. Shutters, mauled by the wind, were parted from their hinges; unprotected glass shattered.

Hannah's contractions returned. This time they were more closely spaced, the pain stronger. Guy was trying to board up a broken window when something made him turn.

"It's all right, dear, we'll be safe enough," he said, mistaking the look on Hannah's ashen face.

"Guy . . . it's . . ."

He dropped the hammer. "My God—your time—the baby!"

"Yes—I'm afraid—"

"My God! My God! We must get you to bed. Here— here, let me help you."

They had fit up the little side room once occupied by Billy Ostler as a bedroom since it shared the main fireplace and was warmer than the off-court rooms.

Guy assisted Hannah into her nightgown, plumping up pillows, lighting the kerosene lamp, bringing a cup of water she didn't want. "I'll go at once to fetch Tess."

"You can't go out in this storm. You . . ." She paused, biting her lip. "The horses . . . are frightened enough."

"It's letting up," he fibbed as the gale pounded at the house, screeching under the eaves. "I'm going." In the yellow light of the lamp his face looked as white as Hannah's. "I'll be back in an hour, an hour and a half at the most."

He jammed his hat on and threw an oilskin cape about his shoulders. "Will you be all right? Should I get Billy?"

"Heavens, no!"

"I'll leave my watch," he said, winding it, putting it on the little side table. "You'll be all right?"

Looking at his worried, frightened face, she felt that he needed Tess Barlow's comforting presence as much as she.

"I'll hurry," he said.

She heard the whoosh of the wind, the door slam.

The wind howled down the chimney, showering sparks. A red ember, popping as it flew in an arc, caught the edge of the hide rug. Hannah heaved herself out of bed and swatted the smoking ember until it died, leaving the smell of singed leather and fur.

She crawled back just as a white-hot hook gripped her loins. She breathed deeply, taking air into her lungs, letting it out slowly until the pain passed. How long did Guy say—an hour? In good weather it took nearly an hour each way. Now with this storm still on a violent rampage, the night black as pitch, it might take three before he returned.

She got out of bed again and brought in another lamp. Then she went into the kitchen and filled the kettle from the drinking bucket and put it on the stove. Next she knotted several towels and tied them to the bedposts. The pains, evenly spaced, were bad but endurable. Perhaps the child wouldn't be born until morning.

She dozed off and was brought sharply awake by a wrenching, clawing monster turning her inside out. A loud groan escaped her lips as she grabbed her make-shift rope, pulling, pulling, her eyes bulging with the effort to keep from screaming. She didn't know why she should hold it in. There was no one to hear her. This time it seemed to take forever until the pain subsided, leaving her drenched in sweat.

The fire had gone out. Levering her swollen, clumsy body up, she climbed out of bed. Her legs felt weak, the burden she carried weighing on her spine, her pelvis. The wind had quieted to a sighing moan, but the rain still fell unremittingly. She replenished the flickering lamps with kerosene and, glancing at Guy's watch, saw to her horror that five hours had passed. Five hours! Where was he? What had happened? Fear made her tremble. He'd had an accident, the horse had bolted, thrown him. Or a falling tree had caught both rider and horse, pinning them under. She thought of Guy in the dark and wet, alone and helpless, his legs perhaps crushed, and for a few minutes she forgot her own predicament.

She was stooping to relight the fire when a searing knife twisted in her belly. She bent her head, gritting her teeth while the pain went on and on and on, increasing, growing larger and larger like a hideous balloon filling the room, the house, the world in red agony. She heard herself scream. Then it was gone, leaving her panting like a winded animal.

Drenched in sweat, shivering with cold and terror, she forced herself to face reality. The baby was coming and she would have to give birth alone. No one to help her. No one to wipe the perspiration from her brow, to rub the back of her neck, to hold her hand, to give her calm instructions and reassuring comfort. Feeling like an elderly invalid, she tottered to the sideboard in the dining room and found a knife and the bundle of clean cloths and the wool blanket she had knitted in preparation for the infant.

Another pain caught her before she reached the bed and she had to cling to a chair until she could move again.

The next hour was lost in a chaotic nightmare where she was torn, pierced, flayed, tortured beyond the limits of human endurance. She wished she were dead, begged for it. She found herself shouting for help, for God, for Guy, for Travis, for Granny. Then through the chaos she seemed to hear Julie's voice saying over and over, "Bear down, push, bear down, push . . ."

"Now!"

Gathering every ounce of her weakening strength in a tremendous last effort, she expelled the child.

It was over. Done, done, done, *done*!

Fighting inertia, the overwhelming desire to sink into profound, blessed sleep, she elbowed herself up and, leaning forward, cut the cord. When she wiped the baby's eyes and mouth of mucus, it began to cry, the purple-red face crinkling up like a monkey's. She wrapped it in the blanket and laid it beside her on the pillows. It was all she could manage before she drifted off into oblivion.

It was morning and still raining when she woke. She felt sticky and sweaty. She had forgotten how bloody a process giving birth could be. The baby began to whimper. She took it in her arms, lifting it, unfolding the blanket. It was a boy, perfectly formed, all ten toes, ten tiny little fingers with their infinitesimal rosy nails were there. Her heart swelled with love. Hers. Her child. And the face, how smooth in sleep it looked, the little rounded cheeks, the rosy budded mouth, the dark lashes incredibly long and thick for an infant. It opened its eyes, blue like all newborns', and for a fleeting moment she saw reflected in that new face the child to come—not Guy's, not hers, but Christian Falconer's.

It was Christian's son she had borne.

Chapter XI

Travis reread the letter, his eyes skimming over passages:

> *Mark . . . seven months old now . . . with my color hair and a mind of his own . . . we've got five new heifers . . . wild mustard has turned the hills yellow . . .*

He paused again on the closing paragraph.

> *Don't give up, Travis dear. I understand why you had to use the money we sent for your train fare to buy food for the children. Chad being Chad and up to his old tricks . . .*

It wasn't Chad. And Travis hadn't used the money to buy food. He had gambled it away. Cards were his bane, a vice so secret Hannah hadn't ever suspected.

> *Guy plans to cut a load of tanbark he hopes to sell in the fall. Perhaps then I can forward enough to cover the cost of a ticket. . . .*

He felt lower than a snake's belly. Hannah and Guy,

short of funds, were probably doing without so they could help him leave Stonebridge. Why had he ever sat down to poker with those two drummers? Sure he'd been pretty lucky now and then in the past. But he ought to have known better. Liquor salesmen were notoriously slick customers, just the kind who could cheat so's you couldn't prove it. He had lost every penny plus five dollars he had managed to filch from the cashbox.

There was no use asking Chad for a loan. He, too, had recently made a bad gamble, in his case a disastrous investment. He had bought a sack full of gold watches from a glib-tongued, bowler-hatted traveler who had convinced Chad that he could sell the watches at double the price he paid for them. In order to acquire this potential bonanza Chad had cleaned out the till and thrown in his horse and wagon to make up the balance of his payment. This time, he had assured Travis, he had hold of a good thing. With his profits he'd be able to afford a new wagon, a horse that wasn't dead on its feet, and maybe even a handsome rig to ride about town in.

The watches had turned out to be brass of shoddy make, keeping poor time or no time at all. The few Chad had managed to sell had been brought back by irate customers who threatened mayhem unless they were reimbursed.

With no money, no wagon, no horse, no food in the larder, and his creditors banging on the door, Chad had appealed to Aunt Bess.

"No," she said, "I've already loaned you much more than good common sense would allow."

She had put on weight since Julie's death, acquiring a partridge plumpness that suited her. Her cheeks had rounded out, her mouth had become less pinched, her nose less prominent. And her figure had actually developed a bosom. In Bayetville she was now considered an heiress and consequently had more than one suitor at her door.

"But the little uns gotta eat," Chad pleaded.

"I'll send over food, but no money."

"That's hard, Bess. You're a hard woman."

"I know it. But you'll never stand on your own two

feet as long as there's someone around to pull you out of trouble."

"This is the last time, I swear. I've taken the pledge, Bess. I ain't had a drop in two days. I even been to church. Don'cha believe me?"

"Worse men than you have come into the fold, Chad. I'd be the first one to shake your hand if you accepted Jesus in your heart."

"I do, I do."

"Well, we'll see," she said, but she did not give him the loan.

Chad came home cursing Bess. He emptied the beer keg, got roaring drunk, and cried like a baby on Travis's shoulder.

Travis got a job helping a man build a house on the outskirts of Bayetville. The kitchen wench who had replaced Lacey was let go and Sue Joy, now thirteen, was considered old enough to take on the household chores. Colin was brought into the taproom to help Chad during those hours when Travis was at work.

Aunt Bess was outraged to see a twelve-year-old nephew of hers serving spirits. She came down to the inn and made a scene in front of Travis, the children, and two men who were having a quiet game of two-handed pinochle over their beer. She scolded Chad, using God as her witness, calling on the ghosts of Granny Julie and her dear departed sister, Mary Louise, to behold the depths to which Chad had sunk.

"It'd be better to sell the child into bondage. Putting temptation in his way. You're a worse fool than I thought."

The two customers, a wagoner and the town smithy, snickered. Chad went red.

"If you had the gumption to put a stopper on your drinking," Bess went on, "you might be able to get this place in hand. With the right management it could earn you a decent living and there'd be no need to have your young son tending bar."

Chad gave her a bitter look. "Would you like to try?" He sneered.

"I'm sure if I put my mind to it I could make Stonebridge a paying proposition."

"What, with a place that sells demon rum?"

"I have nothing against spirits if they are drunk in moderation—that is, by men of suitable age and no kin to me. If Stonebridge were mine, however, I'd make it a real inn. With the new tobacco plant coming in and the sawmill doing so well, Bayetville is growing. It's becoming a real lively town and it could use a decent hotel."

"This is decent enough," a disgruntled Chad maintained.

"Ha!"

But a seed had been planted in Aunt Bess's fertile brain. Before Julie's death her activities had centered around household and church matters. However, since she had come into her inheritance and had achieved the status of a woman of substance, her mind dwelled more and more on ways and means of increasing her legacy. Stonebridge, near bankruptcy under Chad, was a promising possibility. He owed her money she would never collect and what with this latest financial crisis he would be ready to sell cheaply.

Three months later Bess Page owned Stonebridge Inn, lock, stock, and barrel. And it hadn't cost her a cent.

It had all begun when Chad fell ill with a bad case of the flu. Hearing of it, Aunt Bess, good Christian that she was, left her home on Asbury Street and came to Stonebridge to nurse him. She not only tended the invalid but, in her brusque, no-nonsense manner, restored order to the taproom and kitchen. She made Travis quit his carpentry job and put him back behind the bar. A protesting Colin was returned to school. Sue Joy was given set chores, and since she was a terrible (not to speak of, wasteful) cook, Aunt Bess hired a young girl, Elthea Trumbull, to take over that task.

Elthea was the daughter of a local farmer more successful at breeding children than growing crops on his few acres of depleted soil. She was a pretty thing, not yet fifteen, with fine blond hair and delphinium-blue eyes. The eldest of ten, she had been the first to hire

out, working for Preacher Wright while his wife got over
a difficult confinement. It was Mrs. Wright who had
recommended her to Bess.

"Though still tied to her mama's apron strings," she
said, "she's a good worker and does have a light hand
with biscuits."

Aunt Bess paid Elthea's meager wages out of her own
pocket, adding the cost to the monies she had loaned
Chad in the past.

His debt to Bess amounted to a considerable sum. But
then Chad was obliged to everyone in town. Argyle, the
agent for the brewery with which Chad had done business, was pressing to collect the two thousand Chad
owed him. The lien Argyle's lawyer threatened to slap
on Stonebridge, already mortgaged to the hilt, would
have sunk it out of sight.

On the night Chad got up from his bed for the first
time since the onset of his illness to sit at the supper
table, his children barely recognized him. Washed,
combed and shaved, slimmer and sober, he looked like a
different man.

A smiling Aunt Bess, ladling out potato soup, announced, "You children may as well be the first to hear
our news. I am to be the new owner of Stonebridge. I
have promised to pay up all debts and Chad is signing
the property over to me."

No one said a word.

"Nothing will be altered," Aunt Bess assured the
startled faces staring at her. "We will go on as before."

Chad nodded. "Don't look so flabbergasted, Travis.
'Tain't a bad deal. Bess has done right by us. She's a
good woman. She's made a changed man of me. I ain't
had a sip of anythin' stronger than coffee for three
weeks now. And I feel like a young bull. Don't I, Bess?"

Bess blushed.

Travis said, "Well, I'll be a . . ."

"Don't swear, son. Me 'n Bess are goin' to be married soon as we can' get holt of Preacher Wright, ain't
we, Bess?"

Travis, rendered speechless, shifted his gaze from Chad
to Bess and back to Chad again.

Bess dabbed her lips with a lace-edged handkerchief. "Your father has done me the honor of asking me to be his wife and I've accepted."

"Thass right." Chad beamed.

Travis's first thought was, Why did she have to marry him? Certainly not to own Stonebridge. She could have managed that without becoming his wife.

"I'll be your stepmama now," Bess said. "I'll be Mrs. Chadwick Blaine."

That's it, Travis told himself. She won't be a spinster no more. She'll be Mrs. Blaine, a married woman, not the odd one out, an old maid snubbed by the hens in town who bragged on their husbands and children when they had nothin' to brag about. But why Pa? Why take on Chad Blaine when she could have geezers like Simon Lawler, mebbe a little lame, but respectable, a pillar of the church?

A new man. Could it be that Bess, proud to get Chad sober, wanted to show the town what she had done with a sinner? Reformed him. Her handiwork. Or was it just that in order to run Stonebridge right, she had to live there, and the best way to do so without setting tongues to wagging was to marry Chad? To contemplate anything as romantic as those two falling in love or even being fond of one another seemed ludicrous to Travis. It was, as they said in the penny novels, a marriage of convenience. And his father, who never could see beyond the tip of his veined nose, forgettng how strict and tight-fisted Aunt Bess could be, accepted the arrangement, grateful as a puppy with a bone, relieved to have the load of debt and responsibility removed from his shoulders.

"I wish you both a happy life," Travis said, belatedly remembering that congratulations were due.

"Thank you." Bess smiled benevolently.

She would expect him to go on working in the tap-room, of course. Dare he suggest wages? He could ask but it wasn't likely he would get them. Nor would Aunt Bess look kindly on losing him when he told her he planned to join Hannah in California. He wouldn't tell her, he decided. Lucky he had never spoken of it to

Chad or the children either. It was his secret. He would wait it out in silence, and when Hannah sent him the money for his fare he would slip down to the station and take the first train out.

Preparations for the wedding began at once. The date was set for March 15. Invitations were printed up by the Bayetville press, addressed in Aunt Bess's bold, confident script, and mailed. Extra chairs and tables were borrowed and brought in for the taproom. Along with several kegs of beer, meats were set down in the cooler. The bride would wear white. Why not? Though forty, she was still a virgin. She had Mrs. Minsham, the local seamstress, send away to Atlanta for the best white satin and a roll of real Valencia lace. She would have bridesmaids and a flower girl, organ music and Bobby Stuart singing, "Oh, Promise Me." She was determined to make this such a grand event the old biddies who had patronized her in the past would drop their jaws in envy.

Travis, the children, and Elthea were given the task of shelling pecans for the pies and tarts and the huge wedding cake that would be served as part of the buffet supper. As they worked, dipping into the two bulky sacks leaning against the table legs, they spoke of the coming festivities. But the children soon grew bored with what seemed an endless chore and began to quibble among themselves, hurling nuts at each other. An angry Travis packed them off to bed. He and Elthea, left alone, continued their job in silence.

After a bit Travis said, "Seems like a lot of extry work for you."

"I doan mind. It's jist that I've had to give up my day."

Elthea got every other Sunday off, spending that precious, looked-forward-to time with her family. Despite the crowded conditions in the pine log shanty Elthea called home, the Trumbulls were a close-knit clan and Elthea missed them even when away for a short while.

"I'll ask Aunt Bess if she cain't give you two Sundays in a row after the weddin'."

"Oh, would you? Thank you, Travis."

Her smile pleased him, in fact made him feel expansive. He had not been unmindful of her charm before this. He had noticed the blue eyes, the fine-spun golden hair, the pointed bosoms beneath the cotton waist, the moment he had laid eyes on her. Since Elthea's arrival he had often found himself in the kitchen on some pretext or other, speaking casually, looking—but on the sly—not wanting to make it appear he had lustful thoughts.

Tonight with the lamp glowing on her rosy cheeks and haloing her hair, she looked like an angel, but a seductive one. Travis tried to keep his eyes on his hands and the jar filling up with nutmeats, forcing his thoughts away from her. He wanted no entanglements, not even brief ones, for his whole being was bent on leaving Stonebridge. This past year, fired by Hannah's letters, he could think of little else but Sycamore Ranch, the open range, the sea, which he could almost smell. But he was young and his sexual feelings, long kept in suppression, were now rising like yeast, growing, expanding, filling his blood with a longing to touch, to take Elthea in his arms and cover that sweet face with passionate kisses.

"Why are you starin' at me like that, Travis?" Elthea asked, a delicate blush staining her cheeks.

"Didn't mean to. Sorry."

He busied himself by sweeping the empty shells before him into a tin pail. A long silence followed. He was conscious of her, more than ever now. He could hear her soft breathing and in his mind see the gentle rise and fall of her bosom. White breasts, delicate pink nipples. Abruptly he got to his feet.

"I think we've done enough of these damned pecans for tonight."

"But we're 'most through. Just a bit more to go, Travis."

"I could do with a drink," he said, feeling hot and foolish.

"I'll fetch it for you." She rose.

"No, I . . ."

" 'Twill only be a minute. You go on crackin' nuts."

She disappeared down the passage. In a few minutes

she would return with a tot of whiskey. Having asked for it, he would be expected to drink it. He wasn't particularly fond of spirits. He had no head for liquor and knew that the whiskey coursing through his veins would impel him to do just what he was trying to avoid.

He got to his feet and left the kitchen only to bump into Elthea as she was entering the passage. The liquor spilled over him, over her.

"Oh, jeez, I'm clumsy. I didn't mean to . . ."

She laughed. "Well, now, don't I smell like a toper? And yore shirt, I got it all wet." She lifted her apron and began daubing at the dark streaks.

Her closeness, the touch of her warm hands, was too much for Travis. With a gasp he pulled her into his arms, crushing her to his chest, finding the small mouth, claiming it in a hungry kiss. All the held-in longing, the desires he had fought hard to repress, exploded in his head as he devoured her mouth, pouring kisses over her face, her throat, her shoulders. He was desperately, frantically trying to unbutton her waist when she managed to tear herself away.

"No, Travis. It ain't right." Her hand went to her bruised mouth. "You mustn't."

"I can't help it, Elthea. I've been yearnin' to kiss you fer so long."

He took her in his arms again, gently this time, and she didn't resist. Restraining himself, he held her, letting her head rest on his shoulder.

"Don't you like me, even a little?" he asked, brushing her hair with his lips.

"Oh, Travis." She looked up at him, her lashes wet with tears. "I loved you the minute I saw you. I never reckoned you'd love me, too."

"But I do," he heard himself say. "My sweet Elthea." He started to kiss her again, frantic, hurried kisses. She did not draw back but timidly responded, the pressure of her soft, hot mouth igniting him like a brand. His hands found her round warm breasts through the cotton, the nipples aroused, hard and exciting.

Like one possessed, he lifted her in his arms and carried her through the passage to the little curtained-off alcove next to the kitchen where she slept. The rickety bed, an old one salvaged from the attic's castoffs, took up much of the space, and Travis, stumbling, fell upon it with Elthea in his arms.

"Travis," she whispered, "what are you about?"

"I ain't goin' to hurt you, sweetheart. I ain't, I promise." He kissed her passionately, fumbling again with buttons. They kept slipping out of his fingers. His swollen manhood throbbed like a fevered pulse as he tried to undo her bodice. Frustrated, he grabbed the neck of her waist in his hands. She caught his wrists.

"No, Travis! I ain't got but this gown. Let me—"

He hovered over her on his elbows while she wriggled out of her waist and skirt, then her petticoat. She wore no stays, only a camisole and cheap cotton drawers. Impatient, because she seemed to be taking forever, he tore the camisole away. God, oh, God!

"Travis, you rooint my—"

He didn't hear her. Her naked breasts, two soft white mounds tipped in delicate coral, filled his vision. Sweat broke out on his forehead. He had never dreamed of anything like this!

"Sweet, sweet," he murmured, dipping his head, grasping a nipple between his teeth. She squealed and his grip loosened. Gently he licked at the nub, feeling it harden on his tongue. She trembled under him as he shifted his mouth to the other nipple, all the while stroking the tender, firm flesh.

"Travis, don't! You cain't . . . !"

She wriggled and squirmed, but weakly, then with a little moan of pleasure lay still.

Travis had had little traffic with women. The truth of the matter was that Elthea was only the second female he had bedded. The first had been a peddler's wife in the back of a wagon on a pile of empty sacks while the peddler himself was in the taproom quaffing beer. The woman, considerably older than Travis, insisted he suck her breasts before she allowed him to end his blind search for the place that would ease his swollen manhood.

Travis went on sucking and licking until Elthea's ragged breathing told him that she was ready. At any rate, he himself, his orgasm about to burst, could not wait. Lifting himself again, he tore his britches down. Frantically, almost brutally, he kneed her legs apart, ignoring her attempt to bring them back together.

"Elthea . . . please . . . it won't . . ."

And then he was plunging inside, piercing a resistance he was only dimly aware of. He heard her cry out through a roaring in his ears, but no power on earth could stop him now. He plunged again, the velvety sheath closing around him, and a moment later the agonizing tension was suddenly released. He felt himself go into a torrential spasm, a shivering ecstasy racing through his body.

She was crying softly as he took her in his arms. "Elthea, please, don't, don't."

"You rooint me," she sobbed.

"I—I didn't mean—I couldn't help it, darlin'," he protested, feeling ashamed.

"Do you love me?" she asked timidly.

And because he wanted to atone for his behavior, he said, "Would I have done what I did if I didn't love you?"

"Oh, Travis, I love you, too."

In the days that followed Travis avoided Elthea as much as possible. Remorse, shame, and above all anger at his own weakness kept him from the kitchen, his eyes averted at the supper table. Why had he done it? Why had he allowed his lust to get the better of him? It was one thing to thump a woman who didn't much care who thumped her, and another to take a young girl, a virgin, sponsored by Preacher Wright and with a papa who probably owned a shotgun. Worse, far worse, he had told her he loved her. She had taken him seriously too. Most likely she had thought he would soon ask her to marry him. But he couldn't saddle himself with a wife. He'd never leave Stonebridge, never get away.

And yet the terrible thing was he wanted her again. He yearned to kiss and hold her, to uncover those little apple breasts, to feel the sweet nipples growing taut in his mouth, to part her round white knees and enter that secret moist place under the little thatch of blond hair.

He got in a sweat just thinking about it. He had to leave, the sooner the better. Now.

He tried to borrow money from his father—who had none—and from Aunt Bess, who demanded to know what he wanted it for.

"To buy me a bicycle. I could run errands quicker that way."

"You've walked until now," she said. "A young, healthy boy like you doesn't need to ride."

One Sunday night Travis was having a late supper in the kitchen. Elthea had gone home and was not expected until the following morning, so Sue Joy had cooked the meal, hominy and burnt sausage, kept warm on the back of the stove. Travis, having ousted the last customer from the taproom, had doused all the lights except for the one in the kitchen. The family had long since retired to their beds. He was alone with his thoughts, unhappy, depressing thoughts that went around on a treadmill in his head. Money. How could he get his hands on money? Should he write Hannah and tell her he couldn't wait until Guy cut his tanbark? No. He could never explain. How could he confess that he had to get away quickly because he was tempted by the hired girl whom he had already deflowered?

Outside a wind-driven rain rattled the shutters and he didn't hear the knock at the door until a voice called, "Let me in!"

It was Elthea, looking distraught, drenched, her bonnet gone, her hair streaking down her back.

He snatched up his coat from the back of his chair and threw it about her shoulders. "Come, sit by the stove."

Crying and shivering, she sat.

"What is it? Elthea, what happened?"

Between fits of weeping she told him. As a rule, after her Sunday off her father brought her back to Stonebridge on Monday morning. But the one horse they owned— both wagon and plow puller—had gone lame and to save herself a long walk, Elthea had accepted a ride from a neighbor who was driving his rig into Bayetville to fetch a doctor for his ailing wife. They had covered only a few miles when the neighbor began to make lewd remarks, then advances. Frightened, Elthea had jumped from the wagon and hidden in the bushes by the side of the road.

"I could hear him stampin' about. Oh, Travis, I was so sceered."

He put his large hands on her cold, little ones. "I'll kill him! I'll get my rifle and shoot the damn bastard daid!"

"Oh, no, you mustn't, Travis. They'd put you in jail, mebbe hang you. I couldn't bear it." She began to cry again.

He knelt beside her. "Yore makin' yoreself sick, sweetheart. Don't cry no more."

"Oh, Travis."

He put his arm about her and kissed her cheek. "Yore safe now." She whimpered and nestled closer. A feeling of protective manliness swelled his chest. "Little darlin'." His lips strayed to her mouth and he tasted tears in her trusting response. "You'd best get out of yore wet clothes." One arm went around her waist, the other under her legs as he swung her up.

Looking in his eyes she smiled shyly. "I thought mebbee you was mad at me, Travis."

"Now, what ever gave you such an idee?"

He made love to her more leisurely this time, savoring her nakedness, his bare skin against hers. She seemed to like it better, too, the breast sucking, the kissing, her arms around his neck going slack. When he entered her and began to thrust, she moaned but did not struggle or protest. His movements quickened. Faster and faster. Oh, it was grand! Raising her buttocks with his hands, he drove deeply. Ahhh! This was the heaven that Preacher Wright promised, this was the joy, the ecstasy. If it could only last forever, but he was coming, coming. . . . His arms jerked convulsively about her as his orgasm burst like a torrent.

Replete, he kissed her softly, gratefully.

"Travis—I love you. Do you love me?"

"Yes," he said, every nerve, every muscle floating.

"Does that mean we'll be married?"

"Yes," he said, adding, "but not right away."

He shifted his weight, lying beside her in the bed. He

had acted like a lowdown dog for the second time, but now with the wind whistling around the corners of the house, safe and snug, holding the softness of Elthea close to his heart, he felt a comfort and a happiness that had to be love.

He would marry her, make her his wife. And what of Sycamore Ranch? He couldn't give that up. But why couldn't he have both? He could go west, and when he had enough money saved send for her.

He explained his plan to Elthea.

She shifted her head on his arm so that she could look up into his eyes. "Does that mean I'm spoken for?"

"Yes, darlin'." He kissed her on the cheeks, on the mouth, on her pert little nose.

"But, Travis, must we go so fer away? I'd never see Papa or Mama or Tom or Caroline or Betsy, none of my brothers and sisters again. Oh, Travis, I couldn't!"

"Not even for me, darlin'? For yore husband?"

"But why cain't we stay in Bayetville? There's plenty work even if you diden want to work for yore aunt."

"No," he said. "I tole you I wanted to go west. I promised my sister I would."

"But she's got her a man and a baby. It's not that she's all by herself."

"You'll have a man—and later a baby."

"It ain't the same."

"Are you sayin' you won't marry me? That you don't love me?"

"Oh, Travis!" She turned, kissing him. " 'Course, I do. I'd die if I couldn't be yore wife."

"Then it's settled. We'll jest keep it a secret for a while. Yore not even to tell yore ma. Promise?"

"I promise, Travis."

Chad and Bess were married in style, as showy a wedding as Bayetville had seen in a long time. Aunt Bess may have been parsimonious in many matters, but for this affair she had loosened the purse strings and spent with a liberal hand. The guests were treated to a lavish reception after the church ceremony, a supper where food and drink were not stinted. If Chad got a little drunk, he was excused. So many toasts, how could he refuse to toast back? A man didn't get married every day. There were the usual sour asides, claiming Bess must have been desperate else she wouldn't have chosen the town's worst drunk. But all the others wished them well, giving long tipsy speeches, congratulatory testimonials larded with crude jokes. After the guests had eaten their fill the chairs and tables were pushed aside. Old Pa Edgmore and his son, Luke, tuned up their fiddles while eager dancers standing by tapped their toes.

It was at this point that Travis went looking for Elthea, who had disappeared a half hour earlier. He found her sitting in the kitchen, her hands clenched on the table in front of her, her face white as a bedsheet.

"You feelin' sick, darlin'?"

"Yes. I done lost my supper."

"You been workin' too hard. Mebbe you ought to lie down for a spell."

"It ain't gonna help, Travis. Not for what I got." She turned shadowed blue eyes up at him. "I'm goin' to have a baby. We cain't wait to get married. We gotta do it now."

Travis, who had been celebrating rather freely with the others, suddenly went sober.

"You shore it ain't somethin' you ate?"

"Yes. I missed my time. I'm shore."

When he said nothing, her eyes flooded with tears. "Ain't you wantin' to marry me?"

"Yes, yes."

Well, he was in a pickle for sure. But would it make any difference to marry now if they both could get away? How? He had been hoping to obtain an odd job here and there when he could be spared from the taproom, adding what he earned in tips to make up his own fare. Maybe, he had thought, he could even persuade Elthea to put aside part of her wages rather than hand them entirely over to her pa. That way she could get a little nest egg to help her come out to him once he got settled. But if they married now, Elthea's wages would stop. As a husband he would be required to use his tips for little necessities, shoes for Elthea, a petticoat, clothes for the baby.

"You go lay down, Elthea. We'll get married, don't worry, darlin'. I gotta think some."

He went back into the taproom where the noise and music, the babble of voices, the shouts, laughter and scraping of fiddles had grown wilder and more abandoned. Going behind the bar, he poured himself a neat whiskey and downed it like a dose of Doc Pemberley's medicine. As he stood there wiping his mouth with his sleeve his eye fell on the cashbox. It had been his duty during the last week when Aunt Bess was so busy with the wedding preparations to empty it each evening and take the day's proceeds to the bank. He remembered now that it had completely slipped his mind yesterday and today was Sunday. There should be money taken in for two days plus whatever Aunt Bess had collected from the people who usually came in and paid their bills on Saturdays. Aunt Bess, of course, kept the key to the cashbox, but he knew exactly where to find it.

He returned to the kitchen, parting the curtains of the little alcove where Elthea lay, hands folded on her stomach as if already feeling the life growing within.

"Get yore cloak," he said, "and gather a few things in a pillowcase. Whatsoever you think you cain't be parted from. We're leavin' in ten minutes."

"But where? Oh, Travis, I cain't . . ."

"Do as I say, Elthea, else you'll have that baby without a pa."

No one noticed as he slipped upstairs. In Bess's room his hand closed on the key, hidden under a pile of mending in her sewing basket. Next he went to his own room and looked around. He was afraid to pack anything, but he put on his coat and stuffed his pocket with two pairs of clean socks and his tip money. Then he descended the stairs with a forced smile on his face, though his heart was beating like a hammer.

The cashbox was under the counter, hidden from view, so rifling it without being seen was easy. He left a few dollars and some coins to allay suspicion and eased the rest into his pocket.

Edging around the crowd, he made for the stairs again
and had a bad moment when the Moore girl shouted,
"Hey, Travis, come dance with me. C'mon!"

"Later," he mouthed and was relieved when she was
swept away by the bank clerk's son.

He put the key back, making sure the mending looked
undisturbed. Let Aunt Bess wonder tomorrow morning,
not tonight.

Elthea was sitting on the bed, muffled in her cloak, a
frightened look on her face.

"We gotta hurry," he said, taking her hand. If they
walked fast they would be just in time to catch the
eastbound train to Atlanta.

Chapter XII

With Mark in her lap Hannah sat beside Guy in the wagon, waiting impatiently for the King City stagecoach to arrive. Travis's letter, written from St. Louis and reaching them through the Limekiln post office where Guy had gone to pick up some supplies the week before, said that he was on his way. He had outlined his itinerary, estimating that he should reach Jolon (a stage stop to the east of King City) by the twenty-fifth of April. Hannah was not to worry. There was no need to meet him; he would find the ranch on his own.

"He can't possibly know how long and difficult a hike it is over the mountain," Hannah had said to Guy, showing him the letter.

"We'll go down on the twenty-fifth with the wagon and take an extra horse. If he isn't on the stagecoach, we can leave Belle—she's a good steady mare and knows the road—with the stationmaster."

Now that Travis was almost here, Hannah realized how much she had missed him, how long it had been since she had last seen him. When he had written to say he had used the fare money she'd sent him for Sue Joy, Bobby, and Colin, she had been bitterly disappointed. But she had understood and loved him all the more for

185

his sacrifice. She had felt guilty too. She should have been contributing to her brothers' and sister's support. But cash was hard to come by. Everything Guy made went back into stock or seed for Sycamore.

"They're late," Hannah said, her eyes straining across the valley for the first sign of dust that would announce the appearance of the stage.

"It's never on time."

At least, she thought with a sigh, I don't have to go on worrying about the young ones. Travis in his last letter had written that Bess had taken over Stonebridge along with Chad. What a stroke of luck! Sue Joy and the boys might have to toe the mark but they would be decently clothed and fed. As for Chad, perhaps Bess had bitten off more than even she could chew. Hannah could not see Chad reforming for Bess, no matter how she lectured or chastised, and did not envy the troublesome job her aunt had set for herself.

And now, thank God, Travis was out of it.

Sitting there next to Guy, Hannah's thoughts went back to the childhood she had shared with her brother. How close they had been. She remembered how they would hide from Chad under the stairs, holding tightly to one another as he stomped about in one of his drunken rages. She recalled the time they had stolen a cooling blueberry pie from Mrs. Butterworth's kitchen sill, how together they had followed the ice wagon on hot summer days, cadging chunks of ice from Bill Hollister. In those early days Travis had made what would have been a miserable life at Stonebridge bearable. It was only when she had gone off to school and later to Wildoak that they had grown somewhat apart.

Guy suddenly said, "Look! It's coming!"

He helped Hannah and Mark down from the wagon. Her heart thumped with excitement as the coach pulled up in a cloud of dust. The coachman assisted the women passengers to alight: a mother carrying a sleeping baby, an elderly woman who immediately unfurled a large black umbrella, and a young girl, hardly more than child, a pretty little blond thing wearing an old-fashioned poke bonnet. Then Travis jumped out.

Hannah gave Mark over to Guy and ran to meet him. She embraced her brother, kissing him, tears welling up in her eyes.

"I never thought . . . Oh, it's been so long, *so* long! Let me look at you! Travis, you haven't changed!" With a happy sob she hugged him again. "Oh, Travis, there's so much catching up to do."

He untangled himself from her arms. "Hold on, darlin'. There's someone I want you to meet." He turned to the young girl in the poke bonnet who had been standing shyly behind him and, taking her arm, brought her forward. "Hannah, this is Elthea, my wife."

If the ground had parted under her feet, Hannah could not have been more stunned. "Your wife?" The words echoed in her ears.

The girl said, "How do, Miss Hannah," her large blue eyes scared and uncertain in the shadow of the bonnet. "Pleased to meet you."

Travis said, "I thought I'd surprise you."

Surprise? Oh, Travis! "Well, I must say . . ."

What *was* there to say? Hannah tried hard to hide her shock and disappointment. She had urged Travis to come west hoping to free him from the narrow confines of Stonebridge, hoping that in time she and Guy could afford to help him get more schooling, send him to San Francisco, where he could learn a respectable trade like cabinetmaking or typesetting. And now he had a wife! Elthea. From her speech, her diffident air, her clothes—that bonnet!—she appeared to be one of those ignorant farm girls who marry early and start dropping babies almost at once. And Hannah, with a sixth sense that some women develop, could swear that this one was pregnant already. She could see it all. Travis with a houseful of little ones, unable to do more than earn enough to take care of their needs. In addition Sycamore wasn't large enough to support two families, unless by some miracle the price of cattle and ponies tripled. But miracles were too rare to count on. Travis would be bogged down in the same poverty that had kept him chained to Chad and Stonebridge.

"I know it's a bit of a shock," Travis was saying. "But I'll work for our keep, so you needn't worry."

"Of course I'm not worrying," Hannah said. Whatever she had she'd share with her brother. Hadn't that always been the way? Oh, but she had wanted him to get on in the world! Clever and handsome, he couldn't help but make something of himself. And later when he'd marry, it would be to some fine accomplished girl he'd be proud to call wife.

"Elthea is a very good cook," Travis said, putting his arm about her waist.

Hannah immediately felt conscience-stricken. They were here. Her brother and the girl he had chosen for his wife. "Why, I'm glad to hear that, Elthea. I'm not much in the kitchen myself."

She stooped and kissed the girl. Forlorn little thing. It wasn't her fault. "Welcome, Elthea dear. I'm very happy for both of you. And—oh, my!—here we are standing and jabbering away and you haven't met Guy and Mark."

From the beginning Travis and Guy got along well, just as Hannah had anticipated. It was as though they were old friends, reunited after a long absence, no strain in each other's company. For Travis, Sycamore was love at first sight. He wanted to know and to do everything, but since he was still awkward on horseback, he took over the job of mending broken fences and reroofing the barn, tasks that Guy never seemed to have time for. At supper the two men had much to talk about. Guy seemed happy to have a man, besides useless Billy, to discuss his problems with.

Elthea, however, remained shy, hovering on the fringes like a lost shadow. She had trouble mastering the stove—so different from her mama's and the one at Stonebridge, she said. She spent a great deal of time in the bedroom Hannah had fixed up for Travis, the room now shared by the two of them. She was "tuckered" from her trip, she explained apologetically to Hannah.

Hannah, feeling sorry for the girl, attempted to reach her, but without success. Two days after they had arrived she went out to speak to Travis, who was working in the barn, whistling as he hammered.

"Do you like Sycamore?" Hannah asked the obvious.

"It's everything you said."

"Travis—we—we've always been able to talk to one another."

"Yup." He removed the nail he had been holding between his teeth. "That's what I missed. All the time you've been gone. No one really to talk to. Until Elthea came to Stonebridge."

"She worked in the kitchen?"

"Yup. But she ain't one bit like Lacey. She's a clean girl and no half-wit."

"I can see that. But I did think you'd wait awhile before you married."

"I couldn't, Hannah. I got her with child."

"Oh, Travis."

"Now, don't get me wrong. It was no shotgun marriage. I love Elthea just like you love Guy. I didn't want to go away without her."

"Of course, Travis. I understand."

Travis, lonely, a young full-blooded male, and Elthea, pretty, shy, and trusting. How could she blame him?

Hannah tried again to get Elthea involved in the daily life that went on around them. She thought perhaps Elthea, coming from a farm, would prefer working out of doors, not heavy work, but doing simple chores. So Hannah, in a kindly way, suggested that Elthea gather the eggs and feed the chickens. But after several mornings when Elthea came into the house with only a few eggs in her basket, Hannah discovered that the girl was terrified of the rooster who, sensing it, would come at her the moment she set foot in the hen yard. She was no more successful at milking the cow. Elthea had only to approach her when old Flossie fidgeted and kicked. Hannah couldn't understand how a farmer's daughter could be so inept with animals. Hannah herself, with no experience when it came to cows (they had had chickens at Stonebridge), found milking simple. Guy had taught her in ten minutes. "Sit down with authority. Lean your head against Flossie's flank and pull."

Hannah, watching Elthea's fumbling attempt, couldn't help saying, "You've not done much milking, have you?"

"My mama wanted me in the kitchen."

So Elthea went back inside. Though she finally did learn to deal with the stove and put out meals that were sometimes quite good—efforts for which she received high praise and encouragement from Hannah—Elthea remained withdrawn and drooping. She rarely spoke except to Travis. Hannah could hear the murmur of their voices behind the closed door of their bedroom. On occasion Travis's voice rose as if out of patience and Elthea would come in the kitchen the next morning with red-rimmed eyes. It grieved Hannah to think that the young couple were quarreling and when she tried to talk to Travis about it, he said, "She's a little homesick, that's all. When the baby comes, she'll settle in."

Elthea would perk up a bit when Flavia came to visit. It was hard not to be cheered by Flavia. She had a ready smile and an infectious, merry laugh that seemed to make the very freckles on her nose dance. Her tales of life on the Barlow ranch, whether mundane or catastrophic, were told in a light, rib-tickling vein. Hannah liked her. And the feeling seemed mutual. Flavia was a little reticent with Travis but bold with Guy, flirting with him in a way that should have made Hannah jealous. But it was all in fun. Besides, Guy was definitely not the kind of man to stray simply because a young, pretty girl fluttered her lashes at him.

Travis and his wife had been at Sycamore a month when Hannah discovered that she, too, was pregnant. Guy couldn't have been more pleased. Little Mark was almost two now and Guy felt it was time he had a brother or sister. Though Hannah did not share Guy's wish to have a "tribe" (the memory of her own mother, sickly, spineless Mary Louise, pregnant every eleven or twelve months, delivering misshapen, dead babies, was too uncomfortably clear) she was happy to be carrying Guy's child. She hoped for a boy, one that would be truly his and could legitimately carry his name. A son will be my penance, she thought, my atonement for foisting another man's child on him.

She had tried to forget Christian but Mark was a daily reminder. Though the boy had her dark hair with its chestnut highlights and her nose (people were prone to remark on mother and son's likeness), Hannah, when she looked at Mark, saw Christian. He had the same hazel-flecked eyes, the same assertive jaw. Sometimes when he concentrated on an object or became angry, his eyes would narrow like Christian's, and Hannah, catching that familiar expression, would feel her heart constrict. Mark's smile, his laugh, too, were Christian's. It was as though Christian were there to taunt her.

Watching the child, loving him fiercely despite her hate for the father, she prayed that when Mark grew older, the resemblance to her seducer would not become more pronounced. The one fear skirting her conscious mind was that someone—perhaps Travis—at some point would say, "I do declare that child puts me in mind of Christian Falconer." Though Guy did not know the name of the man who had betrayed her, it might set him to wondering, and she did not want to see him look at the boy with doubt in his eyes.

Travis and Elthea had been at Sycamore for two months when an angry letter arrived from Bess.

> . . . *I heard from Elthea's folks that both she and Travis are with you in California. They're upset because Elthea ran off without as much as a goodbye. I'm upset too. Travis, before he left, helped himself (stole, to put a real name to it) to fifty dollars from the cashbox. I'd be obliged if he'd return it.* . . .

Travis denied he knew anything about the money. "I earned that fifty dollars doin' odd jobs and from customers' tips. Chad took that money and he's puttin' the blame on me. I been workin' for nothin' all them years and that old hen has the gall to accuse me of stealin'."

"Then you ought to write and tell her," Hannah suggested.

"Fat lot that'd do. Did you ever try arguin' with Aunt Bess once she got a notion in her head?"

To Travis's relief Hannah accepted his explanation. But the lie (not the theft, for he had already persuaded himself that the fifty dollars were owed him) sat uneasily on his conscience.

Tess Barlow had been ailing for several months now, losing weight, complaining of constant exhaustion that no home remedy or rest seemed able to alleviate or cure. Her sister, Frances Anderson, whose husband ran a sheep and cattle ranch near McIntyre Canyon, insisted she see a doctor. A good one, she said, not one of those quacks in Monterey. She had heard of a physician, Dr. Russell, in San Francisco who dealt in "female trouble" and strongly advised that Tess consult him. For his part, Leonard Barlow felt that if Tess kept taking the medicine he had brought back from King City—Toland's Nostrum, a tonic that claimed to cure everything from dandruff to fallen arches—she would feel right as rain in no time. But Frances swore Toland's was nothing but snake oil laced with laudanum and of no earthly use. Did Leonard want his wife to be a permanent invalid? Or worse still, dead? Leonard, though gruff and undemonstrative, was fond of and dependent on Tess and more worried than he let on. His wife had never been sick a day in her life and, except for birthing the children, never abed in daylight hours. It did not take much persuading for him to agree to let her go. Tess asked Hannah if she would accompany her.

Hannah, her old fear of San Francisco still strong, tried to think of a way to refuse. But the sight of Tess's hollowed eyes and the loose flesh hanging from a figure that had once been stout, alarmed her. Tess couldn't go alone, she needed her.

Guy believed that Hannah, too, would benefit from the trip.

"You can ask the doctor about your condition."

"But I'm all right," she told him. "There isn't a blessed thing wrong with me."

"You had such a hard time with Mark."

"It was my first." They never spoke of her miscarriage. "The first is always hard."

"Well, it doesn't hurt to get a clean bill of health."

Guy drew up a modest list of articles for Hannah to purchase in the city—cambric, tea, vegetable seed, a seven-inch wrench. Elthea would care for Mark, Travis would tend to the hens and cow.

"Flavia has offered to stop by and help Elthea," Hannah said to Guy. It was the night before she was to leave and they were lying side by side in bed. "But I think it's you she wants to see."

"Me?" His surprise was genuine.

"I believe she's in love with you."

"You're mistaken, Hannah. She just enjoys flirting. It doesn't mean anything. I've never in any way encouraged her. To me she's just—well, Flavia."

Guy rose on an elbow to look down at her, and since he couldn't see her face his fingers traced her lips to determine if they were smiling. "You're not jealous?"

"Maybe, perhaps," she teased.

"Oh, Hannah, darling." He hugged and held her. "There's never been anyone but you. Never will be."

He made love to her, putting all the ardor he could muster into it, fondling and kissing, holding back his orgasm, which usually came quickly, whispering endearing words, asking Hannah what would pleasure her. "This?" stroking her breast, something he had never done before. Hannah said, "You're doing fine." She made appropriate sighs and little murmurings in the back of her throat, and when it was over said it was wonderful, calling him sweetheart and love. But long afterward she lay on her side, her back to her sleeping husband, and silently wept. She had the best husband in the world, and she ought to be happy. Why the tears? But to examine the cause of her sadness would lead down an avenue she thought it best not to explore.

San Francisco.

Hannah looked around as if seeing it for the first time. When she and Guy had gone through, en route to Sycamore, she had been too anxious and preoccupied to notice the city. Except for the vague impression of busy street traffic, the clanging of trolley bells and the crowds of people, she remembered very little about it. Now, riding with Tess in an ancient hansom to Mrs. Tivoli's boarding house on Pacific Street, she had the opportunity for closer observation.

She had thought that all big cities were more or less built along similar lines, but San Francisco was different in many ways from Chicago. Whereas Chicago was laid out on a gridiron, flat as a pancake, the streets of San Francisco went up and down steep hills. Occasionally she caught a glimpse of the bay beyond, where fishing boats, coastal steamers, and the tall masts of sailing vessels were outlined against the backdrop of a headland, so different from the rusty-hulled steamers Hannah had seen docked in the noisome Chicago River. No headland or sea smells there. As for the houses, many seemed similar to those in Chicago: frame buildings, two or three stories with fanciful conical towers, bay windows, and jigsaw trim.

From the storefront signs they passed Hannah observed that San Francisco was also a haven for immigrants; Poles, Jews, Italians, Germans, Greeks, and Lithuanians had posted their businesses not only in English but in the languages of their native lands. However, the miasmic depression of the neighborhoods surrounding Hull House in Chicago seemed to be absent along Pine, Jackson, and Kearney streets. Surely there were poor here also, but there was something in the way people— even those shabbily dressed—walked, smiled, and held their heads that gave them an air of optimism. Perhaps it was the legacy of the Gold Rush, a spirit that had imbued the forty-niners with the belief that every man who came to San Francisco could become rich, an equal if not superior to his neighbor.

"I've written to Dr. Russell," Tess said as they neared the hotel. "He is expecting us tomorrow at ten o'clock."

She had forgotten that she had told this to Hannah at least three times. Nervous, clasping and unclasping her gloved hands, biting her lip, a frown of pain between her eyes, she looked white and ill.

"Perhaps it's nothing serious at all," Hannah said cheerfully, also for the third time. "You've been working too hard. This change will do you good."

"The change . . . Well, we'll see."

Dr. Russell's office was on the second floor of a four-story, redbrick building on Market Street. When Tess and Hannah arrived, the waiting room was occupied by a plump, weak-chinned woman with a small boy, a white-haired gentleman who sat rocking and moaning, and a young woman holding tightly to what Hannah supposed was her husband's hand. She was very pregnant and kept grimacing as if she had already gone into the first stages of labor.

The doctor's assistant, a harassed middle-aged female in a starched gray skirt, emerged from the consulting room, took Tess's and Hannah's names, and told them to be seated. It was hot in that small crowded room and the old man exuded an unpleasant odor. The little boy, out of boredom, took to sticking out his tongue at Hannah, ignoring his mother's tired entreaty: "Please don't do that, Johnny." Hannah picked up a tattered copy of the *Lark* but did not read it.

After what seemed hours of waiting, the woman in the gray skirt opened the door and summoned Hannah.

"Perhaps Dr. Russell can see Mrs. Barlow first?" Hannah suggested. She was concerned about Tess, who seemed close to exhaustion.

"You're next on the list," the woman in gray said. "Mrs. Hartwell, is it?"

Tess said, "Go on, Hannah, I don't mind waiting."

Hannah was relieved to find that the doctor was a fatherly type, white-haired with a huge handlebar mustache. He invited her to have a chair, then seated himself at a battered rolltop desk littered with papers, medical tracts, unraveled bandages, and a jumble of vials and pillboxes.

"So you are Mrs. Hartwell," he said in a kindly voice. "And how may I help you?"

She explained her condition and her husband's concern.

"No complaints except the long labor with the first one?"

"None."

He did not ask her to undress but told her to be seated on his examining table. Hannah, perching there, noticed the oilcloth that covered it was not too clean. Beside it stood a glass cabinet with shelves of instruments that appeared frightening if not lethal. After thumping and prodding her chest, back, and stomach, the doctor proclaimed she was fit and should have no fear of not giving birth to a healthy child.

"And many, many others," he added.

"Thank you, Doctor, but I think I shall confine my family to no more than four." Adding, "at decent intervals, of course." Hannah thought this was as good a time as any to ask about the sponge. She had learned from Jane Addams that women could prevent pregnancy by the use of such a device. What kind of sponge and how it could be obtained and inserted she had been too reticent to ask at the time. An unmarried girl—especially one who had miscarried an illegitimate baby—did not make such inquiries. She had understood, however, that a physician might be able to provide such a prophylactic. She wished she had had one the day she had gone to bed with Christian. But their lovemaking had been such a spur-of-the-moment happening, a passionate surge that had taken her completely by surprise. Their combined ardor had swept her up in a tumult of love and desire, and there had been no thought of afterward, of pregnancy or Christian's duplicity.

"I wonder if you could suggest something I might use to limit my family."

"My dear," he said, patting her on the knee, "I don't believe in such contrivances. Aside from being unhealthy, they go against the good Lord's commandment—go forth and multiply. Motherhood is a woman's joy, the crowning achievement of her life."

"But I want my children to have the best, to be educated. If there are more than we can decently support, we will all end up in poverty."

"Tut, tut," he admonished. "One more tiny mouth to feed is hardly a formula for poverty. If you have the unnatural desire to limit your family, practice abstinence, my dear. Abstinence. Explain that to your husband. But don't come crying to me if he seeks his marital rights elsewhere."

Hannah said nothing. Dr. Russell no longer seemed fatherly, but cold and unthinking. She wondered how he would feel if he was constantly pregnant, if he had to go through the trauma of birth over and over again, if he had the care of a flock of babies and the worry of feeding and clothing them.

When Hannah came out, the waiting room had refilled and several people were standing. Tess said, "Hannah, why don't you go down to the little cafe we passed next door? It might take me some while yet. And it would be much pleasanter. Have some coffee and a cruller. I'll meet you there when I'm through."

"Are you sure . . . ? All right, then."

Hannah went out into the corridor and was starting for the stairs when one of the doors opened and a woman, wearing a satin dress with frills and furbelows down the low-cut front, her cheeks and mouth painted bright pink, came out. She was laughing. A deep voice, one that Hannah had heard in dreams she would rather forget, said, "Now mind, Dora, be more choosy in your customers."

"Oh, I will, I will, Dr. Falconer."

Hannah, overcoming initial shock, turned to flee. But it was too late. Christian had seen her.

"Hannah . . . !"

He caught her and brought her around.

They stood facing one another—Hannah, her heart racing, Christian, his eyes blazing.

"Am I that repugnant to you?" he asked angrily.

She should have noticed the plaque on the door. CHRISTIAN FALCONER, PRACTICE OF MEDICINE. It was there, as bold as the brass it was engraved upon. Why hadn't she remained in Dr. Russell's office, hot and uncomfortable as it was? Why hadn't she followed her instincts and stubbornly refused to come to San Francisco? The thing she had feared had happened. She might have guessed that some day she would come face-to-face with Christian again. The not-so-improbable accident had to happen. She knew he was practicing medicine in San Francisco but so were hundreds of others. That Christian should have offices in the same building as Dr. Russell seemed highly unlikely. What was more unlikely was Christian opening his door as she passed through the corridor. But he had.

"Come inside," he said, still with his hand on her arm. "I want to talk to you. Yes. You owe me an apology."

"I owe you nothing." She had found her voice, instilling it with indignation. He was everything she should hate, everything she should scorn. The woman who minutes earlier had emerged from his door was obviously a whore. Did prostitutes compose his clientele? Or had she been closeted with him for another purpose?

"Hannah," he said, his fingers tightening, bruising her flesh, "I must talk to you. Not here. Inside. Or do I have to drag you there?"

"Would you?" she challenged, bristling.

He smiled, the kind of enigmatic smile that men give over the barrel of a dueling pistol—parted lips, cold eyes.

She loathed that arrogant smile, hated it because the shiver that ran through her was half fear, half excitement.

"*Please,*" Christian said in a tone that was more command than request.

A man and woman came out of the adjoining office and gave them both a curious look.

"I can only spare a few minutes," she said haughtily, quelling the trembling inside.

He led her through a waiting room, similar to Dr. Russell's. She was too agitated to notice the people there, except to feel their eyes upon her.

"In here." He opened the door to the consulting room. A voice cried, "Doctor . . . !" He shut the door behind him.

"If you will." He motioned to a chair. He was wearing a gray vest looped with a gold watch chain, but no coat. His shirtsleeves were clipped above the elbow with blue elastic bands. The mustache was gone. Smooth-shaven, he looked trim, lean, handsome.

He sat at a desk, unlike Dr. Russell's, tidy, with neatly stacked papers, an inkwell and a pen to one side. A stethoscope lay curled like a black garter snake on a clean blotter.

"So it's Hannah in the flesh and blood." There was a jeering edge to his voice. "I never expected to see you in this part of the world."

Iron will steadied her heart and forced her to hold his gaze. "I'm married now to Mr. Guy Hartwell. I think I mentioned him to you. He bought a ranch in the Santa Lucia Range."

"I see." He moved the pen a fraction of an inch. "I was under the impression you were going to marry me. In fact, if I remember correctly, I sealed our engagement with a ring."

"I threw it in the gutter," she said, lifting her chin.

A tiny ripple moved across his cheek but the expression in his eyes did not change. "When I called at Hull House I was shown the door. I wrote to your father, to your brother, and to Miss Addams. But only Miss Addams replied and from her I got no information except that you had left Chicago."

"I'm surprised you made the effort. Surprised that you went on with the pretense of an engagement and marriage when you hadn't bothered to break off your attachment to Amanda Cox."

"Amanda," he mocked wryly. "So it was Amanda again."

"Yes. Please don't deny it. I saw both of you at the Palmer House. You were registered there as Mr. and Mrs. Falconer."

He lifted his dark brows in surprise.

"How convincingly you can pretend. You should have gone on the stage, Mr. Falconer. You missed your calling."

"No. It's you that have missed yours. There are times when you are able to put Lillie Langtry and Sarah Bernhardt to shame. You said you loved me. You proved it that afternoon in a way only a woman in love—"

"I don't want to hear about it," she interrupted, the sudden memory of passionate kisses, of strong, stroking hands, flashing through her mind. "It was a mistake. A terrible mistake. I didn't love you. I never did. I love my husband. We have a child, a boy. And now I'm expecting my second."

He was silent, those probing panther eyes searching her face. She felt the iron will crumbling. In a moment he would read the secrets of her innermost soul, ferret out the truth, discover something there she herself had no wish to know.

She rose abruptly. "I must be going. My friend—"

"I don't give a damn about your friend! Hannah—"

"There's no point in further discussion. Good day, Dr. Falconer."

He did not detain her.

Once in the corridor she felt weak, her watery knees threatening to give way under her. It disturbed her to think that Christian Falconer still had the ability to make her tremble. Damn him! she thought angrily. He knows he has this power over me. I hate him for it, I hate myself.

At Sycamore, Travis was going through similar feelings. He and Elthea had just had another of their quarrels. Thus far they had managed to do their fighting behind closed doors, but this time warfare had broken out at the supper table. Elthea had mentioned Mama once too often and it had goaded Travis into a tirade. While Billy Ostler, taking his plate, had quietly slipped out the door, Guy had tried to mediate. But Travis was too riled up to listen and went at her until Elthea ran sobbing from the room.

After she had gone, Travis sat with hanging head, the heat slowly ebbing from his face. Finally he broke the awkward silence by apologizing to Guy. He didn't know what had come over him. It had been a trying day, what with the discovery that a coyote had carried off their best laying hen and a loose bull giving him a merry chase before he could be penned again. He was sorry, real sorry.

But he wasn't sorry. He just didn't want Guy to think badly of him. He hated himself for taking on so in front of Guy, hated Elthea. He knew he should feel pity for her, the wet, tearstained face, the red eyes, the belly swollen with his child. But he couldn't. She had lost her looks, had become what she always was, an ignorant, half-grown farm girl. She did nothing but whine about her mama and her pa and Bea and Caroline and Tom and all the numberless clan she had left behind in Georgia. It would have been easier, and far more pleasant, had she only given Sycamore a chance. But she had been set against coming from the start, and once at the ranch had turned her back on it, saying it was nothing like home.

To Travis Sycamore was more than home. He looked upon it as some kind of Eden. He loved the place, the smell of chaparral and greasewood, the distant roar of the surf on a quiet day, the freedom of wide-open spaces. Here he had no responsibilities, no need to make decisions. Guy did all that. He had only to complete a task Guy set out for him, receiving thanks and praise, neither of which Chad or Aunt Bess had ever thought of giving him. Sycamore suited him. If he had his druthers, he'd stay forever. He didn't want to go to the city and get more learning as Hannah wished. What for, when he was perfectly happy here?

Travis was having these thoughts as he sat milking Flossie one evening. The sun had already gone down behind the cliff and dusk had darkened the lengthening shadows of the barn. Travis found the dimness, the musty sweet scent of old hay soothing. He shifted his cheek on the cow's flank, reminding himself not to doze off, and was just doing that when he heard footsteps. Turning, he saw Flavia on the threshold.

"Oh, there you are, Travis. I'm to tell you supper will be late this evening."

"Thanks, Flavia. Elthea send you?"

"Yes." She came inside. "I stopped by on my way home from the McCrackens'."

"Stayin' for supper?"

"I haven't been asked." She laughed. "I couldn't, anyhow. I got to get on home." She came closer. "Need help?"

"No. I'm about done."

He gave the cow a thank-you pat on her side and stood up.

Flavia smiled at him, dimpling at the corners of her mouth. She had a very slim waist and lovely, large breasts. The nipples straining at the cambric bodice mesmerized him. He wondered how they would feel bared to his hands.

She giggled and he tore his eyes away. "Shore"—he swallowed—"shore you won't stay for supper? *I'm* askin'."

"Would you like me to?" She cocked her head flirtatiously.

" 'Course I would."

"Mmmmm." Her tongue flicked out and caressed her bottom lip. "Well, *you* asking makes the difference."

"Who, me?"

Again she laughed, a gay, happy sound that echoed under the rafters. "Yes, you."

"I thought you was sweet on Guy."

Her nose wrinkled. "Why, Guy is just like a big brother to me. But you . . ." She drew even closer. "You're a very handsome young man, Travis."

He could feel her breath on his face; her eyes, smiling at him, were a smoky blue. And those breasts were almost touching his chest. Travis, entranced, enchanted, felt a growing tightness in his crotch. One part of his mind said, Git goin'. This is 'xactly what happened between you and Elthea, but the other said, I ain't had any lovin' for so long. And she wants it, I can tell.

"I liked you right away, Travis," Flavia whispered. One finger traced his cheek.

He caught her wrist, stared at her, swallowed, then suddenly pulled her into his arms, his mouth claiming the cherry-ripe lips in a hungry kiss. She was soft, yielding, but as the kisses grew prolonged Flavia began to respond, opening her mouth so that his tongue could enter.

"Flavia . . ." Her name emerged raggedly.

His hands moved across and down her back, pushing her buttocks into his yearning groin. She murmured something, her hot breath tickling his ear. His hips rotated and she moaned, clasping him tightly about the neck.

He lifted her and carried her into the shadows.

This was a far different experience for him than it had been with Elthea. His wife had been passive, accepting his lust with a virginal acquiescence, but Flavia matched him in mood, in desire, in wild unbridled kisses, her naked body pressed to his, moving with him. She touched and fondled in a way that drove him mad. Elthea had never touched him *there*. She would have been terrified at the mere suggestion. But Flavia not only cupped his rigid member in her hot hand, she ran her fingers over the sensitive tip, kissed and licked it until the top of his scalp seemed to lift from his head. Where had she learned such tricks, how did she know?

"Hold back," she whispered, his come about to burst.

"I can't . . . oh God!"

He plunged inside and not a moment too soon. His seed exploded, sending him into a convulsive, shivering ecstasy such as he had never experienced before.

As he clung to her in the sweet, euphoric aftermath two thoughts came simultaneously to him—one, that Flavia was not a virgin, and the other, that he was now an adulterer.

Guilt and shame rolled him from Flavia's warm body. What had he done? What if Hannah or Guy should find out? And Billy. He had forgotten about Billy, who slept in the loft above. Had he heard, seen? Would he tell if he had? He and Billy got along, they were friendly, though Travis didn't see much of the old man. Suppose even now he was up there clucking his tongue silently?

Travis sat up, drawing on pants, shirt, boots, his eyes averted from Flavia. She lay on her back, naked, shamelessly uncovered, her head pillowed on her arms, watching him.

"Travis, maybe we could get together like this again."

"No. Not that I didn't 'preciate—but no. I'm sorry. I'm a married man." What if he had gotten her pregnant? He broke out in a cold sweat. It was bad enough the first time, trapped into a marriage with Elthea. But now! What a mess! Hannah would probably boot him off the place. "This ain't goin' to happen again. Do you hear?"

She smiled at him, her eyes soft and liquid. "I love you, Travis."

"For chrissake, I'm married! Worse luck, dammit! Do you understand?"

"No."

Turning, he stamped out of the barn.

Chapter XIII

Hannah and Tess sat side by side on the train. They were traveling home, first to Monterey, then by stage to Big Sur where Leonard would pick them up in the wagon. They had spoken very little. Tess at the window watched the countryside slip by with an unseeing eye, the towns and hamlets indistinguishable from one another. Hannah, immersed in her own thoughts, had not taken much notice of Tess until the train came to a temporary halt in Burlingame.

"We have ten minutes, here," Hannah said. "Shall we get out and stretch our legs?"

"Go on, if you want. I think I'll just sit." She gave Hannah a wan smile.

"Are you feeling poorly, Tess?" She looked much worse now than she had earlier when they had come up to San Francisco. Her skin had a sallow, almost greenish hue, and the pain lines between her eyes had grooved themselves more deeply.

"I'll be all right," Tess said, attempting another smile, little better than the first.

"I'm sure of it. You never did tell me what Dr. Russell said."

"Dr. Russell." Tess's lips twisted in scorn. She turned

her head back to the window. "I know one thing," she went on bitterly, speaking to the window. "It's hell to be a woman."

To this astounding remark Hannah had no reply. She had always thought that Tess enjoyed her role as wife and mother—cheerful, courageous, never complaining, a strong, happy person who seemed content with her life. Now she was saying it was hell.

"You don't understand, do you?" Tess asked, turning back to Hannah. "I wouldn't either if I were young and just starting out."

"But, Tess, you aren't that old. You talk like—"

"I'm going to die, Hannah. Six months, if I'm lucky, a year if I'm not."

Hannah refused to believe it. "You're talking nonsense! Is that what Dr. Russell told you? The old fool."

"He may be an old fool. But he's right."

"How can you be sure? Die of what? Oh, Tess, please . . ."

She took the older woman's hands in hers. They were cold, limp, as if the life had already gone out of them. "Doctors make mistakes. We'll consult another. They have specialists now. Perhaps someone in Monterey . . ."

"It's no use, Hannah. I've suspected something was really wrong and now I know." Her eyes were dark with misery.

Fear brought a lump to Hannah's throat. "It's not like you to be so down. You're tired, you miss your bed. Once you get home and take your medicine, you'll feel better."

"Yes," Tess agreed without conviction, "I'm tired. Truthfully, though, I wish I was going anywhere right now but home."

"Oh, Tess. What is it that ails you?"

Tess shrugged and fixed her eyes on the window again. The train jolted and slowly began to move again. Hannah, leaning toward Tess, saw a tear roll down her cheek.

"What is it?" she repeated, her heart twisting with pity.

Tess took a handkerchief from her reticule and wiped the tear away. "I have a growth—there—you know? The female part where the babies come out," she added delicately. "It's cancer."

"But surely Dr. Russell . . ."

"No mistake. He said so. I believe him. He said . . ." Her voice broke and she strove to regain her composure. "It was God's will. His way to punish the wicked."

"*You,* wicked? Oh, Tess, what a foul thing to say."

"I damaged myself. I did it with a crochet hook." The tears were coming thick and fast now. Hannah put her arm around Tess's shoulders, drawing her close. Crochet hook? What had that to do with anything? Hannah, thoroughly mystified, murmured words of solace.

Tess sniffed loudly as she groped for her handkerchief. "I'm sorry. Made a nuisance of myself. Crying like that. It's not like me."

"No," said Hannah, hoping this was a dark, passing mood, that Tess out of fatigue and illness had embroidered, that she wasn't really going to die.

"You see," Tess said, giving a final blow into the handkerchief, "it first happened three years ago. I couldn't face having another child. Not at my age. I just couldn't. The big, heavy stomach and the swollen ankles and the dizzy spells. And another one when we had so many. What for? I couldn't. I had heard that you could get rid of it by shoving a crochet hook—well, you know where— and you'd miscarry. And that's what happened. I did it twice. Last year was the second time. Dr. Russell knew right away. He said that other women had come to him in the same fix and it served them right."

"No! It doesn't!" Hannah exclaimed forcibly, remembering how the doctor had rebuffed her request for a sponge. "He's an old stick who believes women are nothing but brood mares. You aren't wicked—nor am I."

"You?"

She told Tess about her conversation with Dr. Russell.

"Yes, I've heard about the sponge. From the same woman who advised the crochet hook. She said the sponge was an old wives' tale. It didn't work."

"I don't know," Hannah said. "I don't see why it wouldn't be worth a try."

"The trouble is, we're so *ignorant* about our own bodies."

"We're supposed to be," said Hannah. "It's not something you discuss, especially with men, even your own husband."

Could she have discussed it with Christian? she wondered, his dark brows, the handsome face suddenly imprinting itself on her mind. He was a doctor, he had whores as patients, he . . .

"I'm not going to tell Leonard or the family. I don't want them to know," Tess was saying. "Promise you won't say anything?"

"But . . ."

Tess gripped her hand. "Promise."

"I promise."

In the days that followed, Tess's plight weighed on Hannah's mind. She could not help but imagine how she might someday come to the same impasse. One evening as she and Guy were sitting in front of the fire, Guy mending a bridle, Hannah sewing (she was unable to look at a crochet hook since Tess had bared her soul) she said, "Guy, if I didn't want more than four children, would you mind?"

He looked up from his work, a surprised expression on his face. "Is there any reason?" He paused, his eyes suddenly concerned. "The doctor didn't say—there's nothing wrong with you, is there?"

"No, no, Guy. I'm perfectly all right. Dr. Russell assured me I would have a healthy baby. It's just that I don't want to have a large family."

"Well, I had hoped . . ."

"I know you did, darling. But think of it: five, six, seven tots and how little we could do for them. We'd have a hard time just keeping them in shoe leather."

"You talk as if we'd always be struggling. I mean to do much better. It takes time, Hannah."

"I know, my dear. And I have complete faith in you.

You'll make Sycamore Ranch a profitable venture, I'm sure. Perhaps I'm selfish. I dread thinking of myself going in the same direction as my mother, who had one pregnancy after another, or those women I knew who came to Hull House, old and worn before their time, loving their children but unable to do for them because there were so many. Oh, Guy, I hope you don't hate me for it."

"Hate?" He dropped the bridle as he rose from his chair. "I don't ever want to hear you say that word." He leaned over and kissed her upturned face. "My sweet Hannah. Of course I don't mind, if that's your wish. I'm not a beast, but Guy, your husband, the man who loves you."

She grasped his hands, tears crowding her lashes. "I love you, too, Guy."

And she meant it. Guy was a good man in every sense of the word, selfless, uncomplicated, loving her without quibble or qualification. How fortunate for her that he had come into her life when she needed him most, how fortunate she had not married someone like Christian, who was everything Guy was not: selfish, self-indulgent, deceitful. Guy would never stray. Flavia could toss her head and twitch her shoulders, be coy or bold, but Hannah knew Guy, even if tempted, would never by word or deed be unfaithful. Christian, on the other hand, could go to bed with dozens of women, swear eternal love, and even propose marriage without giving the consequences of his actions a second thought. No threat of hellfire would ever deter him. How could it, when he was a demon himself? Well, perhaps that was too strong, too fanciful, too much like a figure of speech in one of Preacher Wright's thundering sermons. Yet Christian's charm was devilish, hypnotic. Simply being in his masterful arms, feeling the strong heart beat beneath her ear, the hands sliding down her back and up to cradle her breasts, eloquent eyes bending toward her, the mouth meeting hers, so possessive, so thrilling . . .

She caught herself with a start. Guy was observing her. "You seem so far away, Hannah. What are you thinking about? Something pleasant, I'd guess, from the look on your face."

"Oh, yes," she lied quickly. "I was imagining how nice it would be for Mark to have a little brother to play with."

The Panic had finally reached King City. Beginning in '93, it had rolled over the country, leaving a trail of failed banks, mortgage foreclosures, bankruptcies, and unemployment. Now two years later the nation was still in the doldrums. Prices for cattle were at rock bottom. Leonard had never seen them so low.

"Hardly pays to drive the critters to market," he said.

He and Guy, gambling that rates were bound to rise in the near future, kept their herds on the range. Others felt that selling cattle at any price and then using the money to purchase purer breeds—Hereford yearlings, for instance, which would come cheaply now and later would fetch more than range cattle—was a wiser choice. Leonard thought not, and Guy, who had great respect for his neighbor's judgment, followed his example.

But money would be scarce this year. The tanbark, another, smaller, source of income, was still plentiful though the trees were becoming more difficult to reach. Guy was forced to ask the bank for a postponement of his monthly payment. He also went further into debt with the same bank when he borrowed to buy seed for oats and grain that he, Billy, and Travis would plant. Guy's hope was that, if weather conditions permitted, they could reap a bountiful crop and sell the surplus. The future crop, yet unsown, was held as security by the bank.

Elthea had her baby at Christmas, a little girl she named Clara after her mother. Despite screaming throughout the five and a half hours it took her to deliver, Elthea had a relatively easy time of it. Unlike Hannah, who had suffered her ordeal alone, Elthea was attended by Tess Barlow, Hannah, and Frances Anderson.

Flavia had come along to cook and care for Mark while the women were preoccupied with the birthing.

Travis, though somewhat disappointed because it was not a boy, managed to accept the usual congratulations with a smile. When he went in to see Elthea, so small and frail-looking with baby Clara nested under her chin, he felt a few moments of tenderness.

"You all right?" he asked, awkward, his hands shoved into his pockets.

Hannah, tidying up, whispered in his ear, "Kiss her, you fool."

Travis obeyed. "Elthea . . ." He was going to say something about a new beginning but she interrupted.

"I wish Mama was here to see her."

"Yup," he said, stepping back. Mama again. There wasn't going to be any new beginning. She had taken up where she had left off.

"Ain't she purty?" Elthea asked.

"Shore is." How Elthea could see anything pretty in that red, wrinkled creature was beyond him. He tried to think of the child as his but it was hard to make the connection.

"Travis, do you 'magine when the baby is older we might visit home for a spell?"

There was that whine again that drove him around the bend. "I ain't got the money to get there, Elthea," he said roughly. "Georgia is a long way off. Why can't you be happy here?"

Tears brimmed her eyes and rolled down her cheeks. "I know it's a long way off. But I'm so sick for home." She turned her face to the wall.

"You just had you a purty baby," he said. "Now think of little Clara."

"I *am* thinking of her."

"Well, dammit . . . !" Hannah's look stopped him. In a moment they would be quarreling again. Ashamed and angry, he turned and left the room.

Crossing the yard past the henhouse, he went into the barn and took the milking pail from its hook. Milking always made him feel easier. He had been at it a few minutes when Flavia appeared.

This time there was no self-conscious give and take.

He forgot the cow. Getting up from the milking stool, he took her hand and led her to a back stall where a heap of last year's hay made a sweet-smelling bed.

She was hot and quivering under his kisses. Her slim body, the ripe breasts, that entrancing triangle of fur between her legs was given over to him in a frenzy of passion. He took longer than he had the first time and her moans of pleasure as he sipped at her breasts, as his seeking fingers, guided to the moist place, slowly, gently teased, increased his own desire. Now she was begging him to put an end to her torment, panting and gasping, and when he entered her she wrapped her legs about his hips, lifting herself to get the full sensation of each downward thrust. "I love you, I love you!" she cried hoarsely. But Travis, gritting his teeth, soared beyond the reach of her words.

It had rained the third week in December, a series of showers that portended a wet January. But after that rain—nothing. Every morning the sun came up in a blaze of pink and gold, rising high in a cloudless blue sky. The newly sown oats and grain poking green shoots up from the soil seemed to be waiting for the life-giving moisture that would coax them to grow. The wind blew in from the sea with a tantalizing damp iodine smell, the fog bank hanging back on the far horizon. But no water dropped from the heavens. There was still February, Guy said, and March.

One balmy morning Leonard and Flavia stopped by on their way to King City where they planned to sell two of their colts.

"I hope we're not in for a drought," Leonard said grimly, gazing up at the sky. "But it don't look too good."

Flavia laughed. "Oh, Pa, it'll probably pour buckets while we're halfway to King City."

When Hannah asked about Tess, Flavia said, "She's getting along fine. She's making Polly and me new petticoats." Polly was Flavia's younger sister. "Ma sends her love."

To Hannah this seemed a good sign. Tess busy with sewing, sending her love. Perhaps (it was Hannah's daily hope and prayer) Dr. Russell had been mistaken or perhaps Tess's growth had become benign.

So it was with some surprise that Hannah, kneeling in the kitchen garden, thinning out her beet plants, looked up from her task to see Polly loping toward her on the old nag the children used for riding. She was sobbing bitterly.

"What is it?"

The horse, an ancient, jug-eared piebald, its flanks heaving, had stopped short, lowering its foaming muzzle.

"It's Ma—I can't . . . ! Oh, God! She's—something terrible . . ." She began to laugh hysterically.

Hannah dragged her from the saddle, shook then slapped her, but all she got was a storm of incomprehensible words.

Something had happened to Tess, an accident of some kind. That was the only thing Hannah could make out.

She hurried the girl into the house and asked Elthea to tell Guy she had gone over to the Barlows and if she wasn't back by supper he was not to worry.

"You'd best stay here for a while," she said to a still-sobbing Polly. "When you're feeling better and your pony's rested, you can come on home."

Polly covered her face and wept all the harder.

The younger children were standing on the veranda gazing out toward the lane and the gate when Hannah arrived. They had the stunned, dumb look of white-faced cattle. No one spoke or moved as Hannah approached. The two littlest ones, usually so garrulous, clung to sister May's skirts, silently staring at her with round, frightened eyes.

Hannah dismounted and tied her horse to the rail. "Where's your mother?" The oldest boy, Tom, made a movement toward the inside of the house with his thumb. His freckles stood out on his ashen face in startling color.

Hannah entered the house. The main room was both

kitchen, dining room, and parlor with a huge fieldstone
fireplace running the length of one wall. The table had
the remnants of the noon meal, dirty, unscraped plates,
a pot with a few beans at the bottom, a loaf still on the
bread board, knives and forks bundled together as if
someone had started to clear. A fly buzzing over the
empty milk pitcher was the only sound in the room.

Hannah, looking around, stood for a moment gazing
at the fireplace with the odd feeling that something had
changed since she had last been in the Barlow house,
though she couldn't say what.

She called, "Tess? Tess, are you here?"

She turned and went to the door of the bedroom that
Tess and Leonard shared. She paused with her hand on
the latch, suddenly afraid to open it, afraid of what she
might find.

"Tess!"

The door creaked as she inched it open. Peeking fear-
fully around the edge, she suddenly stopped, wanting to
slam it shut, not to look, not to see. But it was too late.
There, sprawled on the floor, lay Tess Barlow, her bloodied face and head scarcely recognizable. A derringer—a
Civil War memento—rested beside her outflung arm.
That was what had looked odd, Hannah thought, her
mind reeling with horror. A gun had been missing from
the pair that had always hung over the fireplace. Tess
had taken the derringer down, gone into the bedroom,
placed it in her mouth, and pulled the trigger.

Oh, Tess, Tess!

There was no doctor to call (too late for that), no
sheriff, no coroner. Miles away from the resources one
could turn to for assistance or guidance in violent death,
Hannah had only herself to rely upon. Later she would
fetch Guy and Travis. But for the present she must deal
with the children, with the bloody mess on the floor.
She could not allow herself the luxury of breaking down.

Forcing her mind to numbness, she stepped around
Tess and was drawing a blanket from the bed when she
noticed the note on the pillow.

"I couldn't stand the pain anymore. I'm sorry. Tess."

She had suffered in silence until the malignancy like a many-tentacled octopus had gripped her in an agony she could no longer bear.

Hannah's eyes filled with tears as she drew the blanket over Tess. Then she went back out to the veranda, where the children still stood in a cluster, waiting, hoping for some grown-up to rescue them from their nightmare.

Tess was buried under a wind-warped cypress on a slope high above the sea. It was a lonely site where on quiet days one could hear the muted roar of the surf far below. Flavia had chosen the spot because she believed her mother would have liked it.

"Mama hardly ever got a chance to be alone," Flavia said with a mature perceptiveness that warmed Hannah. "She loved the sea, Mama did. When she had time—and that wasn't too often—she liked to come here to watch the cormorants diving for fish and the seals sunning themselves. Now she can look all she wants."

Of all the children Flavia had wept the most. She blamed herself for going to King City, for not being home on the day her mother had killed herself. Hannah had tried to explain that it wouldn't have made any difference. Tess had reached the limit of her endurance.

"She's at peace now, she's released from her suffering," Hannah said. "I loved her, too, and God knows I'll miss her. But I can't find it in my heart to fault her for what she's done."

Frances was angry. She felt that if her sister had consulted a doctor earlier she might have been saved. At the wake she blamed Leonard, calling him a skinflint and insensitive. A bereft Leonard ordered Frances from the ranch and told her not to come back. Hannah's efforts to smooth things over were quashed by Guy, who felt this was not the time to interfere in family matters.

The next day Leonard wrote to Tess's other sister, a widow, Ruth Hertzinger, living in Ohio, informing her of Tess's death. Ruth arrived three weeks later, a woman older than Tess but strongly favoring her in the eyes and

shape of the nose. Flavia maintained it was hardly a
visit.

"She likes it at the Barlow ranch. She hasn't got
much back in Ohio. No children. Living with her dead
husband's people. I guess in six months, maybe less,
she'll be my new stepmama."

"Do you mind?" Hannah asked.

"If I did it wouldn't matter much."

February passed with a few tormenting clouds hovering over the crest of the Santa Lucias, but no rain. The
courtyard well went dry and Hannah was forced to lug
buckets of water up from the spring to save her kitchen
garden. The oats and grain withered and died, and in the
meadows last year's dun-colored grass turned gray. There
was no new growth, no mantling of green on the hills.
The webbed, crosshatched earth crackled underfoot. Then
the Santa Ana winds began to blow from the hot dry
valley to the east, drawing the very last vestige of moisture from the already parched and thirsty land.

One afternoon, Hannah, coming out of the house,
saw a column of smoke rising from the northwest field.
Puzzled, she stared at it. A campfire? They had only a
rare transient, a lone hunter now and then. But who
would stop to cook a meal in the middle of the day?

It wasn't a camper. The grass was on fire!

Hannah ran to the barn where Travis was getting
ready to ride out to check on a cow expected to calve
any day.

"There's a fire, Travis!" she exclaimed breathlessly.

He hurried out. "God Almighty! God Almighty!"

"We can't just stand here, Travis. We'll have to put it
out before it spreads. Where's Billy? Billy! Billy!" she
called frantically.

"He ain't here. Guy sent him to look for a lost steer
this mornin' and I ain't seen him since. Probably asleep
under a tree somewhere."

"Wouldn't you know. And Guy gone over to the
Barlows. The three of us will have to do it ourselves."

"Three? You ain't thinkin' of Elthea?"

But Hannah was already running back to the house.

"I cain't leave the baby," Elthea said.

"You'll have to. The children will be all right. Come on, hurry!"

Mounted on horses, leading a fourth laden with hemp sacks and spades, they headed in the direction of the smoke, now billowing in black clouds and fanning out in gray banners across the horizon.

"Thank God the wind is from the east!" Hannah shouted. It was blowing hard, but toward the ocean, and the fire would be stopped either by the steep canyon where the vegetation retained some sea-laden moisture or the sea beyond. As they rode, a herd of bellowing, stampeding cattle came into view about a half mile to the right of them. Packed together, their hooves thundering over the dry ground, long horns glinting in the sun, they charged in mad, unseeing fury, breaking through fences, trampling everything before them. Though they were at a safe distance, a pale, frightened Elthea would have bolted and taken off in the opposite direction if Hannah hadn't guessed her intent. She rode alongside Elthea, blocking her escape. Elthea shouted something but the wind tore the words from her mouth.

When they reached the fire they could see it was eating away more of the meadow than they had first thought. Flames leaped from patch to patch of dry grass, widening laterally along the rim of the cliff. A dead madrone in the fire's path caught, its bleached branches sprouting shimmering flags of flame, then, a few moments later, exploding in a shower of fiery sparks. A stand of twisted pine was next, the fire lapping at the trunks, fingering oily needles, running across the branches, filling the air with the odor of resin and smoke. Flocks of birds flew overhead—turkey buzzards, wrens, bluejays, and gulls—while on the ground, wildlife, the small creatures that inhabited the chaparral and meadows, having lost their fear of horses and humans in the greater terror of fire, scampered and scurried past them.

Travis and Hannah dismounted, momentarily at a loss as to what to do. Neither of them had ever dealt with an actual fire: a pan of grease on the stove flaming ceiling-high, an ember from the fireplace catching a rag rug was the extent of their experience. A brush fire was new to them and the frightening speed with which it traveled awed them. The tall, sere grass was like closely bunched tinder. Crackling and popping, it burned with a hot ferocity that scorched their faces.

Travis said, "Best cut a path along the grass here just in case the wind decides to change directions."

From a sack he took out a scythe. "Only could get my hands on one."

Hannah said, "We'll use our hands and pull."

They moved quickly in three parallel rows, pulling and scything as fast as they could move, Elthea saying she couldn't, Hannah saying she could.

Suddenly the wind died. The fire was raging down the cliffside now, eating scrub oak, chaparral, laurel, and pine at a terrifying speed. A tall redwood erupted in orange flame, then another and another. A great smoky pall, bronze at the center, a dirty gray at the edges, blocked out the sky.

"Keep cutting," Travis urged, "the wind's changed."

They continued to work feverishly though the worst of the fire seemed to have burned itself out on the clifftop. As Hannah bent to her task she felt the sting of a hot ember on her sleeve. Straightening, she quickly smothered it with the hem of her skirt. Then another fell at her feet, where it sputtered, flaring into a tiny flame. Hannah stamped it out. But a few feet ahead a low-lying bush was already burning.

"The shovels!" Hannah shouted.

They all ran back to the tree where the restive horses were tethered and the shovels lay on the ground. Returning to the spreading fire, they worked in sweating fury, using the large flat ends, beating at the hot coals, the incipient little spurts of fired grass, hoping the west wind would not pick up. The blaze was raging far below now, a towering inferno, shooting up, dancing, crackling, leaping, consuming timber and undergrowth with a deafening roar. The smoke rising from the narrow confines of the canyon, which acted like a chimney, blinded them. Choking and coughing, they spanked and whacked, running here and there, snuffing a flame, killing a spark, smacking at the licking, crawling fire that was slowly pushing them back.

Elthea was the first to give up.

"I cain't," she wailed. "I'm a-near to faintin'. I cain't." She dropped the shovel and sank to the ground.

"All right," Travis said. "Are you able to move the horses to that madrone?" He pointed.

"I ain't got the strength, Travis."

"Then get out of the way," Travis said.

Hannah's back and knees ached. Each time she lifted the shovel it seemed to grow heavier, a weight that dragged at her arms. Tears fell from her smarting eyes, streaking her perspiring, grimy cheeks. She could feel the swell of painful blisters on her fingers where they grasped the wooden handle. And yet she worked on, dizzy, her strength ebbing, with no visible sign their efforts were having any effect. The flames continued to hop and skip, igniting the oily greasewood, eating at the bone-dry turf. For every red-hot tongue extinguished, two would take its place.

Just as it seemed she could not raise her arms once more, Guy, Leonard, Mr. Anderson and his two sons, and Mr. McCracken came galloping across the meadow. Jumping from their mounts, they began to beat at the grass with heavy burlap sacks. A few minutes later Polly and Flavia drove up in the wagon loaded with buckets of sand. Water was too precious, Flavia explained to an exhausted Hannah, and sand worked just as well.

It took less than fifteen minutes for them to get the fire under control. Down below, the holocaust had reached the water's edge. It would burn for two days, decimating Guy's tanbark and redwood, leaving a blackened wedge between the walls of the canyon. The charred underbrush would rejuvenate at the next rain, but it would take years for the trees to replace themselves.

On the way back to the house Leonard told a glum Guy, "Lucky for you, you didn't lose more."

"Lost all my tanbark," Guy said in a tired, dispirited voice. "That hurts."

"Look at it this way," Leonard said. "It could have burned over your range, burned your house, maybe even spreading to our ranches. I've seen thousands of acres go up."

The men talked of other fires. "Beats me how this one started," Leonard said. "Usually it takes a bolt of lightning in a thunderstorm to set a blaze off."

It was at this point that Guy asked, "Where's Billy?"

"I don't know," Hannah said. "Travis said he went out this morning and we haven't seen him since. Funny, isn't it?"

"Damned funny. The old coot could have lit our fire. Probably fell asleep smoking, then when he woke and saw what had happened, he scooted off. Would be just like him."

They were never to know for certain whether Billy was the cause of the blaze. When they got back to the house, Guy discovered that Billy's few possessions were gone, the bed stripped of its blankets. Later they heard he had been seen in Jolon, begging a wagon ride to King City.

Washing up at the spring, Hannah felt a sudden pain grip her stomach. It lasted half a minute, then went away. The excitement, she thought, a stomach upset. But as she was helping Elthea in the kitchen the pain returned. This time she recognized it for what it was. Labor pains.

An hour later she lost the baby.

Guy took the news badly. Concerned for Hannah and her well-being, he nevertheless found it hard to hide his disappointment. That night Hannah could hear him weeping as he sat alone in the parlor before the empty fireplace.

She herself cried bitterly for days, inconsolable tears of loss mingled with guilt. She had not wanted more than four, she had told Guy, and now she felt as though she was being punished for putting that limit to a man who longed for children. Of his own. Guy, who did not know he had none. And she had wanted this baby, wanted it with all her heart, looked forward to the child even as she spoke of sponges. Was she wicked, as Dr. Russell had accused Tess? Oh God, she thought, what if I'm destined to lose all my future babies? But I can't think that, I won't. I'll make it up to Guy, she promised herself grimly. I swear I will.

Chapter XIV

The drought continued. It was March now and hope of rain died a slow, strangling death. One of the two field wells—like the one in the courtyard—dried up. The shrunken pond became brackish, covered over with a green slime. While the spring still bubbled weakly, the water it gave was only sufficient for household use. The bleached earth between stalks of papery grass became more and more cracked and fissured, giving little sustenance to the restless cattle. Again Guy led them to the small canyons that had not been burned out and where streams trickled thinly over stony beds.

By April when these streams disappeared and the vegetation on their banks had been browsed to the roots, the cattle began dying for lack of pasturage.

"It's cruel to let those poor beasties starve," Guy said. He, Hannah, and Travis were standing over the corpse of a steer who had literally expired at the barn door. "But I don't know what to do about it."

Even if he had wanted—or could afford—to buy alfalfa and hay, he would have been unable to do so. The large cattle companies in the valley had managed to absorb the smaller farms and so had cornered the feed market for their own use during drought years. They also had the resources to dam streams and irrigate their crops, something the independent ranchers like Guy and Leonard could not do.

"Doesn't seem like there's an end to our troubles," Guy said, still mourning over Hannah's miscarriage. That to him had seemed like the worst of their bad luck. Yet, for Hannah's sake, he tried not to dwell on it. "I'll write to the bank and see if they can't hold us a little longer." They were three months in arrears with their payments.

"Won't the animal hides we've taken from the dead cattle fetch something?" Hannah asked.

"Not much."

Hannah had never seen Guy so worried. Having overcome his initial dismay at the neglected state of Sycamore, he had thrown himself into the job of improving the ranch to the point where it was beginning to sustain them. But now, with bad weather, disease (six steer had to be put down because of black leg only a week earlier), and falling market prices, Sycamore had become a losing proposition.

"Some mornings," Guy said, looking out past the steer's carcass, his eyes fixed on the never-changing blue horizon, "when I go out there and see one of our cows standing in a little hollow against the warm side of an embankment to gain strength from the sun so she can give birth, I want to cry. Chances are a coyote will get the calf anyway. They're getting bolder. Hardly even wait for night anymore." He sighed, turning to Hannah. "Seems to me, maybe I ought to sell."

"Sell?" Hannah was shocked. "Why, you haven't been here three years. It takes five to homestead a place that's nothing but wilderness. I can't see letting Sycamore go before we've given it a good try."

In her schoolgirl days Hannah had never pictured herself on a ranch. She had imagined her future to be involved in teaching, perhaps in a women's college, instructing young, active minds, living in a world of books and stimulating conversation. Somewhere in this daydream a husband had stood in the background, a faceless, kindly male who shared her profession and her aspirations.

But that had been a fantasy. Before Christian. Before Guy. When she married, she had put aside her girlish dreams for good. She had sworn to herself she would make Guy a good wife, a vow redoubled after the birth of Mark. She would not only make him a good wife but do everything in her power to see that he succeeded at Sycamore. She was not going to allow Guy to abandon a project he had looked forward to for so many years. These were unfortunate times, but they would pass.

"We shouldn't even *think* of selling," she said. "Isn't that so, Travis?"

"Shore," said Travis, looking uneasily from Guy to Hannah. The thought of abandoning Sycamore scared him.

"Well?" Hannah asked anxiously of Guy.

He smiled, although Hannah could see his heart wasn't in it. "I guess you're right. We haven't got that much more to lose."

Hannah was disappointed in Guy's answer. She wanted a positive affirmation, an optimistic look into the future. The drought couldn't last forever.

"Wouldn't we feel terrible," she asked, "if we did sell and it rained and rained?"

Guy cracked his knuckles, an annoying habit he had recently acquired. "We can give it another year, I suppose. But, Travis, you don't have to stay if you don't want to. I can't pay you the wages I'd hoped to. If you'd like to leave, go up to the city with your wife and little girl and get yourself a job, I won't object."

"I ain't aimin' to leave, Guy. I like it here."

In the middle of March Guy negotiated a trade with Horace King, owner of a sheep ranch near Anderson's Cove. For allowing Guy to graze his cattle on his property at the creek bottom where the grass still grew, Guy would give Horace one third of his stock. Hannah thought one third was far too much, but Guy said he'd lose close to that number if he didn't get the herd to grass and water.

The day before Travis and Guy were to drive the

cattle down the steep track to Horace's ranch was spent rounding them up. Because the men were too busy to come in for their noon meal, Hannah took it out to them.

"Elthea might have been a little more generous with the biscuits and gravy," Travis grumbled, looking into his dinner bucket.

"I'm the one who dished up," Hannah said. "Elthea's taken Clare and gone over to the Barlows'."

Of late a friendship had sprung up between Polly Barlow and Elthea. What the two girls found in common Travis couldn't fathom, since Polly was fond of ranch life and loved the Coast Range country and Elthea hated both. Maybe, Travis thought, dipping his biscuit in the gravy, Elthea's cottoned to Polly because she listens to her complaints and just nods her head and gives Elthea a big, sympathetic smile. It probably tickles Polly to have Elthea confide in her. I can just hear Elthea sayin', "Yore the only one who's got feelin's around here." And now Elthea was at the Barlows' most likely tellin' Polly all about the fight they had last night. Only this time it wasn't a visit home Elthea had begged and cried for. She wanted to go back to Georgia for good. Well, dammit, let her talk her fool head off. It didn't bother him none.

At suppertime when the men came in from moving the herd into the fenced paddocks close to the house, Hannah was waiting on the porch step. From the set look of her mouth Travis sensed something was wrong.

"Elthea's gone," Hannah said, before he had a chance to speak.

"What y'mean, gone? She still at the Barlows'?"

"No, she's gone. I found this note."

Travis took it in his leather-gloved hands.

Dear Travis,
Im taken Clara home. I stole the egg money to buy me a trane tickut. Tell Hana Im truly sorry. Ill pay her back when I get a job. Dont come after me, Travis. I aint comen back.

                                        Elthea

Ill leave my pony at the Post ranch.

The Post ranch was the last stop of the Monterey coach on its south coast route.

Travis looked up from the note, disbelief in his eyes. "Why didn't you chase after her, Hannah?"

"I just found the note. By now she's probably at the Posts'. The money she took will buy her a ticket on the stage as far as Monterey, but she won't have enough to get her on the train."

The egg money was cash and coins Hannah had earned each summer from the sale of eggs, blackberry preserves she put up, and wild honey she had gathered. Her customers were vacationers at the two fishing resorts on the coast and the camping people at Big Sur Village. She had been saving coins and dollar bills for two years now to buy pipes to carry water into the house from the spring. Providentially she had hidden most of her cache in a tobacco tin kept at the back of her wardrobe. Cash from recent sales she had temporarily put into a jar on the top shelf of the kitchen cupboard. It was this money Elthea had stolen.

"I'll go after her in the morning," Hannah said.

"No," Travis protested. "I'm going to get her now."

Guy said, "Don't be foolish. You can't go galloping over these hills in the dark. Wait until morning. Like Hannah says, she hasn't the money to take her very far."

"But if something happens . . . Dammit, why did she do such a fool thing?"

He was to blame; he knew it. That fight last night probably was the last straw. He'd said a lot of things that were downright mean. And he'd hit her. He had never done that before. She'd made him so mad. But he never dreamed she'd leave. Taking Clara, too. What if she got lost, took a wrong turn, got scared? What if some hunter, some tramp looking for work, found her, beat her up, raped her? He didn't love Elthea but she was his wife and Clara was his daughter. He should have taken better care of her, shouldn't have been rolling in the hay with Flavia.

"What about the stock?" Hannah asked. "Guy, you need Travis to help you in the morning."

"Leonard and I can do it ourselves."

"No, you can't. You know that even with three it takes some doing. You said so yourself. *I'll* go after Elthea. Flavia won't mind coming over and watching Mark."

"But it's my place as a husband," Travis argued. What must Hannah and Guy think of him? Couldn't hold his wife at home. Did they know about Flavia—guess? Oh God, what a fine kettle of fish! Damn Elthea!

"I know it's your place and how cut up you must be," Hannah assured her brother. "But, believe me, I can do as well as you. And you're needed here."

The next morning Hannah packed a small bag with her nightgown, an extra petticoat and a change of drawers, a hairbrush, a toothbrush, and a cake of lye soap. She wanted to be prepared should she need to spend a night, maybe two, in Monterey. The return stage was not always reliable. Guy gave her five dollars. At the last minute she decided to supplement it with her savings—just in case an emergency arose—tying it in a handkerchief and stuffing it down her bosom.

She didn't mind the ride to the Post ranch. Her mount, Theda, a dapple-gray mare, bought from the Barlows the previous year, was Hannah's favorite. Theda seemed to know the trail, stepping along at an easy trot on the level stretches, slowing to a surefooted walk whenever the path climbed a mountain, picking her way carefully down canyon walls. It was dim in the forest, but a pleasant green dimness. As Hannah rode she inhaled deeply of the ferny fragrance of butternut, hedge mint, and maidenhair growing in shady nooks where the water still ran. The crackle of fallen maple leaves under the horse's hooves, the soft wind soughing in the tall pines had a soothing effect, and a time or two she caught herself drowsing in the saddle. If it hadn't been for her errand, she would have enjoyed this break in her routine. What had possessed the girl to sneak away, thinking she could get home with a few dollars? Egg money. Hannah had never been impressed with Elthea's intellectual abilities, but now she wondered if the girl wasn't simpleminded. No, she concluded after some thought, she can be smart enough when she wants to. That she wasn't happy was no secret. Travis had exacerbated the situation by treating her with negligence or anger. If he once loved her, it was obvious that his love had cooled.

Why had he married her?

Probably because he had gotten her with child. Wasn't that the way of men? She was beginning to see that Travis, whom she had always loved and looked up to, had his share of faults. He hadn't really bettered himself by leaving Stonebridge. Though he was no longer under Chad's shadow, his financial situation was, if anything, worse. Back home at least he had been able to earn extra money. Now he was completely dependent on Guy.

And what of me? she asked herself. No, I'm not dependent. I'm Guy's helpmeet, his partner. There's a difference. Last year when they had asked her to take a teaching post at Big Sur School she had refused, though it was something she would have enjoyed doing. But Mark and Guy and the ranch came first. Maybe someday when Mark was older, going to school himself, and Sycamore could afford to hire help, then she'd think about teaching again. But not now.

Hannah reached the Post ranch before noon. She went at once to Barney's stable where she found Elthea's pony, Winkle, her nose buried in a hay box, running up a feed bill they could ill afford.

"Yes, I saw Elthea and her baby," Barney Post said. "They got on the Monterey stage yesterday."

Hannah received the news with disappointment. She had nurtured the hope that perhaps Elthea might have had second thoughts and had spent the night at the ranch with the idea of returning to Sycamore the following day. Now Hannah had no choice but to continue on to Monterey.

She left her horse at the stable and boarded the stage an hour later, asking for an outside seat next to the driver. Inside there were three women, only one of whom she knew. Mrs. Hoskins was the wife of a rancher up near Botchers Gap, a busybody who would bombard her with a torrent of questions Hannah would rather not answer. The fourth passenger was a small man wearing a frayed minister's collar (whether Catholic or Presbyterian was not certain). He had a bewildered look on his face as if he had somehow caught the wrong coach and was not quite sure it would take him back to civilization.

They set off at a smart clip, passing Swiss Canyon and soon after that Little River Hill. Creeping fig, thriving on sea air, covered the cliffs, giving the landscape a look of spring. The ocean glimpsed between canyon walls was emerald green along the shore, fading to apple green farther out, then merging into an aquamarine blue. In the distance Hannah could see the rocky point where there was talk of erecting a lighthouse. She asked the coachman about it and he shrugged in answer.

In addition to her suitcase, Hannah had brought a basket packed with cold chicken, biscuits, a jar of preserved plums, and a water flask. She had already eaten her noon meal and, feeling thirsty, reached in for her flask.

"Wass that you got in the boddle?" the coachman asked.

He had to repeat the question before Hannah understood that he had mistaken the contents of her flask for spirits and that he was very drunk.

"Water!" she shouted over the drumming hooves and the clatter of the rocking coach.

"Wass that?"

Realizing she couldn't make herself understood, she handed him the uncorked flask.

He took a swig, spat, and tossed the flask over the side before Hannah could shout in protest. She could hear the rattle and clank as the back wheels ground over it.

A few minutes later he brought the horses to an abrupt halt, the carriage behind bucking and bouncing as he slammed on the wheel brake. Cries of "God in heaven! What happened?" came from inside.

Where they were, Hannah could not tell. A broken

wooden fence covered with green lichen trailed along one side of the road and on the other the cliff fell away to an outcropping of granite. There was no habitation in sight, not a roof, barn, or hen roost, just the ancient fence with a squirrel perched atop a post stump staring at them out of beady eyes.

The coachman groaned. "I'm turrible sick." He heaved himself up and started to get down from his perch when he suddenly pitched forward, falling past the wheel to the ground below. He lay where he fell, his face in the dust.

The minister and Mrs. Hoskins got out. Hannah joined them.

"Dead drunk," Mrs. Hoskins proclaimed in a disgusted voice.

The minister, looking green and ill himself—though sober—took out a handkerchief and mopped his damp brow with a shaking hand.

"We ought to try and get the driver inside," Hannah said.

By pulling and tugging and lifting they finally managed to double the coachman up and squeeze him through the narrow door, depositing him on the floor. The two women sitting on the leather seats gathered their skirts fastidiously aside.

Mrs. Hoskins said, "I'm no good with horses. Can you handle them, Reverend?"

The minister's eyes opened wide. "No—oh, my, no. I have no idea . . ."

"Never mind," Hannah said. "I'll see what I can do."

She hoisted herself up and strapped herself to the boot. Then, giving the lead horse a light taste of the whip, she urged the team to "giddyup!" They responded, lunging forward, but the carriage, still braked, slid along behind until Hannah remembered and, groping for the lever, pulled it.

Now they were rolling along, the team trotting briskly, tugging at their bits, anxious to reach their buckets of oats at journey's end. Hannah's arms soon began to ache. Her one fear was the the horses, feeling a lighter hand on the reins, might suddenly take it into their heads to bolt. But they clipclopped on at a good pace for a mile or so, until they reached a fork in the road. The horses slowed, seemingly in hesitation. Two weathered, arrow-shaped signs were nailed to a contorted Torrey pine. One read: CARMEL—MONTEREY 15 MI. The other, pointing to the right, said: PALO COLORADO CANYON. Hannah, choosing the Monterey road, spurred the faltering team on with a crack of the whip. At the same moment a skunk scooted across the path, tangling itself in the lead horse's legs. He shied, going up on his hind legs. Coming down, he sprang into a gallop, carrying the rest of the team with him.

"Whoa! Whoa!" Hannah, bracing herself against the seat, frantically jerked on the reins. But she may as well have tugged at the frightened horses with a piece of string. Ignoring her signal—they didn't recognize it as belonging to their gruff master—they galloped faster, racing ahead, thundering on at a mad, hard-driving speed. Hannah pulled and shouted again and again until her throat was raw and her arms felt as though they were being torn from their sockets. The team pounded on, the coach rocking perilously from side to side as it bounced and swerved over ruts. When the road suddenly curved, the horses did not turn with it but ran straight ahead, leaving the road behind, taking off across a flat mesa covered with wild dune grass, charging with an insane swiftness down and over a dry, shallow water course, the stage tilting dangerously, the wheels spinning uselessly for a heart-stopping moment. On they drove. Above the din Hannah could hear the women screaming. All she could do was hang on, giving the horses their head, hoping they would tire and come to a halt. But they continued their breakneck flight, foam from their muzzles flicking back to spatter in Hannah's face. She lost her hat, the wind whipping it off, tearing at her hair, stinging her eyes. It was like a continuing nightmare rolling itself out, the landscape—tufted grass, bushes, stones, pitted gullies—flying past in a blur. Down they went again, in and over a dip. When they emerged,

Hannah's heart contracted in horror. Not a half mile away lay the edge of the high mesa and below it the sea.

Her left hand sought blindly again and again for the brake. Finally she found it and yanked with both hands, using a strength powered by terror. There was an awful grinding, clattering noise. The coach swayed and slid, the rear wheels leaving the ground, tilting Hannah forward, then bouncing down again.

But it worked. The horses, panting audibly, their wet sides heaving, slowed to a walk. Halting, they stood, heads hanging in a vast echoing silence.

The passengers tumbled out. One of the women had fainted and the other was ministering to her with sal volatile. Inside the coach the driver snored on.

"I could kill the drunken sot," Mrs. Hoskins said. "If it weren't for him—are you all right, Hannah?"

"Yes," a shaken Hannah replied.

Somehow Hannah found the road again and they traveled the rest of the way without mishap, arriving in Monterey after dark, hours late. Hannah was so stiff and sore she had to be helped down like an old woman. Thankfully her basket of food and her case, which she had stored under the seat, had not suffered the same fate as the minister's luggage. His portmanteau had worked itself loose from the rope on top of the coach and been lost somewhere on the mesa during their runaway flight. Though they had searched, they had not been able to find it.

Exhausted, grimy, gritty, tasting dust, wanting nothing more than to sink into a bed—any kind of bed— Hannah nevertheless walked from the coach stop to the railroad station. Scanning the waiting room, she saw at a glance that Elthea was not there. Could she have missed her, perhaps crossed paths? It did not seem likely, for they had passed no southbound coach on the way. There was some explanation, there had to be. Tomorrow would be time enough to decide what to do. She was too tired to think, too tired to find a hotel. She sank down on one of the hard waiting-room benches, one arm flung about her bag, the other resting on the basket in her lap. Her head slumped forward and she slept.

In the morning she opened her eyes to the sound of a snorting engine on the track outside the station door. Jumping to her feet, she hurried outside, afraid that the passengers had already boarded and that she might have missed Elthea. But a bearded man in a greasy, peaked cap told her they were loading freight and the train would not be leaving for at least an hour.

In the lady's lounge she brushed her hair, repinning it into a shining dark coil at the nape of her neck. She washed her face and hands and tried to get some of the dust from her clothes. No hat. She missed her hat. But thinking of how close she had come to disaster she was glad to be all of one piece and never mind the hat.

At the ticket window she said that she was looking for her sister-in-law.

"A small, thin girl with blond hair and a light-haired baby girl in her arms," Hannah described. "Have you seen her?"

"Blond hair? Baby girl? Seems I did. Yesterday, or was it the day before? Yesterday. She got on the San Francisco train with a gentleman, older than she. I thought they were father and daughter."

"It could have been someone else, I suppose."

"Could be. He called her Elthea."

Hannah's heart sank. "Can you describe him?"

"Portly. Red whiskers, big nose."

A stranger. God, oh God, who had she taken up with? "Did the man say where in San Francisco he was going?"

The ticket man plucked at his braces, smacking them smartly. "Well—I dunno—seems like I heard him mention the name Glendening. But whether 'twas a place or person, I can't say."

Elthea, after having paid for her stagecoach fare, would have had only a few coins left in her pocket. Hannah could imagine the girl's bewilderment as she stood in the depot staring at the posted fares. It must have been then that the portly man approached her. What had he prom-

ised in return for paying her way to San Francisco? And
once arriving in the city, what then? Surely Elthea must
have understood that she was still a continent away
from Georgia. Oh, the foolish, foolish girl.

"May I have a ticket to San Francisco?"

"One?" the trainman asked.

"Yes, one."

Hannah had no idea how she would go about looking
for Elthea with such meager information. She had only
the name Glendening and a description that might fit half
a dozen men. Yet the thought that she should turn back
did not occur to her. Elthea had been difficult to like.
Except for befriending Polly, she had rebuffed all over-
tures. Hannah supposed it was because the girl was
afraid to forge new ties that might replace the ones she
had with her own people, to her mind an act of disloy-
alty. But whether Hannah was fond of Elthea or not had
little to do with the need to find her. She was kin by
marriage, Hannah's sister-in-law, the child her niece.
And she was so young, so naive. This last worried
Hannah. Afraid for her, and pitying her, too, Hannah
hurried back to the stagecoach depot. There she wrote
out a note and sent it by return coach to the Post
ranch. She knew that Travis and Guy would go there,
anxious to know what had happened, if she did not
come home in two or three days. In her note Hannah
said that she had gone on to San Francisco and, hedging
a little, assured the two men that she had reliable information that would lead her to Elthea.

Hannah slept most of the way to San Francisco, arriving at the Broad Street terminal stiff, tired, but too
anxious to notice. From a woman in the stationmaster's
office she received the first bit of encouraging news.
Yes, there was a hotel named Glendening.

Leaving the depot, Hannah made for the first secondhand clothing shop she could find. There she bought a
cheap flat hat of black straw, ornamented with a gray
velour ribbon, and a pair of cotton gloves to replace her
dirty stained ones. Peering into the mirror the sales-
woman offered, she was satisfied that the hat, not the

most becoming one she had worn, at least made her look respectable.

She took a cable car up Clay Street, a steep hill that ascended from the Embarcadero. The Glendening Hotel was a narrow three-story frame building, its window blinds pulled, the worn wooden steps badly in need of paint. Hannah went in and up to the front desk. The clerk behind the counter was busy putting mail into a rack of pigeonholes. A portly figure with red hair.

"Sir." She rang the little silver-plated bell on the counter, hardly daring to hope that this was the man.

It was.

When he turned, she saw he had the red whiskers and big nose described by the ticket agent in Monterey.

"Well, madam?" He looked her over with narrow-lidded eyes. "Do you wish a room?"

Hannah straightened her spine. "I'm looking for someone. My sister-in-law, as a matter of fact. Mrs. Travis Blaine. Elthea. Small, slender, blond, carrying a baby girl. I was told I'd find her here."

She was immediately sorry she had tipped her hand. Of course he would deny ever having laid eyes on Elthea. Then what would she do?

To her surprise he said, "That one," in a tone of disgust. "She give me the slip. That's the last time I put myself out to help a soul that says she's needy. Said she didn't have a body in the world to borrow from. And here you are, her sister-in-law, come to look for her. A poor widow, she said, her husband dead and she wanting to go to San Francisco to look for work." He leaned on the counter, his face mottled with anger. "So what do I do, wooden-headed, kindhearted gentleman that I am? I promised her a job, bought her a ticket, and then the wench disappeared with never a word of thanks."

His outrage seemed genuine to Hannah. But the "job" he had offered to Elthea was open to question.

"You have no idea where she went?" Hannah asked.

"Didn't I say so? You want know what I think? I think she was lying. I think she had more than the price of her fare. She just saw me as an easy mark. The damned bitch!'' He paused. "What about you? You looking for work?"

"No, but thank you, sir." Hannah left quickly.

On the sidewalk Hannah did not know which way to turn, which way to go. She had eaten the last of the chicken and plum preserves the night before on the train. Hunger and lack of sleep made her feel giddy. She knew she ought to find a cheap cafe where she could have a meal before she fainted and made a public spectacle of herself. Squaring her tired shoulders, she began to walk down the street, trying to look purposeful and not to stagger. Turning a corner, she saw a restaurant, its window dressed with looped sausages. A placard posted on the door read KNACKWURST AND SAUERKRAUT, 15 CENTS A DISH.

After she had eaten and surreptitiously stuffed three heavy rolls into her basket, she asked the stout proprietor who stood at the cashbox for the name of a respectable hotel.

"Clayton's on Kearney Street."

Rooms for fifty cents a night. A bath in the communal tub would cost her extra. The room she was given had an iron bedstead, a commode, and a dresser with a cracked, fly-spotted mirror. After a tepid bath, she dried herself with the hotel's towel, so thin it was transparent. Then she tumbled into bed and slept until the next morning.

Her first stop was the police station. Talking to the small, spindly-looking clerk who took down everything she said, she was suddenly overcome with a sense of futility. The man was being kind. He had already said that Elthea's case was far from unique. Numerous young women came to the city, girls fleeing strict parents or dull husbands, thinking they could better themselves or lead a more adventurous life. They came without money, connections, or skills. Many of them, the little clerk said, ended up on the street or in the cribs of the Barbary Coast.

Listening to him, Hannah felt as though it were Chicago all over again. She remembered her arrival at Randolph

Street station, how confused and frightened she had been, the crowds of milling people, the smell of cooking fat, popcorn, hotdogs, fried chicken, the gnawing hunger, her friendlessness. And then Mrs. Corinth.

"My advice," the little clerk said, "is to put an ad in the paper. Offer a reward for the whereabouts of your sister-in-law. If she's in a brothel—and she may not be—but still if she is, some pimp or madam might read the ad and think it more worthwhile to collect cash on the barrel than to put a green girl out—you did say she was shy, from the country, and with a child?—soliciting. The *Examiner* would be a good bet."

"But I have very little money," Hannah said. "How can I offer a reward?"

The police clerk scratched his two-day-old beard. "*They* don't know that. At least if someone answers—and you play your hand right—you might get a clue as to her whereabouts."

It seemed like sensible advice. The ad might not elicit a single response, she might have to spend the eighty-five cents it cost in vain, but she could think of nothing else to do. The search for Elthea seemed akin to the proverbial hunt for a needle in a haystack.

Hannah took a trolley down to the *Examiner*'s office. Mulling over a form, pencil in hand, she finally came up with:

REWARD for the whereabouts of Mrs. Travis (Elthea) Blaine, 5 feet, 2 inches, blond, blue eyes, small scar over left brow. Has a baby girl who answers to the name of Clara. Please contact Mrs. Guy Hartwell at the Clayton Hotel, 212 Kearney Street.

The day's edition had gone to press. The ad would not appear until the following morning. Hannah returned to her hotel room, but once there she soon found herself pacing up and down, window to door, door to window, until someone on the floor below, objecting to the sound of her footsteps, banged loudly on the ceiling. She sat down on the bed and after a minute got up again and went to the window once more. She had the whole afternoon to while away, an evening and a night. She had stopped in a cafe next to the newspaper office and bought a bowl of greasy stew. It came with a generous portion of bread, and as she had done the previous day, she had purloined the bread, slipping it into her basket. Now she took a thick slice and broke off a piece and began to nibble at it. She wasn't hungry, just nervous. She thought about Mark. Did he miss her? Probably not half as much as she missed him. She wondered what Travis and Guy were doing, if they had been successful in moving the cattle. They must be worried about her. About Elthea. Perhaps they had already gone to the Post ranch and received her message.

She stood up, shaking crumbs from her lap. She couldn't go on sitting, staring at the stained wallpaper, the faded morning glories climbing endlessly up thin lattices of anemic green.

She pinned her hat on and went out. She would search the streets even though she knew that her chances for finding Elthea in the crowded maze of the city were next to impossible. At least it would give her something to do.

Where to go? She remembered the clerk at the police station saying, "Most of them end up in the Barbary Coast."

She had never been to the coast but its vile reputation was well known. The cesspool of the world, Tess Barlow had once called it. Hannah did not like to think of Elthea in such a place, but with Elthea anything was possible. Who would imagine that anyone so shy would allow a man like the red-bearded one at the Glendening to be-friend her?

Hannah got directions to the Barbary Coast from the gripman on the cable car, who added, "It's no place for a respectable woman."

"I realize that, but I'm looking for my sister-in-law." There wasn't any harm in letting people know, especially someone like the gripman who was out in public all day. "She's left home and is here somewhere in San Francisco." Hannah went on to describe her.

"Ah," said the gripman, "in that case I understand. But be careful and leave before dark."

Daytime was bad enough. The cobbled streets were teeming with pedestrians, curiosity seekers, panhandlers, and sharp-eyed runners and pimps. Rubbing shoulders with the crowd were sailors from every port, French, Italian, Greek, Malaysian, German, dark-skinned and light-skinned and various shades in between. They strolled in pairs, trios, and quartets, pointing, laughing, ogling the women. Some were drunk, some very drunk. A man wearing a beret with a red pompom atop weaved along the sidewalk and suddenly went to his knees. He swayed for a few moments in that position as if he were doing obeisance to a pagan god, then pitched forward. He was rolled aside by a couple of laughing seamen and propped against the wall of a wooden building. THALIA DANCE HALL, the sign read. Inside, a piano banged away a syncopated tune to the stamping of feet, shouts and cheers. Hannah caught a glimpse of whirling skirts and trouser legs through the open door.

"Wanna jig, sister?" a bald man shouted to Hannah from a shadowed doorway. "I'll show you a good time."

Hannah crossed the street. Along this pavement was a row of shacks with open windows at which sat prostitutes calling to the men passing by, advertising their wares with bared breasts or spread legs. Most were unattractive, many past youth, some with pockmarked faces, others with haggard, bruised eyes, a sad-looking lot despite the false smiles on their painted lips.

Oh, surely Elthea couldn't be among these? Hannah thought with sick despair. She would die. And what of little Clara? This was a world that existed in limbo, on the lowest rungs of hell. However hard Elthea had worked, however lonely she had been at Sycamore, her life there had been a paradise by comparison.

One woman, noting that Hannah had stopped and was staring at the prostitutes, shouted viciously, "Whatcha lookin' at, sister? You wannna try one of us? There's Bertha." She flicked her thumb at a two-hundred-pound woman with three front teeth missing. "Bertha knows

ways to make a ewe scream with pleasure, doncha,
Bertha? She does it with dogs, horses . . .''

Hannah did not wait to hear more, but fled.

The next morning at ten o'clock, an hour after the
Examiner was out on the streets, Hannah stationed herself downstairs in the little side room the Clayton Hotel
pretentiously called a parlor. There, sitting on an uncomfortable horsehair sofa, she waited for the callers
she hoped would come in answer to her ad.

Her wait was short. The first to arrive was an old
woman, a humpbacked crone dressed in black. "I seed
her, that Elthea," she said, "jist t'other day. She's
staying at the Olympia Hotel.''

"Is she?"

"Yes, she was there. I seed her comin' out the door
with her little girl. She was toddlin' 'long 'side her.''

"The little girl, Mrs . . . ?"

"Jist call me missus.''

"The little girl, missus, is too young to walk.''

The old woman chewed her gums, anger flushing her
parchmentlike face. " 'Lees' you could give me a dime
for my carfare.''

Not wanting to argue, Hannah gave her the dime.

The next to appear were two men, one with a limp,
the other with a broken nose. Both wore drab, dirty
pants and coats without shirts, collars, or ties. They had
seen Elthea on the pier and had followed her to Mrs.
Cooley's boardinghouse, where she had a room. "A
short girl," the one with the broken nose said, "about
so high.'' When Hannah said she would have to corrob-
orate their story, they got angry, demanding the reward
money at once. She was saved from what might have
been an ugly situation by the advent of three other
people, all claiming to have seen Elthea in three different sections of the city. Hannah took down the locations
and the names of the people reporting, but without hope.
She had the feeling that thus far her advertisement had
drawn only those who had no idea of Elthea's whereabouts, but had come with a cooked-up story in order to

collect the reward. That the amount hadn't been specified seemed not to matter.

It was getting on to noon. The spate of callers had ebbed. No one came during the next half hour. But she wasn't discouraged. She felt there had to be someone in the city who had seen Elthea and who had read her ad.

She looked up hopefully as the bell on the outer door jangled once again. There was the murmur of voices—the bell ringer consulting with the hotel clerk. Then a moment later a man in a faultlessly tailored gray suit entered the parlor, a handsome, dark-haired man with an air of masculine vigor.

"Good afternoon, Hannah," Christian said.

Chapter XV

Christian had seen the advertisement that morning.

It was his custom to read the *Examiner* over breakfast, taken late that day because he had been up all night with a difficult confinement. The *Examiner*—Hearst's rag, as he termed it—both amused and annoyed him for its sensationalism, its exposés, and its gross distortions. Sometimes he wondered why he bothered with it, except that he did enjoy Ambrose Bierce's fine, often witty writings and Davenport's clever cartoons. He also found the Personals column entertaining. He was perusing the listings of sad pleas to come home, the boastful self-congratulations, and funny, touching assertions from one throbbing heart to another when the name Mrs. Guy Hartwell leaped out at him.

He reread the notice more carefully. Hannah? Hartwell was not an uncommon name. Someone else? But no, the lost woman was called Blaine, the same as Hannah's maiden name. Hannah was here in San Francisco at the Clayton Hotel and apparently in distress. He did not ask himself, Should I go to her? He knew he would.

He had returned to San Francisco three years earlier after Hannah had suddenly, mysteriously refused to see him. One day they had been a man and woman madly in love, engaged, planning marriage, and the next—nothing, strangers. Enemies. He knew now from their encounter in the corridor outside his office that Hannah's abrupt change of mind had come about because she had seen him with Amanda at the Palmer House. Again Hannah had come to the wrong conclusion without giving him the chance to explain.

And the explanation had been very simple. Amanda, in her usual impulsive, single-minded way, had followed him to Chicago. She had checked in at the Palmer House, registering as Mr. and Mrs. Christian Falconer. Knowing that he usually stayed at the Woolridges' while in the city, she had sent him an urgent note, saying she had an important message from his sister, Sabrina. Would he meet her at the Palmer House for lunch? He should have known it was a trick. But underestimating Amanda's audacity—once more—he had gone. And Hannah, by some freak coincidence, had seen them.

It still angered him to think that Hannah, who had professed undying love, put so little trust in him, even though she had found him in what seemed—on the surface, at least—a compromising situation.

At the time, however, he had been more hurt, more painfully confounded than angry. After trying unsuccessfully to communicate with Hannah and receiving no response from her family, he had lingered in Chicago for a week longer, then left for San Francisco.

Bored with the aimless life he had been leading, the drunken sprees and meaningless affairs with women he had no interest in, he had resumed his abandoned medical practice. He had moved back into the family mansion on Nob Hill as a temporary measure until he could obtain his own quarters. But to his surprise he had found he was comfortable in his old home. His room, furnished in solid teaks and dark walnuts, with its view of the bay, was restful, easy on the nerves after a trying day with patients. The servants, except for a new face or two, were the ones he had known since childhood. Ancient, bent, and considerably slower now, but familiar and patently glad to see him, they seemed to have forgotten or forgiven his earlier pranks and fits of temper. Arthur, his younger brother, had married and was living in Sacramento, where he was practicing law and dabbling in politics. So there were only three of them—his mother Carmella, his father Miles, and himself—left in that big house on Nob Hill.

His mother, thinner now, her hair graying, but her features still retaining strong traces of her youthful beauty, had wept to see him. The tears had come as a surprise. He had thought her affection for him had always been tempered by exasperation and that she found his presence at home uncomfortable. But now she seemed genuinely overcome with joy at his return. Yes, Christian had decided, his mother, like the servants, had forgiven or forgotten and had been sincerely glad to see him.

His father's attitude, however, had not changed.

Miles had always behaved in a cool manner toward him. What affection he had bestowed on his children had gone to Sabrina, his favorite child. Christian remembered that as a small boy he had been eaten with envy, watching his sister cuddled in Miles's arms, coaxed from her tears over a fall, a bruise, or an imagined affront while he, weeping over the same fall, the same bruise, was admonished sternly to be a little man. He and Miles had always been at odds, Miles trying to press his son into the mold of model student, model son, model lawyer, and Christian bitterly resisting the mold every step of the way.

Before going back to medicine, Christian had debated the question, knowing that if he became Dr. Falconer again his father would approve. Then suddenly, for some obscure reason, he realized it no longer mattered. He was twenty-seven years old now, an adult. He was through arranging his life to spite his father. It seemed stupid to go on weighing every decision, asking, "Is this what Father would want me to do?" And then doing the opposite. It was a perverse game that had lost its pleasure. It was beneath him. Whether he and his father would ever be more than polite strangers, he did not know. Perhaps, eventually, they might learn to respect one another, but more he did not expect.

Christian had set up his office in the Kohbler Building

on Market Street. It was in a middle-class neighborhood with a mixture of second-generation ethnic groups, Germans and Italians mostly, men whose fathers had come west too late to share in the wealth of the Gold Rush, but who were shrewd and ambitious enough to prosper in businesses like bakeries, restaurants, and tailoring shops. They now lived in stone-fronted apartments or in gingerbread frame houses crammed with heavy furniture and a wealth of bric-a-brac. They could afford to hire the less fortunate Negroes or Chinese to wait on them, to do their laundry and clean their houses for wages barely above those their fathers had earned as immigrants. Their wives had constituted the greater part of Christian's practice. At first he was a huge success with them; his good looks, his aristocratic manners, his genuine interest in their welfare brought them again and again to his consulting rooms. But Christian soon grew tired, then annoyed at these overweight, idle middle-class women who complained (like many of their Nob Hill sisters) of headaches, stomach distress, coughs, and constipation. Rather than coddle them, as many of his colleagues did—for the encouragement of hypochondria paid well—Christian would speak plainly. His advice to eat moderately, to find useful diversion, and to exercise was met by expressions of shock or resentment. As a consequence his practice dropped off. But he did not mind. He now had the satisfaction of treating really ill patients, those suffering from fractures, hepatitis, acute dysentery, pleurisy, venereal disease, apoplexy, and the like. He adopted a sliding fee scale, geared to the patient's ability to pay. Those who couldn't afford even a modest charge were administered to with the same attention as those who could.

Christian had studied Lister and Pasteur and was conversant with ideas about asepsis and the transmission of disease through bacteria. Unlike Dr. Russell, he did not wear a frock coat—the symbol of the doctor—either in his office or in the operating room. Nor did he believe in the use of leeches, bleeding, and blistering as cures. Though he prided himself on being a modern doctor, he was well aware of the limitations of his profession: Mer-

cury worked only on incipient syphilis, quinine sometimes did and sometimes did not ease his malarial patients.
With advanced cases of chorea, heart lesions, and
pneumonia, he was helpless.

Some of his clients were prostitutes, the girls from the
better sporting houses on O'Farrell Street. They came
with chancres, lung congestion (the beginnings of tuber-
culosis), and botched abortions. Christian fixed them up
as best he would with bismuth and mercury and arseni-
cal compounds. He gave advice on preventing pregnancy and, more important, on how to surreptitiously
inspect the private parts of their partners for any telltale
signs of gonorrhea or syphilis. A few of these ladies he
knew from his salad days. There was no embarrassment
on either side at his new role of doctor. There were a
few reminiscences or perhaps an offer now and then to
pay in kind, which he charmingly declined.

Reflecting on these women who trailed the heavy scent
of patchouli through his office, flaunting scarlet cheeks
and feathery boas at the more conservative matrons in
his waiting room, he would sometimes think of their
hapless sisters who serviced half the naval fleets of the
world from their cribs on the Barbary Coast or who
walked the streets of the Tenderloin. Who took care of
their ills, their sores, their unwanted pregnancies, not to
speak of typhoid and consumption?

He had only been dimly aware of the less fortunate in
his roisterous, devil-may-care medical-school days.
Though he had quit medicine because of Dr. Baumgard's
negligent treatment of a charity case, he had given little
thought to the general plight of the poor. But now he
was beginning to feel that he ought to apply his medical
skills to assisting the needy—go into public health,
perhaps.

Then he would laugh at himself. He had become a
sobersides. That he, Christian Falconer, who had enjoyed the good life—fine cigars, expensive cognac, elegant tailoring, and beautiful female flesh—should reach
the point where he actually contemplated "doing good"
bordered on the absurd. But was it absurd? He saw
things differently now. He had changed. Why this alter-

ation had come about was hard to say. Perhaps it was because of boredom, as he had originally supposed, the wish to immerse himself in other people's problems so that his own would seem minor by contrast, a restless urge to be on the move, perhaps a surplus of energy once devoted to activities that had palled.

Or perhaps it was due to Hannah.

She was never far from his thoughts. Her face, the wide-spaced eyes, the small, slightly upturned nose, the pink mouth came to mind at random moments. Things as simple as the sound of falling rain or the sight of rosy lamplight suddenly blooming in the dark would recall the cottage at Wildoak or that afternoon at the Woolridges' when they had made such passionate love. Sometimes he fancied he saw her in a crowd, the slender figure and slightly swaying hips, her face, all but the chin hidden under the wide brim of a hat decked with flowers. Once he followed a woman for two blocks, certain that when she turned it would be Hannah. It wasn't. It was always someone else. Not Hannah.

He loved her. It was more than her clear gray eyes, more than her passionate nature, the full firm breasts, the soft, silky skin that he cherished. It was Hannah herself. She was nothing like the namby-pamby women he had met at debutante balls and at Greenway cotillions. She had backbone, strength, courage, and honesty, qualities his contemporaries would consider unfeminine. Yet who could be more feminine than Hannah? Certainly not Amanda, whose selfish aggressiveness and whorish appetite had begun to repel him once he saw that she was no different from but far more demanding than the harlots at Mrs. McAllister's.

Hannah was decent. Now that in itself should have turned him away. Christian hated the very word, one that had been thrown at him by both his father and mother since he could walk. He had always recoiled from the company of "decent" women, who eyed his acceptance of a glass of whiskey at tedious functions as if he were drinking brimstone and fire. Yet Hannah was decent in the real sense of the word. A decent human being. For him it added to her intrinsic beauty and made him love her all the more.

She was far from faultless, however. Her mistrust, her refusal to believe him, her jealousy when there was no cause for it had angered him. Leaving Chicago, he had given her up, told himself he must forget her, that surely there were other women who had the same allure as Hannah, a woman yet unknown, waiting for him somewhere.

But he did not forget her, and if there was a woman waiting, she was yet to be found.

"Good day, Mr. Falconer." She clasped her hands tightly as if by so doing she could steady her voice. "And to what do I owe this pleasure?" That was better. Dry, cool, impersonal.

"I read your advertisement, Hannah, and came to see if I could be of assistance."

The advertisement. What was the circulation of the *Examiner*? At least half of its readers must know by now that Mrs. Guy Hartwell was looking for Elthea Blaine. Why shouldn't Christian?

"Thank you for your offer. But it's really not necessary. I have a promising lead and was just about to follow it up."

"Indeed."

She had never been a good liar and Christian knew it. He was gazing at her, his eyes alert, the same keen assessment she had always found so disconcerting.

"Mrs. Blaine, I take it, is your . . . ?"

"Sister-in-law."

"How long has she been missing?"

"Several days."

"And you feel this—ah—'lead' will take you to her?"

"Yes," she answered, replanting the lie in a firmer voice.

"Perhaps I can offer you transportation. I have a buggy outside."

"Thank you, but I can find my way."

Did she sound churlish, ungrateful? It didn't matter. She would not, could not accept his help. Christian was not for her, he was bad luck, unhappiness, pain. She was drawn to him, would always be; his vitality and good looks, the charm, the intelligence that was essentially Christian acted on her like an irresistible magnet. But her love, any sort of relationship with him, was hopeless, had always been hopeless. She was happily married to Guy. *He* was her future, not Christian. If she ever believed in good sense as opposed to emotional foolishness, she did now. She must not let her feelings become entangled with this man again.

"Very well," he said. "Here is my card. If you are not successful in locating Mrs. Blaine, please feel free to call on me. I have connections in the city, a friend who is a Pinkerton agent, a private detective, specializing in finding missing persons."

She took the card. Not to do so would be rude. His eyes flicked over her hands and she was immediately conscious of their reddened skin and broken nails. He was probably thinking how ugly they looked, roughened by frequent use of lye soap and the alkali-hardened water they drew from their wells. She hated herself for being ashamed of her hands, for the way she had quickly buried them in her lap.

"I doubt I shall be calling on you," she said with dignity. "Nevertheless, I thank you again." The words were what courtesy demanded, but the look she flashed him was icy. "And now, if you will . . ." She rose to her feet.

But he was not to be so summarily disposed of. "The child you were carrying?" he inquired.

"Miscarried."

"I'm so sorry."

If there had been pity in his eyes, the faintest hint in his voice, she would have lost control and lashed out at him. She did not want his pity, she did not want his concern.

"Good-bye, Mr. Falconer."

During the next three days Hannah crisscrossed San Francisco not once but several times, pursuing reports of sightings, hunting down rumors and clues. She visited a whorehouse on Taylor Street where Elthea supposedly had become one of the "girls." Not true. Next she stopped at Jules Restaurant on California Street, where someone claimed to have seen Elthea working at the cash register, changing money into five-cent pieces that could be used in the new "5 by 5" slot machines. A woman answering Hannah's advertisement swore that Elthea was working as a maid at the Baldwin Hotel. She was not. Nor—as an old gentleman in a plug hat asserted—was she employed by the Sutro family as undercook.

Up California Street, down Kearney, knocking on doors, going into shops—Mrs. Bradley's Fashionable Cloakmaking, the City of Paris, the White House—Hannah met with the same response. With trepidation she checked the patient rosters at the City and County Hospital on Stockton Street and later St. Mary's, run by the Sisters of Mercy. But it was the same there as elsewhere. No sign of Elthea, not even the faintest clue. The thought occurred to Hannah that Elthea might have managed to catch a train for some point east, if not all the way to Georgia. But Hannah doubted it. Elthea had no money and her experience with the red-whiskered man might have frightened her from taking up with another stranger. Hannah believed that Elthea was still in San Francisco. But where?

Hannah was running low on money. She had optimistically put aside enough for two coach and train fares—hers and Elthea's—back to the Post ranch. What was left would take care of her hotel bill for three more nights and one simple meal a day.

Then what?

She wanted to go home, longed to leave the city behind. She missed Sycamore, Guy, Travis. And most of all Mark. But to return home without Elthea after a search of less than a week seemed unthinkable. She had already written to Guy and Travis, telling them where she was, a cheerful letter in which she said that she felt sure of success. She knew she ought to write again and explain her dilemma and ask Travis to come to San

Francisco. But even if she could afford to wait for Travis, what could he accomplish that she could not?

The three days passed but she stayed on, spending the money she had been saving for Elthea's return fare. Subsisting on bread and coffee, walking rather than taking public transportation, gave her another two days. At the end she was no closer to finding Elthea than she had been from the first.

She had nothing to pawn or to sell. She was going through her purse to see if any loose change had fallen to the bottom when her hand closed on Christian's card.

Dr. Christian Falconer
313 Market Street
Office Hours—9 to 9

If I can be of any assistance . . . But I can't ask him, she thought. I can't. And the next moment—why not? Could she let pride stand in the way? By now she was worried sick, picturing Elthea ill, held prisoner perhaps, mistreated or dead. And the baby. That was the real tragedy. Elthea's flight, though made in desperation, had been a foolish act, but that innocent little Clara should have to suffer for it was doubly distressing.

Hannah knew no one in San Francisco except Christian. He'd spoken of contacts, a Pinkerton man, someone skilled in locating missing persons. How could she return to Sycamore and face Travis with a clear conscience, telling him she had tried everything when she had not?

But it took courage to go to Christian, the kind of courage that made controlling a team of runaway horses seem like child's play.

And yet she knew if she didn't ask Christian for help and Elthea and Clara were never heard from again, their faces would haunt her until the day she died.

He was in shirtsleeves, the stiff white collar setting off his dark skin.

"Hello, Hannah. No luck?"

His handsome face showed no emotion except polite

inquiry, his eyes told her nothing, no surprise, no smug I-told-you-so. Still she had the feeling that he had been expecting this visit. Waiting for her. It annoyed Hannah, but annoyance at this stage would hardly help matters.

"Are you still at the Clayton?" he asked.

"Yes." She had paid her bill that morning and told the clerk she would collect her things and move out at noon. She had to find cheaper quarters. Even so—if she was to stay on in San Francisco—she would be forced to use the money she had set aside for her return. But that was in the future. She would manage. It was the now she was concerned about.

Christian, for his part, had rightly assessed her situation. Her shabby appearance, the cheap straw hat, cotton gloves, and the mended shawl all spoke of her poverty. He tried to lend support in what he felt was the most tactful way.

"I'm living at home now. I wonder if it wouldn't be more convenient for both of us if you put up at my parents' house?"

"What do you mean?" she asked, bristling.

"My meaning is simply this: We have a telephone at the house, making communication between you, myself at the office, and the Pinkerton Agency easier." He paused. "You look doubtful. You suspect me of ulterior motives?"

The stubborn set to her mouth told him she did.

"Well, then," he went on in a level voice, "you are probably right. Since you have alway thought the worst of me, I may as well live up to it. I, of course, shall expect favors in return for my efforts."

There it was. She could refuse, tell him that only a cad would require such a reward. But it was too late to play the lady. "If you wish to treat me like one of your whores, then I have no choice, have I?"

His narrowed eyes went over her, as if gauging her worth. "I'd say you do have a choice."

"I can't go back to my brother empty-handed." Her jawline tightened. "I'll do anything to find Elthea."

"Good. I'm glad we understand each other. Very well, I'll send someone to fetch your things from the

Clayton. In the meanwhile I'll see that my Pinkerton friend starts an immediate investigation. But tell me." He leaned indolently back in his chair. "Why did your brother send a woman to do a man's job?"

Her first impulse was to say it was none of his business. How dare he make Travis out as spineless? But she was not here to argue. "My brother wanted to come but I felt he couldn't be spared. He and my husband were engaged in moving cattle to another pasture where the herd could find better grazing and water. We are experiencing a serious drought at Sycamore."

"I see."

He didn't see. Why should a drought mean anything to him? Yet she had no desire to explain.

"Shall we go, then?"

"As you wish. But won't your parents think your bringing a strange woman home rather odd?"

"I daresay it won't be the first time."

The Falconer residence was less grandiose than the other Nob Hill mansions with their conical towers, peaked roofs, and dormer windows. Its interior, too, though luxurious, was furnished in a less cluttered style than was currently fashionable among the wealthy. Still, to Hannah, coming directly from the drab Clayton—and before that the simple ranch house at Sycamore—the Falconer residence was as overwhelming as the Wool-ridges' had been in Chicago. She tried not to gawk at the entryway rising three stories to a domed amber skylight. Or to stare at a white marble replica of Michelangelo's *David* standing in bold frontal nudity to the left of the staircase. After the butler had taken Christian's hat, gloves, and stick, Christian led her across the terrazzo-tiled floor and opened a pair of oaken doors.

They entered a beautiful room furnished with hand-rubbed black walnut chairs, pearl-inlaid tables, and red plush sofas. On the wall hung paintings—among them an original Whistler, a Rosa Bonheur, and a Millet—and large cheval mirrors framed in gold. There were one-legged mahogany tables holding gold-clasped, vellum-bound books, and cut-glass vases filled with pink hothouse

roses and sprigs of maidenhair fern. Rubber plants and
elephant ears grew in jardinières on either side of a
fireplace manteled in black onyx where a crystal and
gold clock kept time.

Here in the imposing double parlor, referred to as a
"drawing room," Hannah was introduced to Christian's
mother, Carmella Falconer.

"Mrs. Hartwell was at Wildoak for a time. She was
Hannah Blaine then," Christian said.

"Oh, indeed, I remember Sabrina speaking of you,"
Carmella graciously acknowledged. "May I call you Hannah?" There was no trace of shock or surprise, no lifting
of brows as to Hannah's unannounced arrival or to her
shabby appearance, even more frayed and humble-looking
against this exotic background.

"My dear, how good to meet Page's niece and a
friend of Sabrina's. I understood you were teaching school
near Wildoak."

"That was several years ago. My husband and I own
a ranch below Monterey."

"How nice. And you are visiting in San Francisco?"

"Unfortunately not."

Christian explained Elthea's disappearance, Hannah's
search for her, and how he planned to call in the Pinkerton Agency.

"I'm so sorry," Carmella said. "But in the meantime
we will try to make you comfortable. You'll join me for
tea? Tuesdays are my at-home days and I'm expecting a
few friends."

"Thank you, but I think not."

She was in no mood to sit down to tea with a group of
women who might not be as democratic or gracious as
Carmella Falconer, women who would look her up and
down and wonder where Carmella had dredged up this
particular specimen.

"Of course you must be tired. Christian, why don't
you show Hannah to Sabrina's old room? And Hannah,
dear, we dine at eight."

Upstairs, Christian said, "Now, was that as difficult
as you imagined?"

Hannah removed her hat, her cotton gloves and laid

them on the marble-topped bureau. "No. But I can't go
down to supper. Not in these clothes. I simply can't. I'd
feel out of place."

"Nonsense. Did you feel out of place at Wildoak?"

"No. But then Sabrina was young and she and her
husband were trying to make a go of the farm. It was
different, not so—well, elegant. I can't explain. Your
mother's like royalty."

He threw back his head and laughed.

"I don't see why that's so funny."

"Oh, Hannah, Hannah. For all your stiff pride you
haven't lost that wonderful naiveté. My mother—royalty?"
And he broke into another fit of laughter.

Hannah said, "I don't care to be mocked."

"I'm sorry. I'm not mocking you, for how would you
know? It's the notion of my mother being royalty. Hannah, my mother's mother, my grandmother whom I never
met, was a fixture of one of New Orleans's most notorious *maisons de joie*. In other words she was a prostitute."

Hannah looked at him in disbelief.

"It's true. I swear it. So you see I come by my
fondness for whores naturally. Whatever you wear doesn't
matter."

"But it does. I can't go to supper in these clothes.
You must make my excuses."

He strode to the wardrobe and flung it open. "Take
your pick." His hand brushed a row of gowns. "I'm
sure you'll find something here that fits. You and my
sister must be about the same size."

"I don't like being the object of—"

"Charity," he finished. "Really, Hannah, you repeat
yourself. Why don't you look on it as choosing a cos-
tume for a masquerade, if it will make you any happier.
However"—he shrugged—"do as you like. If you decide to sit here all evening and sulk, do so. My mother
may feel slighted but that, I'm sure, is of no concern to
you."

An hour later Hannah's bag was brought up by a
manservant. A maid followed him into the room, offering to unpack for Hannah.

"Thank you, but I can manage."

"Shall I draw Madam a bath?"

Hannah hesitated for a fraction of a moment before answering. "Yes, please."

The bathroom, ringed with mirrors, was huge. It had a flush toilet. Faucets and spigots were fashioned in gold, the ceiling painted with a scene of mermaids sporting in the sea. A rack of white fluffy towels also held salts and oils and a jar of Pond's cream whose label read "For a smoother complexion." Hannah, soaking in the hot water, bubbles of perfumed foam tickling her nose, felt the tension go out of the muscles across the back of her neck. For the first time since she had ridden along the Coast Ridge Road she allowed herself to smile. Though she stoutly refused to be seduced by the luxurious comforts of Nob Hill, she had to admit that the bath was one of the few things she wouldn't mind having at Sycamore.

In the end, driven by hunger and curiosity—for she hadn't met Christian's father—she chose a blue challis gown with overlapping skirts. But—alas!—even Hannah's provincial eye detected it was out of fashion since it had a pronounced bustle. Finding scissors, she removed the offending flounces and perky bow that were meant to sit over a wire contraption strapped on at the rear. The gown was also too tight across the bust and pinched at the waist. Hannah let out the seams on each side, stitching quickly, hoping her handiwork would not be too obvious.

Apparently it was not. Carmella Falconer said, "My dear, you look lovely." If she recognized her daughter's dress, she gave no sign.

Miles Falconer said, "So this is the little school-teacher."

He was a handsome man, dark like Christian, with a wing of white at each temple. His manner was courteous but aloof. Only to his wife did he unbend, at one point giving her a warm, affectionate smile. The few words he spoke to Christian were those he would have used in polite conversation with a stranger, not a son. It did not take long for Hannah to sense the strain between the two men.

In the dining room, under gaslights blinkered with opaque glass shades, they sat at a long polished table that would have easily accommodated twenty. Hannah, unaccustomed to a bare-shouldered gown, felt naked. It did not help to have Christian gazing fixedly at her.

"The blue is charming," he said, embarrassing her, making both his mother and father stare a few moments at her with interest. "Don't you believe so, Mother?"

"Very charming."

To Hannah, who hadn't eaten a decent meal for a week, the supper that night was a feast. She constantly had to remind herself that she must not act like a starveling though she felt like one. She forced herself to take small helpings from dish after dish that was offered by a sour-looking butler: oyster cocktail, cold consommé, fillet of beef, purée of potatoes, alligator-pear salad, cucumbers in aspic. Each course was served with a different wine. The cumulative effect was more than satisfying. Hannah, despite her attempt at restraint, knew by the time the long meal was over that if she hadn't overeaten, she certainly had imbibed more wine than was prudent. She found it difficult to keep her eyes open, much less to walk a straight line from dining room to parlor, where after what she thought was a suitable length of time she excused herself.

In Sabrina's room once more, she quickly got out of her gown, breathing with relief as the borrowed stays were thrown aside. She unpinned her hair and thought of brushing it, but was too tired. Still wearing Sabrina's lace petticoat and camisole, she drew back the bed covers and crawled into the soft warmth of lavender-scented linen. Sinking down into the goose-feather mattress, she fell instantly asleep.

It seemed that she had put her head on the pillow only moments earlier when a soft knock on the door awakened her. She sat bolt upright; the unfamiliar surroundings and her wine-dazed state gave her the illusion that she was still sleeping and this pretty, white-ruffled room was part of a dream.

The door opened and Christian entered. "Did I wake you?"

His sudden appearance frightened her. She had seen him like this in nightmares in which he had come into a room, darkly handsome and threatening, while she lay helpless in a bed from which she could not rise.

"Go away," she whispered.

"I wanted to see if you were all right. You seemed a little—how shall I say?—tipsy at dinner." He gave her a broad, knowing smile. "I brought you a bromide in case you should have a headache." He came closer and seated himself on the edge of the bed.

She was wide awake now. In Sabrina's old room. And Christian was here beside her. The patently thin excuse, the charming smile, the friendly voice, the audacity hadn't changed. They were still his stock-in-trade. She ought to know. He had tried it on her before. And succeeded. Memories of the cottage at Wildoak, the dark-paneled room at the Woolridges', crowded one upon the other. She, succumbing to his wild kisses, listening to his words of love, eager, panting for more. Two pregnancies. Disillusionment. Heartache. It angered her to think that he would still take her for a simpleton.

"Are you here to collect your reward?" she asked tartly. "Beforehand?" She would give her body to him, a body divorced from thought or feeling. But no more.

She felt him stiffen. A steely look came into his eyes. "Hardly. The women I've known always expected to be paid in advance."

Turning crimson, she pulled the edges of her camisole together.

"Modest?" he jeered. "Isn't it rather late for that?"

"You beast! You enjoy gloating, don't you? A bromide, indeed. Did you think I would be gulled by such a flimsy lie? You're a liar. You've always been one."

His face darkened. A pulse beat at the edge of his mouth. "That shrewish tongue again. How deftly you use it."

"Spare me the compliment. I'll sleep with you when you find Elthea. Not before. Now, get out!"

His expression hardened. "Get out!" he exclaimed, incredulous, a scornful edge to his voice. "You expect me to leave with my tail between my legs simply because you have spoken, is that it? Is that how your husband behaves when you issue a command? I don't take kindly to orders, Hannah. You don't know me if you think I do. I'll leave when it pleases me."

"Haven't you always done what pleases you?" She was trembling inside with anger and with fear. His arrogance had never been more blatant, this man who once manipulated her like a puppet on a string. Words were her only weapon. "Isn't that the way of a selfish lecher, to do as he pleases?"

He stared at her. "What did you call me?" There was an ominous steeliness to his voice, a gathering of forces behind those leonine eyes.

"Lecher!" she repeated in defiance. And he was, he was. She had only to remind herself of Amanda clinging to his arm, of the prostitute laughing up into his face, of the countless women he must have had. "Womanizer! Whoremaster . . . !"

He grabbed her shoulders, his fingers digging into her flesh, and shook her so roughly she felt as though her neck would snap.

"D-d-don't. I-I'll ssscream."

He paused, still grasping her bared shoulders, his arms trembling. "Scream, damn you! Go on, scream!" A lock of hair had fallen over his dark brow and his eyes had a savage look as they raked the rise and fall of her breasts beneath the flimsy cambric.

"Let me go!"

"Why? You want me as much as I want you. I know it. I know *you*."

"You're wrong. I hate the sight of you."

"Do you? You pretend to be virtuous, but you're not. You enjoy a man between your legs, the feel of his—"

She slapped him hard across the face. He drew back, putting his hand to his cheek. She took that moment to spring out of bed, but he caught her and hurled her back against the pillows. When she struggled to rise, he anchored her arms at her sides.

"Why don't you scream?" He sneered, leaning over her.

"Christian . . ."

He brought his mouth down, ravaging her lips in a hungry kiss, roughly prying them open, his tongue stabbing, curling, twisting. He caught her mouth again, crushing her already swollen lips. His heavy body, covering hers, pinned her helplessly to the mattress. Her mind cried out—Please don't; oh God, please!—but already her body was beginning to respond to the rocklike hardness pressed against her pelvis. A hot trembling took possession of her limbs. Her breasts burned under his touch.

He felt the tight-strung resistance go out of her and he lifted his head to look down. Her eyes were closed, a slight frown between the arched brows, her lashes dark smudges against her cheeks. So beautiful, so lovely—so obstinate.

Her eyes flew open. "Let me go," she repeated, but there was no anger, only a soft pleading.

"I know you so well," he said, releasing her arms. "I knew you'd come around, my own Hannah."

My own Hannah! How dare he assume she was his, that she would come around! How dare he know and exploit her weakness!

"All you really need is a little coaxing. . . ."

She hit him again and again, first with one fist, then the next. No gentle slaps, but strong, painful blows.

He grasped her hands by the wrists, jerking them upward, pinioning them above her head. Bitch! To Christian this violent attack was a further sign of her duplicity. It was as if she had tricked him once more, soft compliance, a pleading look, then suddenly, for no apparent reason, the abrupt rejection. Heartless bitch! The hot, savage anger he thought he had conquered rose in him, erupting like a molten volcano. Her struggle, the soft, squirming body beneath his, served to inflame him further.

"Damn you!" he muttered. His kisses now were savage, blazing a fiery trail across her cheeks, hot, desperate, angry, lustful kisses. Grasping both wrists cruelly with one hand, he tore the camisole open, exposing her ripe, heaving breasts. The sight of the creamy mounds, the pink buds, twisted his loins. He took a nipple in his mouth and mauled it with his tongue, licking and sucking, until the rosy crest grew hard in his mouth. A shudder went through her body. A moan escaped from her lips as he took the other pink nub in his mouth.

She did not fight him when he let go of her arms. She knew it was a losing battle, had really known from the first. She had struck him as much out of self-anger as anger at him, anger at the circumstances that had brought them together. Nothing would come of this lovemaking. Once it was over, there would be that void once more. She would have to forget him all over again, banish his dark face, the memory of his deep-set eyes, his touch, his passion. To struggle against him, against the torrid heat that raced through her veins and melted her bones was futile.

He was kissing the cleft between her breasts, his hands tracing the curve of her hips, sliding up between her quivering thighs.

"No," she whispered.

"Yes, yes, yes." His hot breath burned her ear. "You were made for me and me alone."

"No," she moaned. His strong hands, his teasing, taunting fingers stroking and caressing, raised her to a fever pitch, the secret place where no man had been but him throbbing and pulsating exquisitely.

She couldn't. He mustn't. It was shameful, disgraceful, sinful, he must stop! But she was powerless to speak, to move. Her senses, like her breath, were caught in a hypnotic web. She felt a rush of hot blood mounting to her face, her whole body trembling in a blaze of passion, her hands clawing, clutching the rough cloth of his sleeves as her torso convulsed into a shattering ecstasy.

Breathing hard, her eyes closed, she heard the rustle of cloth. And a few moments later he was over her again, his naked knee thrusting her legs apart. She gasped as he entered her, his hardness plummeting down, down into her wetness. Out and down again, deep inside as if

to reach the very seat of her soul. Again she felt the
tense trembling, the liquid fire consuming her. Her arms
went about his broad back, her hands raking the rippling
muscles, her hips arching, thirsty, hungry, wanting more
and more, her breath coming in ragged gasps, her entire
being hanging a hairsbreadth away from release, yearning for it, wanting it, until it came, a shuddering climax
one moment before his own.

She lay in his arms as he silently caressed her tangled
hair. She did not think, she did not want to think. But
the thought came, nevertheless, sneaking into her mind
like a thief. This is what it's like to really be made love
to. This is what it's like to have someone more powerful, stronger than I taking me to the outer limits of
passion. He has used me savagely, and I should hate
him, should be ashamed of my own rapture, my own
wild response. And I am ashamed, I am. But, oh, how
pleasant it is to lie in the shelter of his arms, to feel the
relief of sweet surrender.

Chapter XVI

Two days later Elthea was found.

Hannah, sitting in Sabrina's room, had been reading an account of Chinese shrimp camps at Tomales Bay in the *Lark* when the maid came to the door and told her that Dr. Christian wished to speak to her over the telephone.

It was the first time Hannah had used the telephone and it gave her a start to hear Christian's voice, clear except for a slight echo, from so many miles away.

"Mr. Kahn, the Pinkerton fellow, thinks he has located Elthea. He didn't make himself known for fear of frightening her away. *If* that's her. Only you can make positive identification."

"Yes, yes, I understand."

Though Hannah had prepared herself for this moment, warning herself that it might still be another disappointment, her heart quickened. "Where is she?"

"In the Mission district. Living with a man by the name of Edward Maybeck."

"I'll go at once."

"I think it would be wiser if I took you in the buggy. I shan't intrude, but I'll be there in case you need me. Expect me in half an hour."

They spoke little as they drove, Christian skillfully guiding the bay cob through the busy streets thronged with carriages, bicycles, and wagons, moving the buggy smoothly to the right at the clang of a cable-car bell.

Hannah had not seen Christian since he had made love to her. She had anticipated his return the following night by blocking her door and placing a chair under the handle. But though she had slept uneasily, waking at the slightest sound, she had not heard his footstep. There had been no knock or rattling of the knob. The next morning she learned Christian hadn't been home all the previous day or night. Where he had gone, when he would return, was not mentioned. Apparently Christian's unexplained absences were taken as a matter of course because he was a doctor. Or perhaps that had always been Christian's habit, to come and go as he pleased. The thought that he might have a mistress, that he had gone from her bed to another's, had slipped into her mind. But she could not bring herself to ask or even to hint at it.

"We're almost there," Christian said. "I suggest you try to gain admittance to the house if someone other than Elthea comes to the door. Say you are collecting for the poor. Some specific charity, like the Little Sisters' Infant Shelter." He drew the buggy up to the curb. "The place is around the corner. Number thirteen. I'll wait twenty minutes. If you don't return by then, I'll assume you're having trouble and I'll come after you."

Number thirteen was a row house identical to its neighbors, each with its corniced, double-fronted windows, shallow flights of wooden steps and iron rails painted white. Hannah, her mouth dry, her heart thumping, mounted the stairs, paused a moment, then let the knocker fall twice and waited.

A man in shirtsleeves, his soiled white collar unbuttoned, opened the door.

"Yes?" His breath smelled strongly of cheap whiskey. "Whatcha want?"

He was in his early forties, Hannah guessed, a heavyset man, his bald head and hooded eyes giving him the look of a cobra.

"I'm Mrs. Cable." Hannah smiled broadly. "I represent the Little Sisters' Infant Shelter and we are collecting contributions. Have you heard of us?" She spoke quickly, smiling again, for he was starting to close the door. "I'm sure you have. The shelter cares for the babies of working mothers who have no place to leave them. The sisters are in desperate need of funds, any little contribution would help. You look like a kind Christian gentleman, I can see it on your face."

Nothing was further from the truth. But he hesitated. "Well," he grumbled, "wait a minute. I'll see if I can rustle up some change."

He left the door slightly ajar and Hannah slipped through. It was dim inside and it took her a moment or two to make out her surroundings: a fern stand, dark walls, and a staircase. There was a faded portiere to her left, behind which she assumed the man had disappeared. The house smelled of frying bacon.

"Who is it?" a feminine voice inquired.

Hannah moved closer to the curtain, not sure of the voice, hoping against hope.

"Somebody collecting for the Little Sisters," the man said. "I'll give a few pennies just to get rid of her."

A child began to cry. "Hush," the female voice cautioned. "Hush, Clara, darlin'."

Hannah stepped through the curtain, vaguely aware that she had entered a small, stuffy dining room. A grandmother clock on the wall said one-fifteen. But it was the figure across the room that held her attention. Elthea, holding Clara, was standing in the doorway of what appeared to be the kitchen.

"Elthea!"

She froze, her eyes starting from her head. "Oh, God! Oh, God! It's Hannah!"

The man, who had been rummaging in a dresser drawer, looked up.

"Who?" He whirled about. "You! How'd you get in? Whatcha doing in my house?" He turned back to Elthea. "You know this woman?"

"She—she's my sister-in-law." Little Clara had stopped her whimpering and turned wide eyes on Hannah.

"What the hell!" His face darkened. "You tricked me. Get out! Get out, or I'll throw you out!"

Hannah ignored him. "Get your things, Elthea. You're coming home with me."

Elthea threw a frightened look at the frowning man. "Ed—Edward won't let me."

"He has nothing to say about it. Do you want me to help you pack?"

Edward made a threatening gesture toward Elthea. "Stay where you are, woman." She shrank back against the wall. The baby began to whimper again. "And shut that brat up!"

He returned to Hannah. "Now get the hell out! Coming in, fooling me, begging for the Little Sisters. I don't like that." His fists clenched as he crossed over to where Hannah stood. "D'ya hear me?" His hot whiskey breath was like a blow. "I ain't above manhandling a female."

Hannah, her heart skittering in fright, stood her ground. "I don't know how my sister-in-law came here. But I'm sure it wasn't of her own free will."

"So you're sure?" he mocked. "Elthea—do you want to leave with this bitch who says you're her sister-in-law?"

Elthea's lips trembled. "N-no, Edward."

"You see!" Edward said triumphantly. "You heard her. She don't want to go. Now *you* get!"

"I don't believe her," Hannah said in a calm voice that hardly seemed hers. "She's frightened. She's afraid to say what she really wants and that's to go back to her husband. So step aside." When he did not move, she added, "You could be in deep trouble, Mr. Maybeck. I'll go to the police if you force her to stay."

The lidded eyes glared down at her.

Then suddenly the glare, the scowl, disappeared and he gave Hannah a yellow-fanged grin. "You know you wouldn't want to go to the law. Would you? You can't blame me for getting mad. I'm a suspicious man. You might be anybody walking in, asking for Elthea. How'd I know you wasn't some tout from Dupont Street, rounding up innocent birds for the trade, eh? Now, where's this little lady's husband?"

"I can't see where that concerns you." His abrupt turnabout made her wary. Or was he really worried about the police?

"Elthea . . ."

"Is Travis here?" she asked in a scared whisper.

"He's at the ranch, waiting for you." Hannah spoke softly. "He's terribly upset about you running off."

"Is he?"

"He wants you back, Elthea. He promises not to be angry. He just wants you back."

Edward stopped grinning. He looked from Elthea to Hannah. "So he sent you here by your lonesome."

"Yes. And I'm not leaving without Elthea."

"Is that it?" Edward strode to the sideboard, moving, for all his ponderous weight, on light feet. He drew out a long, metal-handled knife that looked as though it had been honed to razor sharpness. "She's staying with me. And you . . ." He pointed the knife at Hannah. "You ain't going to any police."

A stray beam of light glanced off the knife blade as Maybeck twisted it in his beefy hands. An icy sickness lodged in the pit of Hannah's stomach. Yet somehow she managed to keep her voice from breaking. "Are you threatening me, Mr. Maybeck?"

"I ain't threatening. I mean it." He covered the distance between them, bringing the knife up, placing the tip against Hannah's throat. "I mean to slit you wide open."

"Put—put that knife down, Mr. Maybeck." Her heart was hammering against her ribs now. "I have a friend waiting outside. All I have to do is call."

Christian had said twenty minutes. How long had she been here? She glanced at the clock. One twenty-five. Ten more minutes. If she screamed, Christian would never hear her. Keep talking, she told herself, or this brute will kill you before Christian arrives. Put him off, say anything.

"You're lying," the man said. "I ain't seen no one when I opened the door. If you had a friend, he'd be on the street."

"I'm not lying. It's true."

"All right, I'll have a look. But don't you move! If you as much as blink, I'll skin you alive."

Keeping an eye on Hannah, he backed toward the window. Elthea stood against the wall, petrified, white to the lips, her baby lolling on her shoulder.

Every nerve, every instinct urged Hannah to flee. *Run!* Here's your chance! But she couldn't. God knew what this man would do. He might be angry enough to kill Elthea or the baby or both.

Edward Maybeck snatched aside the curtain and made a quick left-to-right scan.

"Ain't nobody there." He came back to Hannah. "Say your prayers." He smiled his cobra smile as he brought the knife up again, pricking Hannah's skin through the collar of her blouse.

"You fool," she said, putting scorn into a voice that nevertheless trembled. "The Pinkerton Agency sent me here. They know who you are."

"It's a lie. You're making it up like you did everything else since I laid eyes on you. Even if what you said is true, I'll be long gone with Elthea before they find me."

Sweat had gathered on Hannah's forehead under the brim of her hat. Surely twenty minutes had passed? But she couldn't tell. Her neck muscles ached with the need to lift her head and glance at the clock. But the knife, gleaming in the dust-moted dimness, mesmerized her. She could not tear her eyes away from the deadly silver blade. So engrossed was she with the knife, so absorbed was Edward in watching her now-obvious terror, that neither of them noticed Elthea lift a china pitcher from the sideboard until it came flying through the air, catching Edward squarely on the side of the head.

He let out a roar and, pivoting about, was advancing on Elthea, knife poised. She screamed just as Christian came through the curtain.

Edward blinked at him for a moment, then, like a raging bull, lunged at Christian, who sidestepped. Before Edward could regain his balance, Christian grabbed the red-faced man by his shirtfront and landed a punch on his jaw. Edward dropped the knife and staggered back. Without giving Edward time to bring up his fists, Christian drove into him again and again, until Edward crumpled to his knees, then to the floor, almost taking Elthea with him. The baby was now howling in terror. Christian picked up the knife and stood over Edward, breathing heavily. Hannah, her heart hammering, saw the mad blaze in Christian's eyes, the savage, feral gleam that was so frightening because it did not fit with the smooth facade of his usual self. It was as if the devil had truly taken possession of his soul and for one moment she thought he was going to drive the knife into the fallen man. Then he opened his hand and the knife fell to the carpet with a dull thud.

He turned to Hannah. "Are you hurt?"

"No," she whispered. The scene, those same words, took her back to the night he had rescued her from the escaped convicts, the night they had become lovers for the first time. He was looking at her now as he had then, a softness in his eyes, a concern that melted her. She wanted to run to him, to have him close his strong arms around her, to have him kiss the crown of her head, to hold her trembling body close and tell her that everything was all right. He must have guessed her thoughts for he took a step toward her. But as he did so Elthea let out a small cry and, with the screaming baby still in her arms, slid down the wall into a faint.

They took Elthea back to Christian's house. She had recovered in the buggy and now she stood in the hall under the amber dome looking lost and frightened, clinging fast to Hannah's hand. The Falconers had gone to visit friends in fashionable Burlingame—"down the peninsula"—for a few days and Christian played host. He had Elthea and the child installed in one of the upstairs bedrooms, although Elthea would have preferred sharing Hannah's. A trundle bed was brought in for Clara, and hot food on a tray.

Before leaving Maybeck's Hannah had quickly gathered up the few things that she recognized as belonging to Elthea. Edward had still been comatose when they had carried Elthea and the baby out. Hannah had assumed that Christian would notify the police at once and have Edward arrested for forcibly detaining Elthea.

"Do you really want to call in the police?" Christian had asked Hannah. "To do so would embroil your sister-in-law in a trial, not to speak of the public scandal. The newspapers are always looking for such tidbits—girl held as white slave—that sort of thing. I imagine poor Elthea would prefer to go home and forget the whole unhappy affair."

Christian had been right, of course. Elthea looked ill, her eyes bruised and haunted. She said nothing about going on to Georgia. In fact she said almost nothing about what had happened to her since she and Clara had left Sycamore. To all Hannah's questions she replied, "I don't know," or "I was so homesick I couldn't think," or "I don't remember." She was worried about Travis, what he would do, what he would say.

"He don't love me no more," she said.

"But he does." Hannah took Elthea's hands in her own. "He wanted to come looking for you the minute he found you gone, he was that concerned."

"He was?"

"Yes. He loves you. We all love you." She kissed Elthea, holding the slim body for a few moments. "We've missed you. I never realized how much." She smoothed Elthea's hair with her hands. "But you're here now, thank God, and we'll be going back together."

Things would be different. Hannah would see to that. She'd have a talk with Travis, remind him that he had married Elthea for better or worse and must be kind to her. She herself would try harder to cajole Elthea into a feeling that she belonged, that she had a family at Sycamore who cared.

"Little Clara misses her papa," Hannah said.

After Hannah had tucked in both Elthea and the baby, kissing them, wishing them pleasant dreams, she returned to her own room.

Opening the door, she found Christian sitting on a

chair near the window. In his waistcoat and shirtsleeves, smoking a cigar, his long legs stretched out, reading a newspaper, he looked as if he belonged there.

"Ah, Hannah." He put the paper aside. "Got the runaways settled for the night?"

"Yes."

It flashed through her mind that this was how it would be if she came into a room that was theirs, hers and Christian's, a bedroom they shared as husband and wife. Christian would be waiting for her, his eyes lighting up, the familiar, loving "Ah, Hannah" on his lips. He would ask if the children had been bedded down, she would say yes and go to him, his arms would open wide. . . .

Fantasy.

Christian had told her long ago that he wasn't the marrying kind, he wasn't a family man. And though he had later claimed he no longer felt that way, she wasn't sure. She would never be sure.

"Have you come to discuss our train fare?" Earlier she had asked if she could borrow the money to get back to Sycamore.

"No."

"Then why are you here, Christian?" There was a tired edge to her voice. The day's events had drained her.

"Close the door, Hannah."

She didn't realize that she was leaning against the half-open door for support until he told her to close it.

"Why are you here?" she repeated.

"I'll explain. But I'd rather the servants didn't hear our conversation."

She gave the door behind her a backward shove and a nerve jumped as she heard it click shut.

"You've already collected your reward." She hated the way those cold words sounded. She didn't mean to be ungrateful for what he had done, even if he did have an ulterior motive. She would have liked to thank him decently without this man-woman thing between them, this conflict of wills.

"I'm not here for a reward, Hannah."

He rose and drew up a slipper chair. "Sit down. There is something I have to say and I'd like you to hear me out. No—now."

She sat primly, smoothing out her skirts. Her eyes fastened on the gold watch chain looped across his fawn-colored, satin-backed waistcoat. When he did not speak, she lifted her eyes.

He was looking at her, a brooding speculation in his eyes. "Sometimes I wonder why you are so frequent a visitor to my thoughts. Your stubborn pride puts me off. If I live to be a hundred, I'll never understand you. Yet in spite of your confounded arbitrariness I love you."

The words spoken so plainly, so matter-of-factly, flustered her. No fanciful admonishments, no sweet nothings, no honeyed flattery. He had not taken her hand, had not moved. He sat gazing at her, an imperturbable expression on his face.

"Don't you believe me?"

She shook her head. There was a sudden thickness in her throat that made it difficult to speak.

"Well?"

"You—you've said that you love me before, Christian. To me loving is being faithful. The two go hand in hand."

"Faithful works both ways, Hannah. You spoke of love, too. You were engaged to me, if you remember. Then you suddenly turned around and married another man."

"How could you expect me to be faithful when I saw you at the Palmer House with Amanda? And both of you registered as Mr. and Mrs."

"That was Amanda's doing."

He went on to explain. She listened, wanting to believe, yet her mind kept asking, Is this true? Has Christian really changed? Were his good deeds, his protestations of love, a charade, a mask hiding the dissolute woman-izer who had seduced, then refused to marry her? Oh God, she prayed, how can I possibly be sure?

"Hannah, I want you to be honest with me. Do you love me? In Chicago you claimed you did. But I want to hear it now."

She got up from the chair and walked over to the bureau. Laid out neatly on the marble top were a silver-backed brush, a stoppered scent bottle, a cut-glass vase, and a box of powder, the toilet articles Sabrina had left behind ten years earlier. She studied the powder box, the faded forget-me-nots on the lid. Countess Estina's Complexion Dust. Hannah had never owned a box of complexion dust in her life.

"Hannah?"

She did not want to think about Christian, about his love, she did not want to think that he was sitting behind her waiting for an answer, an honest answer. She did not want to confess her innermost feelings, the love she had locked away in her heart. She knew now she had never loved any man as she had loved Christian. But she loved Guy, too—a different kind of love, perhaps, not this passion, this tearing pain, this deep-seated knowledge that whatever happened, wherever she was, Christian's face and Christian's voice would always be with her.

"I love you," he repeated. "And I know you love me. I want you to think about it before you get on that train back to Monterey. I want you to think about what the years ahead will be like, Hannah. You don't belong on a ranch. You're not the sort of woman who should be reduced to a menial, who should be slaving for a man you don't really love. Hannah, you love *me*. I want to give you so much. I want to dress you in silk and satin. I want to put diamonds and rubies on your fingers, at your ears, around your throat, because you are made for jewels and beautiful clothes. I want to take you to the theater, to the opera, to the ballet, because you would enjoy those things. I want to see you use your mind, the native intelligence you were born with, reading books, attending lectures, not have to waste yourself in tasks that any dull-witted wife can perform. Do you know what I'm saying, Hannah?"

Was he tempting her, baiting, luring her with the promise of an easy, fascinating life? Luxuries she never dreamed of could be hers. The bath with its gilded taps and mirrored walls. But it was more than luxury he was promising. He was pledging his love.

She looked up from the powder box and saw her face in the mirror, the unsteady mouth, the misted eyes.

"Look at me, Hannah."

She turned. "You must not . . ." she began and couldn't go on.

"I'm asking you to leave Guy. I'm asking you to come to me, where you belong." Neither his eyes nor his voice begged. He was not a begging man. And yet his tone was tender.

"I can't," Hannah said. "I gave my vow. He loves me."

"But do you love him?"

After a long moment she whispered, "Yes."

"You're not being candid, Hannah."

She covered her face with her hands. "Why are you tormenting me?" Her muffled voice shook with emotion.

"You torment yourself, Hannah."

She swallowed. Then, taking a deep breath, she brought her head up. "You say you love me. How can I believe it?"

"I've only to take you in my arms and have you feel the beat of my heart."

"No!" Her cheeks stung with vivid color. Oh, damn him! Yes, damn. Why did he have to be so sure of himself? "You still have the same insufferable arrogance."

"It isn't arrogance, Hannah." He sighed, then shook his head. "I wish you would try to understand. How can I prove myself? What can I do? I won't touch you, Hannah. Not even a kiss. Though I want it badly. I would live like a monk—a month, a year, five, ten, if only I knew that at the end of that time you would come to me."

"As your mistress?"

"As my wife. I can arrange a divorce."

"Divorce Guy? How? I would have no earthly reason. You know how difficult, if not impossible, it is for a woman who leaves a good husband to obtain a divorce."

"Then we will live as man and wife all the same. It is

a much more forthright, honorable arrangement than spending the rest of your life with a husband you don't love. It isn't fair. It isn't fair to him or to you."

How glib he was. How he could twist words to suit his own meaning, his purpose. Yet he wanted them to be together, whether as mistress or wife didn't matter. Mistresses and divorced wives were ostracized from polite society but she didn't care about polite society. She would live with Christian and be introduced as Mrs. Falconer. She would never have to fire a stove, feed a chicken, or milk a cow. She would sit in a box at the Mission Street Opera House, the one she had read about in the *Examiner*, and hear Caruso sing in *La Bohème*. She would watch Ellen Terry at the Lyceum. She would have books to read, the latest fashion magazines to choose her clothes from, a piano to play. She would turn at night in bed and have Christian's strong arms go around her, see his smile at breakfast, feel his kiss on her cheek.

"I want you to be the mother of my children, Hannah."

"Even though they may be illegitimate?"

"I can legitimize them by adoption."

Oh, God, why was she contemplating this insane proposal even for a moment? Christian already was the father of her child, the boy Guy thought was his. Guy would never let her have Mark. She'd have to leave her son unless she confessed that Christian had fathered him, that she, Hannah, had been a liar and a cheat. It would crush Guy. She couldn't.

"Think about it, Hannah."

Did Lucifer in the guise of the serpent so tempt Eve? "I can't." What did she really know of Christian? She knew he had a black temper, that beneath the fine clothes and courteous air lurked a man who could turn savage at a moment's notice. Yet he could be tender, too. Or was his tenderness part of a disguise, like his well-tailored coats and charming manners? His way of life had altered, true. He was no longer an idler but a professional man. But had *he* changed? Had he given up his whiskey and his whores? In her experience men seldom relinquished their vices. Though her father had sworn dozens of times to walk the straight and narrow, he soon returned to drinking just as he had done before.

"I won't press you," Christian said. "If at the end of two days you still want to return to Sycamore Ranch, I'll not stand in your way." He got to his feet. "I don't want you if I can't have your heart as you would have mine. All of it, Hannah. No regrets. It's your—*our*—happiness I'm concerned about. Remember, you have only one life to live."

For a moment she thought he would reach out to her. She wanted him to. She wanted him to hold her against his strong chest, to have him stroke her hair, to banish the confusion and doubt in her mind. But he went to the door and smiled at her, a soft, almost sorrowful smile. "Good night, Hannah."

She spent a sleepless night. Of course she wasn't going to leave Guy. She couldn't leave him, sitting there at Sycamore in the midst of a drought, in debt, working from dawn to dusk, toiling for her and the boy and the family they had planned. She would never forgive herself. What if her days went on as they had in the past, without excitement or surprise, a revolving wheel of routine? She would have more children, be a good wife, a good mother. And if her mind grew rusty and her heart cold and she became another Tess Barlow, at least she could face her Maker with a clear conscience. Yet . . .

You have only one life to live.

It was Christian who put meaning into her life, gave her world color and excitement, Christian whose solid shoulder she could lean on. Whatever his failings, he was strong. He was nothing like Chad, or Travis, or even Guy. Perhaps he *had* changed. And his tenderness, how could she deny him when his hands gently caressed her hair, when he looked into her eyes with a melting softness that spoke so eloquently of love?

Oh, why had she ever met Christian? Why had she ever loved him?

Hannah and Elthea, with little Clara on her lap, were

having breakfast at the long table in the dining room. There were just the three of them. Christian had left early, called out by a woman whose husband had been stabbed in a fight over an unpaid bill. The Falconers were still at Burlingame.

Elthea ate with an exaggerated daintiness. Every now and then she would spoon porridge into Clara's pursed little mouth. Hannah tried hard to converse with her sister-in-law. But she was as chary with words as she had always been. Hannah felt no resentment, however. She understood how difficult it was for the girl to express her feelings to someone like herself, who, in Elthea's eyes, represented authority. Hannah also understood Elthea's fright. Back home in the Georgia hills a wife did not run away from a husband no matter how he treated her. "Until death do us part" was taken literally. Elthea had violated that moral code. (Just as surely as I have, Hannah thought, when I slept with Christian.) I can't blame Elthea. There's no blame in me.

They were nearly finished with the meal when the butler entered.

"A man to see you, Mrs. Hartwell. Says he's your brother."

"Oh! It's Travis!" Hannah jumped up from chair as Elthea paled and wrapped her arms tightly about Clara.

Hannah ran out into the entry hall. "Travis!" She gave him a hug, felt him stiffen, and stepped back. "Oh, Travis! Travis! It's so good to see you. How's Mark? Is he all right? Does he miss me? And Guy . . ."

"Hold on," he said. "Everyone's fine. What I want to know is what yore doin' here." He frowned, pushing his hat back, revealing the white line on his forehead above his tanned face.

"It's a long story, Travis. I've found Elthea and little Clara."

"They here, too?"

"Yes. Come in, come in. Have you had breakfast?"

The butler stepped forward to take Travis's hat. Travis hung on to it. "I don't feel easy here, Hannah. Get Elthea and Clara and let's go."

She linked her arm in his. "Don't be foolish, Travis.

Come in and have a cup of coffee. You've nothing to fear. All of the Falconers are gone."

He went reluctantly into the dining room, feeling as out of place in his patched, dusty overalls and wool shirt as Hannah had felt in her shabby shawl when she first came to Nob Hill.

"Elthea," he said. He leaned over her chair and kissed the baby but not her.

"You mad at me?" she whispered.

"I was at first, but I ain't no more."

He sat down on the chair beside her. The butler, ready to fill Travis's coffee cup, stood with the silver pitcher poised, staring at Travis's hat. Travis sheepishly removed it and placed it on the seat next to him.

"How did you know I was here?" Hannah asked.

"I didn't till I went to the Clayton Hotel. They told me where you'd moved."

"We were going home in a day or two," Hannah said. "You should have waited."

"Couldn't. I was that worried. I had to come and see what happened. Didn't know whether Elthea and the baby were dead or alive."

"I wrote you yesterday and explained everything."

"Well, I'm here."

He looked at Elthea. Her lip quivered as she averted her eyes.

"Why don't you two go upstairs?" Hannah suggested. "I'll take Clara. I'm sure you have a lot to say to each other."

An hour later as Hannah sat in her room dandling the baby on her knee, there was a hesitant knock on the door.

"Hannah?" Travis opened the door. When he saw he had the right room, an angry look came into his eyes. "I got to talk to you."

"You've not handled Elthea roughly?"

"I ain't laid a finger on her. We got along, all right. What she done was wrong, but I'm willin' to forgive her. 'Specially when it weren't her fault."

"I don't understand."

"She come to San Francisco like you guessed. She come on her own. Some kind gentleman she met up with at the Monterey station gave her the money."

This was not quite the way the red-whiskered man had explained it but she let it pass.

Travis went on. "Soon as she got to the city she took a job in a woman's kitchen in one of them big houses on Rincon Hill. A couple of days later when she was out walkin' with little Clara, she got kidnapped right off the street."

"I suspected as much," Hannah said. "She wouldn't talk about it, but I didn't force the issue. She's been through so much."

"She was that. What riles me is how you could come *here*. How could you get anywhere near Christian Falconer? He's nothin' but trouble, Hannah. Ain't you got respect for yore husband, comin' to this fella's house— and I don't know what all."

It was hard to keep her voice steady, harder not to blush. "There was no 'what all,' " she lied. "It was perfectly proper. This is Mr. Falconer's parents' home. The Falconers are decent people. I was well chaperoned."

"Christian Falconer, decent? I'd soon say the devil was decent."

"It was Mr. Falconer who found Elthea for me."

"Easy enough. Elthea says *he* was the one who got her kidnapped and put her with that man."

"What? That's preposterous! How does she know it was Christian?"

"She saw him. He come to that Edward Maybeck's house late one night when Elthea was supposed to be asleep. She crept down the stairs and saw them both in the parlor. Maybeck was askin' for more money if he was supposed to get a punch in the jaw for his trouble. Falconer was going to put up a show, he told Maybeck, so you'd be obliged to him."

"Why—I never!" Hannah exclaimed. "That story is so farfetched, I wonder you give it credence." It was the kind of tale Elthea, feeling guilty, could easily have made up. Did she go with the man willingly, then later

find herself a prisoner? Or was her account simply a
means to gain Travis's sympathy?

"Is Elthea sure that's what happened?"

"Shore as shore," he answered grimly. "She ain't
lyin', Hannah. I know Elthea."

Hannah thought, Suppose, just suppose it is true.
Then why hasn't Elthea said anything about it to me?
Not one word against Christian. Is she afraid? Under his
roof she might fear repercussions. Perhaps her story
isn't all that fanciful.

She remembered how Christian had arrived at the
Clayton the very morning the advertisement had been
published. That was the first he had known of Elthea's
disappearance. Armed with her description, could he
have contacted the Pinkerton Agency, instructing them
to locate Elthea, then arranged for her kidnapping? Was
that why he had been reluctant to call the police? He
had claimed it was because it would embroil Elthea in a
public scandal. But what if the real reason was his wish
to hide the truth? The possibility that the events leading
up to Elthea's rescue might have happened exactly as
Elthea had explained to Travis triggered Hannah's old
mistrust. How could she believe anything Christian said?
Did he *really* love her?

Travis said, "It come as a big shock, did it? Best plan
is to get on home and forget the whole thing. I don't get
why you ain't already left."

"I don't have the money. Mr. Falconer offered to buy
our tickets."

"He did? We don't need charity from Christian Falconer or no one. I've got money and I'll see to them
tickets straight off."

She didn't argue. Somehow in the back of her mind it
had already been decided even before Travis's appearance. She had known she would return to Sycamore.
Whether Christian had lied and, in the last instance,
schemed did not matter. She couldn't abandon Guy. If
Guy had been cruel, selfish, faithless, a drunk, she may
have had an excuse. But he was a good man, a good
husband. He loved her. She had been married to him in
the sight of God, had vowed to be a faithful wife. If she

yielded to Christian and left Guy, tempted by Christian's ardor and his promises to give her the many things she'd never had, then she would be guilty of inflicting pain on a man who deserved better. She couldn't do that. For better or worse she belonged with Guy at Sycamore.

She would try her best to forget Christian. God willing, he would come to mind less and less as the years went on. There would be moments of pain, moments of tender memories, flashes of anger, perhaps. There might even be times in the dark of the night when she would mourn her loss with tears. And if the sight of their son, his frown, the sound of his laughter, stirred up old memories, that was the cross she must bear.

Chapter XVII

It sprinkled some in March, a few brief showers that wet the parched earth at Sycamore and brought a delicate, almost imperceptible green haze to the hillsides. But it was far too late for the oats and barley. Only wild cucumber vines, hardy and impervious to soil or weather, now grew in the withered fields.

Hannah, having replanted her garden, coaxed the new corn, bean, and tomato sprouts along by hauling water from the spring. Each morning, emerging from the house to fill the kitchen water buckets, she would scan the vast reaches of the blue sky for a sign of clouds. Once March passed they could not hope for rainfall until the following winter.

A half-dozen calves had been born to Guy's cows in February. As soon as the young ones had grown out of the wobbly stage Guy and Travis brought the herd— minus the third promised to King—back to Sycamore to feed on the fragile new growth.

Life had resumed its old pattern. It was as if Elthea had never run away. Travis grumbled at her and Elthea wept, but not so the others could see. His promise to be kind and loving was more often broken than kept. Elthea annoyed him. Hannah was certain that Travis held the girl's association with another man against her whenever they quarreled. He had even begun to shout at Clara. Hannah remonstrated with him over this. She conceded (but not to him) that Elthea was not the best of possible wives, but she could not forgive him for taking after the child. Clara was a timid little girl with golden curls and large scared blue eyes much like her mother's. Perhaps this resemblance was what irritated Travis. But it didn't excuse him.

Hannah had given up trying to encourage her brother to better himself. She saw that he wasn't interested in learning a trade, in educating himself, in improving his station in life. What she had thought was ambition had been merely a desire to get out from under Chad's thumb. At Sycamore Travis had found his niche—ranch hand. He liked the outdoor life, the freedom from responsibility, liked the routine of mending fences, hazing and branding cows, checking the wells and water troughs. Hannah had become resigned to her brother's acceptance of things as they were. Apparently he had not even the wish to acquire a piece of land that he could call his own.

She told herself that she did not love Travis less because he did not fit the ideal she had set for him since childhood. He had been her ally, her big brother, her protector. The latter was still a role he attempted to fill. His dislike of Christian, she was certain, rose from his fear that Falconer would harm her. At Stonebridge he had learned of Christian's black reputation and, forming an opinion, had not seen any reason to change it. Nor had Hannah given him any reason, for she never discussed Christian with her brother.

She tried not to think of Christian but memories of him persisted more tenaciously than she had imagined they would. He had written her a letter and, without opening the envelope, she had torn it into shreds and tossed it into the fire. What was the use? She was beyond whatever he had to say, whatever appeal he might make. He might be angry and hurt but she could do nothing about it.

Trying to forget, Hannah had thrown herself into passionate response to Guy's lovemaking, even daring to initiate it herself a time or two, hoping that the yearning fire that consumed her would be quenched. Her wild kisses, her eager embraces, were met with surprise and delight. Guy gave her all he could, but after the first spate of kisses and inexpert fondling, he would enter her and quickly come to climax, leaving her unsatisfied and depressed.

Her wish to have a child by Guy now came close to obsession. Nightly she prayed for pregnancy. The coming of her monthly was met with dismay. If only she could have her husband's baby, a child that would bind her more tightly to Guy. Seeing Mark with Christian's hazel eyes shining out at her was both pain and joy. She worried unduly about him, rarely letting him out of her sight, afraid that some accident might happen, a divine retribution visited upon the son for the mother's sin. She called herself foolish, but still found it hard to shake off the biblical superstitions instilled in her as a child. Watching Mark as he played with a set of wooden soldiers Guy had whittled for him, or with his head bent over a picture book, the cowlick falling across his brow the way Christian's sometimes did, she fought the desire to weep. It was not seemly for a married woman to sorrow, loverlike, over the loss of another man. Granny's ghost standing in the the shadows of her mind would shake her head sadly. But what was seemly and what was bitter fact were worlds apart.

Flavia still rode into Sycamore once a week, bringing bits of local gossip. True to her prediction, her father had asked his sister-in-law to marry him and she had accepted. A wedding barbecue was planned as soon as a minister from Monterey could be brought down.

"April or May, maybe," Flavia said. Word would be spread up and down the coast for people to be ready. Flavia herself was currently being courted by a widower who owned a spread in Indian Valley. A man some twenty years older than she, he was anxious to remarry and produce a son, since his wife had left him childless. Flavia had no mind to accommodate him.

"He's ugly and he smells," she complained. "I don't

care if he's richer than Pa and promises to build me a new house with one of those newfangled tile stoves.''

As always, she flirted outrageously with Guy, which seemed to embarrass Travis, who made himself scarce when Flavia appeared. But Hannah liked the girl, despite her pursuit of Guy. Flavia's cheerfulness, her bubbling sense of humor, lightened the atmosphere at Sycamore—God knew it needed lightening these days— and Hannah looked forward to her visits.

"I don't believe you have a mean bone in your body," Hannah would say, laughing at some quip.

And Flavia would reply, "Yes, I do. What's more, I'm a sinner. Oh, yes." And her pretty face would dimple into a smile.

A foggy, though rainless, summer had passed into early fall when another misfortune befell the Hartwells. Anthrax. Guy first noticed the dreaded pustules, signs of the virulent, contagious, and deadly disease, on a recalcitrant bull he had acquired only two months earlier from a rancher named Turlock in Big Sur Valley. It angered Hannah to think a sick animal had been foisted on Guy.

"Turlock probably didn't know the beast was carrying anthrax," Guy said. "He sold me that bull in good faith. He's an honest man."

"Honest is as honest does," Hannah quoted tartly. She had always admired Guy's confidence in the word of his fellowman, his refusal to believe the worst, but now she wished he had been more skeptical.

The bull died the next morning but not before it had infected some two dozen steer.

Guy and Travis, examining the rest of the herd, moved those who seemed healthy to higher pastures, isolating them in small bunches. The rest, even those who showed only the slightest sign of weakness, they destroyed. It was the only known recourse against this malignant and swift-acting infection, and they hoped by taking these drastic measures they could save the rest of their stock.

The loss of some thirty animals—in addition to the drought—came as the market price dropped even further. The meat-consuming public were now favoring their beef fattened on alfalfa and corn rather than the leaner range-fed steer. The cattle broker, who must bear the cost of putting fat on the animals he bought from ranchers like Guy, paid less for the latter.

Guy, wondering what new calamity would happen next, was plunged into despondency. Travis had seen Guy down before but not the way he was now. It scared him. For the first time Travis began to wonder if the ranch would go under. He couldn't imagine leaving Sycamore. What would he do? There was nothing waiting for him in Georgia even if he wanted to go back. He'd probably have to find himself a job in San Francisco or Monterey. Live in small, dingy rooms with Elthea and the baby, working ten to twelve hours a day with a boss breathing down his neck.

Worse yet, Elthea was pregnant again. Good job she had been back at Sycamore long enough for him to be sure the kid was his or he'd have sent her home to her ma right quick. But he couldn't do that now. He couldn't cast her off no matter how she irked him or how much he wished he had Flavia as wife. Hannah wouldn't stand for it.

After Elthea had run off, he'd hied himself up to San Francisco because Guy kept asking if he wasn't worried. Well, he did feel guilty with her gone that way, not knowing where she was—and his fault. Then when Hannah had found her and they'd come back to the ranch, he thought maybe Elthea'd learned her lesson and they could make a fresh start. But no. Elthea wasn't home two weeks when she began moaning about her mama again.

She'd never growed up, Travis thought. That was the trouble. If she could have been more like Flavia, things would be different. Flavia—now there was a real woman. Maybe she did bat her eyes at everything in britches, and if she was his she'd bear close watching. They'd already had words over her taking after Guy so. But Flavia said it was just a tease. Besides, she didn't want people suspecting she was in love with him. *Him*, Travis. Made the front of his britches swell just thinkin' of the way she moaned and groaned, wanting it hard and fast, sayin' there wasn't a man in the world like him.

He knew he was doing wrong to bed Flavia. And he was scared he'd get her with child. *She* didn't seem to mind. But the idea made him break out in a cold sweat. Travis Blaine, the father of a bastard. But then when you looked at it another way, he wouldn't be the first, would he? He sometimes wondered about Mark—if you wanted a for-instance. There wasn't a bit of likeness to Guy in that boy. He did have Hannah's hair, dark brown with glints of red in it. But the way it grew was different. And the eyes. Hazel, they were called. When he first saw Mark's eyes, he thought they looked familiar. He'd seen the same speckled color on someone else. Christian Falconer came to mind. Those were Christian Falconer's eyes. And that square jaw, too. Not a Blaine jaw. Could it be? His sister and that drunken woman-chaser? No. Impossible. Hannah was such a good woman, decent, virtuous, a much better person than he could ever be. No. It was just happenstance. Plenty of folk had square jaws and cat's eyes; didn't mean a thing.

Leastwise he wasn't going to worry over it. Keeping Sycamore was what took up his mind these days. Guy being so glum about it didn't help. Travis tried to boost Guy's spirits by telling him his luck was bound to turn.

"Look at my pa," he'd say. "Nobody come so near to losin' his place, I don't know how many times, as Chad Blaine. And then at the last minute somethin' happened to let him keep Stonebridge."

"Let's pray you're right."

It was more than rain they needed now. It was money. Hannah suggested that maybe she ought to write to Aunt Bess for a loan and was surprised when Guy agreed. He had always been so independent, refusing to ask either his or his wife's relatives for help. But now he encouraged her to write. He himself sent a letter off to a brother who ran a prosperous truck farm outside of Calumet, Illinois. The answer to both letters came in a surprisingly short time considering the distance and erratic deliveries to their part of the world. The gist of Aunt Bess's terse reply (in which she again reminded

Travis that he owed her fifty dollars) and Edgar Hartwell's long rambling missive was that "money was short." Aunt Bess had added a postscript. "Your pa is drinking again. If he doesn't straighten up, out he goes. For good this time."

"I wish staying off corn whiskey was my only problem," Guy said.

Guy's last hope was that the bank might give him an extension—postpone both payment and interest for six months—if he appealed to them in person. He and Travis went up to San Francisco together. Five days later they returned, both with long faces. The bank had refused to wait for more than sixty days.

"They're getting ready to foreclose, Hannah. The man I talked to was polite, even helpful. He wasn't running the bank, he explained, just working for the people who did. He said we'd come out a lot better if we put the place up for sale. If the price is right, we might get a buyer right away."

"I don't like to think of selling when we've put so much of our lives into Sycamore."

"Neither do I. It makes me sick when I think of it. But what else can we do?"

"There must be *something*. Someone we could appeal to."

Guy shook his head. "Who?"

They were sitting in the kitchen, the pine worktable between them, Guy a picture of dejection, his face haggard, his shoulders drooping. Why, he's given up, Hannah thought. The fight's gone out of him. Looking at the turned-down mouth, the melancholy eyes, it occurred to her that he'd given up before he went to San Francisco. He had only gone as a gesture for her. She remembered how he had said he didn't think he'd be able to accomplish much, that the people at the bank didn't care what happened to ranch folk as long as they got their money. Hannah hated to think of Guy as a man easily defeated, and yet if she looked back over the past two years, she recalled certain signs. The drought, when it first came, had set him to pacing after supper, back and forth on the veranda, from time to time peering at a barometer he had nailed to a post. Optimism had turned to a pessimism he made no attempt to hide. Always one to talk, to make easy conversation, he had often lapsed into long silences. Now Hannah suspected that he had been seriously thinking of selling for some time.

If it were me, Hannah thought, I'd not sell. I would fight. I'd visit every bank and loan shark in the city, use the herd, the horses, the furniture, whatever was worth a nickel for collateral. I never would have come back to Sycamore empty-handed.

Yet pity held her tongue. Guy was the man of the house. She had to allow him some dignity.

"Do what you think is best, Guy." She got up, crossed over to where he was sitting, and kissed him. He threw his arms about her waist, holding her, clinging to her like a child. Then, to her dismay, he buried his face in her apron and wept.

By the next morning Guy had pulled himself together enough to draft a notice for the *Chronicle*. It took him half an hour to get past the heading, RANCH FOR SALE, and five attempts, with Hannah's help, to finish. While Hannah packed him a lunch he saddled his horse. If he pushed Strawberry at a good clip, he'd just barely make the mail pouch that went north on the noon coach from the Post ranch.

Though Hannah and Travis had long since ceased to confide in one another as they had in their childhood days, it was obvious that Travis was taking this latest reversal hard. She knew he was unhappy with Elthea—one would have to be blind not to see it—and that his fondness for Sycamore made up for his disappointing marriage. But there was little she could do to cheer him. Losing Sycamore would be difficult for her, too. She had come to appreciate its beauty, the blue-skied mornings when the rising sun painted the peaks of the mountains in a wash of gold, the summer fogs rolling through the canyons, a fairy mist sifting upward from the trees, the soaring flight of the hawks, the crimson and purple sunsets. But she would survive. She would get on with her life. She was adaptable. In the long run Guy would adjust, too, though his failure at Sycamore would always eat at him like a canker worm. And Travis? She didn't know. Somehow it seemed that he and his family would always be her charge. Travis, she realized, was not able—would probably never be able—to fend for himself.

Hannah and Mark were in the barn currying Theda when Elthea poked her head in the door. "Some man's come about the ranch. You're wanted up at the house."

"What's he like?" Hannah asked, hanging the curry brush up on its peg and rinsing her hands in the water pail.

"Dunno. Guy just hollered from the front room and I went out the kitchen door."

Mark asked, "Must I go, too, Mum?"

"Yes, come along."

Hannah took Mark by the hand and went toward the house. The stranger's mount tied to the rail was chestnut in color, a sleek-coated, silky-tailed Tennessee Walker. A rich man's horse, Hannah thought. All to the good. Once the decision to sell had been made, she and Guy wanted the best price they could get.

The men were in the parlor. She could hear the rumble of voices through the window. But it wasn't until she stepped through the door that she recognized the stranger.

"Good afternoon, Mrs. Hartwell," Christian said, rising from his chair. "I was just telling your husband that we are related in a roundabout way."

Hannah, paralyzed for one long appalling moment, replied, "Yes." The muscles in her face felt tight, a frozen mask that hid the turmoil behind it.

Why had he come? Oh God, why?

"The same Mr. Falconer," Guy was saying, "who was kind enough to help you find Elthea."

"Yes," Hannah echoed in a numb monotone. Guy had never been told the entire story of Elthea's flight. Hannah had persuaded Travis to keep silent on Elthea's claim that Christian had any part in Elthea's kidnapping. For one, she couldn't be sure it was true, and for another, she had felt that Guy would have wanted to inform the San Francisco police and that it would only complicate a matter that was best forgotten.

"My parents send their best wishes," Christian said, smiling.

"Thank you." Hannah's voice had no inflection, a dummy's voice. Her face felt stiff with the effort to control any hint of her distress, the welter of emotions churning inside. Why had fate played this cruel trick again? Was she never to be rid of him, never to be done with the painful constriction in her lungs, the flurried beat of her pulse when she saw him? "I didn't know you were interested in ranching, Mr. Falconer."

He did not seem to hear her. His eyes were fastened on Mark. Hannah's heart lurched sickly in her breast. Her first impulse was to step in front of her son, to shield, to hide him. Would Christian notice the resemblance? God, please no. Would Mark's eyes, the way his hair grew, the mouth and line of jaw be a dead giveaway? She prayed not. She didn't want Christian to know. Not now, not ever. It would be something to hold over her, perhaps to blackmail her with. Christian would not say anything in front of Guy—he was too well bred for that. Or was he?

"My son, Mark," Guy said proudly. "Say hello to Mr. Falconer, lad."

Mark shuffled shyly forward, his little hand reaching out to shake Christian's. "Hello, Mr. Fawkner."

Hannah forced a laugh. "Now run along, darling. Go to your room and play with your drum."

"But, Mama . . ." Mark, drawn to the stranger, objected.

"Do as I say, darling."

Christian watched as the child disappeared. "Fine boy," he said, looking directly at Hannah.

"Thank you." He knows, Hannah told herself. Dammit, he knows! He knows!

Guy said, "Well, then, would you like to look around, Mr. Falconer?"

"Yes, thank you, I would. Oh, and Mrs. Hartwell—I happen to be very much interested in ranching. It's been a lifelong ambition of mine to own a spread in this part of the state."

Liar! Hannah wanted to shout. Why are you here? What do you want?

"Won't you join us?" Christian asked.

"I think not."

"Perhaps we can persuade our guest to stay for supper and the night," Guy said. "It will be too late to start back once we've finished going over the ranch."

"By all means," Hannah said, sure that Christian had timed his visit with just such an invitation in mind.

The men returned in two hours with Travis, whom they had met in the upper pasture. Scowling, he made little attempt to hide his displeasure. Leaving Guy and Christian in the parlor, he came into the kitchen where Hannah and Elthea were fixing the evening meal. Elthea, with Clara on her hip, was stirring a kettle of rabbit stew. Hannah was slicing bread.

"What's he doin' here?" Travis wanted to know, jerking his thumb in the direction of the door.

"Hasn't he made it plain?" Hannah replied. "He wants to buy Sycamore."

"Well, I hope Guy doesn't sell it to him."

"I don't see what difference it makes who Guy sells it to. If he meets Guy's price . . ."

"*If.* Shore, if. The man's oily as a greased pig. Have you forgotten how he grabbed Elthea off the streets, then pretended he found her?" (Elthea, once she discovered Christian was at Sycamore, refused to come out of the kitchen.) "He'll cheat Guy. Then laugh about it to his friends."

"Don't make Guy out for a fool. He won't allow himself to be gulled," Hannah said, wishing she could really believe it. "Besides, Mr. Falconer might be straight in his business dealings, for all we know."

"Yore not takin' up for him, are you?" He threw her a suspicious look.

"No. Why should I?"

"Plenty of reason. But I've no mind to go into it now."

Once Guy and Hannah had retired to their room for the night they discussed the possible sale. Christian wanted to go over the acreage again in the morning and then, he had told Guy, he would discuss price.

"Travis doesn't trust him," Hannah said.

"Travis wouldn't trust anyone who's interested in buying Sycamore," Guy said, getting out of his shirt. "Falconer is *rich*, Hannah. He didn't hire that Tennessee Walker in Monterey. He *bought* it. Just to have a way of getting out here. Says he likes Sycamore and will probably use it as a hunting lodge or summer place and hire a manager to run it. He'll put money into the ranch, Hannah. Do all the things I've never been able to do here. Build a new barn, add on to the house. Get a new breed of stock—ours is so inbred now. I was tempted to ask for the job of manager myself."

"Don't."

"Don't what?"

"Don't ask him."

Guy's eyebrows rose. "Why not? We'd probably see him seldom. It wouldn't be much different—"

"It would be very different. Working for yourself is one thing, but working for someone else is quite another."

"I grant you it won't be the same. But we'd still be here. We wouldn't have to move. It might even be better. I'd be making a salary we could depend on. We wouldn't have to worry if it didn't rain or if a cow got sick or a calf was stillborn. Don't you see, Hannah?"

"No!" She took a deep breath, forcing her voice to a lower pitch. "Can't you understand that we would be put in the position of servants?" And Christian's at that. It was a humiliation she could never explain to Guy.

"We'd be employees, Hannah."

"We'd be serving him just the same whatever you call it. If we sell I'd prefer leaving."

"All right, though it's hard for me to comprehend."

"Why so hard? Would you want to be at someone's beck and call on land that had once been yours?"

"Well, maybe not. But if we leave, I'd have to take a job in the city."

"You could buy yourself a truck farm like your brother's."

"That kind of land is dear, Hannah."

"Well, we'll cross that bridge when we come to it. First we have to sell Sycamore, then we'll see."

She wasn't too concerned about afterward—yet. She

was wondering about Christian. He was up to something. What? She was almost certain he hadn't been telling the truth when he claimed he had always wanted a ranch. Piffle. Was he buying Sycamore out of spite? She and Christian had parted this last time, he in anger, she in secret sorrow. Had his anger been so great as to fire a desire for vengeance? Did he want to punish her through Guy? He could sign a contract with Guy, then not live up to it so that the bank would have to foreclose in any case. How could she make sure? They ought to consult a lawyer in Monterey. They hadn't much time but the longer she thought about it the more imperative it seemed that they have professional advice. Christian was far more schooled in the ways of the business world than either she or Guy. They could use the services of a man trained to handle land transactions.

When she suggested this to Guy, he said, "We'll have to pay him, Hannah. Furthermore I don't see that legal counsel can be of much value. I can read and figure contracts as well as a lawyer."

She forbore reminding him that he had not done too well in buying Sycamore sight unseen five years earlier. The ranch, the house, the stock had fallen far short of what they had been led to expect and there had been no room for recourse in the agreement he had signed. But to point that out now would serve no useful purpose.

She wished she could forget the entire matter and simply let events take their course. But pros and cons, if's and but's continued to harry her long after they got into bed. As she lay tossing and turning next to a sleeping Guy, listening to the distant, lonesome yip-yip call of a coyote, her mind skipped from one anxiety to another. Hour followed hour. Midnight came and passed and still she remained awake.

Finally, in exasperation, she got up and pulled her riding skirt up over her nightgown. She would do what she did on other nights when she couldn't sleep. She would take Theda out for a gallop and ride and ride until she was too exhausted to think. Slipping into shoes and throwing a shawl over her shoulders, she eased herself out of the house.

It was a windless night, awash with pure light from a silver-dollar moon so bright it paled the stars. The out-buildings, the fenced compound and distant hills, thrown into sharp focus, were like black paper cutouts on cream vellum. Hannah led Theda from the darkened barn with-out saddling her. Not wanting to arouse those in the house by the sound of hooves, she walked the horse some distance before she found a tree stump and mounted her. Taking the path through the woods, she emerged on the far side, choosing the left fork that would bring her to the upper pasture. Once on level ground without the impediment of low-hanging branches, Hannah kicked Theda with her heels. "Run, Theda, run! Faster, faster!"

The mare sprang into a gallop, with Hannah low on her back, clinging to the reins. There was something wonderfully exhilarating about riding at a furious clip through the night, with the feel of the sage-scented air streaming her long hair behind her. She felt released, a winged bird soaring high above the sleeping world. Her concerns, her doubts, the indecisions vanished. Syca-more vanished. She was free! She heard her laughter in the wind as they flew past a cow who gazed at them with a foolish, vacant face, a group of munching steer, an immense rock, big as a barn with strange carvings upon it, higher and higher, the horse racing under her, skirting a grove of manzanita, avoiding a barranca, jump-ing a dry creek bed. Up and up they sped, then down hill again, along the edge of the mountain, then down and down once more. Hannah drew Theda up when she realized she was winding the poor creature. She dis-mounted, rubbing the mare's wet flank with her shawl, whispering apologies.

Suddenly the sound of a nicker startled her. Turning her head, she saw Christian's Tennessee Walker teth-ered under a nearby big leaf maple.

"Can't sleep, Mrs. Hartwell?" Christian emerged from the shadows like an unsettling phantom. When she didn't answer, he said, "Obviously not. A pity."

No phantom, but Christian in the flesh. "Why a pity? It should be of no concern to you." She gathered her nightdress closer about her throat. "But since you ask, I don't wonder that *you* have trouble sleeping."

"Oh?" He came closer.

"Why are you really here, Christian? Why this sudden interest in buying Sycamore?"

"I don't know," he said carelessly, hands shoved into his pockets. "A whim, perhaps."

In the moonlight his handsome features looked as if they had been chiseled by a master sculptor. His eyes held an amused glitter.

"Did you think I had some nefarious purpose?" he asked.

"Yes."

"Quite honestly, when I saw your notice in the *Chronicle* I had no idea I would respond to it. But after some thought I changed my mind. Funny, isn't it, but advertisements seem to bring us together."

"I see no humor in this situation. You must have known that your presence at Sycamore would be an embarrassment to me."

"I did. Perhaps that's why I came in the first instant. I was reminded again that you chose Guy Hartwell over me. I wanted to see what kind of man he was, what he had that I lacked."

"You wanted to make trouble, Christian. Guy is unaware of our former—our relationship."

"So I presumed. Although by now he should be fully cognizant of the part I've played in your life."

For a moment the moonlight seemed to darken. "What do you mean?" she asked through dry lips.

"He has only to look at me, then at the child he has always thought was his—am I right, he does believe the lad is his?"

"Why shouldn't he? Because it's true. Mark is Guy's."

"Then both you and your husband are blind."

"No."

"Swear to God." He had dropped his careless, casual tone and his voice had taken on the hard edge of restrained anger. "Tell me Mark isn't my son. Say it, asking God to strike you dead if you're lying."

Hannah shivered and closed her eyes as if to ward off the unspoken curse. He had no right to invoke the name of God. None. Does the Devil call on God? She thought suddenly of Preacher Wright and Julie, whose teachings had run like a thread of guilt through her life and Travis's. Her deceit, her lies, her transgressions were all coming home to roost.

She heard Christian move closer and her eyes flew open.

"Speak up, damn you!"

"Why?" Her throat felt raw. "Why do you put me on the rack?"

"Because it gives me pleasure." He smiled, a smile that didn't light up his eyes. "You wouldn't want to burn in that Baptist hell of yours by insisting on a patent untruth, would you? He is my son, isn't he?" He gripped her arm.

"Yes," she answered in a low voice.

Christian's mouth—the mouth that could be so caressing and tender—twisted in scorn. "And yet you went back to him."

"He's my husband."

"You call that blond fool your husband?"

"Don't," she said. "Don't malign him."

"You malign yourself. And then you have the brass to pose as a dutiful wife when—"

"No," she interrupted, steeling her voice against the sob pressing at her throat. "I won't have you go on this way. What do you want? Do you want to break up our family? Isn't it enough that we're losing our place, everything we've worked for? And now you're here to give Guy the final death blow by telling him Mark isn't his."

"He's *my* son. I should think you would consider that before you speak so melodramatically about death blows."

"You turn everything to your own advantage, don't you? You accuse me of brass when you had the unmitigated gall to fake Elthea's kidnapping, then find her, so I'd fall into your arms out of gratitude."

"What? Oh, my God, is that what she told you? And you *believed* it? No wonder she hasn't shown her face since I've been here."

"She's afraid of you."

"If she's told you such a cock-and-bull story, she has

every right to be afraid. I'd wring the truth out of her. By God, I ought to do it anyway, just on principle.''

"So in addition to everything else, you're a bully."

"Bully?" He laughed, a mirthless sound that chilled her blood. "I suppose one more name doesn't matter. You've called me everything else. Coward, lecher, womanizer, and now bully."

"But they fit you, you're—"

"You talk too damned much!" He yanked her into his arms, clamping her mouth shut with a brutal kiss. She beat at him with clenched fists, twisting her body, trying to bring her knee up to attack him in the groin. But he guessed her intent and growled low in his throat as his hand slithered down her back and pushed her body into the curve of his hips. Only when he felt her relax did he let go of her mouth.

"I hate you! Hate you, hate you!" she whispered hoarsely through bruised lips. "Turn me loose."

His mouth brushed the side of her neck.

"Let me go!"

He laughed softly. Still holding her with one arm, he used the other hand to part the collar of her nightdress. Bending his head, he planted a kiss on the beating vein in the hollow of her throat.

She shivered. "Christian, I beg of you . . ."

He looked down into her eyes with his own moon-shadowed ones. "We're past begging, Hannah. Long past."

She gazed up at him out of eyes suddenly, unaccountably misting.

"If it will make you happy, I'll admit to everything." Tentatively, with fingers that trembled slightly, he brushed back a strand of hair from her forehead. "Well, nearly everything." His fingers lingered for a moment longer on her hair. Then he bent his head again. His lips were soft, but firm and possessive. For one fleeting moment she thought to protest, but the magic that was Christian's was already seeping through her blood. He folded her closer against his chest while his kiss went on and on, his lips moving across her mouth with passionate tenderness. A long sigh died in Hannah's throat as her hands climbed his back.

The arm about her waist tensed, then relaxed. One hand began to caress her, traveling sensually up and down her spine, coming around to stroke the side of her breast. The old excitement gripped her as his tongue parted her lips and teased before it touched hers, then went on to taste and turn, exploring the inner sweetness of her mouth. When his hand slipped down beneath her nightdress and found the white silky mounded flesh, his thumb expertly rousing the nipple, she pushed him away.

"This won't do, Christian."

"It will, it will. You don't hate me, Hannah."

There was something in the way he spoke those words, the words themselves, that got her back up. It gave her the feeling that he was coolly assuming he had only to fondle a breast and she was his. She was no better than the other women in his life who had given in easily, eagerly. In her mind she saw them, their painted cheeks, their overbright eyes. . . .

"Stop!" She tore herself from his grasp and stood facing him. "I'm not your whore, Christian. Nor will I ever be. You think because you've associated with loose women that I'm one, too."

His eyes narrowed dangerously. "You damn fool!" Suddenly, swiftly, before she could move away, he swung her into his arms. She flailed wildly at his head and shoulders but the blows fell harmlessly. Carrying her across the turf, he went under the maple tree and threw her down on a bed of leaves beneath it. When she started to rise, he knocked her back with the flat of his hand.

"Christian! You're not to treat me in this manner, do you hear?"

His silence was frightening, intimidating. She sensed his monumental rage and a quiver ran through her body. She had taunted him and she knew by now the limits of his black temper.

"Christian . . ."

But he was already straddling her on his knees. Bunching her nightdress in his fist, he tore it from her, exposing her breasts.

She brought her hand up and struck him across the

face. He knocked her arm away, wrenching her riding skirt and the bottom half of her gown away, leaving her naked and exposed. Then he fell upon her, raining kisses over her face, her throat, kneading her breasts, biting, kissing, sucking, all in a passion of anger and haste. She found hate coming easily now. He was raping her, taking her against her will. Never in his worst, his basest moments had he behaved in such a bestial manner. But she was powerless to free herself from the heavy strength of his body stretched over hers. Tears of frustration beaded her lashes, trickled down her cheeks. With an elbow he knocked her legs apart and she felt him freeing his swollen organ.

"Please, oh, Christian, no." She closed her eyes, bracing herself against a brutal thrust.

But there was nothing. Only his heavy, hoarse panting. She felt his hands and arms that had pinned her down suddenly tremble. He lowered himself, one hand in her tangled hair, his sweat-beaded brow resting on her wet cheek.

"I can't," he whispered softly. "I can't force you. I love you too much."

She felt the hot rush of tears and bit her lips against the whimper that rose in her throat. But he heard it. He gathered her in his arms and, leaning against the tree trunk, cradled her in his lap, rocking her as he would a child, saying over and over, "There, there, my love. No need to cry. I would rather die than harm you."

She was weeping openly now, ragged, tearing sobs.

"I've made you unhappy."

She nodded. "Yes."

"And you hate me."

"Yes," she said weakly.

"Oh, Hannah, you know that isn't true." He took her hand and placed it inside his shirt against his hard chest. "Listen, my darling, do you feel that? My heart."

Every beat, measured and sure, was a life force that seemed to echo her own. Christian was like her in so many ways. He was strong. He would never give up, never accept defeat. If it were he instead of Guy, he would fight hard to keep Sycamore. And that wildness in him that she deplored, the ungovernable temper, how much of that did she envy, she who had been bound to a life of rigid do's and don't's? Loving him was like racing with the wind, dangerous and thrilling.

She looked up into his face. "Christian, what am I to do with you?"

"You must answer that yourself, Hannah. But for now, let me love you."

Tenderly he kissed the hollow between her breasts. Then cupping one in his hand, he licked at the nipple, taking it between his teeth, sucking until it stiffened. Her hands gripped his dark hair, meaning to pull him away, but when he began to lick the other breast, pursing his mouth to suck the second nipple, her hands faltered and a shudder ran through her.

The small night noises, the horses cropping the grass, the twittering of a night bird were lost to her, blotted out as her senses reeled under the touch of his hands and lips. Gently he brought her down to the ground. Divesting himself quickly of his clothes, he covered her with his hard, lean body, his hands stroking her thighs, raising goose pimples along her arms, sending a quivering thread of fire through her veins. Her hips involuntarily arched as his fingers moved along her flesh, parting the fluff of hair on her mound, entering the warm sweet cave, flicking lightly, lightly.

She heard her own breath coming in labored gasps as her hands held tightly to the corded muscles of his shoulders. Suddenly, with a low moan, he thrust her legs farther apart and plunged down into her again and again, a savage assault that made her cry out in an agony of joy. She clung to him, her whole being battered, drowning in a storm of emotion. When the final thunderous spasm rolled through her and she felt Christian's climax a moment later, she could only wonder how a man and woman could be so in unison, so completely one.

He kissed her damp brow, sweeping her hair from her forehead, lifting himself to look into her eyes again. He didn't have to ask, to wonder. She loved him. There was no way she could hide it.

"You must leave him," he said.

They were sitting quietly under the same tree now, Hannah, her tattered gown tucked around her, her riding skirt covering her legs, nestled in Christian's lap.

"I cannot. Especially now when he needs me." The same hopeless debate.

"He doesn't need you as much as you think. I'll give him the money to restock the ranch, see that he gets transport and a market for his cattle. We'll make it a partnership so that he won't feel he's working for me. We'll treat the entire matter as an advantageous arrangement to both sides."

"And then?"

"Tell him the truth, Hannah, and come away with me."

"The truth will devastate him, Christian. He thinks so much of me."

"And you accused *me* of arrogance."

"Oh, Christian, I can't hurt him."

"We love each other, we have a child. You belong with me."

Was he right? Can love admit doubt?

"Hannah, we've run out of arguments. You must make a decision."

"Give me a day or two."

"I don't see how. . . ."

"Please."

"Very well. But I shan't leave until I have your answer. The right one. Furthermore, don't put abduction beyond me."

She smiled up at him. "Now who is being melodramatic?"

All the next day Hannah went about her chores with a heavy heart. She had experienced this feeling once before, torn between her duty and her love for Christian. Should she leave her husband for a man who had been her bane and her joy, her nemesis and her delight, a man about whom even now she had small, unresolved doubts? But who in this world could be sure of another human being? Certainly she had not anticipated Guy's flaws when she married him. The admiration she had once felt for his courage in adversity had faded. Living with him this past year, with one misfortune following another, she had seen him visibly crumble. She knew now she was the strong one, that perhaps it had been that way from the start. She remembered his disappointment when they first laid eyes on Sycamore, his coming apart when she had had her miscarriage, his look of helplessness as he stood gazing at the devastation caused by the canyon fire. She wondered how it would be in the years to come, if he would lean on her to the point where even fondness would vanish and she would come to actively dislike him. He needed someone who loved him deeply, a strong woman, yet one who could look admiringly up at him as though the sun rose and set in his every move, his every word.

Hannah thought about Flavia. The more she thought about it, the more she felt how well suited Flavia was for Guy, how Flavia's gaiety and ability to take the days as they came was exactly what Guy needed.

Christian is right, Hannah thought. I am not all that necessary to Guy. In time he will forget me, perhaps sooner than I imagine. Flavia will be here, he will turn to her. She will be tender and loving—and worshiping. She will bear sons and daughters for him, as many as he chooses, settling down to make him a loving wife. While with me he will have a woman who loves another man, one who will secretly resent him. And in the end the two of us will grow estranged and bitter.

Christian departed the following day with Hannah's promise that she would meet him in Monterey in two days. He wanted them to leave together but she thought it would be best if she broke the news to Guy alone. Christian had already informed Guy that once he reached San Francisco he would send his agent to discuss a partnership. He was careful—at Hannah's insistence—to make no mention of Hannah herself.

After Christian had gone, Hannah suddenly found herself unable to face Guy. She was afraid he would break down and weep and that his tears—and her pity—would

irrevocably bind her to him and she would lose her one
chance to be free.

Therefore she decided to take the fainthearted way
out and write him a note. She waited another day until
Guy and Travis rode off to the Barlow ranch, where
they were to help Leonard put up an addition to his
barn. Elthea would go with them, taking this opportunity to visit Polly.

When Guy, in a happy mood for the first time in six
months, kissed her good-bye, he said, "Come, Hannah,
aren't you going to kiss me back? I feel this arrangement
with Mr. Falconer will be a new start for us."

She bussed him lightly on the cheek, a kiss that made
her feel like a Judas.

Guy, Travis, and Elthea, along with Clara, would
be gone for at least two days, time enough for Hannah
to get to Monterey with Mark to meet Christian. From
there they would travel together to San Francisco.
Once in the city, Christian would put them up at a
hotel until he could find a suitable apartment or house.
He did not think that Guy would look for them. Nevertheless he felt it would be best to avoid his parents'
house and the possibility of a nasty scene should
Guy suddenly decide to pursue Hannah. After a decent
interval, Christian had told her, he would hire a good
lawyer specializing in divorce, who could free Hannah
to become his wife.

Composing the note was not easy. Hannah, sitting at
the kitchen table, pondered over what to say, how to
break the news to Guy gently. She started off by telling
him how grateful she was for his love and went on to ask
for his forgiveness. As she wrote she heard the front
door open. Thinking it was Mark, she called, "Don't go
past the veranda, darling." But a moment later she
heard heavy footsteps and, looking up, saw Travis standing in the doorway.

Quickly, guiltily, she placed her hand over the page,
irritated at the flush that rose to her cheeks.

"I thought you went off with Guy," she said.

"I did, but I forgot my carpenter's plane. And Leonard doesn't have a decent one. I left it here in the

kitchen cupboard yesterday.'' Then after a small pause.
''Writing a letter home?''

''Yes,'' she lied.

He came around the table. ''Thought you said you
were done with Aunt Bess when she wouldn't loan Guy
money.''

''Well—I—I think it's foolish to carry a grudge.'' She
still held her slightly curled hand over the note.

''Let's see.''

''My correspondence is none of your business.''

''The hell it ain't.'' He snatched the letter from her,
half tearing it.

''Dear Guy,'' he read aloud, shaking Hannah's hand
from his arm. ''I want you to know that I 'preciate how
good you've been to me. No husband could have been
kinder or more lovin'. I pray that you will understand
and forgive me for what I'm about to do. I find I can no
longer go on livin' a lie. I love another man, have loved
him for many years—''

Travis broke off. ''How could you?''

He tore the letter across once, twice, and again. Walking over to the stove, he lifted one of the lids, stuffed the
scraps in, then set a sulfur match to them.

Hannah said, ''I'm going, Travis. You can burn a
dozen notes, but I'm taking Mark and leaving.''

''Runnin' off with Christian Falconer, are you? I might
have guessed. How could you?''

''I can't stay. It's Christian I love. I can't go on
deceiving Guy. The child he thinks is—''

''Christian's. I seen it myself. It's a wonder Guy hasn't.
But he ain't got the smallest suspicion and he ain't goin'
to because yore not leavin'.''

''Listen to me, Travis. Guy will forget me. He'll find
someone else, someone like Flavia—''

''Like who?'' He looked at her in utter astonishment.

''I said someone *like*. I'm no good to Guy loving
another man.''

''You think yore the only person in the world that
ain't got a perfect marriage?''

''I know you're not happy with Elthea, but—''

''I stuck by her.''

"You have. But you wouldn't treat a hound dog the way you've treated her. Oh, I know what you're going to say: 'She asked for it.' Don't you see? I couldn't bear to think that Guy and I might someday come to the same pass. If he ever found out about Mark . . . No. It's best to be honest, to make a clean break. Guy needs someone who can give him an unqualified, wholehearted love."

"Words. All that damned speechifying. Pa was right. The bit of schoolin' you had ruined you. You know well as I if you left Guy it'd kill him. And slinkin' off with that sly devil, Christian Falconer. How long d'you think it would take afore yore fancy man got tired of you and found another foolish woman? More 'n that, Guy's no dummy. He'd be able to figure right quick that he sold you to that bastard for this ranch."

"That isn't so."

"Like hell it ain't."

"Christian would have made the same partnership arrangement with Guy even if I hadn't agreed to leave him."

Travis banged his fist on the table and the inkpot jumped, Hannah catching it before it tipped over. "You think so? You really think so? Danged if I didn't allus believe you were the smart one. But you ain't. Let me tell you somethin, Sis." He wagged his finger at Hannah. "I didn't say nothin' afore this, but I found out somethin' when me and Guy went up to Frisco to talk to the bank. The fellah who saw us was all perlite at first, said wait a few minutes, sir, I'd like to discuss this with my superior. So Guy and I were left sittin' in the office with the wood panelin' and a pitcher of an Indian on a horse on one wall and on t'other wall a brass plate with the names of the board of directors. And lo and behold! One of them is Miles Falconer and another Christian Falconer. How do you like that? Don't shake your head, it's God's truth, I swear. Then the man in the paper collar comes out and tells us sorry, sir, but we can't extend your loan."

Hannah sat very still, staring at Travis. "I don't see how the Falconers . . ."

"Wait! That ain't all. I went back later by myself and

got ahold of the same clerk and I talked to him frank. Yes, he said, Dr. Falconer had left word not to make it easy for Mr. Hartwell. Why'd you think Christian run out here in such a hurry? Because he had Guy on the end of his fork. I wasn't goin' to say nothin', 'cause I thought if Guy could make hisself a good sale, all right. But you ain't goin' to be part of it''

"No! It isn't true."

"He's buyin' you, Hannah. He could have seen to it that the bank let Guy off easy. But no. He's rich, spoiled, and selfish, and he allus gets what he wants. He . . .''

Hannah rose abruptly and walked out of the room. She couldn't bear to sit there and listen to Travis any longer. She went through the parlor and the front door. Mark, sitting on the stoop, spoke, but she didn't hear him. She went down the stairs and across the compound, opening a gate, her feet taking her on the path across the valley. The sun was a gilded ball in an azure sky and the gentle wind, smelling of the sea and wild herbs, teased at her hair. But she felt neither sun nor wind. She went on walking, yanking her skirts every now and again from a thorny shrub or a clump of dried grass. Down past the pond, the salt lick, and a lone madrone she went with no destination in mind, only the need to be moving. Stumbling, her right foot went into a rabbit hole, twisting her ankle. Heedless of the pain, she hobbled on. What was a throbbing ankle? Nothing to the wild hurt that lacerated her heart.

False, false! her mind cried, a trick, a lie! She had been duped once again. But, her heart sobbed, it isn't true! He does love me. He hasn't purposely conspired for Guy to lose his ranch. He wouldn't do anything that low. He loves me, he loves me!

She limped on, climbing a hillock, following the rim of the burnt-out canyon, tripping over a small rock, sending a pair of jays into whirling flight. *It isn't true!* She flung herself down in a hollow, beating at the ground with her fists, sobbing bitterly. He wouldn't, he wouldn't!

But she knew that he would and he had. I ought to feel flattered, she thought dully, sitting up, drying her red, swollen eyes on the edge of her apron. Christian

loves me so much he'd do anything to have me. But she
felt that was only part of the truth. Perhaps he did love
her. But she was the first woman who had resisted him
and some sort of perverted male pride had dictated that
she would be his. No ruse, no deception was too base or
mean for him to use. This latest, this wielding of financial power to gain his ends over a defenseless man and a
stupid (Travis was right) woman was the last straw.

After a long while she rose and slowly made her way
back to the house. Travis was sitting on the step, his
arm about Mark.

"Well?" he asked.

She moved past him into the house. At the kitchen
table she took up her pen again. Ignoring Travis, who
had followed her inside, she wrote:

> *Dear Christian:*
>   *I find I'm unable to leave my husband after all. I feel no*
> *explanation is necessary except to let you know I'm aware*
> *of your connection with the First National Bank. Also, my*
> *husband will not be interested in making any sort of ar-*
> *rangement with you as to the sale or management of Syca-*
> *more. You need not use Mark to blackmail me. Guy knows*
> *his true parentage. Worse luck. Please do not try to contact*
> *me again.*

When she had signed her name, Travis said, "That's
better, Sis."

"Is it?" she asked coldly. "Better for you. You're
afraid Guy would go to pieces if I left him. You're afraid
that he wouldn't care and that if he stayed as manager or
whatever, the burden of responsibility—what to do, where
to move the cattle, when to brand, when to get them
ready for market, and a dozen other decisions that must
be made—would fall on you. And you haven't the taste
for it."

"Sis . . ."

"Never fear. I'll stay. Take this letter down to the
Post ranch and have them send it out on the next stage.
I've written the address on the envelope. And—wait!—I'd
best send a note to the *Chronicle* and tell them to continue publishing the advertisement."

"Why don't you put in it, 'Present owner interested in stayin' on at Sycamore'? Look, Sis, if Falconer was willin', mebbe some other rich nob will feel the same."

"All right," she said resignedly. What did it matter if they remained at Sycamore or never saw it again? It was of little concern to her.

Two weeks later a Mr. Brandon came to look at the ranch. A beefy man in his early forties, he offered Guy a price that was lower than the one Christian had first quoted. But since Guy had not heard from Christian (Hannah, riding down once a week to get the mail at the Post ranch, had secretly destroyed all of Christian's correspondence), he accepted Brandon's terms. Brandon, it seemed, was not interested in a manager. He planned to live at Sycamore and run it himself.

On an early April morning the Hartwells and Blaines packed as many of their personal belongings into the wagon as it could carry and drove away from Sycamore. It was a silent, sad departure for Guy and Travis. But not for Elthea, who had somehow gotten it into her head that they were returning to Georgia.

Just as they pulled past the second gate she turned her head and, looking back, said derisively, "I ain't been so happy to leave a place in all my life. Good-bye to all *that!*"

Chapter XVIII

They were not bound for Georgia, of course, but for San Francisco, where Guy and Travis hoped to get employment. The sale of Sycamore had been far from a bonanza. Guy's creditors, getting wind of it, flooded him with dunning letters, one man presenting himself at the door as they were packing to leave. Guy owed money for nearly everything he had bought in the last two years: seed, branding irons and tack, flour and coffee, boots, a brace of mules and a plowshare, rope, a saw, two sackfuls of oats, a list that went on and on. He might have evaded the vultures—as Travis called them—by simply disappearing into the anonymous maw of the city. But Guy was not one to ignore his obligations.

After the last debtor had been paid off, Guy was left with very little money. The cheapest housing they could find was a dingy, clapboard building on California Street. Much smaller than their quarters at Sycamore, it had two bedrooms, a tiny parlor, and a smoke-blackened kitchen where they took their meals. An odorous outhouse sat at the far end of a narrow, bare, clay-packed yard.

Hannah did what she could to make the place more homey, hanging curtains cut from an old bedcover at the windows and scattering the splintered floors with pieces of rug they had managed to salvage from the Sycamore house.

Guy found employment as a carpenter and cabinet-maker, hammering and sawing from sunup to sundown for a man named Beasley who cheated his customers whenever he could get away with it by using pine instead of oak or redwood. Travis got work in a sugar refinery where the sickly-sweet odor of molasses—a by-product—clung to his clothes and skin, no matter how often he washed or how hard Elthea scrubbed his work pants and shirts.

They accommodated themselves to their changed circumstances as their separate natures would allow, Hannah trying to look to a better future, Travis and Guy sprinkling their conversation with idealized reminiscences of Sycamore, and Elthea still muttering about Georgia.

The year was 1898.

The family had been in San Francisco for only two weeks when the United States declared war on Spain. Living in comparative isolation as they were, the Hartwells and Blaines had heard only vague rumors of their government's "trouble with Spain," but had no idea that a war was in the offing. However, they now learned that the country had been expecting hostilities since the *Maine,* an American naval vessel, had been blown up—allegedly by the Spanish—in Havana Harbor in February of that year. Still, the news did not alarm them. After all, Cuba was only an island thousands of miles away and the Spaniards (who had no right to be in the western hemisphere in the first place) defending it would be a poor match for American soldiers.

Then a few weeks later, on May first, Commodore Dewey sailed into Manila Harbor, in the Philippines, another Spanish possession, completely destroying the Spanish fleet. The sensational, imperialistic newspapers, such as the *Examiner,* were jubilant with patriotic editorials, while the good citizens of San Francisco were asking themselves, Where are the Philippines?

"It's an archipelago, a string of islands in the Pacific between Japan and Australia," Guy explained to Travis

one evening as he sat smoking his pipe over the remains
of a late supper.

Since the outbreak of what was now designated as the
Spanish-American War, Guy had not only taken to smok-
ing a pipe but had also begun to read the *Call* and the
Examiner with avid interest. A fellow employee at
Beasley's subscribed to both papers and gave them to
Guy after he had finished. Though the news was a day
late when Guy got to it, the delay, compared to the scant
information that had managed to trickle down to them at
Sycamore, was hardly noticeable.

"The Filipinos, it says here"—Guy pointed with his
pipe to the paper spread out on the kitchen table—"have
been trying to get rid of the Spaniards for years. Maybe
our intervention will be a blessing to them."

"There's no mebbe about it," Travis replied stoutly.

"Well, now," Hannah said, leaning over Guy's shoulder, trying to get a better look at the article he was
reading, "I'm not too sure of that."

Elthea, banging pots and pans at the kitchen sink,
muttered sourly, "I don't see what all it's got to do with
us."

She wasn't carrying this baby well and, according to
Hannah, had a right to be peevish. Her back hurt, her
ankles swelled, and she slept fitfully at night. Hannah
had tried to persuade her to see a doctor, but Elthea
stubbornly refused. She told numerous stories of girls
and women in her condition who had consulted medical
men, only to have them do indecent things, like putting
their hands up their skirts and touching them you-know-
where. She wouldn't go near a doctor. Her mama had had
ten without the help of a physician and only twice, when
labor was unnaturally prolonged, had she used the services of a midwife. "And none the worse for it," Elthea
asserted.

Within the confines of their small house, the two
couples and their children lived in each other's pockets.
They got along, but Hannah's relationship with her brother
had cooled. Though she kept telling herself that Travis
was not to blame for Christian's duplicity, too many
bitter words had been spoken the day he had dissuaded

her from leaving Guy. She had not forgotten them, but apparently Travis had, for he assumed she was grateful to him for having made the right decision.

Then something happened that further lowered Travis in Hannah's esteem.

One evening, a payday, he came home late, saying he had been robbed of all but two dollars, which he had fortunately taken from his wage envelope and tucked inside a shirt pocket. A pair of thugs carrying knives, he claimed, had waylaid him, threatening to kill him. It was money that was badly needed, for Guy's wages alone were not enough to carry them. But Guy said they would manage somehow and Hannah was only grateful Travis hadn't been killed. However, Elthea, who had been promised a new pair of shoes, pouted for days.

Two weeks later, again on payday, Travis, mingling with the crowd outside the *Call* offices to read the latest bulletin on the war with Spain, had his pockets picked. He had chased the thief—a Chinaman, he said—for two blocks then lost him in a maze of alleys in old Chinatown. He had gone to the police, but they had given him little hope of recovering his money.

A month later when Travis arrived home for the third time with another story of robbery, Hannah suspected something was amiss. She found it hard to believe that he had lost his money through thievery three times in a row. But what was he doing with his pay? Although Travis, like so many laborers on payday, would stop for a beer at a local tavern, he wasn't really a drinking man. What then? Cards? Gambling was the only possibility she could think of.

When she spoke of her suspicion to Guy and suggested he follow Travis from his place of work, Guy equivocated.

"I'm not sure spying on Travis is such a good idea. Why don't you come right out and ask him?"

"He'll deny it. We can't live on just what you make, Guy. San Francisco must be the most expensive city in the world. I owe the butcher as it is, though I buy only the cheapest cuts. Not to speak of our bill at the grocer's. No. The only way to get Travis to confess is to catch him at it. I'll go if you won't."

"That won't be necessary. I'll see what I can do."

The second time Guy trailed Travis from the sugar refinery he saw him go into the Galveston, where card games went on twenty-four hours a day. Guy, sneaking a peek through the swinging door, observed Travis seated at one of the tables with five other men, a stack of coins at his elbow, his hat pushed back from his forehead.

"You should have gone in and dragged him away," Hannah said when Guy came home and reported his discovery.

"And have the whole place down on my neck? It's not that I'm afraid of getting hurt, Hannah. But that mob in there would have killed me. And I have no mind to die in a barroom brawl."

"Then I'll do it."

"You most certainly will not."

Hannah waited until Guy had fallen asleep in his chair with the *Call* in his lap as he sometimes did in the late evenings. Tossing a shawl around her shoulders and jamming a hat on her head, she slipped out the door.

The Galveston was so thick with smoke that Hannah, standing at the door, found herself peering through the haze, trying to make out the faces of the men seated at tables placed as close together as a drawn-out chair would allow. A long, mirrored bar ran the length of the room. At it several customers were drinking. There were no women present, not even bar girls or the female entertainers who high-kicked and cavorted to syncopated tunes of battered pianos in the fancier saloons. This was a serious gambling establishment, several cuts above the dives on lower Market Street, but below those rooms at the high-toned Century Club set aside for gentlemen who wished to wager on a game of bridge or five-card stud. As Hannah moved inside several faces looked up. One man muttered, "No women allowed, honey." Another leered at her, patting an empty chair beside him.

She saw the barman coming around through the little gate at the side, with the intention, she was sure, of escorting her outside. He was stopped by one of the men at the bar. Hannah, watching them both, met the customer's eyes in the mirror.

She froze where she stood, her hand at her throat.

For a long moment their gazes held, a world of memory shadowed by regret and desire. A sudden blaze of anger in the hazel eyes, then nothing. Christian made no move to approach her.

Hannah, shaken by this encounter, turned away, disoriented, forgetting why she was there. Christian at the Galveston should have been no surprise. It was just the sort of place he would patronize, drinking and gambling, and later perhaps sauntering down the street to a whorehouse. Did he prefer the dark ones or one of those overblown blondes with big breasts that he could suck on to his heart's content? Perhaps he had a special doxy, one prettier and younger than the others, a prostitute who knew all the tricks of the trade, bringing him back to her time and time again.

Oh, God, she had to get out, she didn't want to think about it, to be near him.

Then she caught sight of Travis. He was so intent on his game he hadn't noticed the little furor Hannah had caused by her entrance. It wasn't until she stood next to him and the other men at his table paused in their play that he looked up.

He turned white, then red. Hannah said nothing, merely stared at him, as Aunt Bess might have done. He rose to his feet. "Sorry, fellas," he murmured, scooping up a handful of coins.

A man in a bowler snickered. "Wifey come to fetch you, Travis?"

He trailed Hannah out of the Galveston accompanied by catcalls.

Once on the street Travis turned on her in anger. "Did you have to shame me that way?"

"Yes," Hannah said. Shamed. And what of her? Having Christian witness that scene was mortifying. She began walking in the direction of California Street.

He caught up with her. "I was only playing a hand or two."

"I see," she said with biting sarcasm. "Is that what happened when your pocket was picked, when you were robbed at knife point?"

"Sis, I wanted to make enough money to get us out of that house."

"And you thought to do it by gambling? Oh, you fool, you utter fool! From now on, either I, Guy, or Elthea will escort you home on payday."

"You can't—"

"Oh, yes, I can. However, if you object too strongly, you have the choice of going out on your own."

"Well, dammit, maybe I will."

But she knew he wouldn't.

In July the newspapers were full of Colonel Theodore Roosevelt, who had become a national hero by leading a successful charge of his cavalrymen up San Juan Hill in Cuba. And from the Philippines on the other side of the globe came word that the navy had taken Isla Grande and a garrison of thirteen hundred Spaniards without resistance. These victories stirred up a new wave of patriotism. Men in all walks of life were joining up, eager to take up arms to fight for the honor of their country. In San Francisco the hastily formed First California Volunteer Infantry, the Utah, the Washington State and Oregon Volunteers, had already set sail for Manila to the music of bands and the cheering of pretty girls.

"Seems like them folks have better things to do," Elthea said.

"I dunno," replied Travis. The family's surveillance of his every movement rankled. More and more he felt as though he were being held on a tight leash. "They say that bein' in the army is a real man's life."

"Can get you killed, too," Hannah put in.

"C'mon, now, Sis, would you miss me that much?"

" 'Course I would. I still love you, no matter what."

"You'd cry, mebbe, if I got a bellyful of Spanish iron?" he teased.

"You know I would. I don't want you talking like that even in jest," she added.

Guy believed that once the Spanish were defeated in the Philippines, the United States should keep at least one naval base and coaling station there. "Germany or

Japan are sure to move right in if we leave the Filipinos to their own devices."

"A coalin' station!" Travis exclaimed. "We oughta take the whole kit and caboodle. Look at the English fighting the Boers in South Africa. You can bet they won't be givin' it away when they get done lickin' the pickle-headed Krauts."

"Dutch," Guy said. "The Boers are Dutch."

Elthea, who couldn't care less about the war, scanned the papers—moving her lips as she read—for gossipy tidbits and the paid announcements. Advertising was just having its start and both the *Call* and *Examiner* carried these paid entreaties, coaxing the public to try various products. Palmolive urged ladies who wished to preserve their complexions to use their soap. Kodak cameras assured the timid, "You push the button, we do the rest." Jacob's Oil, Royal Baking Powder, and Douglas Shoes touted their wares with catchy phrases and attractive sketches. Elthea was particularly interested in Lydia Pinkham's Vegetable Compound, commended as a cure for a wide variety of female disorders. Elthea, who had persuaded Travis to buy her a bottle, swore that she had never felt better and indeed it seemed to make her less irritable.

Hannah secretly wondered what Christian would have had to say about Lydia Pinkham. She had heard him remark to his mother that he was dead set against patent medicines.

Lydia Pinkham's was not the only occasion when Hannah thought of Christian. Ever since her silent encounter with him at the Galveston, she had been afraid of meeting him face-too-face again. Once, riding the cable car down to the wharf to buy fish—cheaper there than at the local shop—she saw him. The car had stopped to let on passengers and he was at the far curb helping a woman into a hansom, his broad shoulders stretching the cloth of a dove-gray coat. Hannah tried, but could not look away. The woman with him was beautiful, an oval face under a plumed hat, a hand-span waist above silk-draped hips.

Envy stabbed at Hannah, a sharp pain that was sick-ening in its intensity. Who was the woman? His new love? How quickly he had taken on another. Beautiful, smartly dressed, young. Would they go home or perhaps to one of those notorious restaurants that had private dining rooms on the upper floors? Would they laugh together, make love?

Christian. Why should she be jealous when she ought to despise him? Forget him, she would tell herself. He isn't worth a single thought. But on the nights when fog reached its gray tentacles up California Street, wrapping the house in thick mist, and she heard the sound of the mournful foghorns in the bay, she wondered who lay beside him now. To whom did he turn, whispering "my darling"? Who held out slim white arms to him, cradled his dark head on her breasts? She would tell herself fiercely that it didn't matter even as the tears pressed against her eyes.

One evening as Guy was perusing the inner pages of the newspaper he exclaimed, "Look here! A piece about our old friend Dr. Falconer."

Hannah's heart gave a sudden lurch.

"Read it out loud, Guy," she said, though she wasn't sure she wanted to hear. Christian was probably engaged, married, seen in the company of a certain Miss ——. The woman with the pretty oval face.

" 'Dr. Christian Falconer,' " Guy read, " 'the son of our own prominent Mr. and Mrs. Miles Falconer, has volunteered his services to the surgeon general of the United States Army for duty in the Philippines. Dr. Falconer received his medical degree at Rush Medical in Chicago and has most recently practiced in this city. He—' "

"Well, well." Guy paused. "I was wondering what happened to him. I never did understand why he didn't go through with that partnership we had agreed on at Sycamore. Didn't answer my letters, either. Just disappeared."

"He changed his mind, I guess," Travis said.

"At least he could have told me so."

"I guess he ain't the type you can depend on."

"But he seemed reliable."

"Fellas like that are slick, Guy. They know how to fool a body."

Yes, Hannah wanted to interject, they know. They have charm and looks and devastating smiles that melt resistance. They have an aura of self-confidence, of masculinity, of feigned sincerity, and they don't care who they disappoint or whose heart they break. She looked at Guy as he dropped a handful of pennies in the "saving jar," the proceeds of which were to go for a new sewing machine. Thoughtful, kind Guy. Count your blessings, she told herself. But that night it was Christian she dreamed of.

Elthea was due in late August, perhaps early September, she wasn't sure which. But on the twenty-ninth of July she went into labor. She struggled all that day, the pains coming at spaced intervals, then receding, stopping, starting again. She had carried on so during her comparatively easy labor with Clara, it was hard to tell now how much of her moaning and gasping was real. But as the hours wore on, Hannah sensed that this would be a difficult birth.

She sat by Elthea's bedside, mopping her brow, speaking words of encouragement, telling the girl that everything would be fine, that she must be brave. Elthea, gripping the towel rope when a pain struck, would grimace, her eyes standing out, then let loose with a wild animal howl, frightening the two children huddling in a corner of the parlor, clinging to one another, too terrified to make a sound. Hannah would run out every now and then to hug, pat their heads, and reassure them. At noon she fixed a hasty lunch, and then sent them out in the yard to play.

In the evening when the men came home from work, they got their own supper and fed Clara and Mark. Guy was instructed to take them out for a walk. They had no neighbors, no friends with whom they could leave the children. Elthea, never one to make up to strangers, had put off the friendly advances of the middle-aged Greek couple next door by refusing to answer their "good days," calling them, within earshot, "furriners." They had only a nodding acquaintance with the man who owned the saddlery on their right and the brothers who ran a stable across the street. Hannah missed the Barlows, especially Tess, and would have given anything to have her with her now.

"I think we ought to get a doctor or midwife," Hannah advised Travis.

"Elthea says she doesn't put store by doctors or midwives. She'd only kick up a fuss."

"She wouldn't know or care now," Hannah said. "She's half mad with pain."

"It can't last too much longer, Sis."

Elthea's labor dragged through the long, dark hours of the night. Hannah, aching with fatigue, tried to catch snatches of sleep in an armchair Guy had brought in from the parlor. But Elthea, in her lucid moments, when she wasn't screaming with pain, called out for water, for a vinegar-soaked cloth on her head, a fresh pillow, or a neck rub, making it impossible for Hannah to get much rest.

At two in the morning Travis peeped in the door. "Is it comin'?"

"No. It doesn't seem to be. I'm terribly afraid it might be a breech birth."

"Ain't good, is it? What must we do?" He seemed genuinely worried. Travis, at bottom, is a good sort, Hannah thought. He's not in love with Elthea and perhaps at times even dislikes her, but he has never wished her harm.

"Fetch the midwife," Hannah said. "There's one on Sansome Street. Not too far. I got her name and address from the baker's wife when I thought Elthea might need her."

It took Travis a few minutes to get into his clothes, then he was out of the house and on his way. An hour passed. Thankfully Elthea had slipped into sleep. Hannah was just dozing off when Travis returned without the midwife.

"Mrs. Minton won't come until morning. She said lots of women take two days to birth a baby. I told her we

thought it was breech. But she said I could be wrong.
Nine times out ten the nervous pa was always wrong."

The night went on, with Elthea getting weaker and
weaker. Her moans were interspersed with delusions in
which she spoke to her mother, her sisters and brothers.
She seemed oblivious to Hannah, who hung over her,
urging her to fight, to push.

An hour after daybreak Mrs. Minton appeared. Hope
stirred as she briskly entered the bedroom with her little
black bag. She shooed Travis from the room, then drew
back the blanket from Elthea's writhing body. Rolling
up her sleeves, she reached in to give "the mother an
assist."

"Why, it's breech!" she said in surprise. "But it won't
be any trouble to get the mite straightened right side
up."

The child was finally brought from its mother's tormented body. A boy. It was dead. Elthea, lifting her
head to have a look, suddenly began to hemorrhage, and
despite Mrs. Minton's heroic efforts to staunch the flow,
Elthea closed her eyes and took her last breath in a long
shuddering sigh.

Chapter XIX

The monsoon had been blowing for a week.

An incessant, windswept tropical downpour, it drenched Camp Dewey, turning the marshy ground into a quagmire. Water dripped from nipa palms and bamboo, from tent flaps, canvas walls and thatched roofs, and ran in rivulets, puddling into greasy ponds along the ditches. The men were beginning to forget how it felt to be dry. Many of them with only one suit of clothes—heavy duck uniforms that remained perpetually soaked—were reduced to mustering and drilling in a half-naked state. Boots and shoes grew a blue mold a half hour after they were oiled. The long Krag Jorgensen rifles required constant care. Paper rotted, iron rusted, food spoiled, and the heavy, oppressive, steaming air sapped strength and will.

Christian, sitting at the opening of the hospital tent, wondered how long it would be before the men came down with the usual tropical diseases. He, together with his hospital steward, had inoculated the troops for smallpox, but there was no vaccine against dengue, yellow fever, typhoid, and dysentery, all rampant in the Philippines. So far the soldiers, most of them volunteers, seemed to be in good health. But then they had

only been at camp—some twenty-five miles south of
Spanish-held Manila—for a short time.

Though Admiral Dewey had put the enemy fleet out
of commission in the bay, the Spanish still clung to their
strongholds on land. Here at camp the Americans had
built detached rifle pits, some skirting the seashore only
thirteen hundred yards from the formidable sandbagged
batteries of the Spanish, others threaded through thick-
ets of bamboo, pepper plants, and wild hemp beyond the
Pasey Road. Thus far the Americans had not been seriously engaged but had spent their time returning spo-
radic Spanish fire. They were waiting for the word to
move ahead and advance on Manila, bypassing their
Filipino allies, who had taken the brunt of the hard fighting in their bid for independence.

Christian, listening to the patter of rain and the drunken
laughter of a small huddle of men who had managed to
sneak some tuba beer into camp, was thinking back to
the day he had written to the surgeon general offering
his services as a medical officer to the United States
Army.

He had done so out of sympathy for the Filipinos,
rather than from some high-flown notion of patriotism.
One of his patients, Ramon Rizaldo, had been a self-
exiled mestizo, an educated man, who had been forced
to leave his country in fear of his life. Half Chinese, half
Filipino, Ramon had been a leading member of the
Katipanan, an organization of Filipinos revolting against
Spanish tyranny. For centuries Spain had ruled the Philippines as a feudal kingdom, imposing a direct tax on
every native over eighteen, obliging workers and peas-
ants to donate fifteen days of labor each month to their
Hispanic overlords, strictly censoring the printed word,
and summarily executing those who disobeyed.

Christian felt that the United States had taken up a
worthwhile cause in siding with the native Filipinos in
their desire to expel the Spanish and set up their own
form of republican government.

But other factors had also worked to bring Christian
into the war. His bitterness toward Hannah had eaten
into him like acid. She had led him on, then cruelly

disappointed him once too often. What made her so
capricious? Was it because she didn't trust him? Couldn't
forgive him for his dissolute past? Why she should resent women who had never meant anything to him was
beyond his comprehension. And this last time, this note
about the First National Bank, had been a complete
mystery. She couldn't leave her husband. Well, wasn't
that the sort of loyalty he admired? No, it wasn't loyalty. She simply didn't care enough for him. There had
been passion, yes, but not love.

Why, then, couldn't he dismiss her as he had Amanda?
Because she wasn't Amanda. She was Hannah.

Thus far Christian had no cause to regret his decision
to come to the Philippines. He would be doing good
here, embarked on a noble mission. Aguinaldo, the Filipino leader, had already set himself up as head of the
revolutionary government he hoped to model after America's democratic institutions, once Spanish rule was over-
thrown. Encouraging Aguinaldo and his rebel followers
was Consul-General Wildman, who wrote to him from
Hong Kong, calling on him to stand shoulder to shoulder
with the American forces.

"The United States," Wildman wrote, "has not entered the war with Spain for the love of conquest or
hope of gain, but to relieve [the Filipinos] from the
cruelties under which they are suffering."

Christian, reading these sentiments, felt his own feelings
had been reaffirmed. As for lingering thoughts of Hannah,
he was not quite sure that the magic formula of escape had
worked to erase them. Time, he told himself, and patience.
As soon as the men went into action, his mind would
be occupied with more than merely personal matters.

But the action he looked forward to did not materialize. One miserable, steamy day followed another without a sign or word of impending battle. No one could
explain the delay. Christian was not privy to his commander's plans. General Green seemed to be waiting for
some event to take place about which the others could
only guess. Then one evening, just as the men were
beginning to think they had been permanently mired in

Camp Dewey's mud, the troops were ordered to move into the trenches at six-thirty the following morning. Their object was to capture the Spanish fortification of San Antonio.

The day dawned sunless and damp with gray-bellied clouds pregnant with rain hovering overhead. Christian, leaving a hospital steward in charge of his two patients, took his medical bag and, arming himself with a government-issue Colt, joined the rear column. Regiment after regiment, starting out in fine formation, was soon floundering in the drenched foot-sucking fields. Christian, bowed forward, pulling one booted leg after the other out of the gluey mire, gave credit to the men, who, unlike him, were laden with heavy haversacks and rifles. Then, to add to their discomfort, the sullen clouds overhead opened like a water sluice and in seconds the field and the road were turned into a lake.

The lines closest to the sea were bad enough but on the flat the men lay in their pits like drowned rats, holding their guns against the breastworks above the slimy water. The poncho Christian had donned that morning leaked and he could feel water trickling down the back of his neck. He wedged his medical bag between two posts, then removed his felt campaign hat and wrung it out, a wasted motion since it was almost immediately sopping again.

Soon Christian, feeling he was not in a good position to spot a wounded man once the fighting began, hauled himself out of the rifle pit and began inching slowly toward an old monastery where General Green had set up temporary field quarters. Climbing to the roof, Christian had a good view of the surrounding country: flat, drowning in marshy water, spiked here and there with clumps of nipa palms. The men, up to their knees in muck behind the flooded breastworks, had their rifles at the ready. To the left, out beyond the building, was the bay and Christian could see the U.S.S. *Olympian*, the *Petral*, and a captured Spanish gunboat, the *Calloa*, sailing up it in half-crescent formation.

As they passed the monastery their guns suddenly

opened up on the Spanish-held fort. Simultaneously the
Utah battery began firing from their pits, their guns
coughing and spitting smoke into the misting rain. A
huge shell came pulsing over Christian's head. He ducked
and a moment later it exploded, smashing the bridge
before the Spanish position.

Now the ships were pounding the fort with heavy
artillery and quick-firing guns, the walls of the old monastery trembling with the echoing sound. Shell followed
shell, whizzing by with the sound of onrushing freight
trains. There seemed surprisingly little resistance from
the Spaniards. When the smoke cleared, the Spanish
soldiers could be seen for the first time, running at top
speed to the rear of the fort. But some of their comrades
armed with sharpshooting rifles had lodged themselves
in the trees, and before they could be picked off they
had wounded a man. Christian, bag in hand, ran down
from the roof and out of the monastery. The soldier, a
private, lay moaning, half submerged in water. Christian, cutting open his blouse, found his wound to be far
from serious. A ball had gone through the fleshy part of
his right shoulder. A stretcher was brought forward and
the bearers instructed to take the man back to camp.

At the order "up and out!" the men swarmed out of
their trenches. Fording a stream with their rifles held
over their heads, they reached comparatively dry land,
where they knelt. Christian, coming up behind, was
suddenly knocked from his feet by the force of a tremendous explosion. The *Olympia*, with a single shell from an
eight-inch gun, had hit the magazine of the Spanish fort,
hurling brick and mortar sky-high.

"Don't stop! Press on! Press on!"

Christian could hear screams coming from behind the
crumbling walls, but the firing had ceased. As a medical
officer he could have remained safely removed from the
conflict, but he never gave safety a thought as he surged
forward with the others. When they reached the fort,
they found it deserted. The Spaniards had retreated in
such haste they had left their dead and wounded where
they had fallen. Without pausing, General Green's volunteers, in their dash and scramble to get inside and

beyond the fort, ignored the enemy casualties. Christian, however, paused long enough to pull the wounded into shelter and to administer hasty first aid.

The regiment moved on toward Malate, a suburb of Manila. This, too, seemed abandoned by Spanish forces. But as Christian caught up with the Utah volunteers, street snipers hidden in the upper stories of the houses on either side began firing upon them. He and the others scattered, taking refuge behind garden walls. One soldier, not as quick as his fellows, reeled, falling under a hail of bullets. When Christian reached him, he was already dead.

Little by little the Americans advanced down the road that led to Manila, where they could see the Spanish retreating. Christian wondered that more of the men were not killed or wounded, for haphazard fire trailing smoke in the rain-fogged air kept coming from windows along the way.

Finally the walls of Manila appeared. There in one corner streamed a white flag. Surrender! The men threw up their hats and cheered, dancing about, clapping one another on the shoulders. "It's over! We've won!"

The Philippine insurgents, who had been fighting the Spaniards for several years, feeling it was their victory also, broke through with the intent of entering Manila with their allies. But they were stopped by army officers—for what reason Christian could not fathom.

Later he was to learn that the "battle" for Manila had been prearranged between the city's defenders and the American high command under General Merritt and Admiral Dewey. The Spanish, realizing that to fight was futile, preferred surrendering to the Americans rather than to the Filipinos. The few combatants who had been killed or wounded were mistakes, since this was to have been a "bloodless" conquest. Aguinaldo and his insurgents had been ignominiously squeezed out. The islanders who had fought so valiantly, clearing Cavité and the road to Manila for the Americans, were now labeled "an unruly mob intent on looting," "savages," "an inferior race," and, worse still, "nothing more than niggers."

Christian felt depressed when he looked over the lists of casualties, this many killed, this many wounded. That these men had been maimed and had died for no reason except to satisfy the political ambitions of commanding officers weighed heavily on his mind.

In the house on California Street the mood was not any lighter. Since Elthea had died, a pall hung over its occupants. Hannah blamed herself for not insisting that Elthea have proper medical care. Guy tried to assure her that not even the best of doctors could have saved her. But it was Travis who carried on the most. It astonished Hannah to hear him weep, to listen to his verbal breastbeating, his constant "I should have . . ." or "I shouldn't have . . ." Given the circumstances of his quarrelsome marriage, Hannah had not expected him to demonstrate such grief.

"I wasn't a good husband to her," he'd say.

Guy tried to convince him that he had done the best any man could. A lie. No one, least of all Travis, believed it. He was an adulterer. His lovemaking with Flavia, his coupling with her time and time again in the barn, bothered him far more than the angry words he had spoken to Elthea. But God had punished the wrong person. It was he who should have died, not his wife Elthea, whose only sin was wanting to go home to Georgia. The dead baby that had been pulled from her womb as she expired also burdened his conscience. It had been a boy, his son, an innocent soul who had never had the chance to draw breath. Travis would have to answer to God for his death also. For he was convinced by now that had he been a decent husband, Elthea and their child would still be alive.

Preacher Wright's teachings, once laughable, came back to haunt him. The visions of hell, painted so vividly in the preacher's sermons in the clapboard, steepled church back home, rose before him in all their biblical horror. Sometimes he felt he could actually smell fire and brimstone and the acrid smoke of leaping flames. In his dreams he saw Satan glaring at him over his forked wand, the slashed mouth slavering in anticipation. He had done wrong, he had broken commandments, he had lied, stolen, and lain with a woman who was not his wife. He must atone. That was the only road to salvation open to him, the only way he could save himself from eternal limbo in purgatory.

Atone—but how?

He began to think about the war in the Philippines. President McKinley was calling for more volunteers to supplement the troops of the regular army, many of whom were still stationed in Cuba as an occupying force. To offer himself to his country, to embark on a dangerous mission, putting his life in jeopardy for a worthy cause, seemed to Travis fitting. He could think of no other deed that would redeem him in God's eyes. Nor in Hannah's or Guy's.

To all intents and purposes, however, the war was over. Manila had been secured, a treaty signed with Spain in which she had ceded all her possessions—Cuba, Puerto Rico, the Philippines—for twenty million dollars. Still, according to the president, the army was not withdrawing from the Pacific islands. The U.S. was expecting trouble from the Filipino insurgents who were muttering about independent rule.

"Ungrateful bastards," Travis remarked to Guy one evening as he read aloud from an article in *Harper's*.

" 'The insurrectionist party has taken the bit between its teeth and now rushes on with little or no gratitude for the aid which made its existence possible. . . . The fact is that peace and prosperity throughout the archipelago can only be maintained through the assistance of some strong governing force from the outside.' "

"That's us," Travis said.

Hannah snorted. "What makes you think that we possess such godlike wisdom as to take on another nation? It's the 'white man's burden' all over again."

"Well, what's wrong with that?" Travis wanted to know. "It's about time we showed the world a little American muscle and do some good at the same time."

Guy closed the magazine. "You might only be on garrison duty over there right now, Travis."

"Mebbe. But there's bound to be trouble. I just got a feeling them Flips are itchin' to fight."

"Same as you," Guy said, and smiled.

"You betcha."

"I have half a mind to go myself," Guy said.

"What?" Hannah exclaimed.

Guy leaned back in his chair, brought out his pipe, and fiddled with it. "Well, I didn't want to say anything before this but they're laying people off at work. Mr. Beasely is thinking of pulling up stakes and going to Australia. He says there's more opportunity there."

"But you can always get another job," Hannah pointed out.

"Yes. But they're not all that easy to find. Carpenters are in plentiful supply."

"But not as good as you."

"The pay isn't all that much to brag about, Hannah. And with Travis gone . . ."

"Travis isn't going," she said. "That's just talk."

But a week later Travis came home and announced he had joined up with the California Volunteer Artillery.

"Here's my papers, Sis. I'm to report to Camp Merritt for training day after tomorrow."

Hannah was upset, but Guy told her there was no need to be, that Travis would probably see little action.

Guy himself had been thinking more and more about the war in the Philippines. He had not spoken idly when he told Hannah he had half a mind to go. Like Travis, he felt a need to redeem himself. His failure at Sycamore had crushed him, and there were times when he felt he would never get over it. The dream of working his own land had been so long with him, he had been so certain that hard work alone would ensure success . . . losing it all had been a calamity his mind still refused to absorb. He had never imagined that so many things could go wrong. It was more than the drought, anthrax, and falling prices; it was his own mismanagement. He was convinced of that. Others had made it, people like the Andersons, the Pfeiffers, and the Barlows. It was true they had been there for at least a decade, but young

John Morton had started down near Bixby's Landing a year after Guy had arrived and was already showing a small profit. He had learned how to breed cattle and had an uncanny sense for finding water. He had built dams and drilled wells. Morton always seemed to pick the right time to take his steers to market and to know if Jolon's prices might be better than Monterey's or King City's one year and not the next. He was what the Indians called savvy. He was a natural-born rancher.

Guy was not.

He wanted to wipe the slate clean. What better way to do it than to make himself useful to his country? When he returned he would start anew. But joining up was not that simple. He could not leave Hannah and the children to fend for themselves. It would be tantamount to desertion, since his army pay—what was it, five dollars a month?—couldn't begin to keep them.

He said none of this to Hannah, but she was too astute not to guess from his comments, his eager study of newspaper accounts of the war, and his ill-concealed envy of Travis that he, too, would like to take up a rifle and don the khaki and blue shirt of a volunteer. Privately she thought both men were fools. She had not swallowed the rousing rhetoric of the Hearst papers. Neither did she believe, as some editors claimed, that this war was "sacred" or in the least romantic, or that the real reason for going into the Philippines was to free the inhabitants from Spanish tyranny. America meant to make it a colony, one that would open up trade with the Far East. She had read this last in a pamphlet an earnest young man had handed her in front of a shop where she had gone to buy thread.

On the other hand Hannah felt it wise to keep her opinions to herself. She saw how Guy's drooping spirits revived as he read the news of American triumphs: Cuba, Puerto Rico, the Hawaiian Islands, and now the Philippines. He had found something he wanted to be a part of, something that would make him feel like the head of his family, a man again.

And it wasn't as if it were a bloody, raging conflict,

Hannah reasoned. Guy himself had said that the worst of the war was over. It was only a matter of a few native skirmishes now, an opportunity for small heroics at little risk, or simply the job of policing the streets of Manila. Hannah was all for urging Guy to go, but she realized that their precarious financial situation prevented him from doing so.

Quietly Hannah began to look about for some way she could support herself and the children. The Levi Company was calling for girls and women who could run their sewing machines to fill orders for army and navy uniforms in addition to their usual line of denim trousers. But Hannah knew that Guy would never permit her to work outside the home. She thought of taking in sewing. But she had no machine—the old one had broken down before they had left Sycamore and the money in the "saving jar" was not nearly enough to get a new one. Perhaps she might be able to get a machine on credit, or find someone who would give her the loan of a Howe in exchange for piece work at home.

Hannah was mulling these things over in her mind as she stood in the butcher shop waiting her turn. A young woman she had often seen and with whom she had a speaking acquaintance was in the group behind those at the counter shouting their orders.

"There's always such a crush at this hour," said the young woman, who had introduced herself as Sophie.

"Yes, I suppose it's because Donaldson's inexpensive cuts are gone by late afternoon."

"Well, I shall have to buy dearer meat then," Sophie said. "I'm going to work next week at Forstan's. My husband's reserve unit was called up and we can't live on officer's pay. He fairly frothed at the mouth when I told him. But I'm not going to be reduced to begging charity from my folks or his or going back to Ohio to live with them." Sophie paused to glare at a stout woman who was trying to elbow her way past.

"As it is," she went on, "I had to lie to Richard. He was worried about the children. I have two—a boy seven, and a girl five, little dears. I said I had someone who'd take care of them, someone I could depend upon. But I don't. Do you know of any such person? I would pay, of course."

It took Hannah a split second to come to a decision. "I'd be happy to have them. I have one of my own, Mark—he's five—and a niece of three. Her mother's dead and her father's in the army. They'd be company for yours. But naturally I'd have to ask my husband first."

Guy made no objection. He thought Sophie was daft for going to work and her husband lily-livered for allowing it, but agreed with Hannah that the children should not have to suffer for their parents' callousness.

The children were not dears. Petra, the little girl, was spoiled. On her first day with Hannah she rolled on the floor and screamed because she was not allowed to jump up and down on Guy's easy chair. She pinched Clara and made her cry, then later tried it on Mark, who gave her a resounding smack. This set her off into another floor-rolling episode. The little boy, John, though more even-tempered, sucked his thumb and wet his pants. Hannah was to struggle with him for much longer than with Petra until she cured him of these infantile habits. Both posed a challenge. But Hannah thrived on challenges. With patience, perseverance, and discipline tempered with affection, she changed their behavior so that their own mother hardly recognized them. And while they never entirely became "dears," Hannah, in the end, grew fond of them.

In the meanwhile other women who were in the same predicament as Sophie, or who were the sole support of their offspring, or who simply wanted to get rid of their precious darlings for a few hours a day, got wind of Hannah's willingness to care for children. They brought their charges to Hannah's door—all described as "little sweethearts," some with running noses, some weeping bitterly, some mean, some lovable.

Since Travis had gone (his letters from Camp Merritt were a mixture of bluster and complaint) his room and the parlor were turned over to what had now become HANNAH'S DAY NURSERY. Little cots for naps were put up and cupboards for uncomplicated games and wooden toys were built. The backyard was made into a playground. Guy constructed a seesaw, a sandbox, and two swings so that the children could amuse themselves when the weather was fine. It wasn't long before Hannah had to turn people away. Her small house could not accommodate all those who sought her services.

She was taking in good money now, as much as Guy was making at Beasley's.

"There's no reason for you not to join up," Hannah told Guy. "I know you want to. We'll be all right. I can manage."

"Not alone. I can't leave you with all this and no help."

"I could hire another woman, I suppose, but I don't like taking my chances with a stranger."

Guy said, "Why don't you ask Flavia if she'll do it? According to her letters, she's dying to leave the ranch and come up to San Francisco."

It was arranged in a surprisingly short time. Flavia wrote a gushing "forever grateful" letter. She could hardly wait to see them all. Had Travis sailed for the Philippines?

Travis had. On October 14 Travis's regiment, along with the 23rd U.S. Infantry, had embarked for the western Pacific. Hannah, standing on the dock amidst the hullabaloo of shouted farewells, watched the ship pull away with a sinking heart and a rush of tears. She had a sudden horrible feeling that she should have put up some resistance and tried her best not to let Travis go. He would be crossing a vast ocean, arriving in a strange, fever-ridden, dangerous land. And for the first time he would be on his own.

She had turned to Guy with tears streaming down her face. "What if . . . ?"

"You mustn't think of what if, dear. He'll be perfectly safe. He'll have a high old time over there and come home to tell little Clara how he won the war."

But Hannah was left with a feeling of impending doom that followed her home and lingered for weeks after.

Once Flavia arrived, Guy needed little urging to en-

list. He was put at once to drill at the Presidio. Hannah
was surprised at how quickly he acclimated himself to
army life. He had always said he preferred to be independent, so it seemed odd to her that he could submit so
easily to army discipline. But he had, and what's more
seemed to like it. Hannah in her perplexity could only
assume that his days, laid out in neat routine, satisfied
his need for orderliness. Guy told her it gave him a
purpose and a goal which were within reach and he
could go to bed every night and say "that's done" and
not have to worry about tomorrow.

The last week of October Guy was given a two-day
leave in order to say good-bye to his family. His battery
was to sail for Manila on November 6.

Flavia thought he was the "handsomest thing in boots,"
and loved the way he wore his campaign hat with the
brim on the left side dashingly turned up.

"I don't know why Hannah is letting you go. Some
Spanish señorita is sure to snatch you away."

"He won't be that lucky," Hannah quipped, and they
all laughed.

They were having their midday meal. The children
had been put down for their naps, and those who had
outgrown napping were in the play yard, fighting loudly
over sand pails or a turn on the seesaw. The postman
came while they were eating, bringing a letter from
Bayetville.

"Sue Joy," Hannah said with a kind of wonder. Sue
Joy had never written to her or Travis before.

Dear Hannah,

*Aunt Bess and Pa were killed sudden-like on
Wednesday in a buggy accident. . . .*

There was a stunned silence. "My God," Hannah said.
"My God!"

Flavia leaned over and covered Hannah's hand. "I'm
sorry, I'm truly sorry. It must be a terrible blow."

Guy said, "Can I get you something, Hannah? You look
so white. A bit of brandy?"

"No—no. I'm all right. It's the shock. And we—Aunt Bess and Pa and I—we hadn't been writing. I suppose I should have. I don't know. . ."

"My dear, don't fret over it," Guy comforted. "After all, your Aunt Bess's last letter was not the warmest. At least it wasn't one that called for a reply."

"I know, I know. Still . . ." She swept a strand of hair from her forehead. "I can't really grieve for Pa. Maybe that's why I feel so bad. I can't honestly say I'll miss him, or ask God 'Why did it happen?' In a way his death is a blessing. He really didn't seem to get much enjoyment out of life, even when he was full of whiskey. It's terrible not to be able to cry over Pa. I did all that crying when I was a small girl. I can't remember him ever being tender to me or to Ma or to Travis. I'm sorry about Aunt Bess. She was always a strange one to me, someone you couldn't warm up to. And yet it comes as a shock."

She pushed away her plate and laid the letter on the table, smoothing it out with her fingers, reading on:

> *Stonebridge was left to us. But Aunt Bess's money goes to you. Tom Baxter says he will write you about it.*
>
> *Your sis, Sue Joy.*

"I suppose Baxter will sell Stonebridge," she said. "I hope for a good price, enough to keep Sue Joy, Colin, and Bobby until they're on their own."

She turned the envelope over. It had been forwarded from the Post ranch months ago. The letter itself had no date. But Hannah reasoned that Aunt Bess and her father must have died when she and the family were still at Sycamore trying to sell it.

"We might have been able to use that money," Guy said, taking the envelope from her.

"Maybe. But it can't have been much."

But it was. The extent of Granny's legacy, however, was not made known until after Guy left. It was all to the good, Hannah was to tell herself. The irony of it might have made Guy bitter.

Chapter XX

Travis's passage across the Pacific was far from pleasant. The *Ukiah,* an old rust-stained freighter hurriedly transformed and pressed into service as a troop ship, had never been designed to carry more than a crew of fifty. Now a thousand men filled its stinking hold, swinging from layered hammocks or bedded down like packed sardines on its lower decks. What cargo it had once shipped no one knew, but the guess was pigs and untanned hides.

One day out of San Francisco Travis was seized with a heaving, rolling seasickness that kept him hanging over the leeward rail. Finally, when his stomach had accustomed itself to the roll of the ship and he was able to eat, he found the food far worse than the meals that had been served in training camp. Cornmeal mush that was closer to gruel, hardtack, a watery stew that must have been made from fat drippings, rotten potatoes, and weak, tepid coffee. "Better than what we got in the Cuban campaign," a veteran in the war of the Caribbean told Travis. "Soldiers dropping all around because of tainted meat. More of them killed by that damned beef than bullets."

Two of the California volunteers came down with

measles. They were quickly quarantined but not before a half-dozen others had caught it. Travis, having had the disease as a boy, congratulated himself on his escape from this first hazard of war.

The misfortunes aboard the *Ukiah*, however, were not over. Two and a half weeks before the ship reached Manila the coal that fueled the vessel caught fire. The officers, when questioned as to the cause, could give no satisfactory answer but reassured the men that the fire would soon be put out.

"Don't you believe it," said another young man whom Travis had befriended. Gil was originally from the mining country of Kentucky and well acquainted with the dangers of burning coal in a confined space. "Spontaneous combustion is what that is. More likely to happen when you have a poor grade of coal. Them fires throw off gas. One tiny spark and it could set the whole thing off like fireworks, blowing us all to kingdom come."

It was not a comforting thought. Nevertheless it was one they had to live with night and day. The smell of burning coal, the smoke, the heat, drove them to moving their hammocks to the already crowded hurricane deck. Then somehow the coal shifted to one side of the ship and the *Ukiah* wallowed through the seas on her port beam end. The men walked slanted decks high above the sea on one side, while on the other they footed it through the wash of breaking waves.

In the meantime the sweating crew worked valiantly to extinguish the fire while the troops were put through lifeboat drill twice daily.

"This damn tub is a floatin' furnace," Travis said to Gil after another sleepless night when he lay tense, waiting for the sounds of a sudden explosion. "Don't see why we can't abandon ship now."

"Don't know. Mebbe because it's easier to replace us than the ship."

The day before they reached Manila the fire was finally snuffed out. Travis, standing at the rail in the rain as they steamed past Corregidor and the masts of sunken Spanish ships, was never so glad to see land. Like his comrades, he was heartily sick of the *Ukiah* and eager to get his feet on solid ground.

But the orders to disembark were not given. To everyone's bewildered disappointment the ship was ordered to pull anchor and set sail again. They were being sent to a place called Iloilo, some three hundred and eighty miles south on the island of Panay. The Spanish had evacuated the town, leaving it in control of the Filipino insurgents, but what role the troops aboard the *Ukiah* would play on Iloilo was not made clear.

Christmas was celebrated en route. Religious services were held and the usual rations were supplemented with fresh fruit, which had been obtained from native hucksters in Manila. A small band of army musicians who were traveling with the troops played all the old favorites, sentimental tunes that depressed rather than cheered. Most of the men were hardly more than boys and were already suffering from homesickness, a feeling Travis did not share. What was there at home to long for? The dingy house on California Street? The sugar factory? Stonebridge? Sycamore was the only place he missed and that was lost to him forever. He thought of writing to Flavia, but felt it would be pointless. No mail had been sent from the *Ukiah* and no mail had been received. Where all the letters that were scribbled daily by dutiful sons, brothers, husbands, and sweethearts disappeared to Travis could not imagine.

When the *Ukiah* finally reached Iloilo on New Year's Day, the men learned that their orders were not to land unless it could be done peaceably. Apparently the Filipinos, having driven out the Spanish, were not too happy to accept American jurisdiction. Why, then, the Americans on the *Ukiah* asked each other again, had they been ordered to Iloilo? "That's the army," Gil said.

They remained at anchor, day following day in monotonous succession broken only by landing drills that were never carried out. The picturesque scenery of limpid waters, jungle greenery, and distant verdure-covered mountains soon palled. Travis, like his comrades, fretted and swore at the heat. Back home he had been warned of the discomfort of tropical weather, a warning that had vastly underestimated what he would find. Georgia-reared, he had sweltered through many muggy summers, but these had been mild compared to the climate he found in the Philippines. Nothing had prepared him for the sudden bursts of tropical rain, the steaming heat of a fitful red sun, the clouds of insects, or the heavy, suffocating air that had the consistency of soup and kept him in a perpetual bath of sweat.

At long last, on January 29, the *Ukiah* was instructed to return to Manila. A week later the troops finally disembarked. They had been aboard ship for one hundred and eight days.

"So far," Travis said to Gil, "this ain't been much of a war."

Tom Baxter wrote Hannah in the second week of February, a long missive in which he explained that according to Aunt Bess's last will and testament Hannah was to receive the bulk of her money when she died. Apparently Bess was afraid Chad might get his hands on the inheritance and waste it as he had his own. What stunned Hannah was the sum involved. One hundred thousand dollars.

It boggled the mind.

"Flavia, I'm rich," Hannah whispered, breathing lightly, afraid the dream would go away.

Oh, if only she could have had it sooner! Hannah recalled the letter she had written to Aunt Bess, asking for a loan to save Sycamore, and the answer she had received complaining about "expenses" and "poor profits" and how she and Chad had to scrounge to make ends meet. And all the time Bess had been sitting on money that in any case was eventually to go to her niece. Hannah tried not to feel bitter, not to think of the difference a few thousand would have made. They would still be together, a family; Guy and Travis would have never gone to war. Perhaps Elthea would have done better if they hadn't had to move to the city. Breathing the clear coast air and eating fresh wholesome vegetables from the Sycamore garden, she might be alive today. But Bess had been miserly to the end and the money had sat there in Bayetville while they had struggled to save Sycamore.

But it wasn't Hannah's nature to waste time on regret. She was never one to beat her breast and moan about what couldn't be helped. Instead she turned her attention to the good fortune that had fallen to her.

For the first time in her life Hannah had money that wasn't earmarked for basic necessities. Before she spent a penny of it, however, she made sure that her brothers and sister were provided for. To the funds they had received from the sale of Stonebridge, she added three equally divided shares of the Haiti rum stock, which, according to Baxter, should give each of the younger Blaines a good income for years to come. That taken care of, Hannah felt free to do as she chose.

"Will we be giving up the children?" Flavia wanted to know.

"Not all of them. I'll keep those who have working mothers and I won't charge them a fee."

"A free nursery?"

"Why not? I can afford it now. First off we'll get a bigger house in a decent neighborhood. On Bush Street close to the Tivoli Gardens, perhaps. We'll be near a cable car so that the mothers will have ready transportation. Then I'll have Mrs. Smith, who's been giving us a hand now and then, come in regularly three days a week to look after the children so that you and I can have a little time to ourselves. I've never really *seen* San Francisco, have you?" Hannah tucked her lower lip under her teeth, thinking, her eyes suddenly lighting up. "Oh, there's so much I want to do!"

The house Hannah rented (she could not buy it without her husband's permission) had four bedrooms upstairs. The bottom floor consisted of a large parlor with double doors, a formal dining room, a library, an extra guest room, a "conservatory" where potted plants grew, and a huge kitchen. The owners had let it furnished, though Hannah would have preferred to put in her own things. The rooms were overcluttered with knickknacks even for a house of the period. Every available flat surface, every shelved nook and cranny was host to porcelain angels, cherubs, shepherds and shepherdesses, souvenir mugs, paper flowers under domed glass, painted dishes, engraved china bells, cloth dolls, japanned boxes, stuffed owls, and bronzed baby shoes. Hannah carefully packed these items away lest the children break them. The remainder of the furnishings, leaning toward heavy oak and plush, Hannah found suitable. Flavia thought they were more than suitable.

"Heaven," she had said, raising her eyes when she first entered the new house. "Just heaven."

Once they were established, Hannah took Flavia on a shopping spree. For someone who had always had to count pennies, who was accustomed to haggling with the butcher, baker, and greengrocer, and before that to saving what little cash she had to help buy a new steer or replace a worn pump, she quickly learned the art of spending. It took no time at all to dispense with the customary "How much?" and to cease wondering if an item was too costly or to ask herself if she could obtain the same cheaper down the street.

It was exciting to try on silks and brocades, the braided woolen jackets with their pinched-in waists, the wide platter hats garnished with quills and feathers, and say, "Yes, this suits me. Please send it out," and then write a draft with nonchalance. When Flavia chose bright, garish colors, velvet-flounced gowns and plumed hats that gave her the appearance of a Taylor Street demimondaine, Hannah only said, "Buy what you like, Flavia dear."

It was considered permissible (though not preferable) in the late nineties for women to patronize restaurants without a male escort. So Hannah and Flavia treated themselves to an occasional evening of dining out. They ate twelve-course dinners at Henri's or the Poodle, dishes that not even Hannah had tasted in her brief stay on Nob Hill. They partook of blue points on the half-shell, boiled ox tongue in sauce piquante, queen fritters in Madeira, crab creole, saddle of lamb covered with a spinach crust, and chocolate mint puffs oozing with whipped cream. They even dared order a bottle of Pinot Noir now and then.

"We shall get fat at this rate," Flavia giggled, crinkling up her freckled nose. "But I don't much care, do you?"

Hannah herself had to laugh at her sudden carefree, spendthrift ways. The years of penury, where even dreams of fine clothing and good food had been suppressed, fell away. She remembered her time at Wildoak when she had castigated herself for wanting a new gown to wear at Christmas, how she later had refused to be tempted by Christian's promise of luxuries she had never been able to afford. But now she could have them all and be beholden to no one.

She attended lectures at the Forum Club with Flavia, who yawned loudly behind a gloved hand, strolled through art galleries, and fed the bears and monkeys at Woodward Gardens. But for the theater they needed a male companion, so Hannah sent for Flavia's brother Tom. Dressed uncomfortably in ill-fitting, rented evening clothes, with Flavia and Hannah, one on each arm, somewhat dazzled by the two butterflies who had popped out of their drab pupae, he took (or went along with) them to see Sarah Bernhardt in *Camille* and to hear Melba in *Faust*.

Still, beneath all this indulgence, Hannah's common sense did not desert her. She knew that this was just a happy episode, a spurt of extravagance, compensation for a deprived girlhood. She did not wish to go through her money and have nothing to show at the end but a handful of unpaid bills, a few lovely gowns, and the memory of a meal or two. She wanted her bequest to last so that when Guy came home from the war (and he would, God would protect him) they could buy another ranch. Not in the Santa Lucias but a spread in Oregon or Washington, where rainfall was plentiful and the hazards of drought unknown. She had had enough of season after season of sun-bleached skies to last her a lifetime.

Half a world away, Guy, unlike Hannah, was wishing he could see a sun-bleached sky. After weeks of gray clouds and falling rain, he found himself remembering Sycamore and the dry sage-scented air with nostalgia. But he was not sorry he had come to the Philippines. Perhaps his decision, compounded of a desire to reassert his manhood and the honest feeling that volunteering

was his patriotic duty, had not been a sound one. But it had
given him time to think, to sort out his thoughts, to set
new goals for himself. He looked forward to the day
when his term of enlistment was up, when he could
rejoin Hannah. Together they would plan for a new
future. He might go into the building trade on his own,
negotiate for a lease on a dairy farm, an apple orchard in
Washington, or an orange grove in Owens Valley. Any
number of things. For the first time since his debacle at
Sycamore he felt a resurgence of hope.

Because he had been a carpenter, Guy was put into
the Army Corps of Engineers. It was the corps's duty to
accompany the regiment not with Krags or Springfields
but with picks, shovels, and axes. When the line came
to an obstruction in their march it was the corps's job to
remove it. Working in impossibly humid heat, sometimes waist-deep in turbid water, warding off hordes of
flying insects, they broke down fences, repaired roads,
built pontoon crossings over innumerable rivers and
streams, and repaired torn-up railroad track.

One evening the column reached a freight building
about one hundred yards from a badly damaged bridge
that spanned the Rio Grande Cagayan. The Filipino insurgents were entrenched on the other side. The object,
as the colonel explained it, was to take them by surprise. He had breastworks erected shielding the freight
house where two companies with long-range guns would
cover the men as they advanced over the bridge. First,
however, he asked for a volunteer to reconnoiter the
situation.

Guy immediately stood up and called out his name.
Though fifteen others followed suit, the colonel chose
Guy because of his knowledge of bridges.

An hour after sunset Guy, stripped to his undercloth-
ing and wearing felt-soled shoes, began his assignment.
Though the clouds covering the moon made him less
visible, darkness slowed his progress. The bridge was
about eighty yards long. The rails, ties, and upper girders had been removed and Guy was forced to walk on the
lower level of the bridge. He judged the cross girders to

be about seven feet apart and those running the length of
the bridge about four feet distant from one another. The
iron uprights that once held the top portion of the bridge
were still standing and these also hindered Guy's cau-
tious passage.

Dampness and the smell of rotting vegetation rose
from the dark river below him as he moved gingerly
from girder to girder. The wide gaps under his feet
worried him, for one slip and he would fall a long distance, plunging with a loud splash into the murky water.

Suddenly an unearthly scream rising in shrill, uneven
hoarseness pierced the silence. Guy's heart crashed crazily against his ribs and his mouth went dry as he stood
frozen in terror at the unearthly sound, the scream of a
soul in mortal agony. There it was again! Oh, God . . . !

But wait! Wait, don't panic, he cautioned himself. He
had heard that shriek before. Yes. Now he remembered.
It was the cry of the great black cuckoo, *bahow,* emit-
ting its bloodcurdling call. His tongue ran over his dry
lips in relief. With knees still somewhat unsteady, Guy
began again to steathily inch his way forward. Soon the
heavy mass of insurgent breastworks began to take shape
in the darkness. No sound came from it. No footsteps,
no murmuring voices. Were the Filipinos asleep? Or was
someone, a lookout, perhaps, silently waiting, watching
his painful progress across the span? *Careful, careful.*
One accidental bump against a steel girder could send a
reverberating metallic echo along the length of the bridge,
giving him away as surely as a shout.

He was nearly at the end of the bridge when he
paused once more, his head cocked forward, listening.
A moment later he heard the soft, almost imperceptible
tread of feet. It was a sentry, he was certain, and the
man must have been barefoot or else Guy would have
heard him sooner.

Ears sharpened by anxiety, Guy crouched against a
stanchion and waited. The sound of his heart seemed to
boom in the silence. The sentry paused at the end of the
bridge, then started across it, moving toward the spot
where Guy, every nerve and muscle screaming alarm,
lay hidden. Guy without a weapon or even his uniform,
felt exposed, nakedly helpless.

He could make out the sentry now, a small fellow dressed in coarse white cotton, the rifle butt (a Mauser?) cupped in one hand, the barrel resting against his left shoulder. His face was lost in shadow. The man halted so close, Guy had only to reach out his arm and touch him.

Guy's breath stopped in his lungs. His hands, gripping the girder, felt as though ice had melded them to the iron. An eternity passed. Then at last the sentry turned and with a parting look over his shoulder retraced his steps toward the insurgent position.

Quietly, but still using caution, Guy began the reverse passage across the bridge.

He had gone a quarter of the way when suddenly a powerful blow hit him between the shoulder blades.

He never heard the shot that killed him.

Chapter XXI

1900

San Francisco welcomed the new century on a tide of champagne. Noted for its gusty gaiety and lightheartedness, for its freewheeling, hard-drinking, high-living Gold Rush heritage, the city celebrated in a night of wild revelry. Crowds made up of whores, shop girls, factory hands, saloon keepers, financiers, burghers, the "aristocrats" of Nob Hill, pickpockets, saints, and just plain folks sang "There'll Be a Hot Time in the Old Town Tonight" as church bells tolled, foghorns tooted, and fire engines clanged.

Hannah and Flavia marked the occasion by toasting one another with a chilled bottle of Taittinger's.

"To your good health, good luck, and prosperity, Hannah. The best friend a girl ever had."

"The same goes for you, Flavia. And may God look after Travis and Guy and bring them home safely to us."

"Amen."

News from the Philippines was promising. The United States Army and Navy, by a strategy of bold moves, had sent the insurgent forces scampering. Fragmented into small, ineffectual bands, their leader, Aguinaldo, skulking helplessly in the hills, the Filipinos, the *Call* reported, were suing for peace. Now all that remained were a few "mopping-up operations." General Arthur MacArthur explained in a press release, ". . . an ingenious combination of Hotchkiss cannon, Gatling guns and borrowed naval batteries have been mounted on flat cars that will follow the rail system deep into the interior to get at enemy sanctuaries." Pacification and the setting up of local governments was already under way. Volunteers would be sent home as soon as they could be replaced by the regular army men who would take over garrison duty.

Hannah read this last bit of information with mounting joy and relief. She had worried and fretted over Guy's safety since the afternoon he had sailed out of San Francisco Bay even though his last letter had assured her he was not actively engaged in the fighting. "As engineer corpsmen we face more danger from the mosquitoes than bullets," he had written. Still she hadn't felt easy. War was war and in her mind the entire Philippine archipelago was bristling with enemy guns. Now, according to the paper, the men would be returning to their families. Guy, along with Travis, would be coming home. She hoped her wait would be a short one.

She missed Guy. She missed seeing him each evening in his easy chair, the newspaper spread out on his lap, fragrant tobacco smoke rising from his pipe, missed hearing the measured resonance of his voice as he read aloud. She felt guilty because he had so far been unable to share the enjoyment of Granny's money. But she would make it up to him when he returned. ("Making it up" to Guy seemed a recurring theme of her marriage.) She would see that he forgot Sycamore. They would only speak of it in passing, not as a place they were forced to leave, but as an experience that had left many pleasant memories. She would have another child. By then thoughts of Christian would no longer trouble her and what had happened between them would seem like an affair she had read about in a novel, the story of a dashingly handsome but feckless man, and a woman who had thought she loved him.

* * *

Christian himself often felt he was living in a world of fiction, a world imagined by some malevolent monster. He had always thought of himself as case-hardened, a man who had seen and experienced more than one incident of man's inhumanity to man. At home he had tended the slashed arms and chests, the bashed heads of innocent victims who had wandered too late at night in the Tenderloin, and set the bones of those beaten and maimed out of maliciousness or for the few coins in their pockets. He had come upon ragged children, bearing the scars of the whip, the cudgel and rod, some of them no more than tots begging for pennies. He had seen aging prostitutes abandoned and cast aside, gasping their last breath in the reeking alleys of Chinatown with no one to care or ease their dying. Human suffering and human degradation were not new to him.

But here in this country of many islands, where exotic flowers bloomed and where birds of brilliant plumage flitted from branch to branch, he had found the very bottom rung of man's incredible capacity for brutality.

Only yesterday they had moved into a town—Tarlac—they had taken before. During their initial assault they had fired the huts, and the scene of the flames leaping higher and higher under a sky blazoned with the Southern Cross and the screams of those entrapped in their burning homes were things he was not likely to forget. And now they had come back to Tarlac. It was a pattern repeated again and again. Capture a village and abandon it, only to return the next week to capture and abandon it once more. There were not enough troops to occupy each town and hamlet, thus only the important ones were garrisoned. Tarlac was not important, yet the rumor that it housed insurgents had brought them there once more. This time the fleeing inhabitants had left behind their dead and wounded.

Christian was bending over a Filipino who had been shot in the legs. Obviously in great pain, the wounded rebel begged pitifully for water through cracked lips. *"Agua—agua."* He was very young, hardly more than a boy, fifteen at the most, with the round dark face and slightly tilted eyes of a Tagalog. Christian knelt and was uncorking his canteen when an army corporal reached down, sweeping the canteen from Christian's hands.

"Goddammit, Doc. Why the hell are you helping that friggin' googoo?" (The Filipinos had been tagged with "googoos" as well as a variety of other derogatory epithets.) Before Christian could protest, the corporal swung his rifle around and fired, killing the young insurgent instantly with a bullet through the head.

Still kneeling, a blood-spattered Christian had a moment of blank incomprehension before he sprang up, consumed with violent rage, going for the soldier's throat, grabbing it between powerful hands. He wanted to kill him, wanted to throttle the breath from his body, wring his neck, stomp on him, annihilate him as he would a cockroach. He could scarcely see for the dizzy red mist in front of his eyes, the pounding blood in his head, the roaring madness in his ears. Sound and sanity were blocked out in his all-consuming need to destroy. Tighter and tighter he squeezed. The corporal's eyes were bulging. Christian felt tugging hands on his shoulder, on his arms, and he shrugged them off. He was going to kill this man if he died in the attempt, he was going to wipe out the inhumanity of this awful war, the scorched bodies, the torn limbs, the murder of innocent children and their helpless cries for mercy. And he would have succeeded had not the blow of a pistol butt caught him on the side of the head.

He reeled back.

"You forget yourself, Doctor."

It was the company commander, Colonel Hodges. "That man you're trying to strangle is one of us."

"Not one of me," Christian gasped, panting heavily, his tiger-mad eyes blazing behind a curtain of dark, tumbled hair.

The corporal's friends were reviving him with rum. Christian could hear the mutterings, "Damned nigger lover," and knew they were referring to him. He surged forward, but was restrained by the colonel.

"Cool down, doc."

Later that evening Christian was called into the colonel's presence.

"Lucky for you, you didn't attack a fellow officer," he said.

Christian, his anger still simmering, did not reply.

"I am not sure what jurisdiction I have over you," the Colonel went on, "since the surgeon general is your military superior. Nevertheless I shall write in my report that due to heat and exhaustion you lost your head momentarily. It can happen to anyone."

"It wasn't heat and exhaustion, sir," Christian replied. "It was the sheer unfeeling cruelty of the man."

"That's war," the colonel said placidly.

"Not of an enlightened people. *We* are supposed to be the civilized ones, a country that is presumably bringing the blessings of democracy and Christian morality and decency to savages. Now we've reduced ourselves to worse. We are killing women and children with impunity. Only yesterday I heard a man describing an attack on a village by saying, 'This is more fun than a turkey shoot.' "

"Well, son, you got it all turned around. They'd do you in without a second thought were they in the same fix."

"I'm afraid you don't understand. I'm not worried about what *they* do. It's what we do that bothers me."

"You must remember, Falconer, this is a dirty war. They don't fight fair and you know it."

"Yes, it's guerrilla war. The war of the poor who can't afford to put an army in the field and fight by the rules."

The colonel's jowls trembled. "Now, listen here, doc. I've heard just about enough. I'd recommend court-martial if it weren't for you saving so many men under fire. But you've lost your usefulness in the field. I think it best for all concerned that you transfer to a hospital in Manila. Or maybe you'd rather be mustered out?"

There was no question that Christian was sick to death of this war. General Otis, the supreme commander, conducting operations from his office desk in Manila, had proven to be a bumbling idiot who kept sending roseate and false reports of the armed forces' progress home. Otis had insisted time and again that the war was over, the enemy subjugated, yet the fighting went on. He had no grasp of the nature of guerrilla strategy. As a consequence his regiments were undermanned, untrained, and undisciplined. And since President McKinley believed Otis's claim that all was well, he saw no reason to dispatch seasoned troops to the far Pacific.

In addition Otis's bigotry was reflected in his subordinates' behavior. Many of them were veterans of the Indian wars and their contempt for the "natives" won them few allies among the Filipinos, even those who might be friendly, or at least neutral, toward the Americans.

The war, which had started out as one of liberation, had degenerated into a dirty punitive expedition. Even the English, who had far greater experience in empire building and were admittedly not above an atrocity or two, viewed the burning, pillaging, and rape by uncontrolled American troops as "unsporting."

Not all officers and men were of that ilk, however. Christian knew from his own regiment that there were many decent men who had come to the Philippines with the best of motives. Most of them were young, not yet twenty. Enervated by the blazing tropical heat and the torrential rains, plagued by dysentery and fever, hedged by fear of ambush, exhausted by forced marches, they nevertheless managed to endure.

It was these Christian thought of now. He could not desert them. There were not enough doctors as it was to care for the wounded and the sick. He agreed that his usefulness in the field was hampered by his outrage at acts of wanton brutality. He feared the time might come when there would be no one to check him as the colonel had done that afternoon, and that blind with rage he would actually kill a man with his bare hands.

"Perhaps I would consider hospital duty, sir."

A week later Christian's transfer came through and he was on his way to Manila.

*   *   *

Hannah's lips moved numbly over the words for the third time.

> *We regret to inform you that your husband, Corporal Guy W. Hartwell, was killed in the line of duty on May 9, 1900. He was a brave soldier who performed with courage under fire. We hope it will be of some comfort to know that he died quickly without pain. . . .*

Had she gotten the name wrong or mistaken the stark word "killed" with its horrible finality as the more hopeful, but still dreadful "wounded"?

She started to read it once more. "We regret to inform you . . ." She lifted stricken eyes to Flavia, who sat next to her on the red plush sofa in the parlor. They could hear the children at play in the backyard, the everyday sounds of their high-pitched voices and laughter increasing Hannah's sense of unreality.

Flavia took Hannah's icy hand in hers, rubbing it to bring back some warmth.

"It can't be true," Hannah said. "Only yesterday I got a letter from Guy saying he would be mustering out in three months. He spoke of an orange grove in Owens Valley. Apparently he hadn't received the latest news about Bess's money, but I'm sure when he does . . ." She got to her feet. "I put the letter somewhere. You read it, didn't you? And this . . ." She shook her head. "It must be another Hartwell, not Guy."

Flavia said, "Let me get you some brandy."

"No." She pulled Flavia back to the place beside her. "It isn't true. Tell me it isn't true. It's a dream, a horrible dream. Tell me—"

"Hannah, oh, Hannah, please. You've got to face it. Guy is dead."

Hannah sat down abruptly and stared at her, her eyes growing larger and larger. "*Dead* . . ." she whispered. Then, covering her face, she began to sob. Flavia drew Hannah close and put her friend's head on her shoulder. Together they wept, Hannah crushed by guilt and regret, Flavia weeping in sorrow and sympathy.

At last **Hannah** lifted her tearstained face. "You loved him, too, didn't you?"

"Of course I did. Oh, Hannah, he was such a decent man, so kind and thoughtful. We all loved him."

"I don't mean that kind of love," Hannah said.

Flavia's red-rimmed eyes widened. "You mean . . . ?" She shook her head. "No. Whatever gave you—oh, yes, I can guess. Because I flirted with him. But that was all in fun, Hannah. Surely you knew that. Oh God—and now he's dead. You didn't think . . . ? But it wasn't so. He laughed at me. It wasn't Guy I loved, but . . ." She lowered her eyes. "Travis," she whispered.

"Travis? But you never let on."

"How could I? He was married to Elthea. And, oh, I don't know how to explain. There's something about Travis that I can't help loving. He's sweet, not bossy like most men. I know some women would consider a man who doesn't strut and swagger around as weak. Not me. I saw enough of that kind at home. Travis has his faults, I guess, but underneath he's shy and lovable, always trying so hard to do the right thing."

"Did he know you loved him? How did *he* feel?"

"He said he loved me, too, but there was nothing we could do about it. He'd given his word before God to cherish his wife."

Before God. A chill gripped Hannah's heart as she remembered Travis's words: *Do you think it's easy for me to keep my vows?* She recalled the look Travis had given her when he read the note she had written to Guy saying she would leave him for Christian. Had she misjudged Travis? Was he built of sterner stuff than she? Did he have a greater sense of duty, of moral obligation? Or was it his fear of the boiling caldrons and red-hot pitchforks Preacher Wright had so eloquently described that kept him at Elthea's side? Yet, Hannah recalled, he had wept at his wife's death. Was his hypocrisy worse than hers?

But *I* was fond of Guy, she told herself. I did everything I could to make him happy.

Everything except telling him the truth. He never knew about Mark, about how she had committed adultery with Christian, not once but twice. Poor, honest, trusting Guy.

Tears welled up again. Now she would never be able to make it up to him, never help him buy an orange grove or a dairy farm, never give him a child. These past weeks she had pushed all thought of his mortality out of her mind, waiting for him to come home, looking forward to a new venture where they wouldn't have to worry about money, where they could build a contented, perhaps even happy life together. "God, oh God, how can I bear it?" she asked in an agony of guilt and bereavement.

"Don't. You mustn't," Flavia consoled helplessly. Then she got up and rustled about. A few moments later she returned.

"Here's a fresh handkerchief. Blow your nose, darling. And I've brought you some brandy. It will help."

The brandy flowed past the lump in Hannah's throat, easing the constriction in her chest. She finished the glass and Flavia poured her another.

They sat in silence, Hannah working the damp handkerchief into a ball.

Flavia sniffed, wiping away a tear with her sleeve. She lifted the brandy glass and took a long pull. "I pray for Travis every night. He hasn't written me, but I understand. He still feels bad about Elthea." She gulped at the brandy, draining the glass. "He blames himself"— she paused to hiccup—"when it was me who was at fault."

Hannah turned toward her. "You can't help it if you fell in love. Love seems to have no set of rules."

"You don't understand." Her voice had thickened. She's tipsy, Hannah thought. And then with astonishment realized that the brandy had begun to spin in her own head.

"I l-led him on," Flavia said. "We—in the barn—we made love." She shook her head slowly. "Lots of times."

Hannah said, "You're drunk. You don't know what you're saying. You can't mean it. You and Travis?"

"I'm not too drunk to tell you the truth. Me and Travis, yes. In the barn."

"I never dreamed . . . How could you? How?"

But why not? She was in no position to judge Travis and Flavia. What difference did it make if bodies joined on a fine feather bed or on a pile of straw? The sin against the innocent spouse was the same. Guilty, guilty, guilty.

Oh God, what a mixed-up world! Why did it have to be so complicated? Suddenly, impulsively, she reached out for Flavia, hugging her tightly.

"I'm not sorry," Flavia said tearfully. "I said I was but I'm not. I love him. And if he doesn't come back, I—don't know what I'll do, but at least I'll have that memory to live on for the rest of my life."

"Don't talk like that!" Hannah said harshly. "Don't say he won't come back, don't even think it."

"I'm not like you," Flavia continued in a broken voice. "I was never taught the Ten Commandments. Only been in a church two or three times in my life. I know what I did was against the good book's teaching, but I guess I'm just a born sinner. I know it's hard for someone who's decent to understand. *You* would never allow a man who wasn't yours to touch you. You're too fine—"

"No," Hannah interrupted, unable to bear praise she did not deserve. "I'm *not* fine. Flavia, if you only knew . . ."

And then, with remorse, guilt, and brandy still working in her, she heard herself confessing her sins to Flavia, everything since she had first met Christian, her miscarriage, her subsequent meeting with him in Chicago, Mark's true paternity, Christian's attempt to buy Sycamore, her decision to run off with him, and how Travis had stopped her.

Flavia listened in silence, her face slowly losing its brandy flush.

"Now you know," Hannah finished. "You know that my tears for Guy are those of guilt, that I have much more to atone for than you."

"But you atoned," Flavia protested, soberer now. "My own mother couldn't have been more steadfast and worked harder for a husband than you. Everyone knew that if it wasn't for you, Guy would have thrown up his hands long before he did. You mustn't regret anything. As for Mark, he's a child. What difference did it make that Guy wasn't his real father? He raised Mark, didn't he? The boy was his son except by an accident of birth. That's the important thing you have to remember, Hannah."

"Yes, yes," she said, twisting the handkerchief. "I suppose I do have something to be grateful for. Thank God Guy never guessed, never knew."

Chapter XXII

Travis's canvas-shod feet moved noiselessly as he followed the soldier ahead in Indian file along the night trail. The inky darkness under the low interlaced branches of jungle trees cut the men's vision to near blindness. Only by occasionally touching a comrade in front could they keep from getting lost or wandering off.

In the past year Travis had become seasoned not only to the climate but to army routine as well. He, like his comrades, carried one hundred rounds of ammunition strapped in his belt, his Krag Jorgensen rifle slung over his shoulder, and in his haversack three days' rations, a canteen of boiled water, and a rubber poncho. These accouterments, though by no means light, were a good deal less cumbersome than the regulation equipment deemed necessary for the foot soldier in the field. The United States Army, taking its lesson from the guerrillas, had learned from hard experience to appreciate mobility.

They came out of the forest and crossed a rice field where a water buffalo looked up from its grazing to see them pass. Then they were in the woods again, enclosed by the tall mahogany and hardwood trees. They were

marching toward a small rebel-held garrison, intending
to take it by surprise before daybreak.

The excitement of impending battle tensed Travis's
stomach muscles. Travis liked night marches. He liked
the war. In contrast to so many of his comrades-in-arms
who complained about the food, the heat, the loads they
had to carry, their inept or overstrict officers, Travis
found the life of a soldier agreeable. He belonged out-
doors, doing a real man's job in God's own army, not
cooped up inside a sugar factory, working as an anonymous cog in a machine. He was well aware of the many
risks he faced—being shot, cut up by a bolo knife, or
catching a fever—but so far he had been lucky. And if
he said his prayers every night, lived a clean life, didn't
drink the native rotgut vino, or get mixed up with a
googoo whore, he felt he had a good chance of coming
through without a scratch.

It hadn't happened that way with Guy. Travis crossed
his fingers as he thought of his brother-in-law dead these
past nine months. Now there was someone who should
have survived, a fine, upstanding, God-fearing man. Poor
Guy. He'd gotten a bad throw of the dice. When Hannah had written of Guy's death, Travis had been stunned.
Guy had been such an important part of his life. A father
couldn't have been kinder or more generous. Even now
Travis's throat got tight when he thought of it. Guy
dead. Damn those black bastards who'd killed him!

Then a few weeks later he had received a letter from
Flavia full of warm sympathy. That girl, knowing he was
feeling so low, only proved she really did love him. He'd
been afraid to have anything to do with her after Elthea
died; his guilt had been that strong. But now he felt he
had mourned his wife long enough and could turn his
thoughts to Flavia.

He remembered while composing a letter to her how
his vision of her had become so clear—the merry smile,
the white breasts pinked at the tips, the smooth belly
and rounded hips—his britches had developed an embarrassing bulge and he had had to go outside the tent to
cool off. If there had been any doubt in his mind that he
loved her, it had disappeared when she wrote again.

Dear Travis,

You asked how I felt? Nothing has changed. I still love you and I always will. Don't ask me why. I can't explain it, but you're the man for me. And I'm proud of you, fighting for your country. I'm so proud I could burst. I pray that you'll come home safely to me. . . .

She was proud of him. To her he was a man in every sense of the word. Well, when this was over he'd go home a hero. Just surviving in this bug-crawling jungle could make you a hero. But Travis wanted more than survival. He had the feeling that the opportunity for some derring-do in which he'd get a medal for service above and beyond duty, as they said, lay ahead. Not that he was dim-witted enough to take unnecessary chances, but he knew when push came to shove he'd be able to stand tall.

They had been walking for hours. Behind Travis, Ben Fox was breathing heavily. Travis himself felt tireless; he could go on for as long as the captain said, putting one foot in front of the other, feeling the rough, root-splayed ground through the hemp soles of his shoes. Above him the trees were thinning and he could catch a glimpse now and then of the far-flung twinkle of stars in the sky.

The column slowed its pace and Travis guessed they were nearing their objective. His senses became more alert, his eyes straining to penetrate the darkness, his ears alive to the slightest sound, his body tuning itself to a fine pitch.

No one was speaking now.

In the nocturnal obscurity around them the trees and tall abaca plants made whispering sounds. Travis took a firmer grip on his Krag.

From up ahead a shadowy figure detached itself and came quickly down the line. The captain. "Keep moving, boys. Quietly now."

They had reached the outer perimeter of the enemy breastwork. Beyond it Travis could make out the lines of a cuartel, a large nipa-thatched house built on stilts. The column came to a halt. They were so close to the Filipino position Travis could hear the low murmur of their voices. Then silence. A half hour later the sky began to pale. The jungle stirred with clickings and chirpings, bird cries, the rustle of leaves and creaking of branches. All up and down the line there was the muffled sound of breeching rifles.

"All right, boys! Let 'em have it!"

The tension that had built up during the past hour suddenly broke with a fusillade of shots, a whining, spanking barrage. As the American guns spoke the caartel came alive with white-clad figures ducking behind windows and bales of hemp set below the house. Moments later they began returning fire.

Travis, his rifle braced against his shoulder, his hands sweating with excitement, got a guerrilla in his sights and picked him off.

"God damn!" he shouted.

Then another and another, falling like nine-pins. All around him the air clamored with the ricocheting zing and crackling of guns, earsplitting, deafening sounds that were terrifying yet exciting. Ben Fox, positioned next to Travis, suddenly shouted, "Oh, my God!" and crumpled to the ground. "Steward!" Travis yelled for the medico. He hunkered down, reloaded and fired, reloaded and fired, again and again and again. As the sun, an angry red flush under banked clouds, rose, the Filipinos could be seen bursting from the doors and windows of the cuartel, shouting and screaming in panic.

"Get 'em! Get 'em!"

Travis jumped to his feet and ran forward around the breastwork. An insurrecto leaped from a window and landed directly in front of him. A reflex—as natural to Travis now as a knee jerk—recoiled and pressed his trigger finger and the native crumpled in a heap. Travis quickly moved on; the smell of acrid smoke, the noise of battle, the barking of guns, the shouts, the curses, acted like an intoxicant. He stumbled over a fallen Filipino who reached out and caught him by the trouser leg. Before Travis could bring his rifle around, the man slashed him in the leg with a bolo knife. A split second later Travis put a bullet through him and, swinging back, ran on.

It was a complete rout. The captain counted ten dead Filipinos, five wounded, three prisoners (who somehow, mysteriously, would never make the march back to the American base camp alive), captured ammunition, a half-dozen rifles, and a few bolos.

The Americans suffered only three wounded men. Travis's cut, which he dismissed as a mosquito bite, nevertheless was bound up by the medical steward who had accompanied the column. "Better see the doc about this when we get back," Travis was advised. "Even mosquito bites don't heal well in this climate."

Travis ignored the advice. The next morning, back at camp, his wound began to fester. In a few days when the leg turned numb and hindered his walk, he finally went to the company surgeon.

The doctor was a young man wearing spectacles that seemed of little use since he was constantly having to remove and polish the fog from the lenses. But he was able to see clearly enough to assess the seriousness of Travis's condition.

"You'd best get to a hospital in Manila, Blaine."

"Now look here, doc, a dab out of one of them bottles would probably do it."

"You've got a bad infection, soldier. I don't have facilities here to treat it."

Manila! Damn! Well, he'd be back. And soon.

Christian was stationed at the First Reserve Hospital, one of the several military facilities in Manila. Originally the old Spanish Hospital of Manila, it was situated just outside the walled city on the banks of the Pasig River. Christian had visited it briefly before being assigned to his regiment in the field. At that time the army was in the process of cleaning it up, a Herculean task. The hospital under Spanish management had apparently been a throwback to the Middle Ages, when such institutions were looked upon as places where people were sent to die. For years no effort had been made to keep the hospital in repair. Weeds grew in cracks and crevices of the broken-tiled courtyard. Garbage, human and animal excrement filled every gutter, overflowing in heaped piles of filth. Windows were broken, cornices crumbling, walls were grimy with fungus, and the ceilings festooned with giant spiderwebs. Why General Otis chose this unsanitary, malodorous place as a military hospital was inexplicable to the medical fraternity. But given the general's aversion to "coddling the sick," and his belief that most army patients were malingerers, it was easy to understand.

By the time Christian arrived at First Reserve for the second time to become part of its staff, the grounds and buildings had been restored to a fair standard of cleanliness. However, it was overcrowded to an alarming degree. Originally meant for four hundred and fifty patients, it now held over four thousand. The wards that in the pestilential, unhygienic days of the Spanish had accommodated two rows of beds were crowded with four. The cots were so closely placed together there was little room for attendants or doctors to move between them. Poor ventilation, floors that could not be properly scrubbed and disinfected, the lack of light, the incessant moans of the dying, made the sick sicker and depressed the medical staff.

Christian did not waste time in bemoaning his assignment or using his influence with the surgeon general to transfer to the Second Reserve Hospital, a more antiseptic, modern infirmary. Instead he rolled up his sleeves and went to work. Cases of ringworm, dengue, pneumonia, typhoid, dysentery, and malaria far outweighed those suffering from battle injuries. Yet recovery from these wounds was often a chancy thing. As the medical steward had told Travis, the humid atmosphere hindered healing.

Though the First Reserve had sufficient medical personnel and supplies, the conditions under which the physicians and stewards worked were frustrating. Christian's superior, Major Peter Whitelow, a conscientious, hardworking physician, struggled in vain against overwhelming odds to get a new hospital or at least an

addition to their present one. He was told that the end of
the war was in sight and that they would all be going
home soon. Hadn't the rebel leader, Aguinaldo, been
captured? According to General MacArthur, once Aguinaldo signed the oath of allegiance to the United States,
the insurrectos would be flocking into American-held
towns to take advantage of the general's offer of amnesty.

But the insurgents made no grand rush to lay down
their arms. Refusing to admit defeat, they continued to
snipe, to ambush, to attack and disappear.

"Our peaceful approach isn't working," a fellow surgeon complained to Christian. "We ought to wipe the
whole damn lot out."

"We might at that," Christian replied dryly. "I see
where General Smith in Samar has informed his troops
that he doesn't want any prisoners. He's given his men
license to kill and burn, the more they kill and burn—
and I quote—'the better I'll be pleased.' He would like
to make the interior of Samar 'a howling wilderness.' "

"Good. The man's got guts."

"Guts. Killing unarmed civilians? I don't think that
takes courage or bravery."

"Trouble with you, Falconer, you think those people
out there are like us. They aren't. They're barbarians."

"Oh?" Christian said with malicious irony. "And I
was under the impression when I signed up that we were
fighting this war for the benefit of 'our little brown
brothers.' "

While Christian may have been disappointed in the
hospital, he found Old Manila—the city proper—a fascinating place. Built up from a native village of nipa huts
at the mouth of the Pasig River by the Spanish four
centuries earlier, the city was still ringed by the same
fortresslike wall the conquistadores had erected against
the piratical Moors. The streets had changed little in the
last hundred years. Christian would walk them in the
early evening when the worst heat of the day was over
and marvel at the heavy traffic of carriages and cabs, of
carabao-drawn carramatos—two-wheeled covered carts—
bicycles, and sedan chairs. The unpaved roadways were

thronged with fruit peddlers, messengers, friars, sweating porters stripped to the waist, Tagalogs, mestizos, Visayans, Negritos, Japanese, Hindus, Chinese, Europeans, each dressed in their native garb, a kaleidoscope of color and sound. Exploring the Escolta, the main business section, he would saunter into jewelry and clothing shops, selecting baskets, finely embroidered shawls, and semiprecious stones as souvenirs for his mother and sister. Once, examining a lustrous rope of pearls, he pictured Hannah, imagining how the necklace would look draped about her slender throat, the sheen of the pearls enhanced by her petal-smooth skin. The image had poisoned the pearls for him and he had left the shop without buying them. He did not like to think of Hannah; she was part of so many things in his past that gave him pain. He wanted to forget, to forever blot out her face from his mind. Yet the memory of her betrayal, like a scar covering an old wound, ached anew when he least expected it. The echo of a voice, the scent of flowers, a woman laughing would bring Hannah back to him with tormenting clarity. At those moments, he would curse himself as a fool, and seek to lose himself in work, ministering to his patients on the wards far into the night, hoping that in the pain of others he would forget his own.

As much as Christian was intrigued by the life of the old city, when given the opportunity to live away from the hospital he took rooms in the fashionable suburb of Maleta. Here the old Spanish families, the wealthy English and German merchants had built grand houses set in gardens of shrubs and palms, papaya, banana, and the perfumed *dama de noche* trees. Rambling many-roomed mansions with fountain-splashed patios, tiled roofs, and overhanging balconies, they were a sharp contrast to the ramshackle city dwellings of the poor perched on stilts in the marshy swamps outside Manila's walls.

Christian had to admit that his love of fine—or at least comfortable—living had not left him despite his sympathy for the less fortunate. After a trying day, working in stuffy rooms, with the smell of putrefaction in his nostrils, he was glad to take refuge in spacious, airy, well-appointed quarters. And even though he continued to derive pleasure from his jaunts along the city's myriad byways, he preferred coming back to Maleta where he could sink into a cushioned rattan chair with a cool gin and lemon and stretch out his long legs while his Tagalog servant prepared his evening meal.

Because he was a presentable bachelor of obvious means and good breeding, he was asked to parties, fêtes, tea dances, and to the evening concerts on the green at Luneta. Seats in the best boxes at the races were put at his disposal, as were the choice tables at the finest restaurants.

Officers' wives who had marriageable daughters inundated him with supper invitations, few of which he accepted. The daughters, paraded for his benefit like so many pedigreed poodles, were for the most part empty-headed, unmitigated snobs, bigots, and crashing bores. More often than not he would forget his good manners—as he had often done in his younger days—and take delight in shocking his wealthy aristocratic hosts by his unabashed praise of Aguinaldo and his generals, Luna and De Pilar. Sometimes, when stung by some particularly denigrating comment concerning the natives, his anger would rise to a dangerous boil and it was only with extraordinary force of will that he was able to keep from giving the perpetrator a tongue-lashing. Nevertheless, despite his resolve to remain the gentlemen, there were times when the ferocity of his rage would show in his eyes, a savage gleam the ladies mistook for heightened erotic interest, and they would flock about him all the more, preening and coyly teasing for his attention.

The Spanish women were the most beautiful and the ones most closely guarded. Christian would catch glimpses of them riding in closed carriages along the bayside on a Sunday afternoon, their magnolia-white faces half hidden by lacy mantillas, their virtuous reputations protected by a male relative or elderly female chaperone who rode along with them. There was a mystery about them that intrigued him, the dark eyes that beckoned, the kissable yet virginal red lips parted in a half smile. But their allure was never strong enough for pursuit.

The game, Christian decided, was not worth the prize, no matter how lovely that prize might be.

One late afternoon Christian and a colleague, Ted Brown, were sitting in the main office going over their medical records when a young woman came to the door. Dr. Brown looked up and, seeing it was a mestizo—a half-caste—and not a white woman, said, "How the hell did you get past the sentry?"

"Please," she implored, ignoring Brown and addressing Christian, "I must have a doctor."

Dr. Brown bristled. "There's the native hospital on the other side of town. We don't treat civilians, let alone Flips. Now if you'll make yourself scarce—"

"Wait," Christian interrupted. "Is it for yourself?" he asked the girl.

"No, my mother. She's very ill. I'm afraid for her—and I can't get a doctor to come out to see her." Again she looked imploringly at Christian. She had a soft voice and a lovely face, a mixture of Chinese, Malay, and Spanish, Christian guessed. With her high cheekbones, small, well-defined nose, dark hair, almond-shaped eyes, and smooth golden skin, she seemed to have been endowed with the best attributes of her varied heritage. Her English, spoken with a charming lilt, indicated education. But there was something else about her, an intelligence, an air of breeding that impressed Christian. This was no ordinary mestizo.

"What seems to be the trouble?" Christian asked, indifferent to Brown's snort of disgust.

"Stomach. Very bad pains in the stomach. She can hardly breathe. It might be her appendix."

"Sounds like it. I'll come."

Brown said, "You know damn well it's against regulations. Let her go to the board of health hospital."

"Regulations are only meant to be broken, my friend," Christian maintained, picking up his campaign hat and bag.

The girl's name was Maria Delores Isabella Torres. She was a widow, she told Christian as they hurried along the streets, her husband having died of cholera

several years earlier. She and her mother had moved
from Cavite when their house had been burned down in
the fighting. (By which side or how she did not say.) They
had just enough money to open a small shop that sold
trinkets, a few items of clothing, and sweetmeats.

"This is the way we have lived," she said. "Enough
to eat and pay the rent."

"You must have been pretty desperate to come to an
army hospital."

"Desperate, yes. There are so few Filipino doctors
and I knew she was dangerously ill."

Maria and her mother occupied the top floor of a
house whose iron-barred balconies hung over a narrow,
cobbled, twisting street not far from the city's wall. It
had very little furniture: a few rattan pieces and two
mosquito-netted beds that once had seen better days.

Maria had guessed correctly. Her mother, soaked in
perspiration and moaning in pain, had an acute case of
appendicitis. Christian, afraid that she might be going
into peritonitis, had Maria run down to the street and
fetch a cab.

"Anything on wheels—hurry!"

He wrapped the woman in a sheet and carried her
very carefully down the stairs. As he did so he noticed
that she had gray eyes. Somewhere in the past there had
been a Spaniard, a hidalgo, perhaps, for Christian could
see traces of the same handsome lineage in the mother's
features as he could in Maria's.

Christian brought the sick woman to the new hospital
set up by the Americans under the jurisdiction of the
department of health as part of their campaign to win the
natives' goodwill. The hospital, whose facilities included
an operating room supplied with surgical instruments
and ether, had no doctors but employed a trained medical staff.

Maria would not wait outside but insisted on being
with her mother during surgery.

"I may be of help. Please let me stay."

A nurse uncorked a can of ether and administered it
while Maria undressed her mother and draped a sheet
over her upper body and her legs, leaving bare the

stomach, where Christian must make his incision. He chose his instruments from a cabinet and, quickly dipping them in a tray of antiseptic solution, laid them on a small towel-draped table close by.

"Sponges?"

Maria produced them from another cabinet and these also had to be soaked. Deftly, with the skill he had used on many previous appendectomies, Christian cut through skin and flesh. However, when he opened the woman up, he saw that he was too late. The appendix had burst. He cleaned the cavity as best he could and closed the incision.

"Her pulse," Maria said.

It was failing, its beat hardly perceptible. Christian tried a stimulant and gradually the pulse increased and a little color came back into the woman's face.

But her improved condition was brief. An hour later, without regaining consciousness and before Maria could fetch a priest, she died.

While the friar (no priest was available) Maria had managed to procure murmured the prayers for the dead, Maria sat at her mother's bedside and wept bitterly. Christian stood by, feeling helpless in the face of such grief. Maria had been so self-contained, so calm throughout the surgery he had not expected her to break down so completely. He knew he had done the best he could. If he had been able to operate a day earlier, even a few hours, he might have been able to save her mother.

"Have you no family, no relatives?" he asked of Maria.

She shook her head. "No. Only Mama." She withdrew a handkerchief from her sleeve and wiped her eyes with it. "I'm sorry." She lifted her dark eyes, soft and luminous with tears. "I haven't thanked you."

"I wish that I could have helped her."

"It was too late. There isn't a surgeon in Manila who could have done better."

He realized that he ought to go. And yet he was reluctant to leave her.

"Is there something I can do for you?"

"Thank you, but the friar will arrange for the burial."

"Let me take you home. It will make me feel better. I don't like losing a patient."

She did not speak on the ride back to the house but sat staring blindly at the back of the cabman's head.

"Please come up, Doctor," she said when they stopped in front of her door. "The least I can do is offer you a drink."

She had a bottle of English gin. "A customer traded it for a hand-embroidered shirt," she explained. She mixed the gin with lime juice and a little sugar.

"Very good," Christian said.

"But not nearly good enough to repay you for your kindness."

They sat for a while in silence. A moth fluttered under the shade of a lamp she had lit earlier. Its wings beat against the paper shade for a few moments, then it flew off only to return to the beckoning light once more.

"Would you like another gin, Doctor?"

"Yes, I believe I would."

Christian watched as she moved across the room to the small alcove that served as kitchen. She carried herself with a lithe, almost voluptuous smoothness. Though the gown she wore, white cotton without any particular style, hid her figure, Christian guessed that her body was as provocatively sensual as her face.

She set the drink down on the small bamboo table next to him where the moth still thrashed about under the lampshade. As he lifted the glass to his lips, his hands grazed hers and he felt the tremor that went through her body. There was a long tense silence, heavy with unspoken emotions, a prelude like the gathering of clouds before a storm. Christian found that his heart was racing, a pulsing beat that had nothing to do with the gin he had drunk.

"What is your given name?" she asked.

"Christian."

"It suits you." She leaned over and dimmed the lamp. The moth fluttered one last time and fell at its base. She gave Christian a small enigmatic smile, a curve of the lips that could have meant anything. Then lifting her slender arms she began to remove the combs from her black, glossy hair. When she shook her head, the ebony tresses fell in rippling waves past her shoulders.

Christian stared, enchanted, his eyes fastened on hers, which had grown enormous in the shadowed light. The lamp glow and her recent sorrow gave her face a breathless and strangely exotic beauty.

Slowly she began to unloop the buttons of her gown.

"Maria, that's not necessary," he heard himself say, incredulous, because he wanted her, wanted to have her in his arms, to part the tremulous lips of her sweet sad mouth, wanted to possess her, wanted to taste the hidden pleasures that those tip-tilted Oriental eyes seemed to promise.

"But it is," she said.

"I need no payment."

She stepped out of her gown, and with a shove of her ringed fingers, her petticoat slipped from her to lie in a froth of white cotton at her ankles. She wore no corset, only a thin filmy undergarment delicately worked in pale lace. The breasts partly revealed to him were firm and ripe, like satiny, golden fruit. She was bare-legged, her calves and thighs beautifully formed. Christian's manhood grew thick with desire.

"Maria . . ."

She leaned toward him and put a delicate finger to his lips. "I want to ease my sorrow. It is for me also."

He rose from his chair. She lifted her face and he kissed her soft warm mouth. She embraced him, drawing him close, and when he felt the pointed tips of her breasts against his chest, all restraint left him. He slammed her against him, hungrily devouring her mouth, her cheeks, her throat, his passionate kisses moving across her shoulders. In a rage of desire, he tore the filmy garment from her and captured the silky breasts with his mouth, torturing the aroused nipples with pursed and avid lips. It had been so long since he'd had a woman, he could not control the lust that ran through his blood like a raging fire.

"Oh God," she whispered, whether out of protest or excitement mattered little to him now.

Picking her up, he carried her to the bed, her weight

no more than a child's. Frantic with desire, he ripped his clothes off, then for one poised moment stood over her, his eyes raking the full breasts, the slender hips, the dark hair between her legs that hid the wonders he had to explore.

Then he fell upon her, his mouth making a fiery path across her face and down, down the golden body that trembled and moaned beneath him. And now, now, his manhood with unbearable pressure behind it could not wait. He lifted himself and plunged into her. He felt her legs wrap themselves about his gyrating hips as he thrust again and again. His blood molten with heat, he clasped her tightly, riding her until suddenly he erupted in a fiery orgasm, and felt her soft cries of ecstasy mingle with his.

Hannah, oh, Hannah, his mind cried.

Had he said it aloud? he wondered the next morning. If so, Maria made no mention of it. Awakening him with a tender kiss and a soft smile, she said, "I thank you for staying. I don't know how I should have faced the night alone."

They became lovers. It was an affair that arose out of more than physical attraction and passionate lovemaking. Both in their own ways were lonely. Christian felt isolated not only from his fellow physicians in the army but from the American officials and their families who did not share his views. And always there, lurking in the shadows, was Hannah, Hannah's voice, her smile, and the promises she had broken that he would give anything to forget.

Maria also lived a life cut off from close ties. Without relatives, her mother and husband dead, she seemed to have no intimate friends. Christian often wondered why she had made no attempt to enlarge her acquaintance. There were many mestizos in Manila, some like herself, widowed and alone, she could have met at church or in one of the clubs that American army wives sponsored for Filipino women. But she shunned social contacts, confining her activities to the little stall she ran on Estola Street. To Christian she remained a puzzle, a mystery, for she rarely spoke of her past, the life she had lived in Cavite.

Then one night in the sleepy aftermath of lovemaking, Maria confessed that she wasn't a widow. Her husband, as far as she knew, was still alive.

"Why didn't you tell me this before?" Christian asked.

"Because he is with the insurrectionists."

Shocked, he rose on an elbow.

"Then . . ." The thought that she might be an informer struck him like a blow. But why him? He was only a doctor in the medical corps. He was not privy to military movements, not even to political policy. His world revolved around diarrhea and the clap, around the scalpel and lancet.

"Are you disturbed?" she asked, looking up at him out of the depths of dark eyes that still seemed to hold secrets he could not guess.

"Wouldn't you expect me to be?"

"I'm not a spy," she said, divining the source of his uneasiness. "I'm simply trying to get along until my husband returns. I don't know why I told you, except that I—I have a feeling I can trust you. It's more than I can say of the others. The Americans have paid agents, both Filipinos and mestizos, who mingle with the natives. They are especially interested in gleaning information from the families of the men who are fighting in the hills."

So that was why she chose to keep to herself. Still . . .

"Since you are being honest with me, can you tell me why you came to the First Reserve for a doctor?"

"I'd heard about you. Two soldiers who patronized my stall were discussing what you had done to save their lives."

"Was that the only reason?"

She remained silent for a long time, her eyes fixed on the sagging folds of the mosquito net that covered their bed.

"I suspected Mama had appendicitis. I blame myself. I waited too long. But what was I to do? Most Filipino doctors joined the revolutionists at the start. They're gone. Those that remained—well, I didn't trust them. I was afraid any one of them might recognize me."

"Why should that bother you?"

"My husband is a physician. He has given lectures to the medical societies here in Manila in the past."

"Ahhh." He let out his breath. So that was why she had not quailed at the sight of blood in the operating room, why she had known about sponges, about surgical instruments.

"Don't you feel you are taking a chance by telling me all this?" he asked. "I might leave here and go straight to the authorities."

"Yes, you might. But, Christian . . ." She turned to him with her soft, sad little smile. "I don't think you will. At heart I believe you're a decent man, that you are able to see our revolution in the light of your own American one, that you do not consider those who are still fighting 'bandits and thieves,' as your government has labeled them. I may be wrong. But I'm willing to take the risk." She ran her fingers up his arm. "I've grown very fond of you, Christian, perhaps a little in love."

He kissed her forehead, his lips sliding across to her ear, before he moved on to her mouth.

"Do you love your husband?" he asked.

"Yes. Do you think it's possible for a woman to love two men at the same time?"

"Perhaps," he answered, thinking of Hannah. Had she ever really loved him? Did *he* still love her? No, he told himself, that's gone, past. I don't love her. What remains are bitter memories, the ghost of a woman still drifting through my dreams. Perhaps in the end Maria will succeed in exorcising her and I can turn to a new love, be a man whose heart has been finally healed.

But one evening when he came bounding up the stairs calling Maria's name, a gift of hard-to-come-by bonbons under his arm, he found the apartment deserted. The few sticks of bamboo furniture, the lamp, the bed were still there. But Maria's clothes were gone. There was no note, no explanation. Neighbors when questioned could tell him nothing.

"She was not one of us. We do not know."

Her stall was closed. The scant merchandise, the carved monkey-wood bowls, the embroidery work, the coconut sweets, sat forlornly on the counter and the two shelves behind it.

Who or what had frightened her into flight he did not know. Where she had gone, he could not guess. He never saw her again and was not to know until years later that eight months after her disappearance from Manila she gave birth to his daughter in Hong Kong.

Toward the middle of May a fresh load of sick and wounded was delivered to the First Reserve Hospital from the fighting in the hills of Bataan and Luzon. Among them was Travis.

Christian, of course, had no prior knowledge of Travis's enlistment as an army volunteer. But it did not surprise him. The jingoistic rhetoric urging "red-blooded young men" to join the fight and put down a rebellion of ignorant savages was just the sort of bait someone like Travis would swallow. The Georgia cracker in Travis could not help but feel contempt for the smaller (and supposedly weaker) dark-skinned Filipino. That's part of his upbringing, Christian thought. I ought to understand and excuse him. But dammit I can't.

Travis was half in and half out of a feverish delirium when he was brought in. But he recognized Christian, and when he found that he would be put in his care, he raised a loud fuss, calling him a drunk, cursing him with every swear word in his now extensive vocabulary, shocking the Red Cross nurses.

Christian, summoned, stood over him.

"Calm down, Travis. You're in the army, not in some private nursing home. Take your lumps with the others. I no more enjoy treating you than you enjoy having me do it. But I'm your doctor, like it or not. I'll do the best for you I can. And *your* job is to recover quickly so you'll be able to get the hell out of here. Now, let's go to work."

Christian smelled the leg before he saw it, a mass of dark gangrenous flesh.

"Well, doc, are you going to be able to fix this damn leg?"

Christian did not reply, but covered Travis with the sheet. He looked down at him for several moments and watched as Travis's eyes scanned his face, turning from cocky belligerence to fright.

Christian said, "I think, perhaps, you ought to have another doctor."

He went down to the office. "Brown, there's an amputation upstairs. Corporal Travis Blaine. I can't do it."

Chapter XXIII

Dear Mrs. Hartwell:

I am writing on behalf of your brother, Travis, who as you may know was wounded several weeks ago during the fighting north of Legapsi. It was a knife laceration in the leg and had already turned gangrenous by the time he was brought into the hospital here in Manila. In order to save his life the limb had to be amputated. (Dr. Ted Brown did the actual surgery.) Travis is young and tough and is recovering physically. But his mental state is precarious. He has twice attempted suicide. He seems to feel that his usefulness as a man is over, that he can't go back to face a normal life as a husband (he says he's a widower who had contemplated remarrying on his return) or father.

I feel that if you—or the woman he is engaged to—would write some words of encouragement, his depressed state of mind might improve. He can be reached at the First Reserve Hospital, U.S. Army, Manila, Philippines.

Yours,
Major C. J. Falconer.

When Hannah had first opened the official-looking envelope, she had expected much worse, for she had never been informed of Travis's wound. Thank God he was still alive. "He might have been killed," she said to a white-faced Flavia.

"Don't say it! I can't bear the thought. Poor, poor Travis! I'll write to him at once. But—oh, Hannah, what if Travis has already managed to . . . ?"

"He's going to be all right."

The situation, however, must have been serious for Christian to write. The letter addressed and couched in such cold, formal tones served to bring Travis's condition home to her more clearly than any sympathetic note might have done.

A leg amputated! What a pitiable end for Travis, who had gone out to the Philippines with such high hopes. Hannah's heart ached for him. She could guess what the loss of a limb meant to him. Rather than come back a cripple, he preferred to die. Perhaps he thought his disability would affect his performance as a husband. Perhaps he saw no future. He might think that no one would want to hire a one-legged factory or ranch hand. But he ought to know better. There were many men in similar situations who had nevertheless made lives for themselves. She recalled old Mr. Dick, one-armed, one-eyed, who ran a thriving livery stable at home. Mangled during the Indian wars, he had returned to Bayetville a feeble heartbeat away from death. But he had rallied and, borrowing money from his wife's people, had bought his first horse and wagon.

But Travis was not Mr. Dick. In the past he had been easily discouraged by misfortune and apparently this latest catastrophe had been too much for him. He couldn't cope. By now Hannah was well aware of Travis's limitations, yet he was her brother and she loved him. He would always be a part of her, her childhood companion and protector. She couldn't bear to think of him suffering in such distress. Of his possible suicide she did not want to think at all.

Could a letter, a half-dozen letters from herself and Flavia, cure his despondency, make him feel that his

loss did not matter? She did not know. That he himself
had not written was a bad sign. Apparently he did not
want her or Flavia informed of his infirmity.

As far as Hannah could see there was only one thing
for her to do. She had to see him, talk to him. No matter
that Manila was thousands of miles away, that official
obstacles might be put in her path (she was still going
round and round with the army about having Guy's
remains shipped back to San Francisco) she had to make
that journey. Pray God, she wouldn't be too late.

After a great deal of confusion with the military bureau-
cracy, she procured passage on a merchantman carrying
flour, dress goods, and drums of petroleum to the Philippines. A party of bureaucrats destined for the new civil
government set up by the Taft Commission were also on
shipboard. They were accompanied by their wives and
families, a jabbering, gossipy lot who constantly plied Hannah with questions. What was wrong with her brother?
Had her husband been killed in the war, how? Did she
have children, how many? Envious women eyed her
stylish mourning clothes, the black silk gown with its
wide cowl collar and butterfly sleeves, her onyx beads,
and the little gold watch pinned by a black ribbon to her
breast. "Money," she heard one of the wives whisper.
And another: "A widow? I wonder."

Hannah was one of the few passengers who did not
suffer from seasickness. Tense with anxiety, she hardly
felt the roll of the ship, much less pausing to give a
thought to the state of her digestion. To her the ship
seemed to crawl, wallowing its way westward at a leisurely speed. In the dining salon she was paired with a
gentleman from Montana who was interested in buying a
sugar plantation on Leyte. An attractive bachelor, he
had prematurely silver hair that contrasted dramatically
with his young face and sun-bronzed skin. He had introduced himself as Michael Farraday the first day out and
had immediately taken a proprietary interest in Hannah
(again causing whispers). He was often by her side,
solicitously seeking her comfort. Was the deck chair
adjusted correctly, a cushion perhaps, a blanket to cover

her lap? Did she care for a cup of tea, a sandwich? She might have been annoyed had he not been so cheerfully charming.

But even Michael Farraday's attentions could not divert her thoughts from Travis. She kept wondering if the hospital would discharge him, though there might not have been an improvement in his mental state. If that had happened, God alone knew what he would do. Stay on in the Philippines, perhaps. Or, overwhelmed with acute melancholy, succeed in doing what she most feared.

The voyage, which took three and a half weeks, seemed more like three and a half years. By the time they reached Manila Bay Hannah felt as though her nerves had been stretched to the breaking point. Standing at the ship's rail with Mr. Farraday, edgy and impatient, she watched the frenetic activity of the harbor. Gunboats and cutters with their fluttering stars and stripes rose and fell on the tide along with patch-sailed sampans and tall-masted junks. Chugging their way through the murky, foam-flecked waters, tugs pulled strings of cascos laden with hemp. The groans of steamer horns, the toot-tooting of tugs mingled with the cries and shouts of men who were busy loading and unloading vessels flying flags from nations around the world. Beyond lay Luzon, mist-shrouded, its heat already beading Hannah's brow.

Once ashore, her trunks piled into a caraboa-drawn cart, Hannah, escorted by the ever-present Michael Farraday, made for the Tradewinds, a boardinghouse recommended by the ship's captain. After registering she had her luggage deposited in a large room with jalousie windows. A ceiling fan, its polished wooden paddles revolving slowly, barely stirred the air. Without removing her hat, Hannah set out for the hospital.

In the main office of the First Reserve there was some delay as a clerk searched for Travis's record. Hannah sat on the edge of her chair, hands folded tightly in her lap, her foot tapping impatiently. What was taking the fellow so long? Was she destined to go through the same sort of red tape she had encountered at the Presidio?

"Our patients have so few visitors," the clerk said apologetically, riffling through another file. "Almost never from back home."

"Surely relatives are permitted?" she asked with asperity.

"I don't believe there is a regulation against it." He had a pencil-thin moustache waxed at the ends like a dandy's.

It was hot in the cubicle, a stifling, smothering heat. Hannah took out her handkerchief and waved it to and fro, trying to cool her flushed cheeks. Somewhere a fly buzzed annoyingly.

"It was Dr. Falconer who wrote me of my brother's condition," Hannah offered, thinking this information might help. "I'm sure—"

"Ah!" the clerk exclaimed, glancing past Hannah. "Here is the doctor now."

Hannah turned. He was dressed in brown duck trousers, cavalry boots, and a white shirt, the sleeves of which were rolled up to his elbows. He looked different, tired. There were lines at the corners of his eyes and grooved deeply over the bridge of his nose. A streak of gray ran through his dark hair. It came to Hannah as she stared at him in those first few moments that though he must still be in his early thirties he looked much older.

"Mrs. Hartwell!" he exclaimed. But there was no warm welcoming look in his eyes, only surprise. "I didn't expect to see you here."

"I thought it best to come in person."

"I see." His gaze took in the little black hat with its toy soldier plume, the black silk dress, the ebony onyx beads. A flustered Hannah realized that she must look different to him also. He had not seen her in a modish gown since she had borrowed his sister's in San Francisco.

"I want to thank you for writing," she said. He continued to stand in the doorway.

"I think it only decent to write to the families of patients."

"I did appreciate the gesture. How is Travis? May I see him?" She half rose from her chair.

"I'm sorry. I . . ." He hesitated. "Travis died yesterday."

"Yesterday?" A bewildered whisper.

"Yes. Regrettably, he . . ."

Yesterday. She sat down quickly, the room having
suddenly gone dim. *Yesterday, yesterday,* the word repeated itself to the heavy measured thudding of her
heart. The clerk's voice from a long way off asked, "Are
you all right?"

Dead! She was too late. God, oh God! She had had a
premonition all the way across the sea that this might
happen. Yet she had hoped and prayed. He was dead.
Why hadn't he waited? Oh, Travis . . .

The fly continued to buzz. The heat was like a clamp
around her skull. Through a swirling darkness, she heard
a voice ask, "Where's the ammonia, clerk?" She felt a
strong arm go around her shoulders and her head snapped
back as the astringent was shoved under her nostrils.
She opened her eyes and looked directly into Christian's
eyes, strangely green and unreadable.

"I—I'm sorry. It was the shock," Hannah managed.
"May I have a glass of water?"

The clerk jumped up and a moment later brought her
some water in a tin mug. When she hesitated he said,
"It's all right. All our water at the hospital is boiled."

As if she cared.

She couldn't talk. She was afraid that if she did, her
voice would quaver uncontrollably. Tears stung her eyes.
She bit her lip to force them back. Both men were
staring at her, expecting her to break into hysterical
sobbing. She couldn't weep, she didn't want these two
strangers to witness her sorrow. For Christian was that
to her now. A stranger. He was gazing at her as if she
were some sort of mildly interesting specimen. Travis
had disliked him and for good reason. She remembered
him once saying, "Christian spells trouble." And for a
moment the irrational thought that Christian was in
some way responsible for Travis's death sprang into her
mind. She tried to brush it away, but it persisted.

"How—how did he die? He didn't . . . ?" she began,
leaving the question hanging.

"He took his own life after a fashion." Christian had
pulled up a chair and was sitting opposite her. "He
refused to eat. We tried to force-feed him, but he would
regurgitate whatever he swallowed."

"Oh my God! How awful!"

"We did everything we could." His voice was detached, clinical, the tone of a doctor explaining medical procedure to the next of kin. "We have over two thousand men here now, some of them severely wounded, others on their deathbed with fever."

"Yes, yes, I understand." She didn't. Christian was speaking to her factually, without compassion. He had become cold, unfeeling. Had the war done that to him? But, no, she remembered when he had talked about his father, he had used the same disinterested, uncaring voice.

"At least he died in comfort," Christian was saying, "if that's any consolation."

"Comfort?" she asked.

"Comparatively, yes. Dressed in clean pajamas, lying between clean sheets. I'd say that was comfort when you compare how some of our men breathe their last in mosquito-ridden swamps or worse still how the natives die of cholera and dysentery, lying in filthy hovels, some so weak they drown in their own vomit."

Why was he telling her this? What had a native's death to do with Travis?

Suddenly she hated him. He didn't care. Travis was just another body, another corpse. As for her own feelings, Christian was as indifferent to them as he was to Travis's death.

"I'd like to see him," she said.

"I'm afraid that's impossible. In this climate we must bury our dead immediately."

"But such indecent haste! I thought to take him home." She didn't want Travis buried in this unfriendly, alien place any more than she had wanted it for Guy. "I would like the coffin exhumed."

"It's an expensive undertaking."

"I have the money," she said, drawing herself up. Christian seemed to represent all that was bureaucratic and insensitive. She was sorry she had thanked him for anything. "Who must I see?"

"You can write out your request for the clerk here." He rose. "Oh—I'd almost forgotten. Would you like his effects?"

"Yes." And with great effort she added, "Please."

Back at the hotel, sitting on the bed under the whining fan, she stared dully at Travis's haversack. Her mind kept saying over and over, *He's dead. I came too late.* How she could have arrived sooner she did not know. But she had not been in time. He had refused food. He had wanted to die.

What shall I tell Flavia? she wondered. How shall I break the news? I can't lie to her. She'll guess the truth because she already knows he tried to commit suicide twice. Why? But it was futile to go on that hopeless round of speculation again.

She started to unpack his haversack. A water canteen, a piece of hardtack, a pipe, the same corncob pipe she had given him several Christmases ago. He had never smoked it. But apparently he had cherished it, for he had brought it with him to this far country. Her fingers ran over the small, yellow bowl, the long stem. And suddenly the tears she could no longer hold back coursed down her cheeks. Travis, who had been her brother, her next of kin, her family for all these years. Travis who had shared her childhood, whose hand she had held tightly, cowering under the stairwell as her father had raged about. Oh, Travis, why didn't you wait for me?

She threw herself across the bed and sobbed and sobbed.

Later, after she had eaten a bite of supper in the hotel dining room, thankful that it was empty because she couldn't bear to speak to anyone, she took a bath in the clawed tub in the washroom down the hall. Then, donning a cool wrapper, she sat on the bed, her eyes still swollen with weeping, and finished removing the contents of Travis's haversack. There were several carved amulets, a rosary (a Filipino souvenir?), a comb, a bottle of hair oil, a neck scarf, and a letter addressed to her in an unsealed envelope.

She unfolded the page and read in Travis's large script:

Dear Hannah,
I am writing this from first reserve horspital. I've been here I reckon close on to three weeks. This

*ain't the happiest moment of my life. I lost my leg,
Sis, and I can't see comin back to you all half a
man. Don't you cry for me now. And don't Flavia
cry neither. Tell her I love her but I ain't much use
to her the way I am. And Guy's dead. He was like
a brother to me. I can't believe Guy's dead. Still
mebbe he's luckier than most.*

*I'm goin to meet my Maker, Sis. And I want to
do it with a clear conshus. (Did I spell that rite?
You was allus correctin my spellin.) I lied to you
about Christian Fallcomer. He wasn't on the bord
of that bank that wouldn't give Guy his loan. He
never did kidnap Elthea. I wormed the truth out of
her. She went with that man because he promised
he'd take her to Georgia. I didden want you to
leave Guy that's why I tole you that story. . . .*

Hannah paused, looking up from the page, wiping
away a tear as she tried to assimilate what she had just
read. Travis was saying that he had invented those stories about Christian, made up the tales about his being on
the bank board, about kidnapping Elthea. Travis had
lied. Lies she had taken at face value. I mustn't be
angry, she told herself. He's not to blame because I
believed him. *I'm* to blame. I've been blind, willfully
blind, which is worse, much worse. I believed Travis,
took his word without question. His word against
Christian's.

She went on with the letter.

*I lied to you because I diden want you to leave
Guy and I was jellus of Christian in a way, born
with a silver spoon in his mouth and so high on his
horse. But I found out he ain't that way attall.
Leastwise from what I seen now. I never would
like the man, but I gotta take my hat off to him.
He's worked like a black in this place. I seen him
late at night with a lamp in his hand going down
the ward to help some poor bugger what was
moanin or hollerin. And he done all right by me,
Sis. He got the razor out of my hand twicet when I*

*was figgerin to slit my throat. And he talked to me
like a Dutch uncle. I thought I ought to tell you
him being Mark's pa and all. Only thing I got against
him—they say he's been tendin sick googoos—that's
American for Flips—down in Tondino. I don't hold
with that. It's like aidin and abettin the enemy.*

*I ain't a coward, Sis. I was a damn good sol-
dier. There's some talk of me gettin a medal. If it
comes give it to Flavia. One more thing—two. I
most forgot. I gambled the money you sent for my
Calif. fare and didden spent it on the younguns
like I said. And I did steal the money from Aunt
Bess. But I never stole from anyone else. As far as
gamblin, thats been my one weakness. And mebbe
being easy led on is another.*

*I ain't sorry to go, Sis. And don't you be. Kiss
Flavia and little Clara for me.*

> *Your lovin brother,*
> *Travis.*

Hannah's throat felt raw. Misery lay locked in her
chest like a cold claw, a misery beyond words. It was as
if Travis had been there; she could almost hear his
voice. "I didn't want you to leave . . . I was jealous of
Christian."

Oh, Travis! She should have guessed, should have
known.

Yet in a way he could never have forseen, Travis's
letter had laid bare three lives—hers, his, and Christian's. She understood Travis so much better now, his
weaknesses—his gambling, his lying—with a clarity that
wiped away any defense she might have made for him in
the past. He was to be pitied, a child who never grew
up. The wonder was that someone like Flavia could love
him. But strong motherly women often favored imma-
ture men. She thought of Aunt Bess and her father.

But whatever Travis had done or been in the past, he
had made her see things she might never have acknowledged. It was painful but true. Through the years, easy-
going Travis had remained unchanged, childlike, and

deceptive. And how much had *she* changed? How different was she from the seventeen-year-old girl who had run from Christian, angry and pregnant, because she would not wait for him to do "the right thing"? And again in Chicago when she had seen him at the Palmer House with his arm looped through—ah, what was her name? —Amanda's she had not given him the chance to explain but had fled into a loveless marriage. She had never allowed Christian to speak in his own defense, not in Chicago, not in San Francisco or Monterey. Letters, notes, an abrupt good-bye. She thought she knew Christian, but she hadn't known him at all. For he had altered during the years, grown from a handsome dilettante into a man of integrity and courage. Yet she had never forgiven him for seducing her, never forgiven his reluctance to marry her at Wildoak. Wasn't that the essence of it? He loved her and she had treated that love lightly because she hadn't the sense to see the gift he had offered her. She had clung to Guy, Guy was safe, Guy was her excuse. She had lived with him, pretending to love him, pretending Mark was his, thinking that standing by her husband was the courageous thing to do. Now she knew that it would have taken far more courage to breach convention and put her trust in Christian despite Travis's attempt to poison her mind.

But it wasn't too late. It shouldn't be. He still loved her. She was sure of it. Oh, he had been hurt by her and was bitter because she had disappointed him so many times. His coolness at the hospital was only a defense, a shield. He hadn't meant it. If he hadn't cared for her, he would not have watched over Travis so carefully, would not have bothered to write her.

She would go to him, tell him about Travis's letter, ask his forgiveness, humble herself if necessary. She would tell him that she loved him, that she wanted desperately to wipe out the misunderstandings of the past. His pride might be an obstacle, for Christian was a proud man, but she knew she could win him back again. She would convince him that they could start afresh, begin a new life together.

I love him, she thought as she drowsed, sinking into

sleep with Travis's tearstained letter still clutched in her hand.

She awoke early the next morning to the sound of cocks crowing and the rumble of carts passing in the street below. For a few moments her heart constricted as she thought of Travis. But as her eyes fell upon the crumpled letter at her side, her spirits lifted. Travis had wanted her to know that he had been wrong about Christian. "He done all right by me, Sis." Was it his way of saying he had misjudged Christian, that the man she had loved for so long was worthy of that love? They had both done Christian a disservice, but today she meant to make amends. She would go to him at once and ask forgiveness, bare her soul before she lost her nerve.

She decided not to wear the black silk. It was too hot, too heavy. Ostensibly that was the reason, but in her heart she knew her eagerness to appear at her attractive best was closer to the truth. She chose a pastel blue linen skirt and a leg-o'-mutton-sleeved blouse to match. The hat that went with the gown, however, was a problem. It had been so crushed and pummeled out of shape by its journey in her trunk she could not possibly wear it. She would have to go bare-headed and use her white parasol to keep the sun from her face.

When she reached the hospital, she was told by the same clerk she had spoken to the day before that Dr. Falconer had not come in yet. He had been up all night with a young soldier suffering with typhoid and had only gone home toward dawn.

"Could I have his address, please?"

The clerk raised his brows.

"It's a matter of some urgency," she assured him in a crisp voice.

The carramato driver was just as surprised when she gave him the address, for Christian had moved from his elegant rooms in Maleta to Maria's apartment in the native district.

"Is Madam sure . . . ?"

Madam was sure.

The pony-drawn cab followed a tortuous route through

narrow streets. Though it was scarcely nine, the sun beat down with a torrid fierceness that Hannah could feel through the cart's canvas top and her flimsy cambric parasol. Perspiration trickled down the back of her neck, gathering in sticky dampness between her shoulder blades and breasts. The cabman, hunched over the reins, his khaki-colored shirt sticking to his back in dark splotches, sneezed from time to time at the dust rising in irritating puffs from the pony's hooves. They rode for a long while in the heat of the punishing sun, then turning a corner, they jolted into the blessed shadow of a cobbled lane that ran alongside the old wall, a thick fortresslike structure with cannon emplacements. Once this ancient wall had housed churches, monasteries, barracks, and administrative offices. But most of these buildings were gone now, as were the surrounding moats of stagnant water. The Americans had dredged these mosquito-ridden ditches, which had served as the city's sewers, and planted them with grass and hedges. But the stinking odor of feces and rotting refuse still permeated the air.

She tried to divert her mind from the heat and the rank smell by rehearsing what she would say to Christian, what she thought he might say to her. She was in the midst of her imaginary dialogue when the cab stopped in front of a narrow, cavelike door that led to an inner patio.

"Perhaps you'd better wait," she said to the driver.

There was no one about except a small boy in dirty cotton pantaloons. "Can you tell me where I can find Dr. Falconer?" He pointed to the staircase at the far end of the patio.

She climbed the stairs, her heart hammering, no longer sure of the little speech she had been preparing on the way. At the door she hesitated. Then biting her lip, she brought her trembling fist to the wooden panel.

"Who is it?" a deep, sleepy voice asked. She knocked again.

A mutter, a grumble, and the door was thrown open. Christian was dressed only in the bottom half of a pair of rumpled, striped pajamas. Unshaven, his hair in dishev-

eled peaks, he stared at her out of bleary, bloodshot
eyes.

"I'm sorry to have wakened you," she said.

He rubbed his jaw.

"I wanted to see you," she plunged on.

"Can't it wait?" he asked sourly.

For a moment her courage failed and she fought the
urge to turn and hurry back down the stairs.

"No," she said, lifting her chin. "It can't."

He stepped aside to let her pass. Beyond the open
door on the far side of the room in which she stood,
Hannah saw an unmade bed through the gauze of mosquito netting. Beside it on the floor was a squat empty
brandy bottle.

Christian indicated a fluted, high-backed wicker chair.
"If you'll be seated, I'll throw on some clothes. Unless," he added sarcastically, "you prefer me as I am."

Ignoring the remark, she said nothing. It was going to
be harder than she had thought, much harder. Perhaps
she ought to have come at a later hour when she might
have found him less irritable. But she was here now,
and once she left she might not find the courage to
return.

She set her furled parasol across her knees. Removing
a handkerchief from her reticule, she dabbed at her
cheeks. Louvered shutters at the windows cut the harsh
light, making the room dim, but the heat from the street
below still filtered in through the slats, banding the floor
in white dusty motes. There were no rugs on the wide-
planked floor and only two wicker chairs and a small
table, which held a kerosene lamp that needed cleaning.
Moths lay in spread-winged, desiccated death at the
base of the lamp. It was an austere room, unadorned
and depressing. Hannah wondered how Christian, who
had always been so fond of the little luxuries that made
for comfort, could be content here.

When he returned he was wearing the same duck
trousers Hannah had seen him in the previous day. But
instead of a regulation shirt, he had donned a loose-
fitting white tunic similar to the ones the natives wore.
On his feet were a pair of rope sandals.

"I'm afraid I'm not inclined to be very hospitable this morning," he said. "But I could offer you coffee."

"No, thanks. Perhaps later."

He shrugged. "I suppose you're here to ask if I've made arrangements for your brother."

"Well . . ." She hesitated, not quite knowing how to state the real purpose of her visit. "I would like . . ."

"The clerk at the hospital is handling it. Didn't he tell you?"

"I didn't ask." She paused again. "That is not why I came."

"Oh?" He went to a cupboard and brought out a bottle. "Whiskey? Or would you prefer brandy?"

"Neither. It's too—"

"Early," he finished for her. "But I'm sure you won't mind if I indulge. You see I haven't broken all of my old habits."

"Please, go ahead." She wished he wouldn't put words into her mouth. She would have liked a brandy, some whiskey, anything that was strong and fortifying. She needed it. But she didn't trust her hands—now gripping the parasol—to hold a glass.

She watched as he drank. She had almost forgotten how his masculine presence could fill a room. Even in his unconventional garb, he looked more virile, more vibrant, more *male* than any man she knew. He may have grown older, with white in his hair and lines between his eyes, but the muscles of his arms in the short-sleeved tunic still bulged, the column of his throat was still strong. His powerful magnetism was still there, the draw, the pull she had never been able to resist. She recalled with an imperceptible shiver the passionate savage love he had made to her that last time at Sycamore and how much—though she tried not to admit it—she had longed for his touch ever since.

Then the thought suddenly occurred to her that Christian might have married. The newspaper article concerning his enlistment had mentioned no wife, only his parents. And there had been nothing since in the society columns to indicate an engagement or marriage. But he must have had other women; men like Christian did not live in self-imposed celibacy. The bed in the far corner—who had slept in it with him, who had sighed and moaned under his lips, his strong possessive hands, who . . . ?

"Now," he said, seating himself on the opposite chair, a whiskey in his hand. "What is it that brings you here at such an ungodly hour of the morning?"

"I wanted to talk about me—us." She could see that there would be no idle chitchat, no breaking of the ice leading up to her purpose here. She must say what she had to and quickly. She swallowed and, inhaling deeply, took the hurdle. "I know now that I've behaved badly in the past. I've made a terrible mistake. I've misjudged you and I'm sorry. Will you forgive me?"

The words, tumbling out baldly, were stiff and awkward. She saw the look of amazement on his face and her heart sank.

"Forgive you?"

"Yes."

He shook his head. "I'm sure I don't know what you mean." He knew very well what she meant. But it seemed he was bent on making things difficult. "Forgive you for what, Mrs. Hartwell?"

The formal address cut deep. There was no smile, no softening of tone, no chiding reprimand. Not even anger. She could understand anger. But the bland look on his face, the eyes that held only mild surprise, confounded her. Taking another breath, she plunged in again. "I mistrusted you when I had no reason to. Travis— Travis left a letter. In it he confessed that he had lied to me."

She went on to explain, telling him how Travis had convinced her that Christian had been influential in the California bank's decision to deny Guy an extension on his loan. That Christian had counted on Guy's near bankruptcy and had offered to keep Guy at Sycamore in exchange for Hannah's promise to go away with him. And all the while Christian sat, his eyes inscrutable, his face a mask.

When Hannah finished, he did not speak at once. Finally, breaking a long, and for Hannah miserable, silence, he asked, "Why are you telling me all this?"

It was wrong. Everything was going wrong.

"Because I—I love you," she stumbled, her eyes raised to his. "I've always loved you."

"I don't believe it." He got up abruptly and went to the cupboard. Opening it, he reached for the whiskey bottle, than changed his mind. Closing the cabinet, he turned and faced her. "You've never loved me, Hannah. Oh, you might have thought you did a time or two, having been swayed by my ardor, for you are a very passionate woman, but passion is not quite the same as love."

She blushed, the blood rising from her throat and flooding her cheeks. He seemed not to notice her discomfort.

"No. It's not the same." He shrugged. "Hardly. Any woman who takes the word of a jealous, weakling brother over that of a man she professes to love . . ."

"You mustn't," she began, the old need to defend Travis rising unbidden.

"Mustn't what?" he asked caustically.

"Travis is dead," she said. "Why put the blame on him now?"

"I don't blame him. Why should I? Unhappy, misguided fool. I blame *you*. You left me sitting there in Monterey, waiting for a woman I thought loved me. And what happened? I received a letter from her, this same woman, mind you, who once swore there was no one in the world she cared for but me, this same woman writing that after all she found she loved another man. No mention that the son she bore would never know his real father, only some nonsense about duty and respect. . . ."

"That's not quite true," she challenged.

"The gist of it is." He came and sat down again, the anger fading from his eyes. "What does it matter? It's all in the past. Over and done with."

"No! Oh, no!" She wanted to tell him how his face had rarely left her thoughts, how she had missed, longed for him, the countless nights she had wept for him. She searched for the words to describe how she had tried to love Guy, but couldn't how many times she had wakened from a dream thinking that Christian lay next to her. "Can't you see . . ." she began, but the chill look in his eyes stopped her.

"I *do* see." He went on. "Why at this late date you conclude you love me I can only guess. Travis's letter, you say. But I wonder if this love of yours doesn't have more to do with with your present situation. You are free now. Guy, Travis informed me, is dead. You're a widow, still young, and I see by your fashionable attire no longer without ample funds. Perhaps there is a shortage of eligible men, someone to match your elevated status in life, a shortage possibly brought on by our ill-advised war in the Philippines. While I—modesty aside—am unattached and fairly presentable. Perhaps—"

"Wait!" she cried, rising to her feet, her pride stung to the quick. He did not want her. He no longer cared; she was nothing to him. She would not throw herself at a man who had no desire or need for her. Had she thought to humble herself, to beg, to go down on her knees? Though her heart ached, she could not. Nor would she stoop so low as to use their son as bait.

"It would be kinder or perhaps more courteous, yes, courteous, if you would simply say you don't love me and leave it at that."

"Very well. Any love I once had for you has long since vanished."

She walked to the door.

"Allow me," he said, springing up to open it.

She did not look at him as she passed, head held high, the tears he would never see lodged in her throat.

Chapter XXIV

Hannah had made arrangements through the American consulate to have Travis's remains shipped back to San Francisco on a troopship. They had not yet located Guy's grave, but she had received assurances that once found, his body would be exhumed and also returned. However, she herself was unable to get passage for another two weeks.

In the meanwhile she wrote to Flavia. There were no words, no pat phrases to soften the blow, no opportunity to lie and say that Travis had died bravely in battle. Christian's letter had anticipated his suicide. She could only quote Travis's farewell note, embellishing it slightly, saying that his last thoughts had been of her. She wished that she and Flavia could be together to share their grief, to weep for a man they both had loved.

But now there was nothing to do but wait for her ship. She tried to occupy herself, tried to make her days busy, filling the long hours sightseeing and strolling the bay front with Michael Farraday, playing whist with the ladies at the hotel and shopping for souvenirs. She purchased carved ivory knickknacks, paper fans, plaster saints, tortoiseshell combs, rattan mats, backscratchers, a set of mahjong tiles, teacups, hanging baskets, coral necklaces, more things than she could possibly give away or want for herself. Yet none of these trinkets, no game of cards, no promenade with Michael Farraday, so charming and attentive, could keep her mind from Christian or ease the dull ache in her heart. It seemed all that had mattered had gone out of her life. Guy and Travis dead, Christian no more than a bitter memory. Thoughts of tomorrow, next week, next year frightened her. She saw the future stretching into an infinity, a nameless black void without purpose or meaning. Years and years to be spent going through the motions of living with only regret for company.

Is this the way Travis felt, she would ask herself, before he willed himself to die?

But I'm not Travis, she would argue. I'm Hannah. I've endured two miscarriages, death, illness, fire, drought, and poverty. And I survived. I have Mark. I mustn't forget Mark. I have my—his, our—son.

But somehow it didn't help.

The deaths of Guy and Travis had been final and beyond her power, but for Christian's loss she had only herself to thank. She hadn't trusted him. She hadn't had the courage to leave Guy and follow the instincts of her heart. She had listened to someone else. Any hope of she and Christian making a life together was gone. Over, finished.

Sometimes when her despair was at its darkest she would remember with a faint rise of hope that Christian and she had parted several times before, and that he had always come back into her life. Chance, fate, his perseverance had brought him to her again and again. When he reflects on it, she thought, he'll deplore that scene in his rooms. He'll reproach himself for dismissing me so uncaringly. He'll come looking for me, say he's sorry, swear he's never stopped loving me.

But Hannah knew she was grasping at straws in the wind. Looking back through the years to when she had first known Christian, she saw that it had always been her decision to cut ties with him, *her* decision to sever the relationship and never see him again. On how many occasions had she told him (or written) that she really didn't love him? It was different now. The situation had been turned around. It was Christian who had said, "Any love I had for you once has long since vanished." He had shut the door in her face. He wouldn't change his mind. He had meant what he said. His disinterest had been written plainly in his eyes, his face. Implacable. A stone wall.

She was thinking of that stone wall the next afternoon as she meandered through the botanical gardens on the arm of Michael Farraday. She had abandoned her heavy mourning as a concession to the climate and wore a powder-gray muslin gown sprigged with purple violets, the fashionable hem showing an inch of ankle. A gray, shallow-crowned straw hat trimmed with a bunch of cloth violets and a gray parasol completed her outfit.

It was siesta time. Farraday and Hannah were the only ones walking the gravel paths in the oppressive heat. The gardens, a riot of color and fragrance, had been planted by the Spanish who had brought in exotic trees and shrubs from the outlying islands. Branches of purple-, cream-, and salmon-throated orchids festooned ipil, red narra, and fronded palm trees. Ferns of every variety and description grew in shaded nooks under cinnamon and bamboo, while beds of some unnamed flowers on spongy stems bloomed in yellow and scarlet and delicate lavender profusion.

Michael Farraday gave it all perfunctory notice. His full attention was focused on Hannah. He had postponed his trip to Leyte where he was to look over the site of a possible sugar plantation. It was of minor importance, he had told Hannah. He had put himself at her disposal, whatever she wanted to do, wherever she wanted to go would be his pleasure. It was no secret at the Tradewinds that he was enamored of this young, beautiful widow. Hannah had tried to discourage him by saying she was still in love with her husband, a lie that did not trouble her conscience. These last few days she had moved through a dull, barren wasteland where things like a conscience no longer seemed of importance.

Mr. Farraday was speaking. "The war isn't finished, no matter what pap they print in the papers back home.

I doubt if I would have considered buying property here
had I known the true story. Now there are rumors of an
insurrection in Bantagas. Have you heard? Mrs. Hartwell,
have you . . . ?''

"What? Oh, yes, I believe I have."

"Of course, I own considerable acreage in the States,
ten thousand on the Canadian border. I have a large
house there. You must come and visit."

"Of course. That would be pleasant."

Cumulus clouds drifting across the sky veiled the sun,
but the heat had not diminished. The air simmered, a
damp steaminess rising from the lush vegetation. Hannah's head had begun to ache.

"Shall we find a cool place to sit?" her companion
suggested.

They sat on a wooden bench under the wide, spreading
branches of a banyan tree. The leathery leaves flapped
and rustled in a sudden breeze. A brightly colored bird
feeding on the red fruit suddenly cried out in anguish.

"Ah, I believe it's getting a little cooler," Michael
Farraday said, fanning himself with his straw boater.

The clouds had become denser and darker, moving
swiftly in from the sea. The breeze quickened to a stiff
wind. In a few moments it began to rain.

Michael managed to secure a carramato and they started
out for the Tradewinds. Soon it was pouring, a steady
sheet of rain that came through the holes in the cart's
canvas top, drenching their hats and shoulders. The
dusty street turned quickly into a quagmire, sucking at
the wheels and at the pony's hooves, threatening to
upset them as they jolted from one oozing pothole to the
next. When they came in sight of the bay, they saw that
it had been whipped to a froth, the cascos and smaller
boats tossing and heaving like corks. Some had already
broken away from their anchorages and were smashing
into the larger vessels.

At the Tradewinds servants hurried about taking in
awnings and umbrellas, nailing down heavy veranda
furniture, and boarding up the windows. The guests
were cautioned to remain inside.

"We may have a typhoon on our hands," the landlord-

host, a portly Englishman, told them as they gathered
for an early tea. "It's the tail end of the season, rather
late in the year for such a storm. Perhaps we'll only get
a bit of rain and a little wind."

But as the afternoon advanced the "bit of rain and
little wind" turned into a full-fledged storm. The dimness in the parlor was dispelled by the lighting of kerosene lamps and candles. Their wicks, fluttering and
dancing from the drafts sweeping under the door, gave
the illusion of cozy snugness. The guests laughed and
joked as the rain thrummed on the roof and slashed at
the boarded windows. However, the laughter soon died
as the wind's velocity increased, growing stronger minute by minute. By four o'clock it was howling like a
pack of mad dogs, tearing at the building, clawing at the
doors, thudding and thumping loosened shutters. It was
now carrying before it uprooted shrubs, palm fronds,
and rubbish, hurling this mass of wreckage against the
walls of the hotel, a barricade that seemed to become
more and more flimsy to the people cowering behind it.

Hannah ran up to her room. Gathering clothing, books,
papers, toilet articles, she crammed them into her trunk
and shoved it under the bed. The board and batten
Tradewinds swayed as she came back down the stairs.

The din and roar outside had reached terrifying proportions. That was not all. Flooding water caused by the
rain and the high tides in the bay had overrun the veranda and was lapping at the door.

"We must all go down to the cellar," the landlord
shouted. "It's waterproof, I assure you. Ladies and gentlemen, please be calm. It will soon be over."

Michael Farraday took Hannah's arm. "You mustn't
be afraid," he said, giving her a confident smile. "These
things never last, I'm told."

It was a fabrication neither of them believed.

In the cellar there was two feet of water and in it
swam a half-dozen rats.

The guests chose to take their chances with the parlor. Cracks under the doors and low windowsills were
stuffed with towling, pillowcases, and rags.

Presently the wind abated and then died. The rain

stopped. The doors were opened and the water swept
from the parlor floor. Venturing out behind the landlord,
Hannah saw a three-quarter moon shining peaceably
amid a thousand twinkling stars.

"The eye of the storm," Mr. Svenson, a white-haired
South China Sea veteran, said. In his late sixties, the old
Swede claimed to have weathered dozens of typhoons
over the last forty years. "What we've had is only a
preliminary. We're in the eye of the storm now. When
the wind changes direction, you'll see what a typhoon
can really be like."

He was right. An hour later the tempest bore down on
them from the north, a lashing, violent assault of wind
and rain. Roaring like a hundred tumbling waterfalls, it
slammed into the house, attacking it with relentless fury.
Again and again it worried and shook the Tradewinds
like a jungle beast with a captive prey in its jaws. How
long the hotel could continue to take such an onslaught
was a question no one dared ask aloud.

A woman began to weep, another went into hysterics,
gesticulating wildly, shouting and laughing shrilly. When
her husband struck her across the face, no one thought
him a brute. In fact they were grateful. With raw nerves
and pumping hearts they huddled together, listening,
waiting. The few brave souls who attempted conversation soon lapsed into silence, except for one woman,
Sally Young, an inveterate chatterer. Nothing, not even
the eruption of heaven and earth, could still her tongue.

No one listened.

The landlord brought out several bottles of brandy.
There were no refusals as the glasses were passed around,
not even by the Methodist minister who had lectured
only the day before on the evils of drink. Hannah, sipping her share, felt temporary relief, a warm relaxation
that spread through her chest and down to the tips of her
fingers. But a moment later the wind seemed to pick up
in fury. A board was ripped from a window as if by a
giant claw, a shattering of glass, and the savage intruder
rushed in, dousing and overturning lamps. Two small
fires on the carpet started by the lighted kerosene were
quickly snuffed out with sofa pillows.

In the darkness there was a scramble for candles and matches. When the tapers were lit, the beleaguered guests could see that the water had begun to creep under the door, an insidious, greasy swamp that was slowly covering the floor again. Once more the landlord suggested they seek refuge in the cellar. He had a gun, he said, and he would shoot the rats.

"Now, Nigel," Mr. Svenson remonstrated, "if we're getting flooded up here, can you imagine what the cellar's like? The water'll be up to our gizzards."

"You're wrong," the landlord said. "I just had a look. It's built of concrete and pretty watertight." He lumbered off to find his gun.

There was no real place to hide, no place that was safe. The outside world was a chaos of uprooted trees and nipa huts torn from their foundations, cart wheels, furniture, storefronts, and wooden planks flung about with a force that could kill any living thing they struck. The streets, the Swede maintained, would have disappeared under swiftly running water, carrying with it the splintered remains of entire neighborhoods. The ramshackle huts that housed the poor, he said, were always the first to go.

While the landlord searched for his gun, a debate went on about the cellar. Someone suggested retiring to an upper floor, a plan that was quickly vetoed since it was felt that the roof was in imminent danger of being blown away. Michael had another look at the cellar and came back shaking his head.

Suddenly they heard a loud rending, grinding noise just outside the door. The landlord waded to a peephole in one of the boarded windows.

"The veranda! It's been torn away!"

Hannah's feet and the hem of her skirts were soaked. The water was cold and the chill air current that blew in from the broken window made her shiver. Someone, she didn't notice who, said it was past midnight. As if time mattered. The world had reduced itself to a whirling mass of nothingness such as it might have been at Creation. She prayed, strangely enough not for herself but for Christian. Somewhere in this wracked city, he was sitting out the storm, too. She hoped at the hospital, safe behind its mortared walls. He did not want her, she would never be his, but she could not bear the thought of harm coming to him.

"Mrs. Hartwell?" Michael Farraday was at her side. "I think you'd best climb onto a chair. Here, let me help you. You'll be perfectly comfortable on the arm." Others were finding similar perches. They were like people lost in a wild sea, afloat in a flimsy craft, hoping vainly for a letup in the violent upheaval, not daring yet to think of rescue.

Then with a cataclysmic roar the wind ripped the roof away, shearing it off as if it were a matchbox cover. Beds and chests tumbled and crashed from overhead. The hysterical woman jumped down from a table, bleeding from a cut on her face. Her husband lay crushed under a trunk. Michael Farraday was bending over him, trying to push the trunk from his body, when a flying timber caught him on the side of the head. Hannah ran to him just as the ceiling and walls caved in.

Hannah floated up from some dark lower depth and opened her eyes to another darkness. She could see nothing and for one horrible moment thought she had gone blind. The sound of wind and rain had ceased, but there was a slight lapping, gurgling noise of water. She could not tell if she had been unconscious for minutes, hours, or even days. The back of her head ached, a pain that throbbed in nauseous waves. She tried to move and the debris around her shifted, pinning her more firmly. She was afraid to try again, afraid that some heavy object would knock her insensible again.

I must lie here patiently, she told herself. Rescue will come. The storm has blown itself out by now and those who escaped it will be put to work searching for survivors. She strained to hear voices. But there was nothing, except that strange bubbling sound and she realized she was lying half in and half out of the water.

She dozed and woke, dozed and woke. Time had ceased to exist, only the numbing pain was real. When she slept now, she dreamed she was back at Sycamore, running across the lower field bright with spring green and dotted with poppy gold, her hair flying in the sea wind, racing toward her husband who stood under a madrone tree, his arms outstretched. She flew into his embrace and he lifted her, kissing her with hungry passion. She tangled her hands in his dark hair, wanting more, her mouth moving with his, laughing as he brought her down, baring her breasts to his seeking lips. "Christian," she moaned. Her husband, her love.

The dream melded into another. She was still at Sycamore, walking arm in arm with Christian on a path in the woods. Above them the live oaks arched cathedrallike, their leaves making a shifting pattern of dark and light at their feet. Mark ran ahead, gathering acorns, dashing back every now and then, opening his small fist to show them what he had found. They were a family; they were happy. So happy, her heart swelled with joy. Then suddenly Christian paused and, looking down at her with a cold smile, said, "It's over, done, finished."

She awoke, her face wet with tears. The darkness was still there like a shroud wrapping cold clammy fingers around her. Her ears strained to hear a creak, a shuffle, a movement, a murmur, a voice. Nothing. Even the lapping sound had ceased. The puddle under her had receded and she was lying in muddy dampness. She tried to call out but her sandpapery tongue stuck. Thirst had parched her lips, dried her mouth. Water, she thought, if only I could have a drink of water, a small cup, a sip, a few drops to wet my tongue. Her mind filled with images of water: rushing rivers, sparkling lakes, dimpled ponds, water pouring from a dewy pitcher, water from a tap, dribbling from the lip of a pump. Even at Sycamore in the worst of the drought they had had water. Her whole body yearned to put her lips to a dipper full of cool crystal water from the quenching spring that came bubbling up at Sycamore. But she wasn't at Sycamore, she was here in Manila, thousands of miles away. Thirsty, so thirsty. She cautiously moved her hand, thinking to find some moisture to bring to her mouth, but as she did so a board clattered and a drift of plaster fell upon her face.

Why was no one coming? Why hadn't she heard even

the faintest sound of movement? They were all dead. Everyone at the Tradewinds had perished in the collapsing building. Everyone but herself. Rescuing teams passing the destroyed hotel would hurry on to where they could see or hear people calling for help. They would assume from the shambled heap of fallen timber and from the silence that all within had died.

The Tradewinds. She wanted to laugh at the irony of it. The Tradewinds, her tomb. Oh God, what a way to die! How long would it take? How many days? And the rats would feast on her body. Already, it seemed, she could feel them crawling on her legs, nibbling at her toes. *Help!* her mind shrieked. *Help!*

Suppose there were *no* survivors. Suppose every man, woman, and child in Manila had been wiped off the face of the Earth, the ships at sea and in the bay sunk without a trace? The thought was like an abyss opening under her. Panic twisted her stomach, shriveled her heart, while her mind reeled, trying desperately to hold to sanity.

Had she said that life without Christian was not to be borne? Yes, yes. Then what mattered?

But Hannah's instinctive will to survive was stronger than she had imagined. She knew she would never— *couldn't*—give up. Help would come. She wasn't going to die. She couldn't give up. She had a son. For Mark she must go on, she *would* go on. Thinking of him, she recalled the storm-tossed night when she had given birth to him with no one to help her, she remembered how she had cradled him in her arms, looking down at her son's face to see an echo of Christian's. She remembered his first laugh, his first babble, his first word, his first step. She thought of him now, waiting for her, asking Flavia, "Will Mama be home soon?"

She wanted to weep, but the tears had dried in their ducts. She could only breathe a despairing sigh, a sound deep in her throat that was more animal than human.

"Hannaaaah!" a voice called from a long way off.

She was hallucinating again. Was this the final stage, when the mind, unable to function, turned from reality to fancy?

"Hannaaah?"

Another voice, closer, shouted, "Here! Here! I saw something move. Careful!"

"Hannah?"

It wasn't fancy. The voice . . . But it couldn't be. Her lips formed his name, and using all her will and strength as though this was her last, dying gasp, she cried, "Christian!" But the cry was only a desperate groan.

"Here! Someone's here! Move that board. Slowly, you fool!"

The scrape of wood, a clatter, voices, many voices, a weight shoved aside, a chink of light, then a flood of blinding sunshine, so painfully bright it made her close her eyes again. She felt arms lifting her, her head cradled against a muscular shoulder. A mug was placed to her lips. She drank. Strong, sweet, cold tea—ambrosia. She gulped at it, but before she could have her fill it was snatched away.

"Not too much at first," Christian said. His voice was cool, professional.

"Oh, Christian—" she whispered.

"There isn't time to talk," he interrupted, carrying her in his arms as he picked his way through the rubble. "We have so many who need our attention."

Hannah, even in her dazed state, caught the impersonal "we," but at the moment she was too relieved by her rescue to give it much thought. She was placed on a litter and lifted into a horse-drawn ambulance. As they jolted along the streets, her poor head and bruised body were bounced unmercifully and she lost consciousness again.

When she came to, she found herself lying in a hospital bed. Someone had removed her muddy, sodden, clothes, had bathed and dressed her in a clean cotton gown. Her eyes rolled from one side to the other.

"Miss!" she called to a passing Red Cross nurse. "Where am I?"

"St. Christopher's."

"Is there . . . ? Am I . . . ?"

"You're fine. Nothing broken. A concussion, but not a serious one. You're luckier than most. The typhoon killed thousands."

"The people at the Tradewinds?"

"From what I've been told, you, a portly gentleman—the landlord, I believe—and a Sally something-or-other were the only ones who came out of that place alive."

"Is there any word about a man named Michael Farraday?"

"I haven't heard. But if he was at the Tradewinds, I'd say he didn't make it."

Poor Michael. Handsome, devoted Michael who had been so good to her. Now he would never have his sugar plantation, never go back to his big house, his ten thousand acres on the Canadian border, never smile in his charming way. And the others, in those last hours they had become a sort of family, the old Swede who had lived through forty years of typhoons, the hysterical woman and her husband, the ladies with whom she had played whist. All dead now but three.

Hannah gingerly felt the lump at the back of her skull. Lucky, the Red Cross nurse had said. Yes, she was lucky. Christian had found her—and then apparently had gone out of her life again. Or had she imagined Christian? The voice and the strong arms, the hard shoulder, had that been part of a feverish dream?

"Hannah!" The perfunctory call of her name roused her from a doze.

She opened her eyes and looked up to find Christian standing over her, a frown between his eyes.

His sudden appearance startled her, set her heart to beating crazily. She wet her lips. "Christian! I didn't think . . ."

"Think?"

"I would see you again," she answered, bewildered by his presence, hoping against hope that the frown would dissolve into a smile. "Thank—thank you for saving me. . . ."

"Thanks are not necessary."

She stared at him for a moment. "You're angry."

"Can you blame me when you keep coming back into my life, turning up again and again like a bad penny? It seems I'll never have done with you."

"Then why are you here?" she asked in a voice free of emotion. She would not return anger for anger. She was tired, weary of the fight. They would never see eye to eye.

"You are not the only patient at St. Christopher's," he said. "Furthermore I feel partially responsible for you being in Manila. If I hadn't written, you would be safe at home."

"You can't mean that it makes any difference to you now. Nevertheless, I'm grateful. . . ."

"Like the thanks, I can do without the gratitude."

He *was* angry. But why should he bother to confront her with his ire? She searched his face as if to find a clue. To her it seemed that there could be only one reason for his presence at her bedside.

"I don't think you mean that. You always did have a rotten temper. *That's* not changed."

"No."

He sat down on the narrow bed beside her.

Her hand crept uncertainly over the bedclothes and covered his. He let it rest there and gazed at her for a long time, the anger gradually fading from his eyes.

"Christian . . ." A faint smile curved her lips. "I can't believe you came by to see me purely out of professional interest."

He shrugged and looked away for a moment. "Perhaps you're right. I must be a fool, a masochistic fool who keeps returning again and again for punishment." He paused for a moment, looking down at her hand. "I could never be sure of you. Even now. Never be sure you wouldn't change your mind tomorrow or the day after."

"Yes." Her smile now was one that mocked and teased. "Kiss me, Christian."

She started to rise from the pillows and winced at a sudden stab of pain.

"Careful!" He lifted her gently and gathered her close, not kissing her, just holding her. Then he began absently stroking her head as it lay on his shoulder.

People from the other beds stared. The Red Cross nurse, in passing, gave them a sharp glance. Neither of them noticed.

"Oh Hannah, Hannah, what am I to do with you?"

"Love me, that's all I ask."

He brushed her hair with his lips. "I didn't think I ever could again. But when they told me they thought everyone at the Tradewinds had died, I couldn't, I wouldn't believe it. I had to find you, Hannah. I knew that I had been an utter cad. I lied to you about not loving you when you came to my rooms. I was angry, hurt, I said some bitter things—just as I did now—things I didn't mean even though I understood how Travis had managed to come between us."

"Oh, Christian, what does it matter now?" She touched his face.

He went on holding her. She closed her eyes, listening to the strong beat of his heart.

"Hannah," he said at last, "how would you like being the wife of a doctor in faraway places?"

"You mean like a missionary's wife?"

"Not quite." He laughed. "I haven't grown a halo, not by a long shot. There's still too much demon in me, a devil I can't promise will disappear. But I belong here with the people of these islands. I want to help them the best way I can. It will be a hard life, not easy for you or for Mark. Heat, insects, tropical diseases, a rainy season that never seems to end, lack of conveniences . . ."

"Christian!" She placed her fingers over his lips. "Are you trying to talk me out of it before I say yes?"

He pushed her hand away. "My darling, did you ever think I'd take no for an answer again?"

And he kissed her, his loving arms and lips telling her more than any words could that he meant what he said.

Bestselling Writer of Romance and Suspense...

PHYLLIS A. WHITNEY